WESTERN

Rugged men looking for love...

Fortune's Lone Star Twins
Teri Wilson

Her Temporary Cowboy
Tanya Agler

T0363356

MILLS & BOON

Teri Wilson is acknowledged as the author of this work
FORTUNE'S LONE STAR TWINS
© 2024 by Harlequin Enterprises ULC
Philippine Copyright 2024
Australian Copyright 2024
New Zealand Copyright 2024

First Published 2024
First Australian Paperback Edition 2024
ISBN 978 1 038 90774 5

HER TEMPORARY COWBOY
© 2024 by Tanya Agler
Philippine Copyright 2024
Australian Copyright 2024
New Zealand Copyright 2024

First Published 2024
First Australian Paperback Edition 2024
ISBN 978 1 038 90774 5

® and ™ (apart from those relating to FSC®) are trademarks of Harlequin Enterprises
(Australia) Pty Limited or its corporate affiliates. Trademarks indicated with ® are
registered in Australia, New Zealand and in other countries.
Contact admin_legal@Harlequin.ca for details.

This is a work of fiction. Names, characters, places, and incidents are either the
product of the author's imagination or are used fictitiously, and any resemblance to
actual persons, living or dead, business establishments, events, or locales is entirely
coincidental.

MIX
Paper | Supporting
responsible forestry
FSC® C001695

Published by
Harlequin Mills & Boon
An imprint of Harlequin Enterprises (Australia) Pty Limited
(ABN 47 001 180 918), a subsidiary of HarperCollins
Publishers Australia Pty Limited
(ABN 36 009 913 517)
Level 19, 201 Elizabeth Street
SYDNEY NSW 2000 AUSTRALIA

Cover art used by arrangement with Harlequin Books S.A.. All rights reserved.

Printed and bound in Australia by McPherson's Printing Group

Fortune's Lone Star Twins
Teri Wilson

MILLS & BOON

Dear Reader,

Welcome back to Chatelaine, Texas, and the world of the legendary Fortune family!

This is my first book for the long-running Fortunes of Texas series, and I could not be more thrilled to be part of this amazing collection of books. This latest Fortunes of Texas miniseries is called Digging for Secrets, and *Fortune's Lone Star Twins* is the fourth book. Make sure to pick up the first three books in this miniseries to get the full effect of everything going on with the Fortune family in Chatelaine, Texas. You can find them at Harlequin.com or any online retailer.

Did you know that the Fortunes of Texas has been an ongoing series for more than twenty years and has included some of Harlequin's most beloved authors? I was so honored to write this book, and not just because I've lived in the great state of Texas for my entire life, y'all.

Fortune's Lone Star Twins tells the story of Tabitha Buckingham and West Fortune. In the opening chapter, Tabitha gets the shock of her life when her long-lost fiancé comes back from the dead. But soon, West is the one who's the most surprised when he discovers he's the daddy to one-year-old twins. And that's only the start! This story and the entire miniseries are full of dramatic twists and turns.

Look for more from the Fortunes in the rest of The Fortunes of Texas: Digging for Secrets miniseries, coming soon!

Happy reading,

Teri

DEDICATION

In loving memory of my sister-in-law, Ramona Bonnet.

We miss you so much, Mona. xoxo

CHAPTER ONE

"BLESS YOUR HEART, Tabitha. Do you have any plans for Mother's Day later this month?"

Tabitha Buckingham bristled as Courtney Riddle blinked her tacky eyelash extensions in her general direction. The other four moms in her weekly moms-of-multiples playgroup immediately followed suit, blessing Tabitha's pathetic little heart in silent unison.

For the record, her heart wasn't pathetic, and it most definitely didn't need to be blessed. Here in Texas, that saying was more often a passive-aggressive insult than an expression of genuine concern. Tabitha had lived in the Lone Star State her entire life. She knew Texas girl snark when she heard it.

Or maybe Tabitha was simply so well acquainted with this specific form of regional vernacular because her heart had been blessed on a daily basis for the past nineteen months straight.

The *other* playgroup moms meant well. All of the members of the group had met during their pregnancies at a special Lamaze class for moms of multiples. After navigating the ups and downs of their unique pregnancies together, they'd decided to keep the group intact and start visiting once a week for baby playdates. While the moms sat cross-legged in a big circle, the babies and toddlers crawled, pulled up and played with a variety of brightly colored toys in the center of Courtney's expansive playroom. Tabitha didn't know what she would've done without the other moms—with the obvious exception of today's host, who never missed a chance to remind Tabitha that she was the only single mother in their ranks.

What, exactly, was Courtney's point? It wasn't as if Tabitha could forget.

Hmm, I haven't seen the father of my children in a while. I wonder where he is...

Oh, that's right. He died before I could even tell him I was pregnant. Silly me, his brutal murder must have slipped my mind.

She could chalk a lot of mental fog up to baby brain, particularly in the early months just after the twins had been born, but Tabitha had never once forgotten what had become of West Fortune. Bless her heart, sometimes she really wished she could.

"It's okay, hon. We know that West would do something sweet for you for Mother's Day if he was still here." Patsy Mercer, one of Tabitha's best friends in the playgroup, reached over and gave her hand a squeeze. "God rest his soul."

Tabitha's throat went thick at the mention of West's name. She didn't care a whit about being pampered on Mother's Day, though. Courtney had just waxed poetic for five full minutes about how she expected her husband to make her breakfast in bed for the special day. "Real, homemade waffles, *not* the frozen kind," she'd been sure to specify with a loaded glance at Tabitha.

On the one-year anniversary of West's death, Tabitha had broken down crying in the frozen food aisle of Great-Store, the big box store that was the only place in town to buy groceries. Time had been such a blur of round-the-clock feedings and diaper changes that she'd regularly lost track of what day of the week it was, much less the exact calendar date. But then she'd glanced at the expiration date on a box of frozen waffles and somehow, she'd known. Her *soul* had known, even though she'd done her level best not to dwell on West's passing. She had twin infants to raise, a home to take care of and a small web design business to run—all by herself. Her former fiancé was gone, and nothing was going to bring him back.

Of course Courtney had stumbled upon Tabitha's rare moment of weakness in the grocery store and taken the opportunity to remind her that organic, homemade waffles were far healthier for growing babies than processed, frozen alternatives. Tabitha had simply blinked away her tears and pretended to listen while her mind spun with memories of West's gruff laugh, his deep Texas drawl and the way her heart always turned over in her chest when he glanced up at her from beneath the brim of his black Stetson. Tabitha had always teased him about his black hat. He'd been an attorney—a county prosecutor. Quite literally, one of the good guys.

Black Stetson notwithstanding.

Tabitha had refused to keep listening to Courtney's lecture about *proper nutrition* for children while memories of West tugged at her heartstrings. In the end, she'd tossed the box of waffles into her shopping basket with a tad too much force and pushed her cart straight past Courtney, accidentally rolling over the pointy toe of the other mom's designer shoe in the process. That little mortifying incident had taken place more than six months ago, but the pesky woman obviously wasn't ready to let it go.

"It's fine," Tabitha said around the lump in her throat. "*We're* fine. The twins and I have plans with my sisters for Mother's Day."

Liar, liar, pants on fire.

Tabitha had no such plans with Lily and Haley…yet.

She and her triplet sisters had been separated as infants after their parents were killed in a car accident, but they'd reconnected now as adults. Lily and Haley had even been Tabitha's birthing coaches. She made a mental note to call them and set something up.

"What are you doing for Mother's Day, Patsy?" Tabitha cast a beseeching glance at her friend in an effort to steer the conversation away from West's gaping absence.

Mother's Day, she could handle. Thinking about West and how different everything would be if he hadn't been shot and killed by a vengeful ex-con he'd helped put in prison? Not so much.

Patsy brightened. "We're having a Mother's Day brunch with my parents after church on Sunday. Last year Gabe gave Mom and me matching orchid corsages to wear for the day."

The mom sitting on Patsy's other side pressed a hand to her heart. "I just love that sweet Southern tradition."

Tabitha nodded and awwwed along with the rest of the group, even though she'd completely forgotten that Mother's Day corsages were a thing. Something told her she wouldn't be getting a flower to pin to her dress this year.

"You know what? This morning has been crazy. The boys didn't get their regular nap before we came today," Tabitha stood. She needed to get out of here. This nagging sense of wistfulness was getting to be too much. Because, truth be told, she had no reason whatsoever to expect that things would've been different even if West were still alive. "I should get Zach and Zane and put them down for a bit before it gets too close to dinnertime."

"Are you sure? The boys seem fine," Patsy said, casting a glance toward the center of the room where the twins were pounding the colorful keys of a musical activity table with their pudgy little hands. One of Courtney's little girls toddled between them, playing along nicely with Zane and Zach. Thankfully, Courtney's twins hadn't seemed to inherit the mean girl gene. Not yet, anyway.

"You know how it is. Kids can be fine one minute and cranky the next," Tabitha said as she maneuvered the boys into their double stroller. Zane grinned up at her, and for a second, his eyes looked so much like his daddy's that Tabitha's smile went wobbly. She swallowed. Hard. "Sorry to cut things short this time."

Courtney stood to walk Tabitha to the door. Playgroup never met at Tabitha's house because her tiny two-bedroom home in Chatelaine's town center was already a tight squeeze with two babies—never mind ten more.

"Don't you worry a bit about having to go. I just can't imagine how difficult things must be for you, doing it all on your own." Courtney batted her ridiculous eyelashes, and Tabitha's teeth ground together.

Don't say it. Please don't... I'm begging you.

"Bless your heart."

TABITHA MADE THREE full loops around Chatelaine in her small SUV before heading to her house near the center of town. Full disclosure: she hadn't exactly been truthful about the twins missing their morning nap time. The boys had slept like little angels while she'd gotten caught up on a website design project for a new client based in San Antonio.

But after the onslaught of feelings at playgroup, she could use a little quiet time before she jumped back into her workday. Tabitha doubted she'd get much accomplished today, anyway. The high school student who usually helped her out with the twins in the afternoons had recently given her notice because she'd made the cheerleading squad. Tabitha was thrilled for her, of course. In small-town Texas, football and cheerleading were Very Big Deals. Unfortunately, juggling two babies while also working at home wasn't exactly small potatoes either.

Like most babies, Zach and Zane loved the soothing motion of a moving automobile, so taking the scenic route home seemed like a mighty fine idea. Not that there was much to see in Chatelaine, which by Texas-sized standards, was truly a one-horse town. Aside from GreatStore and the Chatelaine Museum, the only highlights were the collection of grand, arched gates that led to tree-lined paths and sprawling ranches just outside of town. And the mines, of course.

For a while, Chatelaine had attracted prospectors and fortune hunters, convinced the town held an underground treasure trove of gold, silver and copper. That had been years ago—way before Tabitha's time. The mining operations came to an abrupt end after a terrible tragedy in 1965 when one of the mines collapsed, but tourists and hikers still came to town to explore the abandoned mines. Some of the properties featured guided tours and gift shops. Tabitha's stomach rumbled as she passed a hand-painted sign advertising homemade fudge at one such establishment.

Nope. She made an abrupt U-turn and guided the car back toward home. *Not going there—not today of all days.*

The last gift West had given her had been a batch of fudge from that very shop. "Sweets, because I'm sweet on you," he'd said as he'd handed her the white box, tied with a pink satin ribbon. When she'd opened it, she'd found an engagement ring nestled inside, sparkling like mad among the chocolate. Tabitha still wore the ring on a chain around her neck, tucked beneath her clothes so no one could see. Her little secret.

Which *definitely* needed to stop. She had no right to

wear that diamond solitaire anymore, but after West died, she simply couldn't bring herself to stop. Even if sometimes it made her feel like the biggest fraud in the world.

"We were broken up," she whispered.

Tabitha had only uttered those words out loud a handful of times. For months after West's murder, she hadn't told a soul. Why would she? West was the love of her life. Breaking off their engagement had been the hardest choice Tabitha had ever made, and when she'd finally done it—once she'd finally managed to tell him that they couldn't have a future if he didn't want children—it had all been for nothing. West had been shot and killed the very next morning before anyone found out they were no longer getting married. And irony of ironies, completely unbeknownst to her, Tabitha had already been pregnant with West's babies.

Once she found out she was pregnant, she'd confided in her sisters about the breakup. Recently, she'd also shared the truth with Bea Fortune, West's cousin. Bea had been over visiting the twins and blurted out that she'd recently discovered she was pregnant. Entrusted with Bea's news, Tabitha had shared her secret truth, as well. But they were the only three people who knew.

Tabitha's memories of the night before West's murder felt so surreal now, almost like a fever dream, and she couldn't force herself to face them. When snippets of their breakup came back to her during the funeral, she'd nearly vomited in the church pew. Later that afternoon, after she'd watched the two little lines appear on an at-home pregnancy test, she'd taken her engagement ring out of her nightstand drawer and slid it onto the delicate chain West had given her the previous Christmas. Both the necklace and the ring were crafted from gold from a mine owned by the Fortune family out in West Texas—

not the Chatelaine mine, but another one that held hidden treasures deep underground. In the beginning, Tabitha had loved wearing something with such a meaningful family connection. But now, after the split and West's shocking death, it seemed like a bad omen—as if her engagement ring had been cursed by the same twist of fate that had brought down the mine in Chatelaine all those years ago.

"We were broken up," she said again, louder this time. Maybe if she repeated it enough times, she'd finally internalize the truth and those fleeting, what-could-have-been fantasies would stop invading her thoughts in her most vulnerable moments.

One of the twins stirred at the sound of her voice, and Tabitha stole a glance at the rearview mirror. Zach's tiny rosebud mouth puckered and he let out a whimper.

"It's okay," she soothed. "Don't cry, sweetie. Everything's okay. We're all okay."

Because they *were* okay. She and her babies were just fine on their own. Tabitha had experienced another silly moment of weakness, that's all.

Still, she tugged the chain from beneath the collar of her blouse and wrapped her fingers around her engagement ring, squeezing it tight. The metal was warm from resting in the secret place against her heart. She held it for a beat, savoring her good memories of West—clinging to them while once again pushing their breakup to the back of her mind, one last time.

Zach settled back into a quiet sleep as the car crawled through tiny downtown Chatelaine, and Tabitha let out a sigh as she turned onto her street. She was happy to be home—away from the wistfulness that had come over her at playgroup and back to her normal life with her boys. All she'd ever wanted was to be a mom. She knew she was lucky to have been adopted after her parents' accident, even if it meant being separated from her sisters. But her adoptive parents had always held her at arm's length, and Tabitha had yearned to feel like part of a real family for as long as she could remember.

And now she was. The twins were everything to her. What more could she possibly want?

She shifted the SUV into Park and gathered her purse, phone and diaper bag before climbing out of the car. It always took three separate trips to unload everyone and everything after an outing, so she left the windows unrolled. The twins slept soundly while a spring breeze ruffled their soft, downy hair.

Tabitha had just finished fiddling with her key ring and grabbing hold of the house key when she looked up and saw a man sitting on her front steps.

"Oh." She stopped dead in her tracks.

Was she seeing things? Why was there a stranger on her porch? And why was he wearing a black Stetson pulled down low to cover his face?

Tabitha's heart thudded so hard and fast that she couldn't breathe. The diaper bag slid from her shoulder and fell to the ground with a thud.

West.

No. It couldn't be. That was impossible. Lots of men wore cowboy hats around here. This was Texas, after all.

She blinked hard, squared her shoulders and marched forward. But her hands trembled so badly that her keys jangled like church bells.

"Can I help you?" she managed to sputter.

That hat…that sculpted jawline…those impossibly broad shoulders. They were all so familiar that Tabitha wanted to drop everything, sprint toward the stranger and throw herself into his arms.

Thankfully, she still had enough sense to realize she

shouldn't. *Couldn't.* Dead ex-fiancés just didn't appear from thin air and pop up out of nowhere. She hadn't somehow conjured the father of her children simply because she'd been thinking about him. Tabitha didn't know what was going on, exactly, but one thing was certain. Whoever this man was, he wasn't West Fortune.

But then he lifted his head and aimed his attention squarely at her. His eyes were covered with sunglasses. Aviators, like West had always worn. And even though Tabitha couldn't see past the dark lenses, she could feel his stare. It burned into her with the heat of a thousand Texas summers.

Everything seemed to move in slow motion as the man stood and walked toward her. Tabitha felt like she was looking at him through a long, dark tunnel. Her head went fuzzy, and she couldn't hear anything but her pulse throbbing in her ears. Thump, thump, thump. Then he removed the sunglasses, his gaze collided with hers and Tabitha's knees turned to water.

"Hi there, darlin'." His voice was quiet. Tender. And his expression bore only a ghost of a smile.

It was him.

How?

Why?

What was *happening*?

"West?" she breathed, and then the whole world tilted sideways as she slunk to the pavement.

CHAPTER TWO

WEST SENT UP a silent prayer of thanks that he managed to catch Tabitha just before she hit the ground. As many times as he'd imagined this homecoming...*longed* for it...he'd never envisioned it involving a near-concussion.

Hadn't he hurt Tabitha enough already?

Idiot. He cursed himself. In hindsight, he should've figured out a gentler way to break the news of his "resurrection." But how? He'd gone straight to Tabitha's house the second he'd crossed the town border into Chatelaine. West didn't want to risk anyone else seeing him—not even his family. Tabitha deserved to hear the truth from him and him alone, to see for herself that he was really alive...

Even if she might not love him anymore.

"West?" She blinked up at him as he cradled her head in his hands. They were sprawled in the middle of the sidewalk that led up to her quaint little porch and, Chatelaine being Chatelaine, their dramatic reunion hadn't gone unnoticed.

Across the street, Betty Lawford paused from trimming her rosebushes to sneak a sideways glance at West as he helped Tabitha to her feet. She squinted at him, and he waited a beat too long to avert his gaze. Betty's mouth dropped open and her gardening shears slipped from her gloved hands.

Cue the small-town rumor mill in three...two...one...

"Let's get you inside, darlin'," he whispered into Tabitha's ear.

A lock of her wavy blond hair tickled his cheek, and the sweet familiarity of her honeysuckle scent nearly brought him to his knees. He'd never forgotten that scent—not even once in all the time he'd been away. For nineteen long months, West had closed his eyes and tried to conjure it up late at night when loneliness wrapped itself around him, as thick as a blanket. All he'd wanted was to come home. Not just to Chatelaine…to West, *home* still meant Tabitha.

It always would.

"I'm fine," Tabitha said as she scrambled to her feet, but the tremor in her voice betrayed her. "I just…"

She looked up at him. *Really* looked, and the tears that pooled in her eyes made West's gut churn in a way that was far more painful than any damage the man who'd been hell-bent on destroying him could've done.

"Come on, now. Don't cry." He cupped her elbow and steered her toward the house, stepping gently over her bags, still strewn on the sidewalk.

Had she been on a trip somewhere? Her handbag looked like it had grown three sizes since he'd been gone, and she'd also been carrying a bulky duffel bag—baby blue, covered with little teddy bears doing cartwheels

"Here, let me," West said, taking the keys from her hands and unlocking the front door.

Tabitha stepped inside and lingered in the front entrance as if in a daze. Then she reached a shaky hand toward him and placed it on his chest, right over West's pounding heart.

A smile blossomed on her lips. "You're really here. It's you."

"It's me." *Not a ghost and not a dead man.* West's throat grew thick. He'd waited so long for this day, and in his lowest moments, he'd feared it might never come. There was so much to say, but now that he was here, he didn't even know where to start.

Start with "I still love you." How about that?

He rested a hand on top of hers, still pressed against his heartbeat. "Tabitha, I—"

"The babies!" she blurted, eyes going wide.

West had been so wrapped up in what he'd been about to say that it took a beat for her words to sink in. Even then, they still didn't make sense. "The what?"

"The kids are still in the car. I was going to unload everything first and then go get them, but then you, well…" Her face flushed. West was guessing "you came back from the dead" sounded too ridiculous to utter aloud. "I need to go get them."

She brushed past him, headed back out the door toward her car, still parked at the curb with the windows unrolled. West narrowed his gaze at the backseat and could just make out two tiny blond heads and the headrests of two bulky car seats. His heart sank all the way down to the soles of his custom-made, leather Lucchese boots— one of the few remaining vestiges of his former life that he still owned.

Tabitha has children?

He wasn't sure why he was surprised. She'd made her feelings clear during her big breakup speech. Tabitha wanted a family. She wanted kids and a white picket fence and all the things that West hadn't been able to promise her. Of course she'd moved on.

His gaze flitted around the living room, hungry for details. But there wasn't a family photo in sight, so he blew out a breath and forced himself to walk back outside where Tabitha was unbuckling one of the seat belts and talking to the kids in a singsongy voice that made his heart feel like it was being squeezed in a vise.

"Here, hold Zane for a minute. I'll go get Zach." She placed a baby into his arms.

"Um..." West stiffened.

"Seriously?" Tabitha's eyes flashed. "He's a baby, not a porcupine. You'll be fine holding him for half a second."

Across the street, Betty Lawford had given up any pretense of clipping her roses and was now watching with unabashed interest as she watered her sidewalk with a garden hose.

The baby stared up at him and made a happy gurgling sound as he reached for West's Stetson with a pudgy fist.

"Oh, no you don't, buddy." A smile tugged at his lips, and he relaxed a little as he readjusted his grip on the child.

The tiny thing was as light as a feather and had a sweet little dimple in his chin, like the one West's brother Camden had when he was a kid. And suddenly, he was drowning in grief—grief for what he'd lost when he'd been away, grief for everything he'd willingly given up when he'd told Tabitha he never wanted to be a father, grief for the long "dead" West Fortune.

Because he wasn't that guy anymore. That life was buried and gone, as evidenced by the fact that he was now holding a baby who belonged to Tabitha and another man. His stomach tightened, and he looked away, focusing on some random spot in the distance, above the boy's head.

"Are you coming, or has holding an infant rendered you paralyzed?"

West snapped his head toward the porch, where Tabitha stood glaring at him with the other baby balanced on her hip.

"We're coming," he said and somehow managed to gather her previously discarded bags in one hand without dropping the tyke in the other as he made his way back to the house.

It wasn't as if West disliked babies. They were fine. Wonderful, even. So long as they belonged to someone else. West's upbringing had been far too tumultuous for him to believe he could ever be a decent father. His parents had made one another miserable for West's entire childhood. There'd been cheating on both sides and so much screaming that West routinely fell asleep at night with his head buried under his pillow and his hands clamped over his ears.

He didn't know what he would've done without his two brothers, Camden and Bear. Bear was only a year older than him, but when West was particularly upset or scared, Bear would crawl into his bed and tell him an adventure story to distract him. Kids shouldn't have to rely on their siblings for a sense of stability, though. Somewhere deep down, West was messed up. When his parents were killed in a plane crash five years ago, he'd hoped he could finally shake the bad memories and learn to let it all go. But after he asked Tabitha to marry him and she'd started talking about kids, he'd gotten a sick feeling in the pit of his stomach every time the subject came up. How could he possibly have a family of his own when all his memories of childhood were so tied up with misery? West wouldn't know the first thing about building a happy home for an innocent child like the one in his arms.

By the time he stepped inside the house, Tabitha had already settled Zach on a blanket in the center of the living room with a collection of brightly colored stackable cups. The baby attempted to stick one of them inside another as Tabitha plucked Zane from West's arms as if rescuing the child from some mortal danger.

That was on him, he supposed. He'd never given Tabitha

any reason to believe he was good with children. Because he *wasn't*. West didn't have the first clue what to do with a baby.

That was probably beside the point, though. He still had plenty of explaining to do, and he wanted to get it done and get out of here before Tabitha's husband came home. Chatelaine was a small town. He'd have to meet the man eventually, but not yet. Not today. Not until he'd had a little time to come to grips with this painful new reality.

Would time really help, though? If the past year and a half had taught West anything, it was that he'd never stop loving Tabitha, no matter how many days, months... *years*...slipped by.

"I'm sorry," he said quietly. "I shouldn't have just shown up like this, out of nowhere. But when I got word that it was safe to come back, this was the only place I wanted to be. Here...with you."

Tabitha's expression softened, but there was still a wariness about her that hit him square in the heart. "I don't understand, West. Everyone thinks Trey Mendez shot and killed you."

In his capacity as lead county prosecutor, West had been responsible for putting Mendez in prison three years ago. He'd worked on that trial night and day for weeks. The defendant had been a high-profile member of a Mexican drug cartel responsible for bringing large amounts of narcotics and other illegal contraband across the border. It had been the most important win of his entire legal career.

And then, the same day that Tabitha had broken off their engagement, Mendez's shady lawyer had managed to get his client released on a technicality.

"It was in all the papers, West. Witnesses saw you get shot. There was a *funeral*." Tabitha's voice broke on that last word, and something inside him broke along with it.

He swallowed hard.

"Mendez shot me—that much is true." West rolled his shoulder. He still had some residual stiffness and intermittent pain from the gunshot wound. He'd been lucky, though. An inch to the left, and the bullet would've hit his subclavian artery, and there would've been no need to fake his death. His demise would've been one hundred percent real. "You probably know this already from the news coverage, but it happened on the riverbank near the Fortune ranch. I'd gone out there to think things over after you and I…well…anyway, Mendez found me there the following morning. He shot me from far off, near the back side of the ranch, where the drop into the river is at its highest point. After I fell backward into the water, I stayed under long enough to convince him I was dead."

West's body had never been recovered, obviously. But he'd emptied his pockets of all his personal effects, hoping they'd wash up onto the shore. A fisherman found them in a shallow creek the following morning, and Trey Mendez was caught and convicted almost immediately. But his ties to the cartel ran deep. West knew better than to show his face until the man was dead and gone. So he'd hunkered down and stitched himself up with a needle and thread and a bottle of good whiskey. Then he'd found a job on a ranch and gone underground.

She shook her head, as if she couldn't believe what he was saying. "But I still don't understand. Why didn't you come home once you were safe?"

"He threatened you, Tabs. He said he was going to kill 'my pretty fiancée' to get back at me for getting him put away. The only way to keep you safe was to let him, and everyone else, think I was dead." West had given up his life to save her, and he'd do it again in a heartbeat. No matter what the cost.

Tabitha wrapped her arms around herself, and her bottom lip began to tremble. "But we were…"

Broken up.

Neither of them wanted to say it, but the truth hung over them anyway, stealing all the oxygen from the room.

West took a deep, ragged inhale. "I know, but it didn't matter, Tabs. Mendez wouldn't have believed it. He would've thought I was lying just to keep you safe."

One of the twins let loose with a stream of baby talk, and Tabitha blinked, as if waking up from a trance.

Her head snapped toward the windows facing her quaint, shady street. "Where is Trey Mendez now? You don't think he's coming here, do you? The children—"

West rested his hands on her shoulders, and even that simple contact was almost enough to bring him to his knees. It had been so long since he'd touched her, kissed her, loved her. And yet being this close to her was like muscle memory. Every part of him remembered what it felt like to hold Tabitha Buckingham in his arms.

"They're safe. You all are, I promise," he said with an undeniable ache in his tone. "Mendez died in prison this morning. As soon as I got word, I came straight here."

Home. That's what he'd meant to say. *As soon as I got word, I came straight home.* The instant West found out it was safe, he'd come back to the only home he'd been dreaming of since he'd been away. At least he'd caught himself before he'd said so out loud.

This was another man's home, not his.

"It's all over, Tabs. You've got nothing to fear now." His gaze cut toward the twin boys, playing with their toys, clumsily stacking the cups with their little pudgy hands. Why did it hurt so much to look at them? "Your kids are safe. Everything's okay."

Was it, though? A world where Tabitha's heart belonged to someone else didn't seem like it would ever feel okay.

He didn't have a choice in the matter, however. While he'd been stuck biding his time, the world had moved on without him. He'd have been a fool to expect otherwise, especially when he'd let Tabitha walk away without a fight.

Regret burrowed deep as he took in her familiar features. She looked exactly the same. Same light blond hair, same sparkling blue irises—the exact color of the wild bluebonnets that blossomed across Texas every spring, transforming the landscape into a sea of dusty blue-violet that stretched out all the way to the horizon. It was going to take him some time to come to grips with the fact that even though things might look the same, deep down in his soul, everything had changed while he'd been gone.

But then Tabitha's graceful fingers toyed with the gold chain around her neck, and she absently fiddled with whatever charm or pendant hung from the delicate necklace as she seemed to do her best to absorb everything he'd just told her. West glanced at her hand, fluttering as nervously as a bird searching for a place to land. And that's when he saw it…

The ring. *His* ring—the one that had been crafted from gold from the Fortune family mine. The one he'd hidden in a box of chocolate the day he'd asked her to be his wife.

Hope welled in his heart as he lifted his gaze slowly to meet Tabitha's, and for a tender, breathtaking moment, their eyes met. The present suddenly looked and felt a lot more like the past, and West could almost breathe again. She still wore his ring. That had to mean something, didn't it? Then one of the babies started babbling again, and the moment turned bittersweet.

Confusion gripped him, rooting him to the spot, even as a part of him felt inexplicably drawn to the boys. He studied the dimple in Zane's chin. *Just like Camden.* Then West went numb all over as he realized Zach had one too.

He glanced back at Tabitha, searching her gaze for the answer he was in no way prepared to hear.

"West." The smile she offered him was so steeped in vulnerability that he felt it deep in the pit of his stomach. "Meet your twin sons."

"My sons?" West swayed slightly on his feet, and Tabitha was almost glad she wasn't the only one who'd just experienced the shock of a lifetime.

Her ex-fiancé had just *come back from the dead.* Was she living in a soap opera now, or had the loneliness she sometimes battled late at night finally become so intense that she'd started hallucinating? Those seemed like the only two options. West had explained what happened, but she still couldn't seem to reconcile his version of events with the reality she'd been struggling to accept for the past year and a half. So much loss. So much grief…grief so thick that if she hadn't had the twins to worry about, she might have let it consume her.

The boys had saved her. Once Tabitha found out she was pregnant, she had a reason to get out of bed in the mornings. She hadn't been at all sure how she would do it all on her own, but knowing she would soon have two tiny, helpless babies to take care of was enough to help her put one foot in front of the other. So that's what she'd done. Day after day after day…until slowly, the twins became her whole world and West became her past.

Except now that past was standing right in front of her, shell-shocked to discover that he was a father.

"Yes, Zach and Zane. They're turning one year old in just a few weeks." She bustled toward the boys, trying her best to tamp down the urge to throw herself protectively in front of them. But that was crazy, right? West was their daddy, and he was a good man.

A good man who told you he never wanted children, she told herself. As if she could've forgotten that devastating little nugget.

She sat down cross-legged on the blanket and pulled the twins into her lap, facing West, and ran a hand over each of their downy heads. "This one is Zane and this one's Zach."

West came closer, lowering himself down in front of the boys. He reached out a hand and Zach grabbed hold of it, balling West's finger into his little fist. Zane let out a squeal.

A look of wonder splashed across her ex-fiancé's face for a beat, replaced quickly by bewilderment as he swiveled his gaze back and forth between his sons. "Are they identical?"

Tabitha laughed, despite the absurdity of the situation. "You're not seeing double. Yes, they're identical."

"Identical twins." He gave his head a little shake. "Wow."

"Yeah. It's kind of crazy, isn't it?" She nodded, remembering the afternoon she'd found out she was carrying twins.

It had been an appointment for a routine sonogram early in her pregnancy. She'd expected to come home with a blurry image of West's baby to tack to the front of her refrigerator with a magnet. Instead, the doctor had grinned widely at her and asked if she was ready for the surprise of her life. Afterward, she'd gone out for ice cream with her sisters and smiled so much that her cheeks were sore by the time she finished her three scoops of mint chocolate chip. A moment of pure joy amid so much darkness.

"Can I hold them?" West asked. The uncertainty in his gruff tone just about broke Tabitha's heart.

"West, they're your children. You don't need to ask permission." She didn't know where they went from here, but she'd never try and keep the twins away from their father. They could figure things out, even if they were no longer together.

Because the fact of the matter was, they *were* still broken up. Just because West wasn't really dead didn't mean they were back together. Tabitha had ended their engagement when he'd told her he didn't want children, but there was so much more to it. She'd played second fiddle to his career for a long, long time, and it was his job as a county prosecutor that had landed them in this terrible mess. Tabitha couldn't pretend otherwise, no matter how very badly she wanted to.

You need to protect your heart, she reminded herself as she all but melted at the sight of West gathering the two small boys in his arms. Never in her life did she think she'd witness a moment like this one. It felt like a gift straight from heaven.

"West, I'm so sorry about everything that happened to you. It must have been so hard to leave everyone and everything you knew behind." For *her*. He'd done it for her. Tabitha was still so mad at him for so many things, but that one truth threatened to make her want to sweep them all under the rug.

Still, couldn't he have somehow sent her a message to let her know he was alive?

Her stomach squirmed. *What part of broken up don't you understand?*

"I'm the one who's sorry." West shook his head. "You've been taking care of two babies all on your own."

"Not completely alone. Lily and Haley have been a huge help. They were even my birthing coaches. Can you believe it?" She smiled, proud of all the progress she and her sisters had made on their relationship. Tabitha had wanted to be close to Lily and Haley since she'd first learned she had birth sisters.

But West's smile went sad around the edges. He hadn't been there for the birth of his children, and no matter where they went from here, nothing would ever change that.

Tabitha was suddenly exhausted. This was all too much to take in, especially the painful, overriding truth of this heart-wrenching homecoming: West was back, but he didn't want to be a dad. He'd said so himself.

You're still on your own in this, and don't you forget it.

"I should get the twins down for their nap," she said as the boys began to fuss.

"Okay, I'll help." West stood, a twin tucked into the crook of each arm. "Lead the way to the nursery?"

Who was this man, and what had he done with the real West Fortune?

Tabitha swallowed around the lump lodged in her throat and showed him the boys' room with its whimsical elephant mural she and her sisters had painted during the pregnancy. The nursery was a small, modest affair, just like the rest of the house, but what it lacked in space it more than made up for in warmth and coziness. The whole room was decorated in soothing shades of blue. A rocking chair stood by the window, and among the stuffed animals lined up on the bookshelves, sat a framed photo of West.

His gaze snagged on it just as they finished getting the babies situated in their side-by-side cribs. He looked at it for a long moment, and when he turned back toward Tabitha, she was almost certain she saw tears in his eyes.

"I can't believe these precious wonders are mine," he whispered. "They're perfect, Tabs."

She bit down hard on the inside of her cheek to keep

herself from crying. He was really and truly here, and he was saying all the right things. The urge to throw herself into his arms and kiss the stuffing out of him was almost too much to bear.

"Can I ask you something?" he murmured, shifting closer to cup her cheek in one of his big, warm palms.

Wild horses couldn't have made her turn away. "Ask me anything. I'm sure you have a lot of questions."

"We both do. That's why I think it's best if I stay here for a while." He moved the pad of his thumb gently over the side of her face.

"In Chatelaine?" Tabitha swallowed. Where else would he go? West was a legend in this town.

But that wasn't what he'd meant, and they both knew it.

"Here with you and the boys. Let me stay, Tabs. Please? The thought of you is what kept me going the past nineteen months. Your beautiful face, what we had together… I know there've been ups and downs, but you're everything to me."

"West, we can't just—" Tabitha shook her head, desperately needing to think. She couldn't automatically jump back into a relationship with both feet. It wasn't just the two of them anymore. She had the boys to think about.

"You broke my heart," she finally said, because it was the truth, and she couldn't just forget it had ever happened. When she'd ended the engagement, he'd told her maybe it was for the best. He hadn't even put up a fight.

"I know I did. I know, sweetheart. And I know I have a lot to prove now that I'm back." A muscle ticked in his jaw. "All I'm asking for is a chance to show you how different things can be, and a chance to get to know my kids. Children were never part of my plans, but they're here now. And now that I *am* a dad, I want to be the kind of father these little angels deserve. My life is starting over, and this is the only place I want to be." He aimed a purposeful look at the babies, tiny chests rising and falling in a sleepy rhythm. "Right here, with all three of you."

"What about your work?" She wiped a tear from her cheek. "Will you go back?"

She wasn't even sure why she asked. Even if he said no, she knew she couldn't trust it. That job had meant the world to him.

"I don't know." He shook his head and sighed. At least he was being honest. She had to give him credit for that. "The only thing I'm sure about right now is that I want to be a good dad. Let me stay. Please? Even if it's just for a little while."

It was everything Tabitha had wanted to hear two years ago, but so much had changed since then. How could she possibly believe him?

"This house is too small for four people, even when two of them are babies." Tabitha glanced toward the living room and her resistance wavered…ever so slightly. "You'd have to sleep on the sofa. Understood?"

"Understood." He beamed at her, and butterflies took flight in her belly, just like they did back when things were simpler.

Back before West had died and come back to life. Back before they'd become parents. Back before he'd broken her heart into a million pieces.

That battle-weary heart of hers clenched, reminding her that it was little more than scar tissue now. She had no intention of giving it away again. Not to West, or anyone else. Not ever.

Tabitha smiled through her tears.

What did I just agree to?

CHAPTER THREE

THE FOLLOWING MORNING, West watched the sun come up as he sipped a cup of coffee on Tabitha's front porch. He'd been up for hours already.

The sofa was plenty comfortable. He had no complaints about that whatsoever. But he'd been working as a ranch hand for the past year and a half on a huge cattle farm out in West Texas, doing the kind of manual labor he hadn't done since he'd been a teenager. Life in the saddle started before sunrise, and West's body hadn't gotten the message that he was home now with his head resting on a soft pillow in Tabitha Buckingham's cottage in Chatelaine instead of sleeping in a bunkhouse with a dozen other cowboys.

Even if he'd been able to instantly adjust to his new surroundings, West wouldn't have gotten more than a few fleeting hours of shut-eye. His mind couldn't stop spinning.

Twins.

His boys slept just down the hall. He was a *father*. He'd come home to reclaim his life, only to find that that life looked completely different than the one he'd left behind. His heart was full to bursting in a way that he'd never dreamed possible.

West drained his coffee cup, eyes trained on Betty Lawford's roses across the street. The colorful blooms seemed brighter than they'd been yesterday. His gaze drifted upward. And the soft pink sky over Chatelaine felt more expansive than ever. It was a whole new world, and even though West had a long way to go to earn his place in it, his heart stirred with hope. The West Texas ranch belonged to another lifetime—one that he had no intention of returning to ever again.

He went back inside the house, moving as quietly as he could in his sock feet, Wranglers and a plain white tee. His first order of business when he'd gotten up had been a phone call to his brother Camden, which had been full of yet more surprises. He'd put off telling his family he was really alive until he'd gotten a chance to see Tabitha face-to-face. As much as he loved the Fortunes, he hadn't wanted to risk Tabitha hearing he'd faked his own death from someone else. Now that he'd had coffee and put the sofa back together, he wanted to try and get the twins changed and ready for the day before she woke up. No time like the present to start acting like a real, hands-on dad.

The boys were both stirring quietly in their cribs when West entered the nursery. Their big blue eyes swiveled toward him, and he held his breath, worried they might burst into tears at the sight of a stranger. A father suddenly appearing out of nowhere couldn't be easy on a kid, even an infant. But one of the babies smiled, then the other. They pulled themselves up and reached plump arms toward him, eager to be held.

The sweet moment quickly descended into chaos. West had never changed a single diaper in his life, let alone two. But he somehow managed to get both boys cleaned up and dressed in soft, baby-blue onesies by the time Tabitha entered the room.

"Good morning," she said in a singsong voice as she tied the sash of her bathrobe into a knot, nearly plowing straight into West in the process.

"Oh. You're up already." She stumbled to a halt, gaze

flitting from the baby powder spread liberally all over the carpet to the pile of discarded diapers beside the changing table.

"It took me a few tries to figure out how the self-adhesive tape on these things works," West admitted, patting Zane's tiny bottom. The baby was nestled in his arms, while Zach did a little dance in his crib and babbled at his mama. Trying to hold both of them at the same time first thing in the morning had proved more challenging than wrestling an alligator. "And I was aiming to get everything cleaned up before you got up. I just…"

"But you got the twins changed and dressed? All by yourself?" Tabitha was staring at him as if he'd sprouted another head overnight and already placed a black Stetson on top of it.

"I guess I did." He gave the baby in his arms a crooked smile. "We figured it out, didn't we, Zane?"

Tabitha let out a quiet laugh.

"What?"

She shook her head. "It's nothing. You did a great job, West."

"Something's funny. Come on now, darlin'," he said, and her cheeks went pink at the endearment. He supposed he was going to have to stop talking to her like he used to… like she was still his. Old habits died hard, though. Especially when those habits had been the subject of his every fantasy for the past year and a half. "Tell me."

She bit back a smile, eyes flitting toward the twin propped in the crook of his elbow. "That's not Zane. It's Zach."

So much for nailing the fatherhood thing.

"Oh."

"Don't let it take the wind out of your sails. You did

great," Tabitha said, graciously ignoring the explosion of baby powder and the wad of discarded diapers.

West blew out a breath. What kind of dad couldn't tell his own children apart? Not a good one, that's for sure.

"Trust me. It's an easy mistake to make." She laid a hand on his forearm, and the moment her fingertips brushed against his bare skin, she shivered.

Then she jerked her hand away and pasted on a nervous smile.

West crumbled inside. The sight of her obvious discomfort around him was almost as upsetting as the fact that he couldn't tell which twin was Zach and which one was Zane.

"When was the last time you made that mistake?" he asked, arching a brow at her.

Her hand fluttered to her throat. *"Me?"*

West nodded. "Yep."

"A while." She swallowed, and West traced the movement up and down the slender column of her throat. "But I'm with the boys every day. Don't be too hard on yourself. You'll learn, West."

Would he, though? Or was he doomed to make the same mistakes his parents had made when he'd been a child? The past had a tendency to repeat itself. Shame washed over him at the very thought of it.

You're not your father. You're here *now.*

"What time did you get up?" Tabitha asked as she pulled her robe more tightly around herself.

He hated that she felt so nervous around him. Absolutely despised it. "I got up a few hours ago. Couldn't help it. Days started early back on the ranch."

Her forehead puckered. "The ranch?"

They still had so much to talk about, so much to say.

And yet somehow none of it seemed important compared to the two little lives he was now responsible for.

"When I was in hiding, I worked as a ranch hand on a place out in West Texas," he said.

"I see. I guess that explains the tan." Her gaze flitted to his biceps, and her flush grew a deeper shade of pink. "And the muscles."

"Baling hay and working with cattle will do that."

"I suppose that was quite a change from working as a prosecutor." Tabitha cleared her throat, and her gaze sharpened the way it always did when the subject of his job came up.

She had every right to be upset about his career and what it had done to their relationship, now more than ever.

West nodded. "Indeed."

Tabitha brushed past him to lift Zane from his crib. The child cooed and let out a stream of baby talk that sounded an awful lot like *mama*.

"Mamamammammma." Zane's little face split into a wide grin, showing off his four teeth.

West could only stare in wonder. "Did he just say mama?"

"Sort of." Tabitha moved her hand over the infant's slender back in soothing circles. "They both started saying it a few months ago. Their very first word."

"That's…amazing." West's throat went tight. He knew better than to ask if they could say *dada*. They had no reason at all to know that word.

"Do you want to help me feed the boys breakfast?" Tabitha asked, throwing him a bone.

He nodded. "Yes, please. I'd love that."

West studied every move she made as she sliced up a banana, cooked two helpings of breakfast cereal and scrambled an egg on the stove. Then he helped get the boys settled in their highchairs and clipped bibs around their necks, wiped chins and did the airplane food thing with tiny spoons and forks.

The sheer amount of effort it took to take care of the twins' most basic needs was overwhelming. By noon, West was more exhausted than from a full day in the saddle.

She's been doing this all on her own for nearly a year.

He wasn't sure how it would be possible to make everything up to Tabitha, but he was determined to give it his best shot.

"I should get some work done. I have a few clients waiting on new website designs." Tabitha gestured toward her laptop, sitting atop a small table off to the side of the kitchen after they'd gotten the twins down for their afternoon nap. "Have you thought about contacting your family and letting them know you're back?"

West scrubbed the back of his neck. "I did that first thing this morning. I called Camden, and once he got over the shock of hearing from me, he got me caught up on everything that's been going on with the Fortunes."

Tabitha shot him a knowing grin. "You're not the only one with a surprise up your sleeve."

Of course she knew. Chatelaine was a small town. No one could keep a secret here—all the more reason he'd had to go into hiding.

"So have you met this mysterious 'step-granny' of mine who managed to get nearly all of Elias and Edgar Fortune's grandchildren to pick up and move here to Chatelaine?"

According to Camden, the only holdout was their other brother Barrington, more commonly known as "Bear." Thus far, Bear had refused to respond to the cryptic email that had been sent to all the grandchildren from a woman purporting to be the widow of their long-lost grandfather Elias Fortune. The woman had summoned all six of

Elias and Edgar's grandchildren to Chatelaine to settle Elias's estate.

The other Fortune grandchildren—those of Edgar and Elias's brothers Walter and Wendell—had been notably left out. While Edgar and Elias had a reputation as the black sheep of the family, Walter and Wendell were the golden boys. Quite literally. Back in the 1950s, they'd struck gold in West Texas. Given Elias and Edgar's penchant for getting into trouble, they'd kept their successful mine a secret, leaving the headstrong brothers to mine for silver in Chatelaine. That venture had ended in disaster—the great Chatelaine mine collapse in 1965. Fifty miners had lost their lives.

Walter had since passed on, and Wendell had settled right here under the alias Martin Smith. But he'd recently been outed as Wendell Fortune, the owner of Fortune's Castle in Chatelaine, the epicenter of all the current family drama.

West hadn't been altogether surprised that Bear was avoiding the current situation in Chatelaine. Elias had fallen off the map years ago, after the collapse of the Fortune family silver mine. No one had heard from him in decades, much less known that he'd passed away and left a widow behind. Still, the fact that no one seemed to know Bear's whereabouts made his radio silence for the past three months somewhat concerning. Bear wasn't the best with correspondence, but after what West had been through, he needed to know that every member of his family was safe and sound.

He'd need to deal with that sooner, rather than later. It ranked right up there with *learn how to be a father* on his to-do list.

"Have I met Freya Fortune?" Tabitha nodded. "Of course. Since she gathered everyone up and got them here to Chatelaine, all your relatives found out about the twins. Everyone has been great about keeping in touch and sending baby gifts. I know they're all going to be so happy to hear you're alive, West. But you should probably prepare yourself. I have a feeling your homecoming is going to be a tad overwhelming."

As if anything could trump learning that he was a dad to twins.

West opened his mouth to respond, but before he could get a word out, there was a soft knock on Tabitha's front door.

She stiffened. "Are you expecting someone?"

"Tabs, I told you not to worry. We're safe." West's gut churned. The woman he loved didn't feel safe in her own home, and it was all his fault. "I promise."

She nodded. "The past twenty-four hours have just been a lot. Whoever that is, let's just hope they don't wake the boys."

Tabitha hurried to the door, and West came to stand behind her. Through the door's double-pane window, he spied an older woman with a stylish ash-blond haircut with bangs. At first he thought it might be Betty Lawford from across the street, bringing by a casserole or something as a guise for satisfying her curiosity about West's sudden reappearance. But this woman was no Betty Lawford, in her trademark housecoat and curlers. Whoever this was, she was dressed to the nines in a crisp white blouse with a wide, turned-up collar and slim black trousers. West was pretty sure her gold *H* belt buckle was designer.

"You wanted to know more about your mysterious stepgranny. Well, here's your chance." Tabitha's gaze shifted toward West. He knew exactly what the sudden sparkle in her eyes meant. *I told you to prepare yourself, cowboy.* "It's Freya Fortune."

"FRESH SQUEEZED LEMONADE." Tabitha set a tray containing three frosty glasses on the coffee table in her crowded living room. If she'd known a guest was coming, she probably would've picked up the twins' play blanket and toys.

She *definitely* would've put away the folded quilt and stack of pillows currently sitting at the foot of the couch, broadcasting the fact that West had spent the night there.

She pasted a smile on her face and pretended nothing was amiss, despite the way Freya's left eyebrow ticked skyward when she'd first noticed the neatly folded bedding. "From my lemon tree in the backyard."

"How nice. Thank you so much, Tabitha," Freya said.

Tabitha sat down beside West on the sofa, thighs pressed together since the blanket and pillows occupied a good deal of space. She didn't dare move them, lest she draw more attention to their presence. West's family had no idea they'd broken up before he went missing. Like everyone else in Chatelaine, the last thing they'd expect was for Tabitha to have him sleep on the sofa after finding out he wasn't really dead. For all they knew, West was simply her long-lost fiancé and the father of her children. Why wouldn't she welcome him back with open arms, right into her life?

And her bed.

Tabitha couldn't even think about going to bed with West right now. Scratch that: in reality, she'd thought of little else in the past twenty-four hours. Which was a problem. A *big* one.

She snuck a sideways glance at him as he picked up one of the glasses of lemonade and offered it to Freya, sitting across from them in one of Tabitha's shabby chic floral chintz armchairs. The scales probably tipped more toward the shabby side than chic, but she'd done her best to make a cozy, happy home for her and the boys. When her adoptive parents found out she was pregnant with twins, they'd

reacted by throwing money at her. It was their go-to solution for dealing with problems of any and all variety.

Tabitha had insisted she didn't need their financial help.
What she wanted most was for her mom and dad to act like
normal grandparents and shower the boys with affection.
To spoil them with love instead of expensive gifts and offers to buy the three of them a big new house.

That wasn't the Buckingham way, though. Her parents
weren't neglectful or cruel. Tabitha had lacked for nothing
growing up. She'd just never felt like she truly belonged in
their high-society world of country clubs, private schools
and children who were raised by nannies instead of their
mothers. So it hadn't been much of a surprise when she'd
found out she'd been born into an entirely different family. She'd been a *triplet*!

Tabitha probably shouldn't have been surprised she'd
ended up with twins. Multiple births ran in families. But
the last thing she'd expected after becoming a pseudo-
widow was to see a pair of little pink lines on the pregnancy test she'd taken solely to convince herself that the
nausea and exhaustion she'd been experiencing since
West's sudden death were part of the grieving process.

The surprises just kept on coming, didn't they? The biggest shock of all was sitting right beside her, looking as
manly and rugged as ever—and very much *alive*—among
all her vintage, romantic decor.

Why, oh why, did he have to look so good? The old West
Fortune had always made her go weak in the knees, but
this new version of West was almost too much to resist.
The physical work he'd been doing while in hiding showed.
His T-shirt strained across his firm back and chest. The
weariness he'd carried in the lines around his eyes while
he'd been a prosecutor had all but disappeared. For as
long as Tabitha had known West, there'd been a restless-

ness about him that always made her feel like a part of his mind was always someplace else. But now he seemed as still and solid as a rock.

Or maybe, after changing an average of one hundred forty diapers a week for the past year, she was just a sucker for a man who seemed dead set on figuring out how to be a hands-on dad.

You can't trust that, and you know it. The twins are a novelty to him. Once he goes back to work, he won't have time to play house anymore.

He was simply telling her what he knew she wanted to hear. West had always been good at that. He could charm the skin off a rattlesnake. It was part of what made him so good in front of a jury.

Tabitha dragged her gaze away from West's cattle-wrangling biceps and forced herself to pay attention to whatever Freya was saying.

"Again, I'm so sorry for turning up out of the blue like this. I came as soon as I heard the news." The older woman paused to take a sip of her lemonade.

"Well, it's a pleasure to meet you, ma'am," West said with a nod.

Freya waved a hand, "Oh, honey. There's no need to *ma'am* me. We're family."

"So I hear." He rolled his left shoulder—a new habit he'd developed in his absence.

"I'm not sure what all Camden and Tabitha have told you, so I'll just start at the beginning. A few months ago, your grandaddy, Elias Fortune, got very sick and fell into a coma. I'm sorry to say he never recovered. As you know, he'd been away from Chatelaine for a long, long time. After the silver mine collapsed all those years ago, he left and never looked back. The memories were just too painful."

West nodded, his expression inscrutable.

Freya's version of past events was more than a tad sugar-coated. Everyone in town knew that Elias and his brother Edgar had been at least partially responsible for the tragedy at the mine. They'd blamed the foreman, who'd died in the collapse, along with forty-nine other miners. Then they'd quietly left town to start over in Cave Creek, where a new generation of Fortunes had been born. But Elias and Edgar soon skipped town yet again, and from there, no one knew what had become of Elias.

Until Freya showed up, that is.

"Your granddaddy left a Last Will and Testament, and I'm here in Chatelaine to make sure his final wishes come to fruition. He left everything to you, your siblings and your cousins, West." Freya paused, toying with the silver bangle bracelets on her wrist. "For a very specific purpose."

West glanced at Tabitha. She'd heard about the terms of Elias's will from her sister Lily, who was married to West's cousin Asa. But this was Freya's moment, not hers.

The older woman took a deep breath. "Elias wanted to make amends for all the wrongs he and his brother bestowed on the Fortunes, so he left instructions for his assets to be used to make each of your wishes come true."

West's brow furrowed. "I'm not following."

"I'm here to do as your granddaddy spelled out in his will. In order to do that, I just need to know one thing." Freya's eyes glittered. "What's your most fervent wish?"

"My most fervent wish," West echoed.

"Yes. Just say the word, and I'll see to it that your granddaddy grants it from the grave." Freya threw up her hands. "You've been gone quite a while, West. I'm sure there are plenty of things you need. A new house where you and your sweet family can start over, perhaps?"

Tabitha flew to her feet. "I should check on the twins."

She couldn't stay here and listen to this anymore. *Shouldn't.* This was personal Fortune family business, and despite what everyone still thought, Tabitha wasn't West's family. He was the father of her children, but that's where their connection ended. Full stop.

And the fact that she had no idea how he would answer Freya's question wasn't lost on her. Once upon a time, she knew everything about West Fortune. Those days were over, though. She didn't have a clue what he wanted anymore. They'd been living completely separate lives for nearly two years. Time and circumstances had changed Tabitha so much that she was a whole new person now. A *mother*. It would've been ridiculously naive to think that West had remained exactly the same.

Then why won't you give him another chance?

The thought made her breath catch in a way that was equal parts tempting and terrifying. She pushed it away before it took root.

"I just heard one of the babies cry," she blurted.

"I didn't hear anything," Freya countered.

West eyed her with concern. "Are you okay, sweetheart?"

I'm not your sweetheart. She felt empty inside, hollowed out by grief. She'd felt this way for so long that she no longer knew how to fill up that emptiness with something good and pure—something that might just be within arm's reach. If only she could believe.

"I'm fine." A bald-faced lie. "Like I said, I need to check on the boys. You two visit for a while."

Once she'd excused herself, Tabitha fled to the comforting familiarity of the nursery. The boys were still fast asleep, so she sat down in the rocking chair all on her own, wrapped a knitted throw over her shoulders and quietly rocked back and forth. The motion of the chair helped calm the jumble of thoughts and emotions that had her so tied up in knots. She'd been a mess since she'd found West waiting for her on her front porch yesterday. It felt good to do something normal again—something she'd done a million times before.

Whenever Tabitha felt overwhelmed or couldn't sleep at night, she came here and sat in the dark with the twins. Just being near them kept her grounded and reminded her what was truly important. So long as her boys were safe and sound, everything was okay in her world. She could deal with the rest in due time.

But she hadn't had a second to catch her breath since West's return. He was *right there*, all the time. Before their breakup and before his disappearance, she would've given anything to have so much quality time with the man she loved. Now, it was just confusing.

Had she done the right thing when she'd ended their engagement?

She wasn't sure anymore. In all the months he'd been gone, she'd never once wavered on this point. As much as she'd missed him and mourned his loss, she knew she'd made the right choice. West hadn't wanted a family and he hadn't made her a priority in his life. Not truly.

Things seemed so different now. But Tabitha wondered how long it would last.

She closed her eyes and dropped her head against the back of the rocker. Thanks to the tiny size of her living quarters, West's deep voice carried from the other room. Was there nowhere she could go to escape the man?

"My most fervent wish? That's easy. I don't even have to think about it."

Tabitha stopped rocking and strained to hear more, even

though it mortified her to her very core that she was so invested in his answer.

"I want to be a good dad," he said, voice firm with conviction.

Tabitha's throat closed as he went on.

"It's so strange. I never wanted kids…could never imagine it. But the instant I learned those boys were mine, I felt bonded to them. Like I'd give my life for them. Is that crazy?"

"That's not crazy at all, West. That's love," Freya said, and Tabitha could hear the smile in her voice, even from the other room. "And that's exactly why I know you'll succeed in being a great father."

"Thank you for saying that, but you don't even know me."

"I know enough. Trust me, just being here counts for a lot. That's what children want most—your nurturing presence. Shower them with warmth and affection, and you can't go wrong. You'll learn the rest along the way."

There was the unmistakable sound of boots against the hardwood floors, which meant West had stood up. Apparently, the visit was winding to a close.

His voice grew quieter as they moved toward the front door. "This advice is just the thing I needed to hear. You know, Freya, for someone who doesn't have kids, you sure are knowledgeable about parenthood."

"Your granddaddy and I weren't blessed with children, but I had a daughter a long time ago. It feels like a different life now. We grew estranged, and it's the single biggest regret I've ever had," Freya confessed, and the sadness in her tone brought a tear to Tabitha's eye.

She froze, unable to even wipe it away. Freya had *a daughter*?

"I'm sorry to hear that," West said.

"It's water under the bridge, but don't you worry. We both know you won't be making that mistake." The front door swung open on squeaky hinges, but still she couldn't bring herself to move. "Tell Tabitha thank you for the lemonade, and I'll come back soon so I can give those two babies of yours a squeeze."

Tabitha's throat closed up tight. Her eyes burned from the effort it took not to break down and cry.

Why couldn't she have Freya's unshakeable trust in West? He wanted to be a good father. It was his most fervent wish, and this time he hadn't said it just for Tabitha's benefit. Freya had offered him a *house*, and still all he could talk about was how much he loved Zach and Zane.

Before yesterday, if someone would've told her that West was really alive and he was coming home, her reaction would've been pure, unparalleled joy. But seeing him again stirred up so many conflicting feelings, especially when he'd jumped to the immediate assumption that she'd moved on with someone else. He'd seriously thought she'd married another man and started a family!

How was she supposed to wrap her mind around that?

Tabitha sighed. The man sleeping on her couch was the West she'd fallen in love with, but at the same time, he was also a complete and total stranger.

Even so, maybe it was time to take him at his word.

CHAPTER FOUR

LATER THAT EVENING, Tabitha didn't know what to do with herself while West single-handedly got the twins dressed in their pajama onesies and read them a bedtime story. Once again, he got the boys mixed up and accidentally dressed Zane in the onesie that had Zach's name embroidered across the chest. But other than that tiny mistake, he did a great job.

"You don't need to hover," he told her as he re-dressed the babies in the correctly monogrammed pajamas. "I've got this."

She lingered in the doorway to the nursery for a beat, but finally went to the kitchen to pour herself a glass of wine once West was settled in the rocker with the twins balanced on his lap and a picture book in his hands.

He was their dad. She needed to let him figure some things out on his own, just the way she'd done after she'd first brought them home from the hospital. It was part of the bonding process. West had already missed out on so much. She knew she needed to give him some time and space with the boys on his own so he could get to know them. It was just so hard when she was accustomed to doing it all by herself. Day after day...

"Success! They're both down for the count." West raked a hand through his hair as he joined her in the living room. When his gaze landed on the laptop balanced on a pillow on her lap, a furrow formed between his brows. "You're working?"

Tabitha nodded. "Yes, but I'm just finishing up. Since I had a little bit of free time, I wanted to catch up on a website I've been building for a new florist in San Antonio."

"I don't know how you can think straight at this hour." He shook his head and came to sit beside her on the sofa.

"It's only eight o'clock." She closed the laptop and set it on the coffee table beside her glass of wine and the baby monitor, although the square footage of her cottage pretty much made the second item unnecessary.

"Right, and between the twins and your job, you've been going nonstop all day. If I had to read a legal brief right now, I wouldn't be able to make a lick of sense of it." He dropped his head on the back of the sofa and blew out a breath.

"West Fortune, are you saying that two sweet, almost-one-year-olds are harder to take care of than an entire ranch full of horses and cattle? Because that's definitely my takeaway from this discussion." She gave him a playful poke in the ribs.

He grabbed hold of her index finger before she could snatch it back, and before she realized what was happening, they were casually holding hands…as if doing so was normal. As if they were a regular married couple who'd just put their babies down for the night.

"That's precisely what I'm saying." West turned her hand over in his and stared for a beat at her bare ring finger.

Her engagement ring still hung from the gold chain around her neck. She couldn't bring herself to remove it. Hiding it away in her jewelry box seemed wrong, and yet sliding it back onto her finger didn't make sense either. West was back, but they were still stuck in some strange romantic limbo. Tabitha couldn't seem to figure out whether she should take a step forward or backward. Both options felt equally terrifying.

West's gaze shifted from their linked hands to her face, and his expression turned so achingly tender that her mouth went dry. "I'm here now. You don't have to do it all anymore. Let me help, Tabs."

"I'm trying," she said, but it was so much easier said than done. Couldn't he see that?

She'd worked hard at building this life. It was simple, and yes, it was exhausting at times. But it was *hers*. She'd made a happy home for herself and her boys without any financial assistance from her parents or any full-time help. When West had been presumed dead and she'd found out she was pregnant, Tabitha had felt like the ground had suddenly disappeared from beneath her feet. She didn't know how she'd ever manage things on her own.

But like the good, strong Texas girl that she was, she'd pulled herself up by her bootstraps and become the best mom she could possibly be. Her twins were healthy and happy. Her bank balance was modest, but she'd managed to stash away enough savings for emergencies and create a business from scratch where she could be her own boss and work from home around her children's schedules.

"What are you so afraid of?" West asked softly, and the pad of his thumb began to move in slow, gentle circles over her palm, soothing her before she could protest and pretend she wasn't scared.

The truth was she was terrified to her very core. Once she let this man in, there was no going back. She couldn't go through losing him. Not again. She'd barely survived it the first time around.

"I just need some time, okay? This is all a lot. My head

hasn't stopped spinning since you showed up on my front porch yesterday."

"That's fair." West nodded and squeezed her hand so tight that she thought he might never let go. "But tell me something. It's been hours since Freya left. Are you going to tell me what's been going on in that pretty head of yours all day, or am I going to have to guess?"

West still knew her well enough to know when she was overthinking something.

Tabitha could remember a time when he had told her that one of the most important aspects of his job as a prosecutor was being adept at studying human behavior. To know when witnesses were lying and when they were being truthful, to be able to tell when they actually remembered something and when their subconscious was merely filling in the gaps, to know when to push someone into talking and when to back off. But the way he'd always been able to see her inside and out was uncanny sometimes. She'd thought that after so much time apart, he'd no longer be able to read her like a book.

Wrong.

"Did you mean what you said when she asked you about your most fervent wish?" she asked, because she just didn't have it in her to try and hide the truth. What was the point?

"Why, Tabitha Buckingham." West's eyes went wide in mock astonishment. "Were you eavesdropping on my private conversation with my step-granny and widow to my long-lost grandfather?"

She loved that he could still make her laugh, even when the ground beneath her feet had started to feel so shaky again. "A little bit, yes."

"I meant every word." The smile on West's lips faded, and suddenly he was looking at her with such earnestness that she couldn't remember how to breathe. "But I understand why it's hard for you to believe that, sweetheart. All I'm asking is for a chance to show you how much you and those boys mean to me. I know it won't happen overnight, but that's okay. We have all the time in the world now."

Did they?

Because it didn't feel that way. He'd been gone so long that a part of Tabitha wanted to consume him completely, just to make up for lost time. Tomorrow wasn't a promise or a guarantee. She'd lost enough people in the course of her lifetime to have that truth engraved on her heart from now until the end of time.

Maybe that's why, instead of pulling her hand away and going to bed—*alone*—like she should have, Tabitha did the one thing she couldn't stop thinking about. She shifted to sit in his lap, wrapped her arms around his neck and kissed West Fortune with every pent-up ounce of longing that she'd been trying her level best to pretend she didn't feel. And it was such a relief to let it out, to pour all of her grief and need straight into the only man who'd ever held her heart, that she couldn't seem to stop—not even when her fingers found their way to the buttons on West's shirt. Not even when he groaned into her mouth as her hands slid over his bare chest. And *especially* not even when he picked her up, carried her to the bedroom and kicked the door shut with the heel of his boot.

A shiver coursed through her as he lifted her dress over her head. West hadn't seen her like this in so long. She'd given birth to two children since they'd last slept together, and she half expected him to look at her like she was a stranger. But instead, his gaze landed on the chain around her neck and the gold ring resting against her heart.

His lips curved into a tender smile, and he hooked a fingertip in the chain to reel her in for a kiss.

Tonight wasn't a pledge or a promise. West had said so

himself just a few minutes ago. This moment was something else entirely—it was about remembering. Remembering who they both were and what they'd meant to each other, once upon a time. It was about rewriting the last two years and finding that elusive happy-ever-after. Not for tomorrow, but for yesterday. For those two innocent souls who'd once been on the verge of standing before God and promising to love, honor and cherish each other til death do them part.

Tabitha missed the people they'd been back then—back before work had begun to consume West and things had spiraled so wildly out of control. Everything had been so simple once upon a time. So pure.

So she closed her eyes, returned West's kiss and did her best to fall into yesterday.

WEST DIDN'T WANT to open his eyes the following morning. Somehow he knew if he did, the magic spell that he and Tabitha had managed to weave the night before would be broken in the cold light of day. Sure enough, once he dragged his eyelids open, he found himself alone in Tabitha's bed. The sheets beside him were cool to the touch, and her pillow barely had the slightest indentation.

Who knew how long he'd been lying there by himself?

He sat up and scrubbed a hand over his face. This wasn't good. He'd taken things as slow as possible last night and tried his hardest to follow Tabitha's lead. But she'd been in such a rush. He'd never felt as though they'd really connected. Every time he'd tried to pull back and meet her gaze, she closed her eyes. When he'd whispered sweet nothings in her ear, he hadn't been sure he'd actually gotten through to her. It almost felt as if she'd been somewhere else entirely instead of the here and now, with *him*, in this place where he'd hoped they could build a new beginning.

When he got up and left the bedroom, he found her already dressed and put together in the kitchen, even though the twins were still sleeping soundly in the nursery. She had a mountain of fruit on the counter in front of her, along with a line of plastic containers with lids, and seemed to be in the process of meal planning for the twins for what looked like an entire year. Possibly the rest of their lives.

"Good morning," she said, focusing intently on the mango on her cutting board instead of looking him in the eye. "Sorry if I woke you. I couldn't sleep."

West surveyed the countertop and arched a brow. "I can see that."

"Can I get you a cup of coffee or something? A banana, maybe?" She held up a piece of fruit, and as soon as their eyes locked, her bottom lip began to quiver. Just the tiniest bit. If West had blinked, he would've missed it.

He took the banana and set it back down on the counter. "Thanks, but no. Talk to me, sweetheart. What's really going on here? You seem upset."

She took a deep breath. "I'm not upset. I'm just…"

"This is about last night, isn't it?" West asked, stating the obvious. If he'd done something wrong, he wanted to know about it. Losing his life had humbled him every which way, and he didn't want anything coming between them again. Not if he could help it.

"I'm not ready for this." She gestured to the empty space between them, which felt impossibly big all of a sudden. Like a wide, endless cavern. "I thought I might be, but I'm not."

"I understand," he said quietly.

It's going to be okay. You just got back. There's still time to be a family together. Just because she's not ready now doesn't mean she'll never be ready.

At least they'd had last night. It had been so good to hold

her again, to love her. It hadn't been perfect, but that didn't matter. And now, the memory of it gave West a glimmer of hope that they could somehow find each other again.

"Last night was a mistake," Tabitha said, and he wasn't altogether sure if she was trying to convince him or herself.

Either way, he died a little bit inside. *Please don't say that. Loving you would never be a mistake.*

"I see." He nodded. His mouth had gone dry as a bone. He needed coffee…or water…or to just go back to sleep and convince himself that this conversation wasn't really happening. That it was all just a bad dream.

It wasn't, though. It was as real as all those long, lonely months he'd spent on the run. He'd finally come home, and somehow, he still hadn't made it all the way back.

West knew he had no one to blame but himself. He'd been the one to push Tabitha away when she'd started talking about children. She'd wanted it all—the white picket fence, lemonade stands on hot summer days and pony rides during rodeo season. And she'd had every right to expect it, because they'd been engaged to be married. But as the wedding date grew closer, it had all started to feel impossibly real. He had no business raising kids. What if he ruined them? What if history repeated itself and he screwed everything up, just like his parents had?

The shame of his childhood crept in until it was overwhelming, and instead of sharing those thoughts and fears with his beautiful fiancée, he'd pushed her away. He'd thrown himself into work, because that was what he was best at—putting bad guys away. It was honorable and meant that West was a good man. A man who was nothing like his dad.

Did it, however? Look where it had gotten them.

"It's okay, Tabs. Really. I just want to be in your lives, no matter the terms. I'm not going anywhere. You have my word." He reached for her hand and squeezed it tight. "I'll go back to staying on the couch. If you still want to let me stay, that is?"

His heart was in his throat. What if she said no?

She lifted her chin and gazed up at him, and for a moment, West was convinced she was about to send him packing. But then the twins began stirring in the nursery. Happy, gurgling baby sounds drifted toward them from the hallway.

Tabitha's eyes went soft, and the space between them felt less daunting. She was right there again, just an arm's length away. Close enough to touch, to kiss, to love.

"Of course you can stay. The boys would like that very much." She smiled and West felt it down to his soul. "So would I."

At least she still wore his ring on the chain around her neck. The thin band glimmered in the sunshine streaming through the kitchen window. Like liquid gold, like hope itself.

This wasn't a happy-ever-after, and it might never be. Tomorrow was full of unknowns, as West knew all too well.

But it just might be a start.

CHAPTER FIVE

TABITHA HAD TO tell her sisters about West. Or maybe she simply had to get out of the house. She hadn't set foot out in the real world since her twins' dad had turned up out of the blue, and things had begun feeling much too cozy. Too much like a family, which they weren't.

Which was probably why she'd let down her guard last night.

No more. She'd woken up feeling intensely vulnerable in West's arms in the wee hours of the night. Was she really going to give him the chance to break her heart again? She couldn't. It was too soon, and she couldn't trust whatever she was feeling for him again. It had only been two days, for goodness' sake. Anyone could throw themselves into fatherhood and family life for forty-eight hours.

After the painfully awkward morning-after conversation, Tabitha sent an urgent text to her sisters and all but fled to the Cowgirl Café to meet Lily and Haley, who'd dropped everything they were doing and come straight to the restaurant while West stayed home with the twins.

Having the sort of freedom for an impromptu girls' lunch in the middle of the day was a novelty that Tabitha was in no way accustomed to. Under normal circumstances, it would've thrilled her to pieces. But there was no world in which her current circumstances would've been described as normal. She'd left *normal* behind the very instant her dead ex-fiancé had tipped his Stetson and called her "darlin'."

"So what's the big emergency?" Lily plucked a fry from the enormous platter of chili fries in the center of the table, gaze swiveling between Tabitha and their other sister, Haley.

"Don't look at me. Your guess is as good as mine." Haley shrugged one slender shoulder and reached for her cherry Coke. "Tabs, is everything okay? And where are the twins? I thought your babysitter had to quit because of the cheer squad."

"She did. The boys are actually with—um—" *With their daddy. You know, the love of my life, who we all thought was dead.* She couldn't just blurt it out like that, although the temptation was real. It might be nice not being the most flabbergasted person in the room for a change.

"They're fine," she said simply, resting her hands on the table. She stared longingly at the chili cheese fries. The Cowgirl Café in downtown Chatelaine never disappointed. Tabitha and her sisters had been regulars since the restaurant's recent grand opening, so summoning them here with a text message had seemed like a good idea earlier this morning.

But the establishment was owned by Bea Fortune, one of West's cousins. Tabitha hadn't seen Bea bustling around the restaurant yet, but she was bound to turn up sooner or later. If Freya had already heard about West's return, the rest of the Fortunes had to know too. It was a wonder the gossip hadn't reached her sisters yet. The chili cheese fries could wait. She needed to go ahead and drop the bomb before someone else did.

"Tabitha, you wouldn't believe what I overheard Betty Lawford saying this morning while I was at GreatStore buying a dog bed for Max." Lily jammed a fry into a pile of chili in a way that could only be described as aggressive. "I was *livid*."

Haley held up a hand. "Wait. You bought Max *another* dog bed? Didn't Asa already buy one…or three?"

"Yes, but now Max has gotten accustomed to having one in nearly every room at the ranch. I figured another one couldn't hurt." Lily bit her lip. Tabitha would've bet good money she'd purchased more than just the one bed. Lily worshipped her sweet new rescue dog and vice versa. "Anyway, that's not the point. Just as I walked past the gardening aisle, I overheard your neighbor telling someone that she'd seen West. *West Fortune!* Can you believe it. She tried to say she'd spied him alive and well and drinking coffee on your front porch this morning."

Tabitha nearly choked on her Dr Pepper. The bomb had already been dropped, apparently.

"I set her straight right away. That kind of talk is just hurtful. The past two years have been hard enough without subjecting you to false hope," Lily huffed.

"Oh my gosh, what is wrong with people? Tabs, just ignore that nosy busybody." Haley's forehead scrunched and her drink paused en route to her mouth. "But wait. Was there really a man drinking coffee on your front porch this morning?"

Guilty as charged.

Listen to her. Even her internal thoughts were starting to sound like something West would say in a courtroom. He'd been back in her life less than forty-eight hours, and everything was changing. Was it really so bad that she just wanted this crazy ride to stop for a second so she could get off and catch her breath?

"As a matter of fact, there *was* a man on my porch this morning." Tabitha took a deep breath. "And that man was indeed West Fortune."

A chili-laden fry fell from Lily's hand and landed on the table with a splat.

Haley blinked. "I don't understand."

That makes two of us. Tabitha could still barely wrap her head around it herself.

She spent the next few minutes getting her sisters caught up while the untouched chili fries grew cold and the chili congealed. No one cared about food anymore. West Fortune was *back from the dead*.

"This is amazing! I just can't believe it. I'm so, so happy for you, Tabs." Lily reached across the table to take both of Tabitha's hands in hers.

That was what did it. Her sister's kind words seemed to reach deep into Tabitha's chest and tear her heart in two as easily as if it were made of paper. A sob escaped her and then another, until she was reduced to a bawling wreck right there in the Cowgirl Café among the bandana-style napkins and mod Western decor.

Haley gently dabbed Tabitha's face with one of the aforementioned napkins. "Tabs, what's wrong? West coming home is a good thing."

"I know it is. It's just a little…*overwhelming*. That's all." She lowered her voice until it was barely above a whisper. "We were broken up, remember? But now he's back, and somehow it doesn't feel that way. It almost feels like we're still engaged to be married."

"Maybe this could be your second chance." Lily's eyes sparkled.

Haley smiled in such a hopeful way that Tabitha's heart wrenched. "Do you think things between you might work out?"

"To be honest, I'm not sure there's an us anymore." Why did things seem so uncertain in the light of day? When it was just the two of them, Tabitha could almost imagine a future with West. But the moment the real world crept in, so did her doubts. Case in point: this morning. "He told me he was adamant about not wanting kids before, but you should see him with the boys. He's trying really hard to be a devoted father. It's all so bewildering."

"I'm sure it is, but does it have to be? All that really matters is how you two feel about each other." Lily squeezed Tabitha's hands so hard that her knuckles turned white, which only made her more emotional. All Tabitha had wanted since she first learned she was a triplet was to feel close to her sisters. She just never imagined it would take a soap-opera-level crisis in her personal life to get there.

"You still love him," Haley said. A statement, not a question.

"I do, and I know he loves me too." Tabitha closed her eyes against the memory of West's crestfallen expression this morning when she'd told him that sleeping together had been a mistake. Trying to force the image away didn't do any good at all. The devastated look on his face was seared into her mind's eye for all eternity. "But the choice to be a dad wasn't his. I keep thinking about what might happen once everything settles down and life goes back to normal."

"I think the lesson from all of this is that we never know what might happen in the future, but you shouldn't rule out the possibility that you and West can work things out," Haley murmured.

Lily nodded. "That's right. The only thing you can do is take things one day at a time."

One day at a time. Tabitha took a shuddering inhale. She could do that, couldn't she? West had waited nineteen long months to come home, never losing faith that it would happen someday. What must that have been like, knowing that everyone he loved had gone on with their lives thinking he was dead? Had he read his obituary in the *Chatelaine Daily News*? Had he imagined the funeral and all the tears shed by his loved ones? After West's death and subsequently learning she was carrying his babies, Tabitha's grief had been suffocating. It had been like losing the love of her life all over again, only this time the loss was permanent. Crushing.

But she'd only lost West. West had lost everything and everyone he'd ever loved, all in one fell swoop.

Tabitha couldn't imagine living a day in his shoes when he'd been in hiding. He must've grieved the loss of West Fortune as fervently as everyone else had.

If he could hold out hope indefinitely, never knowing when he could come home, surely she could learn to take things one day at a time. They'd leapt in with both feet last night, and look how that had turned out. No wonder things had been so awkward and she'd felt so vulnerable. She'd acted as if the past two years had never happened, as if she and West were the same people they'd been before they'd broken up and he had been forced to go into hiding.

They weren't the same people. The old Tabitha Buckingham was as much a part of history as the old West Fortune. Her sisters were right. Before they could move forward, they needed to get to know each other again.

Baby steps, Tabitha told herself. Just like Zach and Zane learning to balance on their precious little feet. After all, they were the most important part of this equation. The twins were everything. If she and West were ever truly going to be together again, they'd do so as a family. White picket fence and all, just like Tabitha had always dreamed of…

Which was exactly the sort of happy-ever-after fantasy that had torn them apart the first time around.

WEST HEADED STRAIGHT to his brother Camden's ranch after Tabitha returned home from lunch with her sisters. If she needed space, he was determined to give it to her. They'd rushed things last night. He knew that now, and he couldn't afford to make that kind of mistake again.

He'd spent the past two years in a race against time. Waiting, waiting, waiting...never knowing when it would be safe to come back home. A day hadn't passed without West knowing precisely how long he'd been away.

But now time was back on his side. There was no more need to worry about the passing minutes, days, weeks... *years*. Still, he couldn't help feeling like he had to make up for lost time. He wanted his life back, damn it. Every lost, lonely second of it. When Tabitha kissed him last night, every last remaining shred of his patience had crumbled. He'd actually been fool enough to believe that all their problems had vanished the moment he'd crossed the Chatelaine town border.

It's going to be fine, he told himself again. Whatever Tabitha needed, he'd do it. They could get past this. They had to.

He took a deep breath as he lingered on the front porch of Camden's ranch house and looked around. His brother had done well for himself. The aptly named Chatelaine Ranch was located off the highway, down a long dirt road that led to the shady, somewhat secluded property. West had driven past the ranch offices when he'd first arrived and then various buildings earmarked for the equestrian riding camp and school his brother was working on getting started. The ranch house sat by itself on the back side of the property, overlooking a wide green pasture.

Before he had a chance to knock, the door swung open.

"Well, aren't you a sight for sore eyes?" Camden said as he wrapped West in a big bear hug. "Welcome home, brother."

"It's good to be back. More than a bit surreal, but good."

Camden pulled back to look him up and down. "You look good, man. Less lawyer and more cowboy. It suits you."

"You think?" West pulled his black Stetson down lower over his eyes.

"Okay, so the hat isn't new. But the tan from being in the saddle all day certainly is. And your Wranglers are a fair bit more worn-in than they used to be. If you're not careful, I'll put you to work here at the ranch. I'm always looking for good help." Camden winked.

"Don't tempt me with a good time," West said.

In a way, those days at the ranch out in West Texas had been a blessing. The work had been physically demanding enough that he hadn't had the time or energy to dwell on his circumstances. It wasn't until the lights went out at the bunkhouse every night that his mind wandered back to Chatelaine. Then he'd fall into a deep sleep and dream of sultry nights in South Texas. Of Tabitha. Of home.

He couldn't work as a ranch hand here in Chatelaine, obviously. He was an attorney, and the whole point of coming home was to get his life back. West just hadn't allowed himself to dwell on that part yet, seeing as his job had been a point of contention between him and Tabitha. Now more than ever before, seeing as it had been the entire reason he'd been forced to go into hiding.

"Nice place you've got here, Cam." West nodded toward the paddock where a pair of glossy chestnut quarter horses grazed.

"You want a tour?"

"I'd love one."

His brother showed him around the ranch, from the main house to the barn, the stables and beyond. Afterward, they settled on the broad back porch of the ranch house with ice-cold bottles of beer.

Camden couldn't seem to stop stealing glances at West and grinning from ear to ear. "Man, it's so good to see you. I still can't believe it. You're *alive*."

"And I'm a *dad*." West took a long pull of his beer. "But I suppose I don't need to tell you that. I'm the last one to know."

"Twins." Camden let out a low laugh. "I bet that was a surprise."

"You have no idea." Sometimes he still couldn't believe it, even after the two or three dozen diaper changes he'd racked up since he'd been back. At least he'd figured out which side was the front of the darn things and which side was the back. Now he just needed to master the fine art of telling his children apart. "It was a good one, though. The best news I've ever heard."

"Was it?" Camden arched an eyebrow beneath the brim of his cowboy hat. "As I recall, you've always felt a bit ambivalent about fatherhood. Not that I blame you. Our parents weren't exactly the poster couple for parenthood."

"Not at all." West gave his brother a tight smile. There was no need to get into specifics. They both remembered the slamming doors and screaming fights that punctuated their childhoods on a regular basis. Try as he might, West couldn't forget those dark days, and he knew Camden well enough to realize neither could he.

Kids shouldn't be forced to be part of a family dynamic like that. Innocent children deserved better, which was why West was determined to be a better man than his father was. No matter what it took.

"And you're right. Kids were never part of the plan, but now that they're here..." West sighed. He just couldn't put the feeling in words, no matter how hard he tried. "I love them. I don't have a clue what I'm doing when it comes to taking care of them, but I do love them."

Camden's green eyes went soft. "That's all that matters, bro. You'll figure out the rest. After all, you've dealt with some of the worst criminals in the state of Texas. Twin one-year-olds have got to seem easy by comparison."

West snorted. "You'd be surprised."

Camden shook his head and laughed. "Do you have any idea how grateful I am to see you again?"

"I think I've got a good idea." West's heart swelled. He had more to be grateful for than he deserved.

"Especially with Bear falling off the face of the earth and all. I've missed my brothers, man. I finally got a text from him two days ago and all it said was that he'd try and get to Chatelaine soon. That he's got 'a lot going on.'" Camden made finger quotes around that last part.

He and West exchanged a glance. *Yeah, here too.*

"Does he know about me yet?" West drained what was left of his beer.

"Not yet. I needed to see it myself to believe it." Camden pulled his phone from the back pocket of his Wranglers. "I'll text him right now. I'd call but we both know he'd never answer."

He tapped out a message and within seconds, Camden's phone chimed with an incoming text.

"It's him. Wonders never cease. If I'd known that all it took to get him to communicate was a resurrection, I would've tried to arrange for one sooner," Camden said, squinting at the screen. "He says to tell you he's happy you're alive, and he'll come to Chatelaine before the end of the month. That's a promise."

West nodded. "Good. It'll be great to see him again, and he's got a lot to catch up on around here."

Surprise twins, West back from the dead, Freya Fortune turning up out of nowhere and their grandfather's eccentric Last Will and Testament. What next? Amnesia?

Camden tapped the neck of his beer bottle against the one in West's hand. "Ain't that the truth."

CHAPTER SIX

THE FOLLOWING MORNING, West paid a visit to the local law enforcement offices. He'd been dragging his feet on coming face-to-face with the sheriff since he still wasn't sure what to do about his career prospects, but as a former officer of the court, he had a duty to explain how a man who'd been declared legally dead had turned up alive. He couldn't keep putting it off, especially now that word was beginning to spread.

"Well, as I live and breathe." Sheriff Cooper's eyes lit up the second West strode into his office. He removed his feet—clad, as always, in worn brown leather cowboy boots—from his desk and stood. "So the rumors are true. You're really alive."

"Looks that way, doesn't it?" West removed his hat and extended his hand for a shake, but the older man came around the front of his desk and pulled him into a hug instead. He pounded hard on West's back, as if proving to himself that West wasn't merely a ghostly apparition.

"Do you have any idea how much we've missed you around here?" the sheriff said, eyes crinkling in the corners. "I cried like a baby when I heard that you were back from the dead. It's like a miracle, son. Tell me everything."

So West did. He took a seat and explained what had happened on the day Trey Mendez found him on the riverbank, how he'd faked his death and left just enough personal possessions behind to convince the outlaw he'd truly been murdered. The sheriff listened, riveted, until West finished.

Then he let out a long, low whistle and sat back in his chair. "Like I said, a miracle."

"Let's hope the state bar agrees," West said. Without a law license, he couldn't work. As nice and quiet as the past few days had been, he had twins to provide for now. Tabitha had been doing it on her own for far too long.

That was going to change. The rest of their future was still undetermined, but West was adamant about making parenthood easier on Tabitha.

"Don't you worry about the state bar." Sheriff Cooper waved a hand as if batting away a pesky insect. "Our office will help you get the legalities straightened out as quickly as possible. Chatelaine still needs you, West. *We* need you. When can you come back to work?"

And there it was—the very question West had been trying to avoid.

"You mean as a staff attorney or something, right? I'm sure the county prosecutor position has been filled." West couldn't imagine his job being kept open for so long. It just wasn't possible.

"Oh, no. I mean head honcho, just like before. We've had an interim county prosecutor since your disappearance. There was no reason to keep your desk vacant, but you left some pretty big shoes to fill, West. We've been searching for a fully qualified candidate for quite some time. You're not an easy prosecutor to replace. As fate would have it, the perfect person for the job just walked into my office and is sitting right across from me." The sheriff shot finger guns at West.

Message received. The job was still his if he wanted it.

West cleared his throat. "I don't know, Sheriff. I appreciate the offer. You know I do, but it's a lot to think about. I just got back, and my life isn't as simple as it used to be."

"Ah, right. The twins." Sheriff Cooper flashed him a smile. "How are the little rug rats doing? Their first birthday has got to be coming up soon, right?"

West swallowed and a wave of shame instantly engulfed him. He knew the twins were almost a year old, but he had no idea what their actual birthday was. Father of the year material, he was not.

"I, um…" He shook his head.

The sheriff averted his gaze, and the easy, breezy vibe of their conversation shifted as the older man graciously made excuses for West's obvious cluelessness. "Well, like you said, your life isn't quite as simple as it used to be. I'm sure there's a lot to catch up on."

It was more kindness than West deserved, at least in his own estimation.

"You know what we need?" Sheriff Cooper eyed the desk pad calendar that took up the majority of the wooden surface of his desk. "A party."

He slammed his palm down on the calendar for added emphasis.

"A birthday party?" West asked, still thinking about the twins and their upcoming milestone.

"No." The sheriff shook his head and then shrugged. "Well, yes. That, too. But that's your department. I'm talking about a party for you."

Out came the finger guns again.

West shifted uncomfortably in his chair. "That's really not necessary."

"On the contrary. It's *very* necessary. You're a bona fide town hero, West. And after everything that's happened, now you're a Chatelaine *legend*. Let the community give you a proper welcome home, son. I insist."

West tried to beg off. "I really don't think…"

"Stop." Sheriff Cooper held up a hand. "Consider it done. We'll have a picnic party in the park and invite the entire town. You've made a tremendous sacrifice for the good of Chatelaine. It's the very least we can do. Does this Saturday work for you?"

West tried to imagine the look on Tabitha's face when he went home and told her the sheriff was throwing him a literal party. She'd assume he'd already agreed to go back to work as the county prosecutor, no matter how fervently he denied it. This couldn't end well.

"Good. It's settled, then," the sheriff said, mistaking West's silence for agreement. "Saturday, it is. Make sure you bring those sweet boys of yours. And Tabitha, too, of course."

Right, because nearly everyone in Chatelaine thought they were still engaged, West's former boss included. Now wasn't the time to set the record straight on that matter. His life was already front-page news. And he wanted to protect Tabitha and the twins from as much of that attention as possible.

"Of course," West echoed.

What else could he say?

"We'll be there with bells on."

TABITHA TOOK A deep breath as she pushed the twins' double stroller up one of Chatelaine Park's shaded walking paths late Saturday afternoon.

She thought she'd been prepared for this. A welcome-home picnic in the park sounded thoughtful and sweet. Was she thrilled that it had been Sheriff Cooper's idea? Not exactly. The man worshipped the ground West walked on and she had no doubt that he'd move heaven and earth to get West back to work as the county prosecutor. Still, it was a lovely gesture, so when West had come home from the sheriff's office the other day and told her about the party, she'd ignored the warning bells going off in the back of her head and told him she was happy for him. Of course she'd attend the picnic with him, and the boys would come too. It would be just the sort of family outing she'd always dreamed about.

Or so she'd thought.

"Wow." She blinked at the massive banner strung from two of the park's tallest trees. *Welcome home, West Fortune!* The lettering on the banner was so big that it could probably be seen from space. "This is really something, isn't it?"

West's gaze shifted to the white tent that had been assembled beneath the banner, complete with a podium and enough balloons to send the entire setup airborne. His forehead crinkled. "I guess Sheriff Cooper wasn't kidding when he said he wanted the whole town to come out for this."

"Apparently not." Tabitha pasted on a smile. This day was about West, not her. He deserved to be welcomed back to Chatelaine with open arms, even if this "picnic" was more along the lines of a state fair than a simple small-town party in the park. "I'm happy for you. Chatelaine loves you, West. Our town is a safe place to live and raise a family, largely because of you. It's good that the community appreciates all the hard work you've done on behalf of the county."

"Thank you for saying that." He wrapped an arm around her shoulders and pressed a chaste kiss to her forehead.

A ridiculous shiver coursed through her. They'd been tiptoeing around each other the past few days, pretending their night together had never happened, but her body betrayed her at even the most casual contact.

"But this doesn't mean I'm going back to work as the county prosecutor," he said.

Tabitha nodded. "I know. You mentioned that already. A few times, actually."

The furrow in West's brow deepened. "Tabs, I—"

Before he could finish whatever he wanted to say, Sheriff Cooper came bustling down the path toward them.

"The man of the hour is here! And you've brought your beautiful family. Look at how much those twins have grown." He gave West a one-armed hug before leaning in to kiss Tabitha on the cheek. "I'm so happy for the two of you. I know you're even happier than the rest of us to have West home, as fit as a fiddle."

"The boys and I are thrilled," Tabitha concurred.

"Good, good. Now we just need to get your man back to work. Chatelaine needs him." The sheriff shot her an exaggerated wink. "Maybe you can help me twist his arm and get him to take his old job back."

Her stomach instantly hardened. Why did she get the feeling that there was more to this party than a simple welcome home?

West swooped in with a reply, saving her from having to stumble through an awkward response. "Now, now. This is a picnic, isn't it? No work talk."

Sheriff Cooper held up his hands. "Okay, okay. I'll try to keep a lid on any more job offers. But come Monday, look out. In the meantime, come with me, West. You've got to see the spread we've got set up over by the tent. Hot dogs, with all the fixings. Big ole slices of watermelon. It's like the Fourth of July." He held a finger to his lips. "Don't tell anyone, but we might have some fireworks planned over the lake tonight."

Fireworks? Tabitha thought she might be sick. This was definitely more than just a picnic. It was a full-on parade, with maybe a touch of bribery thrown in for good measure. The county courthouse was probably rolling out a red carpet for West right this very second. He'd never be able to resist this kind of star treatment. Who would?

"You don't mind if I borrow West for just a minute, do you?" The sheriff didn't wait for an answer. He threw an arm around West's shoulders and hauled him away, toward the festivities.

West held up a hand in a parting wave, and Zane and Zach waved back at him from their stroller.

"Ddddddada," Zane said, his pudgy little hand flailing wildly. And then, more clearly, "Da-da."

"Dada," Zach echoed. "Dada, dada, dada."

Tabitha gasped and knelt down beside the stroller. "That's right, boys! Dada. There's your daddy!"

She waved alongside them, and her heart leapt straight to her throat. They'd just called West daddy...and he'd missed it, because he was busy being courted by the sheriff.

It wasn't West's fault, obviously. He could've just as easily been leaving to go to GreatStore or Camden's ranch. And it wasn't like he was going to live on her sofa and be a stay-at-home dad for the rest of their lives. Eventually, he'd be going back to work somewhere. If the sheriff wanted to give him his old job back, it only made sense to accept the offer. West loved that job.

Still, the idea of the man she loved going back to prosecuting criminals made Tabitha's stomach churn. It wasn't just the fact that his long work hours and his tendency to become consumed with his trial work had been a point of contention between them. That job had put West in harm's way. Tabitha, too. What if he prosecuted another psychopath who ended up getting off on some sort of technicality and the bad guy came after Zach and Zane?

A chill wracked through her at the very thought.

"Tabitha, are you okay? You look like you've seen a ghost." Lily came jogging toward Tabitha on the walking path with her dog Max scampering alongside her.

Not a ghost. Just a glimpse of what our future might be like if West goes back to work saving the world. How many times could one man come back from the dead?

She stood, cleared her throat and tried to push away her anxiety. West had point-blank told her that he hadn't accepted the sheriff's offer...yet. "Fine. I was just surprised, that's all. The boys just said *dada* for the first time! West was waving at them from across the park, and out it came."

Lily's hand flew to her heart. "Oh, that's so special! What amazing timing. West is the man of the hour, after all! Good boys."

Max spun three quick circles at the end of his leash and let out a yip, prompting a fit of giggles from the boys.

"I wasn't talking to you, silly. I mean the twins. You're a good boy too, though." Lily gave the dog a quick rub behind his ears before offering Zach and Zane each a high five. "My nephews, the geniuses."

"Oh, good. Here you both are. Say cheese." Haley snapped their photo with her cell phone as she came walking toward them from the tent area.

"Was that for your iPhone photo gallery or the *Chatelaine Daily News*?" Tabitha teased. Haley worked as a freelance journalist, with dreams of becoming a serious investigative reporter. Much to her frustration, thus far, the majority of her earnings came from writing fluff pieces for the local paper.

"Both." Hayley shrugged. "Yes, you're my family and I'm saving this picture because you all look adorable. Love the matching outfits on the boys, by the way. But this event is front-page news and I need some pictures to accompany my article."

Tabitha's gaze darted toward Haley. "Front-page news? Are you serious?"

"Yes, this is Chatelaine, remember? And West is a town hero now—a 'legend.' Word has it that's what the sheriff is going to call him in the speech he's about to give."

Of course Sheriff Cooper was planning on giving a speech. Tabitha wondered if he also intended on mentioning the job offer in his remarks. She wouldn't be surprised.

"So if you're writing this up for the paper, what happened to that top secret project you mentioned a while back?" Lily asked.

"It's still happening, and it's still top secret." Haley mimed locking her lips with a key.

Tabitha looked at Lily and shrugged. So much for finding out what their sister was up to.

"Come on, we don't want to miss the big speech." Haley snapped a few more quick photos before leading the way to the tent, where West stood just to the right of the podium and a beaming Sheriff Cooper.

Tabitha glanced around at the crowd and her heart warmed. Nearly the entire town had turned out to welcome West home. Lily's husband Asa waved at her from the Cowgirl Café food booth, where he helped his sister Bea Fortune serve customers. Tabitha waved back. She couldn't help but feel a bit overcome by all of the love being heaped on West.

He deserves this. A warm, fuzzy feeling came over her. *No matter what happens between West and me, he's a good man.* Years from now, she could show Zach and Zane the article Haley wrote for the paper and tell the boys all about how their daddy was a town hero. Maybe they'd even remember being there, tucked into their stroller in their matching cotton muslin shortie rompers, printed with whimsical cowboy boots and horseshoes.

Doubtful, but it was a nice thought. In any event, she was glad she'd have the photos to share with them when they got older.

But just as the sheriff tapped the microphone to begin his speech and the cheers of the crown died down, Tabitha caught a snippet of a nearby conversation that put an instant damper on her excitement.

"Bless Tabitha's heart. I can't imagine being in her shoes," someone said in a voice with a syrupy-sweet Texas drawl. "West had to fake his death in order to protect her from that awful man, and she didn't even know he was alive. She thought he was dead this entire time, just like the rest of us. Such a shame. He missed the birth of his twins and everything."

West was back, alive and well, and people were still blessing her heart. Would it *ever* stop?

She shifted from one foot to the other, and tried to concentrate on what Sheriff Cooper was saying, but then another voice chimed in.

"I'm sure that's what Tabitha wants everyone to believe, but I heard something entirely different went down. Rumor around town has it that West freaked out when he found out she was pregnant with twins, so he faked his death instead of dumping her. He just upped and disappeared, leaving her to raise those two little boys on her own."

What?

Tabitha's entire body went cold, despite the warm breeze and the sun shining high in the big Texas sky. Not one word of the gossip was true. Tabitha knew that much for certain. She didn't even know she was pregnant until after West had been "murdered," so there was no way West could've known.

True or not, though, she was awash in humiliation to be the subject of such a degrading rumor. Was this really what people thought of her? Of West?

She blinked hard against the sudden sting of tears as Courtney Riddle's face came to the forefront of her mind. Her comment from playgroup the other day rang in Tabitha's head like a terrible bell.

Bless your heart, Tabitha. Do you have any plans for Mother's Day?

The urge to turn around and see if Courtney was part of the conversation taking place behind her was almost overwhelming. She knew she should rise above the gossip and hold her head high, but what she really wanted to do was march straight over there and give the busybodies, whoever they were, a piece of her mind.

"Don't listen to them," Lily whispered as she took hold of Tabitha's hand. "They're just mean girls, and you know the truth about West. He loves you, and he loves his boys. That's the only thing that matters."

She's right. Tabitha nodded, shot her triplet a watery smile and thanked her lucky stars once again that her biological sisters were back in her life. Then she took hold of Haley's hand, so the three of them were linked together. The Perry sisters—they'd been lost to each other and now they were found again, just like West. She had so much to be thankful for.

But a little bit of the shine had worn off the day all the same, leaving her feeling like she was holding on tight to a piece of the fool's gold that was still buried beneath the very ground on which she stood.

CHAPTER SEVEN

WEST HAD NEVER shaken so many hands in his life.

Once the sheriff had finished his effusive speech, he tried to make his way back to Tabitha and the twins, but he couldn't take a step without someone wanting to shower him with well-wishes. It was nice, but also humbling. He didn't deserve a ticker-tape parade. The man he'd been before and the decisions he'd made hadn't always been honorable. Life was more complicated than that. This was his second chance in more ways than one, and he didn't want to screw it up.

"Howdy, brother." Camden grinned as West finished shaking yet another hand. Then, once they were alone— relatively speaking, of course—he gave him a one-armed hug and handed him a red Solo cup. "Try this. It's home-made root beer from Bea's new place, the Cowgirl Café."

West took a sip. It was frothy and sweet, with hints of vanilla and sugar cane, and it might have been the best thing he'd ever tasted. "This is delicious."

"Right?" Camden nodded toward the café's booth, just to the left of the tent, where a line of people stretched all the way to a cluster of picnic tables covered in red-check-ered cloths. "I just saved you at least a half hour of stand-ing in line. Although, since you're the town hero and all you could probably cut straight to the front."

"Stop," West said, frowning into his root beer. He didn't feel like a hero. Heroes didn't typically leave a brokenhearted woman and two fatherless babies in their wake. "Have you seen Tabitha? I keep trying to make my way toward her, but now I don't see her anywhere."

"She's around here somewhere with Lily and Haley." Camden's gaze swept the crowd, and he shrugged. "Don't worry. We'll find her. Real quick, though. Is the rumor I'm hearing true?"

"Rumor?" West tensed. "What rumor?"

"According to the Chatelaine grapevine, you're going back to work as the county prosecutor."

West shook his head. "Nope. Not true—at least not yet. Sheriff Cooper made me an offer, and I told him I need to think about it. I loved the job—you know that—but in retrospect, I'm not sure it's the best thing now that I have a family. And I guess I've also come to realize there's more to life than work."

"Totally understandable. And you know there's a job for you at the ranch if you want to keep your cowboy hat on. I was serious the other day when I mentioned it. I could use some help getting the legalities and insurance paperwork straightened out for the equestrian school. It's all a lot more than I'd anticipated. Even part-time help from Chatelaine's most capable attorney would be appreciated." Camden sighed.

"I'll keep that in mind. I've got a lot to think about, but know that you can always come to me if you're feeling overwhelmed, brother." *Family first*, West thought. From now on, that was his new motto. It would just take a little getting used to, that's all.

"Thanks, man." Camden's eyes lit up as his gaze landed on someone just over West's shoulder. "Hey, look. I told you we'd find her."

West turned to find Tabitha pushing the twins' stroller

toward them. Zach and Zane were both fast asleep with their little blond heads nestled together.

"Hi, Tabitha. Good to see you." Camden gave Tabitha a hug and pointed his cup toward the stroller. "Look at my nephews. They're adorable, even when they're unconscious."

"I think they're worn out from all the excitement." Tabitha laughed, but her smile didn't quite reach her eyes. "Actually, I have big news for the town hero here."

She gave West a gentle shoulder bump. "The twins called you dada earlier when they were waving at you."

"They did?" Now *that* was something really worth celebrating. Joy filled West like sunshine.

"They sure did." She grinned up at him, but something still felt off.

He wondered if she'd ever really let him back in, or had he missed his chance for good? West had never allowed himself to think that way since his return, but lately the thought had begun to burrow its way into his consciousness. Like a burr in a horse's mane that ended up working its way under the saddle pad and causing all sorts of trouble.

"That's the best news I've heard all day," West said, and he meant it. He squatted so he was on eye level with his sons and wished they'd wake up and say it again.

But they were far off in dreamland, a world away from Chatelaine Park and the homecoming that still felt somewhat like trying to fit a square peg into a round hole. And West was more aware than ever that *he* was the square peg. He was the problem that still needed fixing.

"I think we should have a birthday party for the boys." He stood and fixed his gaze with Tabitha's. "What do you think?"

Her eyes widened in surprise. "Oh, sure. I'm sure Zach and Zane would love that."

"Great. It's a date, then." West nodded, but there was still one detail to figure out. "When exactly is their birthday, though?"

Camden's eyebrows rose before he could hide his surprise at the question. Then he quickly dropped his gaze toward the concrete floor of the park pavilion.

"It's the thirtieth," Tabitha said with a nod, completely unfazed, and West realized she hadn't expected him to know the date.

Fair, given the circumstances, but he still felt like an imposter dad asking the question. When West had been in third grade, his father had forgotten his birthday, prompting another explosive fight between his parents. Like father, like son?

No.

West's jaw clenched.

Not if he could help it.

"The thirtieth," he echoed, and then he wrapped an arm around Tabitha's shoulders and pretended not to notice the way history kept worming its way between them.

For better or for worse.

TABITHA COULDN'T STOP thinking about the gossip she'd overheard at the picnic. Three days had passed since the celebration, and she still hadn't mentioned it to West. What was the point? At first, she'd kept quiet because she hadn't wanted to ruin the day for him. Whether or not the sheriff's intentions were a bit self-serving didn't really matter. She wanted West to remember being honored by the town, not being bad-mouthed behind his back.

Afterward, she still couldn't bring it up because, much to her astonishment, the day after the picnic, he'd signed up for an online course in rearing twins. While she worked on her web development business, West either spent his time with Zach and Zane or put together elaborate organizational spreadsheets for everything from meal planning to bath times. More than once, when she'd stolen a free moment to zip into the kitchen to pre-pack a few lunches for the boys, she'd found the task had already been done. Now when she opened her refrigerator, color-coded containers were all lined up in a neat row—blue for breakfast, red for snacks, yellow for lunch and green for dinner. He was trying so hard. She didn't have the heart to tell him that someone had been saying such awful things about the two of them. As the days wore on, it seemed less and less important, even to Tabitha.

Late Tuesday afternoon, she managed to finish a site design for one of her top clients a full week before her deadline. After months of barely keeping up, it felt like a full-blown miracle.

West was busy with more meal planning while the boys sat in their matching highchairs munching on peas and carrots.

"Do you want to share a pizza tonight after the boys finish their dinner? And maybe a glass of wine?" she asked as she closed her laptop.

West popped the lid on a green Tupperware container, looked up and grinned at her. "That sounds perfect. If I eat another well-balanced meal, I might not know what to do with myself." He shot a wink at one of the babies. "No offense, Zach. I know how much you love your veggies."

"West." Tabitha bit back a smile. "That's Zane."

"Of course it is." West sighed, but he didn't tense up the way he usually did when he mixed up the twins. It was nice to see him developing a little confidence in the daddy department—yet another reason not to mention nasty town gossip.

Tabitha joined him in the kitchen and once plates were cleared and chins wiped, the boys sat on their blanket in the living room with a stack of chunky puzzles. The doorbell rang as West helped Zach fit a zebra puzzle piece in place.

"Oh, great. The pizza is already here." Tabitha handed Zane a monkey puzzle piece and pointed to the spot where it went. "I'm famished."

"I'll get it." West stood and ruffled Zach's hair. "Be right back, munchkin."

He jogged to the front door in his sock feet, but instead of opening it, he turned back to face Tabitha after he'd glanced through the peephole.

"What is it?" Tabitha asked.

"Well, it's definitely not the pizza." West arched an eyebrow. "It's Freya Fortune."

"Again?" Another impromptu visit from West's newly discovered step-grandmother? Things were beginning to seem a little strange in that department.

"This is weird, isn't it?" West mused, raking a hand through his hair.

"Not as weird as us leaving her standing on the porch for several long minutes." The older woman was probably just lonely. There were a lot of Fortunes, after all. It might take her a while to figure out where she fit. "Go ahead and let her in."

West nodded and swung the door open. "Freya, what a surprise."

"I hope you don't mind that I popped by again. I promise it's not going to become a habit." Freya held up a giant shopping bag from GreatStore. "I just wanted to bring by a few gifts for the twins."

"Oh, that's lovely, Freya." Tabitha beckoned her inside

while West held the door open for her and relieved her of the burden of the overstuffed shopping bag.

"Something tells me you might have gone overboard," he said, pretending to struggle to pick up the bag.

"Oh, stop." Freya laughed and gave him a playful swat. "You know it's a grandparent's job to spoil the little ones. That goes double for great-grandparents. And, look! There they are. Zach and Zane, aren't you two just too precious for words?"

West ushered Freya inside, and after letting the twins rip open their packages, the adults sat on the sofa to watch the boys explore their new toys on their play blanket.

"Thank you again, Freya. This was really sweet, but West was right. You definitely went overboard. Promise me you're going to come empty-handed to the boys' birthday party later this month," Tabitha said.

"We'll see about that." Freya winked. "I'm not making any promises."

Zach picked up a plastic mallet and banged away on a colorful xylophone while Zane clapped along with the uneven beat.

"They really are the sweetest children. Although, if I'm being totally honest, the gifts weren't the only reason I wanted to come by." Freya shot West and Tabitha an apologetic glance.

"You don't need an excuse to visit the boys. You're welcome here anytime," Tabitha said. The surprise visits were admittedly a little odd, but she didn't want the older woman to think she had to back up a dump truck full of toys to the front door every time she wanted to come over.

West leaned forward on the sofa, narrowing his gaze slightly at Freya seated across from them. Tabitha could practically hear his brain click into lawyer mode. There was still so much about her they didn't know. Which meant there was no doubt in Tabitha's mind that West would want to find out more about this stranger who'd recently turned up in everyone's lives. "Was there another reason in particular that you wanted to see us?"

"Yes, there is." Freya cleared her throat as she gazed wistfully at the twins. "Last time I was here, I mentioned I had a daughter and we'd become estranged."

"I'm so sorry about that, Freya. That must be really hard," Tabitha said. She couldn't imagine being separated from either one of the twins for any reason—not even when they were older and all grown up. It would have felt like losing a big chunk of her heart.

What must have happened to cause such ill will between Freya and her daughter?

"It is." The older woman's eyes grew misty. "I guess I'm just feeling a little vulnerable and exposed after sharing such difficult and personal information with the two of you. I don't talk very often about the estrangement. In fact, I can't remember the last time I told anyone about my daughter. I haven't seen Renee in many years."

"As you know, the Fortune family is well acquainted with estrangement, so we can sympathize," West said.

We. As if they were a couple…a *family.* Tabitha waited for the inevitable wave of anxiety to wash over her at the idea, but it never came. Not this time.

"Maybe you should try reaching out to her. Time has a way of healing old wounds." Tabitha stole a glance at West. Over a year and a half had passed since she'd ended their engagement. Thinking about their breakup was feeling less and less like pressing a tender bruise, especially now that he'd come home.

"I don't even know where Renee is. I haven't spoken to her in decades." Freya shook her head, her hand fluttering to the silk bow at the collar of her blouse like a nervous bird.

Decades?

Tabitha was at a loss for words. A mother and child, separated for twenty or thirty years... She couldn't fathom anything sadder.

"Have you ever tried to find her?" West asked.

She nodded. "Several times throughout the years, but I haven't had any luck."

Tabitha's chest felt heavy all of a sudden. "I'm so sorry, Freya. You must be heartbroken."

"We're glad you opened up to us about this." West reached for the woman's hand and wove his fingers through hers. "If you ever need anyone to talk to about Renee, we're always here for you."

Longing whispered through Tabitha as West caressed the back of Freya's hand with slow, tender circles of the pad of his thumb. Regret tugged at her heart. All over the world, there were people like Freya, separated from their loved ones for all sorts of reasons. Tabitha was one of the lucky ones. She'd been miraculously reunited with her sisters, and after so many months of missing West and wishing she could see him again, yearning for him to know his children and be part of their lives, her wildest dreams had been granted. He was back, and he was sitting right beside her, giving her every indication that he wanted to start over.

And still Tabitha was afraid to open her heart and let him all the way in. Maybe she needed this heart-to-heart even more than Freya did.

She offered West's step-granny her sincerest smile. "One more thing, Freya. Don't ever give up. Trust me on this—life has a way of surprising you when you least expect it. Prayers are answered every day, and dreams really do come true."

Was it really so hard to take the biggest leap of all and believe in a happy-ever-after?

CHAPTER EIGHT

THE NEXT DAY, Tabitha decided she couldn't keep postponing the inevitable, and she did the one thing she'd been dreading since West's return to Chatelaine. She called her adoptive parents.

She'd put it off far too long already. Thus far, she'd managed to limit recent communication with the Buckinghams to text messages and emails. In any other family unit, that probably would've seemed strange. Her former fiancé had come back from the dead, after all. If news like that didn't warrant a phone call, what did?

But her parents had never been warm or fuzzy. Tabitha couldn't remember the last time that Lyle or Grace, or her adoptive brother Alec, had called her out of the blue. Why spend aimless minutes chitchatting when you could shoot off a text instead?

"Tabitha?" Her mom sounded confused when she answered the Buckingham landline, as if she'd briefly forgotten she had a daughter.

Tabitha knew better than to take it personally. What else should she expect from the couple who'd adopted her purely because her blond hair and blue eyes matched the toddler Grace had given birth to a few years prior? Lily and Haley had been raised in foster care after their parents' accident, while Tabitha had drawn the lucky straw. She'd grown up in a mini mansion, she'd gone to all the best schools, and she'd been showered with every material thing a little girl could ever want, including a pony. But she and Alec had also spent more time with their nanny than they had with their parents, all the way through high school.

Still, things could've been so much worse. She was the *lucky* Perry triplet. Tabitha never knew whether to feel guilty or grateful about her good fortune. Most of the time, thinking about it just made her sad.

"Hi, Mom. Happy Mother's Day," Tabitha said.

"Mother's Day is still a few days away," Grace Buckingham said, sounding even more baffled.

Tabitha should've stuck to texting.

"I know, but you mentioned that you and Dad have that golf tournament on Sunday, so I won't get to see you on the actual day." It was a relief, honestly. Tabitha wanted to spend a quiet day with her boys instead of trying to make two babies behave at the Buckinghams' country club, where they always insisted on going for special occasions.

"Well, thank you, then. And thank you for the article you sent over from the *Chatelaine Daily News*. It looks like West is going to have his old job back in no time."

And there it was—the other reason Tabitha had been reluctant to speak to her parents. If Sheriff Cooper was the president of the West Fortune fan club, then Lyle and Grace Buckingham were surely co-VPs.

Not that they'd spent much time with him. They hadn't had to. His law degree and last name said it all.

Tabitha bristled. "That's not what the article said, Mom."

"Honey, it sounds like you need to learn how to read between the lines. The sheriff threw the man a party and the entire town came. The handwriting is on the wall. You should be thrilled."

So, so thrilled. Tabitha squeezed her eyes closed tight. Of all the things that had originally made her fall in love with West, his job and legendary Texas family ranked dead last on the list. Tabitha had fallen in love with West's earnestness. His integrity. And the way he cared so much about others. It wasn't the trappings of his legal career that drew her to him, but rather the way he believed so strongly in protecting the innocent.

Look where that got us, she thought with a bittersweet clench of her heart.

"West hasn't made any decisions about his future yet," she said in as firm as a voice as she could muster.

"Surely that doesn't include the wedding. The twins are about to turn one year old, Tabitha. It's high time their parents get married. Please tell me you've set a date," her mother said. Because goodness gracious, what must her country club friends think?

"West has only been home for a week. Give us time." Tabitha took a deep breath. She knew she should've told her family she'd broken off the engagement, but once West had been declared legally dead, she just didn't have it in her to relive that awful fight. Especially not with the Buckinghams. "Things are complicated."

Grace huffed out a breath. "I don't see why they should be. He's living with you, isn't he?"

"For the boys. West needs to get to know his sons." She needed to switch gears and fast. There'd been a reason for her call, and it was *not* to discuss dates for a hypothetical wedding that technically no longer existed. If she didn't put an end to the West talk, her mother would start tossing out ideas for venues and wedding planners and caterers, just like she'd done before. *Only the best for the Buckinghams!* It was the family motto, after all. "Would you like to have lunch tomorrow? As an early Mother's Day celebration since you and Daddy have plans on Sunday?"

"Oh." Grace paused for a beat. Clearly the idea of making alternate plans so she could actually see her daughter for Mother's Day had never crossed her mind. "That sounds nice. We can meet at the club."

Tabitha much preferred the Cowgirl Café in Chatelaine or, if she insisted on someplace fancy, the Chatelaine Bar and Grill. But, of course, her mother would expect her to schlep all the way to Houston with the twins so they could see and be seen at the posh country club.

She really shouldn't complain, though. The drive wasn't bad. The boys liked looking at the cattle and hay bales through the car windows on the way. And this was supposed to be a Mother's Day celebration. "Super. I'm looking forward to it, Mom. I'm sure the twins will be happy to see you."

"Perfect. I'll make an eleven a.m. reservation for six." Grace's voice was already drifting off, even though the call hadn't technically ended.

"Wait!" Tabitha blurted. "Six? But it's just you, me and the boys."

"Don't be silly, honey. Your daddy will want to be there. And we haven't seen West in years. He'll be there too, obviously."

Obviously.

Tabitha bit her lip and tried to think of any and every reasonable excuse for West to stay back in Chatelaine. But within seconds, it was too late. A click followed by a dial tone sounded from the other end. Her mother had already hung up the phone.

Grace Buckingham had spoken.

WEST REMOVED HIS Stetson with one hand and kept hold of Zane's car seat with the other as he and Tabitha entered the Buckinghams' country club. Tabitha held Zach's car seat and seemed to stiffen a little the moment they crossed the threshold of the stately building. West understood. With its huge white-columned exterior and marble tiled entrance, the River Oaks Country Club felt like it was a world away from Chatelaine. A different planet, even. Try as he might, he could never picture Tabitha growing up in a place like this.

She had, though. She'd done it all—tennis lessons, horseback riding, all the rich girl hobbies. And the moment she'd been old enough to choose a life for herself, she'd hotfooted it back to Chatelaine, where her birth parents were from. She'd been determined to build her own life there, and she'd done just that, without the Buckinghams' help. It was one of the things West admired most about her. Her resilience, her love for her roots, her fiercely independent streak…even if he was still having trouble getting fully back in her good graces due to that hard-fought independence of hers.

"Thanks for this," Tabitha said as she blew out a big breath. "I don't know what I was thinking. I should've just told my parents the truth instead of asking you to pretend we were still engaged."

"It's one meal. I think I can handle it." He shot her a reassuring wink. West knew he probably shouldn't read anything into the fact that she was so hesitant to tell the Buckinghams the truth, but he couldn't help seeing it as a tiny spark of hope. If she wanted to act like they were still a real couple, he was all for it.

"I'm a terrible liar. They're going to know we're faking it."

"No, they won't," West countered, because *he* wouldn't be faking anything. He still loved Tabitha with his whole heart. "Trust me."

Her lips quirked into a smile. "You seem awfully sure of yourself, cowboy."

"Always." He blew her a kiss.

Tabitha's face went as pink as the bouquet of fresh peonies that stood on a polished oak table in the center of the country club lobby. Then she spotted her father bustling toward them from the dining room and relaxed as she assumed the air kiss had been for his benefit.

It hadn't.

"West, Tabitha. Here you are!" Lyle Buckingham gave West a hearty slap on the back. "So good to see you, son. You gave us a real scare, you know."

"I'm sorry, sir. It couldn't be helped."

"Of course it couldn't. You did what you had to do. *Heroic*—that's what it was." Lyle bent down to give Tabitha a kiss on the cheek. "I hope you know that most men wouldn't have made the kind of sacrifice that West made for you."

"Um." Tabitha's blush deepened at least three shades as she held up her left hand and wiggled her fingers to show off her engagement ring. "You're absolutely right. He's a keeper."

West wrapped his free arm around Tabitha and gave her shoulder a squeeze. *We've got this.* "Shall we get seated, Lyle? We don't want to keep Grace waiting."

"Certainly. Then we can dote on our grandbabies for a bit. Right this way." Lyle took Zach's car seat from Tabitha and led them down a hallway with plush red carpet toward the dining room.

Grace Buckingham sat at a table for six in a prime location, overlooking the club's vast, emerald-green golf course. When she spotted their group approaching, she waved but didn't get up.

They spent several long moments exchanging greetings and getting the twins situated in their highchairs, and then

Tabitha handed her mother a clear floral box containing a single purple orchid.

"Happy early Mother's Day, Mom," she said.

"Thank you, honey." Grace cast the flower a curious glance. "But what is this, exactly?"

"It's a wrist corsage. Just a sweet Southern tradition that I'd forgotten about. You know how I love flowers, so I thought it might be fun to make it a new Mother's Day family tradition of our own." Tabitha opened the box and gently plucked the orchid from inside. "I got purple because I knew it was your favorite color. I can help you put it on."

She held the flower toward her mother.

Grace held up a hand. "Oh, I don't think so. Not now. That's a little gauche for our surroundings, don't you think?"

Tabitha's face fell, and West had a very sudden, very real urge to sweep her and the boys off and disappear again. They could all vanish together this time.

"It's very thoughtful, though. Thank you." Grace replaced the orchid in the box and tucked it away in her handbag, where it would probably never see the light of day again. "So, when is the wedding?"

Nothing like cutting straight to the chase.

"I already told you, Mom. We haven't decided yet." Tabitha unfolded her napkin and placed it in her lap. "West has only been back a week."

"Well, honey." Grace cast a pointed look at the twins. "Don't you think you two need to make this official sooner rather than later?"

As if two one-year-olds cared a whit about their parents' marital status.

"Don't worry, ma'am. The boys couldn't be happier. They're little love sponges. Tabitha has done a phenomenal job raising them," West said, perhaps a little too sharply.

But he wasn't going to sit there and let anyone imply that the life she'd created—the one that filled her with so much joy—was anything less than perfect. "That being said, I'd marry your daughter right this minute if I could."

Tabitha let out a strangled laugh.

He arched a brow at her and reached for her hand under the table, giving it a squeeze, so she'd know he was telling the complete and utter truth.

"If we're going to have it here at the country club, we need to reserve a date as soon as possible. I checked with the staff and they're booking eighteen months out, if you can believe that. *Eighteen months.*" Grace sat up a little more primly. "Not to worry. I pulled some strings, and I think we can sneak you in much sooner. There are only two dates this summer to choose from so we should probably do it now."

Tabitha shook her head. "We've already talked about this. West and I want to get married in Chatelaine, remember?"

Lyle and Grace exchanged a glance.

"But honey, that was before," Lyle said with exaggerated patience, as if talking to a child.

West thought he might need to hide Tabitha's steak knife. Possibly her fork, as well.

"Before what, exactly?" Tabitha asked in clipped syllables.

"Before your fiancé came back from the dead." Grace sighed. "Honestly, Tabitha. West was already a Fortune and the county prosecutor. Now he's a genuine Texas *legend.* He's going to go down in history. Your darling boys might even read about him in their schoolbooks someday."

"West Fortune can't get married at that tiny church in Chatelaine," Lyle said with a shake of his head.

Now West might need to hide his own cutlery. This was getting out of hand.

"West Fortune is going to marry Tabitha Buckingham wherever her heart desires," he said flatly. He met both of her parents' gazes and held direct eye contact until they each looked away, focusing instead on the crisp table linens or the ridiculously opulent crystal water goblets. "Understood?"

Grace sniffed. "Of course, it's *your* wedding. We just want the very best for the two of you, that's all."

"Mom, the best doesn't always mean the most expensive or the fanciest. To me, the best means the most meaningful. The most special. And what's really going to make our wedding special is the two of us. Our boys. Our *home*... and that's in Chatelaine, not here." Tabitha face lit up as she talked about their wedding. It was almost as if she thought it might really happen someday.

Which West wanted more than anything in the world.

When neither one of her parents said anything in response, she pushed her chair back and placed her napkin in her empty seat. "If everyone will excuse me, I need to go to the ladies' room."

"That's fine, honey. We'll keep an eye on the boys. We brought them each a little present." Grace reached into her bag to remove two small packages wrapped in matching baby-blue paper. As she did so, the corsage box tumbled to the floor.

Grace didn't notice, but Tabitha did. The purple orchid sat there on the floor, forgotten. She left the table without another word.

"Mama?" Zach's tiny forehead puckered.

Beside him, Zane swiveled in his highchair, looking for Tabitha.

"Mama will be right back, kiddos. I promise," West said.

Grace set the wrapped gifts on their respective high-chair trays and the boys immediately tore into the wrapping paper, happily distracted from their mother's absence.

"I'll be right back, as well." West pushed back from the table before anyone could protest.

As expected, Tabitha hadn't needed to visit the ladies' room. He found her in a cozy nook just off the entrance to the dining room, sitting on a velvet settee surrounded by bookshelves. She gave a little start when he made his way around the corner shelf and sat down beside her.

"You're here," she said quietly.

And I always will be. "I wanted to make sure you were okay. That was a little intense back there."

"But how did you know where to find me? This place is huge." She gestured to the country club's high ceilings and green toile wallpaper. Just around the corner, a grand, curved staircase swept into view.

"You told me about this little nook on our very first date." The memory filled West's chest with warmth. "You said your mom and dad loved to spend time at their club when you were a little girl, but you never liked it here. So you'd sneak off to a hidden reading nook by the dining room and hide until someone came and found you. You said it was always your brother Alec."

"It was always Alec." She nodded, eyes shining bright. "I can't believe you remember that story. Our first date was years ago."

"I remember everything, sweetheart. And I clung to those memories while I was in hiding. They're what kept me going. All I wanted was to get back home." He swallowed, trying his best not to say everything that was in his heart. It wouldn't be fair. She wasn't ready to hear it yet… but he just couldn't keep it inside anymore. "All I wanted was to get back home to *you* and tell you how sorry I was for breaking your heart. I'd have given you the world for another chance. All the babies your heart desired."

"Maybe you were just lonely and missing home," she said, her voice cracking ever so slightly.

"I know exactly who I was missing, babe." He lifted her hand and pressed a tender kiss to her knuckles.

She smiled at him and then cupped his face in her hands and kissed him as gently as if he might break. No, as if *they* might break…as if one wrong move or word might tear apart the new, fragile connection they'd been building. She didn't rush like last time, when they'd been in such a hurry to come together. They'd been chasing a memory then, but this wasn't yesterday's kiss. It belonged to this moment and this moment only.

Her lips were warm and honey-sweet, because Tabitha had always been every bit as beautiful on the inside as she was on the outside. She represented everything West had always wanted when he was a kid. Kindness, goodness, stability. *Love.* Maybe that's why he'd run scared before. He couldn't imagine a dream like that ever being real. Surely he'd screw it up somehow.

But West had done enough running for one lifetime. His boots weren't budging. Not anymore.

"Why are my parents like that?" she murmured when she pulled away, eyes shining bright with unshed tears. "I never felt like I fit in here, and every time I come back, it's always the same. I'm nothing like them."

"You're not, and that's okay, because the person you are is beautiful. No matter what anyone says or how they make you feel. You're perfect just the way you are, Tabs."

"I like that you think so, even if it's not true." She let out a quiet laugh. "I'm hardly perfect. Case in point—I roped you into this lunch so we could lie to my family."

A grin tugged at the corner of his mouth. "I think we nailed it."

"Seriously, West. Thank you for this. You were amazing in there." Her gaze went soft, like she was looking at him through rose-colored glasses. It had been a long time since Tabitha had looked at him like that, and that one look meant more to him than all the hero talk in the world.

Hers was the only opinion that mattered.

"Anything for you, darlin'."

CHAPTER NINE

AFTER THE DISASTROUS lunch at the country club with the Buckinghams, Tabitha forgot all about Mother's Day. In her mind, the holiday was over and done with. She'd tried her best to celebrate her mom and, as per usual, Tabitha and Grace weren't on the same page. They were hardly even in the same *book*, for that matter.

Funnily enough, the things West had said to her while they'd been tucked away in the reading nook had truly made her feel better. She didn't fit in with her adoptive family, but she definitely belonged in Chatelaine. The moment they'd crossed the town border on their way back home, she'd finally been able to breathe a little easier. There was no way on God's green earth they were getting married at her parents' country club.

You're not getting married at all, *remember?*

Tabitha toyed with her engagement ring, which was once again sparkling on her ring finger. She'd placed it there before lunch with the Buckinghams for obvious reasons, and three days later, it was still there, shining like a star in the sweeping Texas sky.

Tabitha really needed to get a grip. She and West still weren't together as a couple. After they'd come home from the day trip to Houston, they'd slipped right back into their co-parenting routine as if the kiss in the reading nook had never happened. Tabitha wasn't sure what to make of it. A part of her thought that West was simply honoring her request for time and space, which should have been a relief. It was what she wanted, after all.

But another part of her knew the truth, and that truth was becoming harder and harder to ignore: her resistance was crumbling.

Their kiss the other day had been nothing like the night they'd spent together. She hadn't been kissing the man who she'd loved and lost. When she pressed her lips to his at the country club, she'd been kissing the new West Fortune. She'd been kissing the man who'd rocked their babies to sleep at night, who'd thrown himself into fatherhood with every last bit of his heart, who'd been putting her needs first for a change and had still yet to commit himself to returning to work at the prosecutor's office.

It couldn't last, though, could it? This little slice of heaven was only temporary. Things would have to change, eventually. West had wanted to devote precious days to getting to know his children, but they couldn't stop time forever. Their world would start spinning again soon, and Tabitha didn't know what would become of these new, overwhelming feelings that were blossoming in the most secret parts of her heart.

So she did her best to mirror West's behavior and threw herself into parenthood. They ate together, cooked together, cared for the boys together…and then at night, they went their separate ways. West on the sofa in the living room and Tabitha alone in her bed, where she sometimes dreamed that this simple time could stretch clear on into the horizon, where the setting sun always made the wide-open spaces of rural Texas look like liquid gold. Precious and priceless, like the fantasy that the miners had been chasing all those years ago. The only thing she'd change would be the sleeping arrangements. She ached for West every single night.

Pretending they were still engaged had apparently gone straight to her head.

Tabitha swallowed as she folded a pile of freshly washed onesies in the nursery. She needed to stop letting her feelings get to her and remember why she and West were living under the same roof. He was here for the twins, not her.

"Knock, knock." West rapped his knuckles softly on the half-closed door and poked his head inside the room. The boys were still fast asleep, lying on their tummies in matching poses. Identical twins to their very core. "What's going on in here? It's barely the crack of dawn."

"Just doing a few chores before the babies wake up and the day descends into chaos," she whispered.

"On Mother's Day?" West gave her a stern look and shook his head. "I don't think so. C'mere."

He gestured to her with a beckoning finger. How could Tabitha say no? He was barely awake, with charmingly rumpled bedhead, and he'd still managed to remember it was Mother's Day, whereas the date on the calendar had completely slipped her mind. She'd woken up with the sun and moved quietly about the house while everyone kept sleeping.

Tabitha actually loved being the first one up. It warmed her heart knowing that the people she treasured most in this world were all safe, sleeping peacefully under the same roof. It was such a simple little thing to take pleasure in. But once upon a time, it had seemed like a pipe dream. How things had changed.

She placed the folded onesie on top of the pile and slipped out of the nursery, following West through the dimly lit hall until they were in the living room.

Tabitha blinked. Everything looked different than it had the night before. Yellow-and-white streamers hung from the ceiling and a banner that said Happy Mother's

Day was draped from one end of the big picture window to the other. A silver ice bucket sat on the kitchen counter with a foil-wrapped bottle propped inside, right next to a pitcher of what looked like freshly squeezed, pulpy orange juice and four thin champagne flutes.

"When did you do all of this?" She swiveled her gaze back to West, who seemed to be hiding something behind his back.

He shrugged one shoulder, and the plain white tee he always slept in stretched nicely across his chest. "Mostly last night after you went to bed. I wanted to surprise you. Happy Mother's Day, Tabs."

All her breath seemed to bottle up tight in her chest as he produced a small florist's box from behind his back—clear plastic, with a corsage made of four buttery yellow roses nestled inside. The flowers were trimmed with white lace and attached to a bracelet of faux pearls.

"Oh, West." Blinking back tears, Tabitha pressed her fingertips to her lips. It was undoubtedly the most beautiful wrist corsage she'd ever seen.

West gave her a crooked grin, and what he said next made it all the more special. "For my yellow rose of Texas. There are four rosebuds there, one for each of us—you, me and the twins. I'm sorry I wasn't here to celebrate last year, but we can make this our own family tradition, starting right now. What do you say?"

Tabitha's heart hammered against her rib cage. He'd really been paying attention at lunch, hadn't he? Her efforts to start a tradition with her mom hadn't panned out, so he'd put that shattered dream back together and made it their own.

"I love it," she whispered, and this time she wasn't simply trying to be quiet because the twins were still sleeping. Her throat was clogged with emotion and all the things she suddenly wanted to say…things she knew might get her in trouble.

"Here, let me." West opened the box, releasing the sweet perfume of the roses into the air. Tabitha's head spun. "Give me your hand."

She let out a soft laugh. "Now? I'm in my nightgown."

"They'll complement each other beautifully." He winked as he took her hand and gently slid the flowers in place on her wrist.

She turned her hand to and fro, marveling at the tiny arrangement and all that those four roses symbolized. Not just a tradition, but a promise. A future, all wrapped up in soft yellow petals and lace. "I can't believe you did this."

"Just wait. There's more," he said.

Tabitha's forehead scrunched and she glanced around, searching for his meaning. That's when the number of champagne flutes on the counter finally struck her as odd. "Four glasses? Are we expecting company?"

Right on cue, the doorbell rang.

"SURPRISE!" HALEY AND Lily gushed in unison when Tabitha opened the door.

Her sisters were both still dressed in their pajamas—Haley in demure polka dots and Lily's decorated with tumbling puppy dogs who seemed to bear a striking resemblance to Max. Haley carried a cake stand with a beautifully frosted yellow cake sitting atop it, and Lily had an armful of gift bags.

Tabitha shook her head. "What's going on here? It's not even seven o'clock in the morning."

"Hence our attire," Haley said with an arch of her eyebrows.

"It's a surprise Mother's Day pajama party." Lily flashed

West a grin over Tabitha's shoulder. "It was West's idea. He wanted to surprise you."

Haley's eyes sparkled. "Did it work? Are you surprised?"

"Surprised would be an understatement." Tabitha laughed and held the door open wide. "Come on in. Please. The boys aren't even up yet."

"Oh, that was intentional. You're not lifting a finger this morning, hon. Zach and Zane's aunties are here, and we're getting the boys up and dressed and fed and all that jazz while you put your feet up and enjoy some cake for breakfast." Haley set the cake plate down next to the ice bucket on the kitchen counter. "Did I mention the cake is mimosa flavored? Orange layer cake with silky champagne cream. Lily made it from scratch."

Tabitha gasped. "You're kidding. I don't remember the GreatStore café serving anything that fancy back when you worked there, Lily."

"That's because this cake is special, just for you." Her sister pulled a face. "But this is my first time trying the recipe, so no promises."

Tabitha took a big inhale. "It smells fantastic. I'm sure it will be amazing."

"Who wants mimosas? I'm ready to pour," West said as he plucked the champagne bottle from the ice bucket.

Haley and Lily both raised their hands.

"Me too, most definitely," Tabitha said.

"That's a given. You get the first glass." West handed her a champagne flute.

She took it but hesitated before taking a sip. "I'm pretty sure I hear the boys stirring in their room."

"No worries. That's our department today." Haley bustled toward the nursery with Lily hot on her heels.

"Try and save us some cake and bubbly, though," Lily shot over her shoulder.

"As if we could consume all of this by ourselves." Tabitha laughed.

Her quiet morning was suddenly filled with the sounds of babbling babies and celebration and more joy than she'd ever thought possible to fit into her modest little cottage. It was such a stark contrast to Mother's Day last year, when she'd been nine months pregnant with swollen ankles and practically on bed rest as she prepared to give birth to twins. As exciting as that time had been, it had also been bittersweet. A day hadn't passed when Tabitha hadn't mourned West. Not just for herself, but for her children. She'd thought they would never know their daddy… had been convinced she was all they'd ever have. Just her and the memories of the man who'd never even known they existed.

And now here they all were, together. Everything she'd been too afraid to hope for, to *pray* for, had somehow still come true. It was almost too much to believe.

Tabitha opened the gifts from her sisters—a scented candle that smelled like the Southern Magnolia trees that grew in Chatelaine, a box of the fudge she loved so much from the gift shop at the mine, a cozy sweatshirt that said *Twin Mom, Doubly Blessed* on the front. Nothing fancy or over-the-top like the gifts the Buckinghams always heaped upon her at Christmas or her birthday. Just little things that showed how well her sisters knew her.

"This is too much, y'all," she said with a catch in her voice.

"It's your very first Mother's Day as a mama," Haley countered, snuggling Zane against her chest. The boys loved cuddling with their aunties. While Zane was happily tucked into Haley's arms, Zach played with a lock of Lily's dark hair.

"And we all wanted to celebrate you." Lily handed Tabitha a small gift bag with a profusion of tissue paper peeking out of the top. "And we saved the best one for last. Go ahead, open it."

The gift bag was lighter than air. Tabitha removed clump after clump of tissue paper, prompting giggles from the twins, who seemed to think it was a game—especially once West wadded the paper into balls and started juggling, putting on a little show for them.

Finally, Tabitha managed to unearth a small silver picture frame at the bottom of the bag. She reached inside for it, certain it must be one of the pictures that Haley had snapped at the picnic in the park the other day. But no…

This photo was older. The image, grainy. But Tabitha knew all four faces by heart.

"Is this…" Her throat closed up before she could finish.

"It's us," Lily said with a wobble in her voice. "When we were babies. And look, there's our mother."

Tears formed in Tabitha's eyes as she scanned the photo, hungry for details. Being adopted by the Buckinghams, Tabitha didn't have a single possession from her infancy. She no longer even had the Perry name. The only way she even recognized the woman pushing the baby stroller in the photo as her mother, Laura, was from newspaper photographs that had appeared in the *Chatelaine Daily News* after the car accident that claimed her parents' lives. When Tabitha first moved to Chatelaine, she'd researched everything she could about her mother and father. The paper had printed old high school graduation photos of her parents, and until now, they were the only faces she'd had to put to their names.

"I can't believe this. Look how beautiful she is." Tabitha

ran a trembling fingertip along the outline of her mother's face, round like Haley's. But she had Lily's freckles, and looking at the sparkle in the woman's kind eyes was like peering straight into a mirror. They'd each inherited a part of their mother and still carried her memory with them, wherever they went, for all the world to see.

The sisters were just babies in the photograph, sitting side by side in a wide, triple stroller. Lily was in the middle, flanked by Haley on the left and Tabitha on the right. She could recognize them easily, even as infants.

"Where did you get this?" Tabitha pressed the picture to her heart. What a treasure, and to receive it on her very first Mother's Day was a gift beyond anything she could've imagined.

"Val Hansen found it in some old boxes she'd been going through after selling us the ranch, so she gave it to me. There was so much going on with Asa at the time— our marriage, and realizing we were really and truly in love. I was overwhelmed, so I kept the photo to myself at first. I told Haley about it at our wedding reception, and we thought it would be a nice surprise to get one framed for you for Mother's Day." Lily's forehead creased with concern. "You're not mad we waited, are you?"

"Are you kidding? This is the best present I've ever received." *Other than West coming back.* Tabitha snuck a glance at him and for once hoped he could read her mind.

The tender smile that came to his lips told her he just might.

"The picture was taken at the dude ranch. See the way the trail curves into an S shape?" Lily pointed at the ground in the photo. "I can show you that exact spot the next time you're out at the ranch. Maybe you can pose with the boys in their stroller in the same spot, and we can re-create it."

"I *love* that idea," Haley said.

"Lub," Zane babbled. "Lub, lub, lub."

"That's right, baby." Tabitha ran her hand over her son's soft hair. "Love."

She was full to bursting with it. Forget Courtney Riddle's big plans for breakfast in bed. This had to be the best Mother's Day celebration in the history of motherhood. And it was all because of West. He'd done this. He'd put this crazy pajama party together.

For her.

"Thank you for all of this," she whispered in his ear later, when she and West were cutting the cake in the kitchen. "This is the perfect day. I really mean it. You were right, you know."

"I'm right about a lot of things," he teased. "Could you be more specific?"

"About what you said in Houston. It's okay that I'm not like the Buckinghams…that I never felt like I fit into their world. I know they love me in their own way, and it's probably the only way they know how to love. They really do want the best for me. Lyle and Grace Buckingham will always be my parents. Alec will always be my brother." Tabitha swallowed around the knot of emotion that had formed in her throat. She wasn't sure she could get the rest out without breaking down in tears, but she had to say it. She wanted to remember this day and what it felt like to truly know her place in this world. "But the people right here in this house are my *family*. Zach and Zane. Lily and Haley."

She rested a hand on his firm chest, kissed him softly and smiled into his eyes. "And you too, West Fortune."

Then neither one of them said another word. They didn't have to. The moment spoke for itself, steeped in sweet buttercream and new traditions. But somewhere in the back of her head, Tabitha heard a still, small voice.

You still think your resistance to this man is crumbling? Oh, honey. It's already nothing but a pile of rubble at his boot-clad feet.

CHAPTER TEN

"WEST, YOU'RE GOING to spoil the boys if we don't stop shopping," Tabitha said the next morning as he crammed no less than half a dozen massive shopping bags from GreatStore into the trunk of her car.

She knew they should've taken West's pickup truck on this little shopping expedition. Or maybe even a horse trailer.

"There's no such thing as spoiling babies on their birthday. They're only turning one once." West pulled the list he'd been consulting all morning from the back pocket of his Wrangler jeans. The paper ruffled in the spring breeze as they stood in the parking lot.

Tabitha peeked at it, mentally checking off one item after another. "Surely you've gotten everything on there."

The list was sweet, really. West had compiled it after doing a copious amount of research on the parenting sites he'd been reading lately. Over the past few days, he'd done a deep dive on the best developmental toys for one-year-olds and pledged to buy them all…in duplicate. Two of everything—two sets of sensory blocks, two pop-a-ball push toys, two zoo-themed wooden activity cubes, and the list went on. Tabitha had no idea where they were going to put it all. He'd even bought the boys a ball pit—assembly required, which would no doubt be a treat that would keep them up late the night before the party. At least Tabitha had managed to talk him into getting only one of those.

"It's a lot, I know." West tucked the list back into his pocket. He removed his Stetson to rake a hand through his hair and then jammed the hat back on his head. Tabitha bit back a smile thinking about the matching baby cowboy hats currently occupying one of the shopping bags in her trunk. "I'm just excited about their birthday."

Tabitha had a feeling there was a lot more on his mind than simple excitement. Enthusiasm didn't require a printed list that had been cross-referenced across three different websites. "I know you are, but maybe there's something else going on here."

"We forgot the board books. Damn, I knew we'd missed something." West turned back toward the store.

Tabitha grabbed hold of his elbow and reeled him back toward her, like he was one of the calves he'd roped during his days as a ranch hand in hiding. "Whoa there, cowboy. We've done enough damage at GreatStore. Let's go to Remi's Reads. Afterward, maybe we can grab lunch at the Cowgirl Café since Lily and Asa are watching the boys."

"Sounds good." West nodded, but he still had that glazed look in his eyes that he always got when he was thinking about something else. Tabitha had seen that expression countless times, usually the night before a big jury trial. In this case, she suspected his mind was spinning with tricycles and other assorted baby paraphernalia.

She dipped her head to catch his gaze. "But first, I want you to know that you don't need to make up for the time you've been away. You're here now. The boys adore you. They're not even going to remember that you missed the first eleven months of their life."

West swallowed. She could see his Adam's apple move up and down his muscular neck. "Is my guilty conscience that obvious?"

"Yes, counselor, it is." Tabitha held her pointer finger and thumb a fraction of an inch apart. "Just a little bit."

"Kids with involved fathers have better overall emotional well-being," he said, and the underlying sorrow in his tone as he parroted one of the parenting articles he'd read made her want to cave and go back inside GreatStore for another ball pit.

"West, the twins have that. You're *here*." And he wasn't going anywhere. Wasn't that what he kept saying?

They still hadn't figured out a permanent arrangement or even discussed their future as a family, but she had stopped wondering if she might wake up in the morning and find him gone. All this time, she'd been holding her breath, waiting for the inevitable freak-out once reality sank in and West realized the lifelong implication of being the father of twins. The man who'd never wanted children to begin with was a daddy. Times two.

Tabitha hadn't fully recognized that the joy she felt upon his return had been tempered with an underlying fear that he'd bolt at the first sign of spit-up or a dirty diaper. Loving babies when they were clean and cuddly and smelled like baby powder was easy. But in real life, those moments were few and far between. It wasn't until after the Mother's Day surprise party yesterday that she'd finally begun to breathe a little easier.

West nodded. "You're right. I'm here now." Then he flashed her one of his crooked smiles that she loved so much. "But I still want to stop by Remi's Reads for those board books."

"Super, but then I'm cutting you off from parenting magazines. At least until we find a place for all of these gifts." Had they gotten enough wrapping paper and tape? They were going to be wrapping presents after the twins went to bed from now until the party next weekend.

"Yoo-hoo! Tabitha!"

A chirpy voice rang out behind them, and she didn't need to turn around to know who it was.

"Ugh," she muttered.

West's gaze drifted over her shoulder, no doubt landing on Courtney Riddle and her eyelash extensions flapping in the breeze. "What's wrong? Who is that?"

"One of the moms in my playgroup. She can be a bit of a mean girl, but overall she's harmless," Tabitha said under her breath as Courtney came bustling toward them pushing a shopping cart. Her twin girls sat in the cart's double-wide child seat area, dressed to the nines in matching floral dresses with massive bows in their hair. Just like always.

No bow, no go. That was Courtney's motto for her girls when it came to going out in public. Tabitha wouldn't have been surprised if the phrase turned out to be their very first words.

"Howdy, you two." The woman gave Tabitha a loud, smacking air kiss beside each cheek before turning her gaze on West. "Lookie, here. If it isn't Mr. Chatelaine himself, West Fortune."

She shoved her hand toward him, wiggling her hot-pink manicure. "Courtney Riddle. I'm a dear friend of Tabitha's. We met while she was all alone and pregnant, bless her heart."

Tabitha could see West's jaw clench as he shook her hand. "It's a pleasure to meet you."

"The pleasure is all mine. What are you two doing here?" She craned her neck to see inside the back of Tabitha's car. "And where are those precious twins of yours?"

"We're shopping for Zach and Zane's birthday," Tabitha said, being extra careful not to mention the party. As much as she'd come to rely on the playgroup moms, Courtney was the last person she wanted to invite into her home. "My sisters are watching the boys."

"Oh, that's a shame. I thought perhaps you'd called that nanny I told you about. I know it's been such a struggle for you to keep up with work without any help at home." She picked an invisible spot of lint off the Peter Pan collar of one of the twin's dresses.

West's jaw clenched again, this time so hard that Tabitha was pretty sure she heard his teeth clang together.

Oblivious, Courtney turned her smile on him. "That was such a lovely party in the park the other day. The sheriff certainly seems thrilled to have you back. So have you made things permanent yet?"

What?

Was the nosy mom asking if they'd run off to the chapel and gotten married the second he'd come back from the dead?

Tabitha's face went as hot as the Texas sun in high summer. "Courtney, West and I—"

Her voice drifted off. *West and I what, exactly?* She still had no clue how to complete that sentence. Not that it was any business of Courtney's.

Courtney flicked her wrist. "I mean with the prosecutor's office, of course. Everyone is just dying to have you back there, West. Chatelaine needs you, good sir."

Tabitha and West hadn't discussed the sheriff's job offer for days. She'd actually allowed herself not to think about it after the lunch at the country club in Houston. That day had seemed like something of a turning point. But now here it was—the job offer of West's dreams—thrust right back to the forefront of Tabitha's mind, thanks to her playgroup nemesis.

"Nothing official," he said. "I'm still mulling over my options."

Tabitha's heart sank, despite every effort to remind herself how present West had been since he'd gotten back. Deep down, she'd even started to believe he was going to turn the job down.

Why was this decision taking so long?

"Well, good for you. You've been away an awful long while. No sense rushing into a serious commitment." Courtney's eyes flitted over hers, as if mentally blessing her poor, sad heart yet again.

Why did it feel like they were no longer talking about a job?

"We should get going," Tabitha said crisply. "We still have a lot of birthday errands to run."

Courtney gave her heart an exaggerated pat. "Oh, how sweet. Don't let me keep you. Will we see you at playgroup tomorrow, Tabitha? We missed you last week. Didn't we, girls?"

The twins swiveled their big blue eyes toward Tabitha.

Confession: Tabitha had skipped playgroup last week on purpose. She'd told herself there was no reason to go since she was so preoccupied with West's return. But in truth, she simply hadn't been ready to face the questions that Courtney and the others were surely waiting with bated breath to ask. It was one thing to admit to her sisters that she didn't know where she and West stood, but there was no way she was going to have that conversation with anyone else, least of all Courtney Riddle.

"Sure, I'll be there," Tabitha said, purely because it was the easiest way to extricate herself from the current third degree in progress.

"Wonderful. See you tomorrow, then. Toodle-loo," Courtney chirped, and then she hiked her designer handbag up further on her shoulder and aimed her shopping cart toward the GreatStore entrance.

Tabitha sighed the second she was out of earshot. "I told you. She's…a lot."

"Yeah." West let out a laugh, but it didn't quite meet his eyes. "Bless her heart."

FOUR TODDLER BOARD books plus one adult-sized tome on raising multiples later, Tabitha and West exited the bookstore and nearly plowed straight into Freya Fortune on the sidewalk.

Hmm, Tabitha thought, *this must be the day for awkward, accidental run-ins*. Maybe they should've stayed home and shopped online instead of venturing out into the world at large.

She immediately chastised herself. Freya seemed like a genuinely nice, albeit lonely, person. The total and complete opposite of Courtney, whose flippant comments about West and commitment had thrown Tabitha for a loop. He hadn't seemed quite like himself since they'd bumped into her in the GreatStore parking lot, either. They'd been having such fun earlier, shopping for gifts and party decorations for the twins. But now things between them felt off, and Tabitha didn't like it. Not one bit.

It was probably just her imagination. She really shouldn't let Courtney get under her skin. Somehow that woman knew just what to say to tap into Tabitha's deepest insecurities. And to top it off, now she was going to have to show up at playgroup tomorrow. Oh, joy.

But she didn't need to think about that right now. Tomorrow was another day, and Freya was standing right in front of them looking a bit shaken. Her sleek hairstyle wasn't as polished as usual, and there were worry lines around her eyes. Tabitha hoped she hadn't followed their advice about trying to track down her long-lost daughter and gotten bad news.

"Freya, are you okay?" she asked gently.

The older woman stumbled backward after their near collision in the doorway of the bookstore, and West took hold of her shoulders to steady her. "Careful, there. Let's go sit down somewhere for a few minutes. You look like you could use someone to talk to."

Again.

West aimed a meaningful glance at Tabitha. She knew precisely what he was thinking, because the same thought was spinning through her mind as well. Their encounters with Freya seemed to be getting progressively stranger.

"West." Freya blinked. "Tabitha! I'm so happy to see you. Sorry for bumping into you like that. I'm afraid I'm a little frazzled today."

"No worries at all," West said as he steered her toward one of the park benches that lined the streets of downtown Chatelaine.

Old wagon wheels served as armrests, with crossed pickaxes etched onto a metal plate on the bench's backrest—an homage to the town's mining history. Freya took a seat in the center of the bench and Tabitha sat down beside her.

West crouched down and smiled up at his step-granny. "Anything in particular on your mind, Freya?"

The older woman folded her hands in her lap, unfolded them and folded them again. Clearly, something was wrong.

"There is, actually." She nodded, and then dropped her voice to a loud whisper. "I think someone is following me."

Tabitha looked around, but the street was mostly empty and quiet. It was the middle of the day on a Monday, and this was Chatelaine. Anyone trying to follow Freya would've stuck out like a sore thumb.

"Not now. At least I don't think so. I haven't seen her since I left my motel a little bit ago." Freya let out a breath.

"So it's a woman who's following you?" West asked in as calm a voice as Tabitha had ever heard him use. He was so great at this. His years of advocating for crime victims and questioning witnesses certainly showed.

"Maybe not following. Maybe just...*watching* me, somehow?" Freya shook her head. "I can't be sure. It's that new young woman in town. Her name is Morgana Mills. Do either of you know her?"

Tabitha shook her head. "Bea might have mentioned her once or twice, but I've never met her."

"Unless we crossed paths at the picnic last week, I haven't met her either," West said.

"She's a maid at the Chatelaine Motel where I'm staying." Freya gestured toward the tail end of the downtown area, where the old motor lodge stood just off the beaten path.

West nodded. "I know the place."

Everyone in town knew the motel. It was as old-school as an establishment could possibly get, with slightly peeling exterior paint and rosebud-pink sinks and tubs in all the bathrooms. But it was clean and respectable, run by Hal Appleby, a kind widower who'd lived in Chatelaine all his life. Pretty much everyone who passed through town, both visitors and those who eventually ended up putting down roots, had stayed there at least once in their life.

"My room is on the first floor. It's one of the big ones with a kitchenette. I think Morgana's room is on the second floor, right above mine." Freya's mouth twisted. "Anyway, when I first wondered if she might be watching me, she didn't work there. I just kept bumping into her around town, and the next thing I knew, boom. She got a job at the very motel where I'm staying."

Tabitha wanted to be sensitive to Freya's feelings, but this entire thing seemed pretty far-fetched. "Do you think it might be just a coincidence? There really aren't that many places to stay in Chatelaine, and if she's new in town, she was probably looking for a job. I'm sure Hal jumped at the chance to get some extra help."

"I'm telling you there's something off about that girl," Freya insisted.

West regarded her thoughtfully. "Besides the fact that you get the feeling she's watching you?"

"Yes. I heard she's been asking people around town about the old silver mine collapse. Now why would a total stranger, a *newcomer*, be poking her nose into that? Hmm?" Freya crossed her arms and let out a huff.

Something seemed off about this entire exchange, but Tabitha couldn't put her finger on it.

"Who *is* this woman?" Freya demanded.

"Like I said, I don't know. But if I learned anything in all my time as prosecutor, it's that the truth always comes out." West rested his hand on Freya's knee and gave it a comforting pat. *"Always."*

She shot him a skeptical glance. He and Tabitha clearly weren't making her feel any better about the mysterious Morgana.

"I have to go," Freya said, standing up abruptly.

"Right now?" Tabitha asked, but the older woman was already in motion, tearing past West, who was still crouching in front of the bench.

He rocked backward on the heels of his cowboy boots as she bustled into a nearby shop. Then he stood, brushed off his hands and narrowed his gaze in the direction where his step-granny had just disappeared.

Tabitha gathered the bags from the bookstore and came to stand beside him. "That was odd, wasn't it?"

"Very," he said flatly.

"Do you think she's just confused? Freya can be a bit eccentric, but she usually seems as sharp as a tack for a woman who's pushing ninety." Besides, it was Elias who'd had the idea to make all of his grandchildren's most fervent wishes come true. Not Freya. She was simply here in Chatelaine to do her late husband's bidding and bring the family back together.

Wasn't she?

"I don't think she's confused, but I do have a theory." West's gaze fixed on hers, and his lips pressed together in a hard line. He didn't look at all like he was turning over some vague idea in his head. He looked more like a man who'd just made up his mind with absolute certainty. "I've met all sorts of people in my day."

"And?" Tabitha prompted.

A muscle in West's jaw ticked. "And Freya Fortune is hiding something."

CHAPTER ELEVEN

"So I was thinking of going to playgroup with you today." West closed the book he was reading—*Double The Pleasure: Raising Twins*—and set it on top of his ever-growing stack of parenting books on the end table beside the sofa.

Tabitha blinked. "You what?"

"Isn't your moms-of-multiples playgroup today? You told your friend Courtney you'd be there." West reached for his coffee.

Sunshine streamed through the front windows of the cottage, and beyond the sheer curtains, he could see Betty Lawford sneak a glance at him as she trimmed her roses. She'd been doing that a lot lately. If she didn't give it a rest, she wouldn't have any roses left.

West waved at her, and she waved back.

He and Tabitha had just spent the early morning hours getting the boys changed and fed and then changed again. Now they were down for a short nap, giving the adults a few minutes to regroup. And to play nice with the nosy neighbors, apparently. What could it hurt? West was back in Chatelaine to stay. Betty might as well get used to it.

"So, about playgroup?" he asked again.

West and Tabitha had mulled over the strange encounter with Freya over dinner last night and hadn't managed to figure out what was going on there, leaving his mind to wander back to the issue of playgroup and the mean-girl mom he'd met in the GreatStore parking lot.

Not that he'd particularly enjoyed that little encounter.

Tabitha let out a nervous laugh. "First of all, I'm not sure I'd call Courtney my friend, exactly. It's more like we coexist in playgroup together."

No surprise there. West hadn't gotten the impression they were close. "And second?"

"It's usually just moms." Tabitha shrugged. "We started out as a sort of support group during our pregnancies. We all met in a special childbirth class for mothers of multiples. Twins and triplets are considered high-risk pregnancies, so the hospital offered a special class just for us. We started meeting outside of class for smoothies. Then, once all of us had our babies, we decided to keep getting together once a week."

West chose his next words carefully. Tabitha was a grown woman, and this was really none of his business. She'd been handling things on her own for nearly two years. But Courtney Riddle had rubbed him entirely the wrong way yesterday, and he couldn't shake the feeling that there was a reason Tabitha had skipped her weekly playgroup last week.

"Can I ask why?" He dropped his gaze to his coffee cup. "Because correct me if I'm wrong, but you don't seem to enjoy it much."

"It's fine. Honestly. Most of the moms are perfectly lovely, and Courtney—" Tabitha rolled her eyes "—is just Courtney. I don't let her get to me. It's nice for the boys to have friends."

West held her gaze until she looked away, focusing on some invisible spot in the distance. When she did, his throat went thick. He'd been thinking about the exchange with Courtney all morning, wondering why Tabitha would want to spend any time at all with someone who seemed to be interjecting little digs into the conversation at her expense.

That didn't seem like the woman he knew. She valued her independence. She hated when the Buckinghams treated her that way, so West couldn't figure out why she'd willingly let somebody else talk down to her.

But now he realized why. Playgroup wasn't just about the twins. Zach and Zane weren't the only ones who needed friends and a support system. Tabitha did too. She'd been lonely.

He blamed himself. He'd left her high and dry, pregnant and alone. Perhaps that's why Courtney's faux sympathy had gotten to him. The things she'd said had been true.

We met while she was all alone and pregnant.

He felt sick just thinking about it. It hadn't been intentional. He'd had no idea she was pregnant, but facts were facts.

"I don't want to intrude. I just thought it might be fun seeing the boys interacting with other kids their age. Forget I mentioned it," he said, not wanting to push. Things between them had gotten easier. More natural. But he didn't want to disturb the delicate balance they'd managed to find over the past week and a half.

West needed to accept that there were certain things he'd never be able to do, no matter how hard he tried. He'd never be able to be there for the birth of his sons. He'd never be able to go back in time and rub Tabitha's feet after a hard day of working all through her pregnancy. The prospect of raising twins on her own couldn't have been easy.

He didn't want her to feel that way anymore, and it was time to do everything in his power to make sure she didn't. Which meant he needed to have a chat with Sheriff Cooper.

West couldn't take the job. He didn't even want it. In all honesty, he wasn't sure how his professional life would look going forward. But he did know that working as the county prosecutor was no longer a good fit. He needed to close that door firmly behind him, once and for all.

He turned toward Tabitha. "Tabs, about the sheriff—"

But she wasn't paying attention. Her eyebrows were drawn together, and her pretty bow lips were pursed, like she was turning something over in her head. Overthinking again.

Her gaze flitted toward his, eyes sparkling with sudden determination. "You know what? I think Zach and Zane would love it if you joined us."

It was the last thing he'd expected her to say.

His head drew back to search her expression. She seemed serious. "Really?"

"Yes, and why shouldn't you get to see how nicely the boys play with their friends? It will be a nice change of pace for playgroup. It's not like there's a *no dads allowed* rule or anything. It's just never come up before." She stood and began gathering the twins' things, packing them away in their diaper bag.

In went a stack of disposable diapers, baby wipes, hand sanitizer, a Tupperware container of Cheerios and two fresh changes of baby clothes. Then she grabbed a few bottles, burp cloths, baby sunscreen and two tiny shade hats. She glanced around for more.

West had packed less stuff when he'd returned from his trip to the great heavenly beyond. Just how long did playgroup last, exactly?

"You're sure about this? I don't want to intrude." He followed her as she flitted around the living room and kitchen area and held up his hands. The chat about his future job prospects would have to wait. Tabitha had suddenly morphed into a woman on a mission.

"Absolutely. Like I said, Zach and Zane will love it."

She brightened, and all at once, West was struck by how much she'd opened up to him since he'd been back.

Things were changing. She trusted him again. He'd turned back up in her life out of the blue after breaking her heart, and she'd welcomed him into her home. Her life. Her children's lives.

He didn't deserve any of it. No amount of resolve on his part could change the past. What's done was done. But maybe, just maybe, having her welcome him back into her heart wasn't a pipe dream, after all.

"And you know what?" she asked, her pretty bow-shaped lips curving into a smile so tender and gentle that it seemed to reach inside West's chest and soothe the regret that he'd carried back home with him. His knapsack might've been as light as air, but the baggage he'd been toting around since his childhood had nearly broken him. For years.

The more he got to know his sons, the more he began to believe that he might finally be capable of setting that baggage down. Oh, how he wanted to.

"What?" he murmured, reaching down to touch her face. She was so damn beautiful that it took his breath away. He'd thought he'd remembered everything about her—every detail of her flawless face, every variety of her laughter, every curve that he'd once kissed, touched, adored...

West had dwelled on all those things for so long, wanting...hoping...remembering... He'd never expected to be surprised or caught off guard by the way he felt around her. But memory was just time caught in a bottle. This was different. This was real, and it was everything he wanted and more.

He wanted to kiss her so bad that it hurt, but he'd made her a promise and he intended to keep it. She needed time and space, and he wasn't about to push. So he gave her cheek one last caress before tucking a lock of her hair behind her ear and then shoving his hands into his pockets.

"I'd love it if you came, too," she said, and West thought that maybe his brother had been right.

Maybe they could figure things out. Maybe they could be a real family. Maybe West Fortune had truly come back to life.

AN HOUR LATER, Tabitha stood beside West on Courtney Riddle's front porch, wondering why on earth she'd agreed to bring him to playgroup.

She'd lost her head for a minute. That had to be it. His interest in the boys and their friends had tugged at her heartstrings and hit her square in the chest. And then he'd given her that look—that certain, specific tilt of his head that reminded her so much of her boys.

Sometimes the expression on his face bore such a resemblance to Zach and Zane that her breath caught in her throat. Technically, it was the reverse—the twins looked like their dad, not the other way around. She was just so used to seeing their tiny faces every day, with their pudgy cheeks and bright blue eyes. They'd become her entire world, and West's memory was just that. A memory.

Not so much anymore.

Then he'd towered over her in all his masculine, cowboy glory, and the joy in his eyes when she'd said yes, he could come, nearly swept her clear off her feet.

Who are you kidding? West Fortune swept you off your feet ages ago, and your toes still haven't touched the ground.

When he'd reached a hand toward her face, Tabitha had thought he was going to cup her cheek and run his thumb gently across her bottom lip like he used to do when he wanted to kiss her. Her mouth had tingled in anticipation. But instead, he'd simply tucked a wayward lock of hair behind her ear.

She was pretty sure she'd had a dollop of pureed apricots from the twins' breakfast stuck somewhere in her bangs, but West hadn't seemed to notice. He'd always had a way of looking at her that made her feel like the most beautiful woman in the world. It was comforting to know that some things never changed, even when everything in their lives had gone so topsy-turvy.

Tabitha took a deep breath now and tried not to think about his warm, solid presence standing beside her on Courtney's porch. This was about the twins, not her—and definitely not about the sparks that had suddenly seemed to be flying all over the living room earlier. Her little house was far too small. West was always *right there*. That was the real problem.

Sure it is, her subconscious screamed. Even so, getting out of the cottage had suddenly seemed like the best idea she'd ever heard. She lifted her free hand and pressed the doorbell with what might've been excessive force.

West gave her a sideways glance, but she kept her attention glued straight ahead. How was she going to explain his presence? For all Courtney's bragging about the virtues of a nuclear family, Tabitha had never once witnessed a father darken the door of their weekly play date.

The door flew open, and she flinched. At first Courtney didn't notice anything unusual. Her head was turned, and she was saying something to another mom. When she finally swiveled to face them, it almost seemed like an afterthought.

But then her gaze landed on West, holding a twin in each arm.

Courtney's mouth dropped open an almost comical

amount. Her eyes slowly moved over to Tabitha. "Tabitha, hi. I see you've brought company."

"I hope it's okay that I'm joining this week," West said, all politeness and charm.

Their host practically melted on the spot. "Of course. We're happy to have you. Come on in."

More astonishment ensued as they stepped inside Courtney's cavernous living room. The moms couldn't have been more stunned to find a dad among their midst, particularly one who'd recently come back from the dead. West got the boys settled in the middle of the play area and after a flurry of introductions, he almost had a handle on which babies belonged to which moms. As the kids played and West chatted with the other parents, Tabitha realized she was actually having a good time.

"Can I help with anything?" she asked Courtney when it was nearly time for snacks. Much like her daughters' meticulous bow collection, Courtney kept play hour carefully organized. Healthy snacks were served to the kids at the half-hour mark, on the dot.

Courtney's gaze drifted toward West, who was helping Zach toddle around with a walker wagon. "That would be great. It seems your man has everything under control."

Her man.

Happiness coursed through Tabitha. Was West hers again? Did she want him to be? "Whatever you need. Just let me know."

"Could you grab the ice pops out of the freezer in the kitchen? I need to change Dotsy's diaper real quick." Courtney scooped one of her twins into her arms. "I'll be right there to get the napkins."

"No problem."

Tabitha wiggled her fingertips in a little wave to West, mouthed she'd be right back and made her way to the kitchen.

As many times as she'd been in the woman's palatial home, Tabitha never failed to marvel at how spacious it was. The kitchen was self-contained, instead of simply divided from the living area by a countertop, like Tabitha's home had been designed. A sleek island stood in the center of the space and a massive stainless-steel refrigerator took up a good portion of the opposite wall. A collection of cheery, posed family portraits were stuck to the front of it with alphabet magnets.

It took her a minute to figure out the fancy fridge. When she opened the freezer door, the ice pops were right there in the front—homemade, of course, in a variety of fruity flavors on colorful, toddler-friendly plastic handles. Had she expected anything less from Super Mom?

But as she removed the tray of freeze pops, Tabitha spied a familiar yellow box with red lettering situated directly behind it. Her eyes went wide, and she nearly dropped the ice pops in her astonishment.

Frozen waffles?

No way. This couldn't be happening. It just wasn't possible.

Oh, but it was. And not only was there a box of preservative-laden frozen waffles in Courtney's freezer, but they were the brand that Tabitha preferred. The *same exact* waffles that had prompted Courtney to lecture her about the evils of processed foods in the freezer aisle at Great-Store on the one-year anniversary of West's death.

Tabitha couldn't believe her eyes. She just stood there, reveling in the sight of a simple box of frozen breakfast food. Bless Courtney's heart, the waffles weren't even whole grain. Clearly, the queen of the playgroup wasn't quite as perfect as she wanted everyone to believe.

"You're really lucky, you know."

Tabitha nearly jumped out of her skin at the sound of

Courtney's voice behind her. She slammed the freezer door closed, turned around and did her best to pretend she hadn't noticed anything amiss.

But they both knew she had. The look on Courtney's face said at all. For once, her perfectly lined lips weren't curved into a condescending smile. She simply looked tired…every bit as exhausted as Tabitha felt after a full day of juggling her web design business with taking care of Zach and Zane.

"Excuse me?" Tabitha said. She must've misheard things. Surely Courtney hadn't just called her lucky.

"I said you're really lucky. None of the other dads have even thought about coming to playgroup. My husband sure hasn't. This would be the last place he'd want to be on a weekday morning."

And all at once, Tabitha understood. All of Courtney's posturing hadn't been a show for her and the other moms. It had simply been the other mom's way of convincing herself that her life was as flawless and wonderful as she wanted it to be. Underneath it all, she was just as overwhelmed as the rest of them were. Maybe if Tabitha hadn't been so mired down herself, she would've seen it.

She probably should've responded to the "lucky" comment, but instead, the words that popped out of her mouth were ones she'd been holding back for days. "It was you gossiping about West and me at the picnic, wasn't it?"

Courtney took a deep, pained breath and closed her eyes.

"I knew it." Tabitha set down the ice pops with a clunk. "Why, Courtney? I don't understand."

"I'm sorry. I really am. It's just that sometimes I get so…" She paused, and Tabitha had no idea what was coming next. *"…lonely."*

"Lonely? *You?*" Tabitha swallowed back her disbelief.

"Yes. Raising twins is hard. You know that even better than the rest of us, because up until now you've been doing it all by yourself. And the crazy thing is, I actually envy you."

"Courtney, trust me. I get lonely too—more than you could possibly imagine." It hurt Tabitha to admit it, but it was the truth.

Lately, though, she hadn't felt lonely at all. She liked having West stay at the house far more than she was ready to admit.

"But you were alone." Courtney's head gave a little shake, and tears swam in her eyes. "Being lonely by yourself is one thing, but being lonely when you're in a relationship is another."

Oh. So all the barbs and little digs had been about Courtney's marriage. They'd had nothing to do with Tabitha or West at all. Not really.

"Courtney, I'm really sorry." She had every reason to be angry at Courtney. The woman had made her life miserable on more than one occasion, but Tabitha couldn't bring herself to feel anything but empathy.

Even when West had broken her heart and told her he never wanted children, she'd never doubted the depth of his devotion toward her. She knew West cared about her even when he disappeared into his work and resisted talking about his childhood. He'd never stopped loving her. Deep down, she'd always known that's why he hadn't fought her when she'd broken off their engagement. She'd wanted him to fight so badly. Wanted him to kick and scream and rail against the idea of being apart. Instead, he'd quietly agreed and walked away...

Because he loved her. And when you cared deeply for someone, you wanted them to be happy. West had wanted her to have everything she'd ever dreamed of—the kids, the family, the white picket fence.

Tabitha had been alone in the dark days that followed, but she'd never felt unloved. That's why it had been so hard to let go of West's memory. That's why she'd still worn his ring on a chain around her neck. He'd been gone, but their love had remained.

Maybe it still did.

"I'm the one who's sorry." Courtney gave her a wistful smile. "Can you ever forgive me?"

"Of course. And if you ever need to talk about things, I'm here, okay?" Tabitha nodded toward the freezer. "But if you show up at my house, I'm definitely serving you frozen waffles."

"I'd like that. Those things are so good," Courtney said as she dabbed at the corners of her eyes with a napkin.

"*So* good," Tabitha agreed.

The other mom sniffed, squared her shoulders and blew out a breath. It was strange seeing her so vulnerable, and Tabitha wondered if she realized it made her seem far more beautiful than her lush eyelashes and expensive clothes.

"Shall we get these ice pops out there before they melt?" She held one up. It was shaped like a strawberry, attached to an easy to hold plastic ring for babies and toddlers. Courtney really was great at this sort of thing.

"Let's do it." Courtney straightened a stack of polka-dot napkins, then paused. "Can I say one more thing, though?"

Tabitha nodded warily. What now?

"He still loves you, you know."

"I—" Tabitha's mouth went dry as her heart began to pound in her throat.

"He really does. Can't you see it? Because all the rest of us do. It's written all over his face every time he looks at you and every time he looks at those boys of yours."

Courtney's smile turned a little less sad and a little more genuine. "I know things are complicated because he's been gone so long, but you really are the lucky one. If he still loves you and you love him, maybe that's all that really matters. Perhaps it's really just as simple as that."

Right then and there, a piece of Tabitha's heart melted along with the ice pops in her hands.

Perhaps it is.

CHAPTER TWELVE

WEST HAD NEVER seen a woman look so much like a spooked horse as Tabitha did the following evening as she was headed out for a girls' night out with her sisters.

"Are you sure about this? Because I don't have to go. It's just Ladies' Night at the Chatelaine Bar and Grill. It happens every week." She gnawed on her bottom lip as she switched her handbag from one shoulder to the other.

"And when was the last time you, Haley and Lily actually went to Ladies' Night together?" West plucked Zane from his highchair.

The twins were in the middle of dinner. Zach's plate was nearly empty, but thus far, Zane hadn't done much but fuss and smear his food around.

"Well…" Tabitha pulled a face. "Technically, we've never been. But—"

"No buts." West held up a hand, and little Zane mimicked him, doing the same in West's arms. "You're going. I can handle the boys on my own. I promise."

She deserved a night out with her sisters. What's more, she needed it. Tabitha never stopped doing for others, and West knew how badly she'd wanted to reconnect with Haley and Lily, now that they were adults.

Her sisters loved spending time with the twins. That much was obvious. But the girls needed alone time, too— time to nurture their newfound bond. West could certainly appreciate that, after having been isolated from his family for nearly two years. He'd been in contact with Camden daily since his return to Chatelaine and was eager for Bear to turn up back in town so they could reconnect.

"You know, I really do think I'm getting the hang of this fatherhood thing," he said as he wiped orange sweet potato from Zane's chubby fingers.

"Don't say that. As soon as you do, something will no doubt spin wildly out of control." Tabitha dropped her handbag on the table by the front door. "Trust me. A few months ago, I was all caught up with work and the babies stopped teething, and I was so delighted about all of it that I told Bea I'd finally gotten things under control at home. Then, the next day, all three of us caught a stomach bug. It was a nightmare. You have no idea."

West carried Zane to the door, took Tabitha's bag off the table and replaced it on her shoulder. "Bye, sweetheart. I want you to have a good time with your sisters tonight. The twins and I will be just fine. If anyone gets a stomach bug, you'll be the first to know. Cell phones exist for this very reason."

West was determined not to call her, though. He was the twins' father, not their babysitter. He should be capable of watching his own kids by himself for a few hours while their mother had time to herself.

Tabitha's eyes narrowed. "You're really sure about this?"

"One hundred percent." He gave her the most tender look in his arsenal. How would he ever feel like a read dad unless he acted like one? The past few weeks had meant more to West than he ever could've imagined, but they'd almost been like a dream. If this was going to be his life, he wanted to be *all* in. "I need you to let me do this, Tabs. Not just for you, but for me, too. Okay?"

That seemed to convince her.

"Okay." She nodded, rose up on tiptoe and brushed her lips against the corner of his mouth. The nervousness in her expression faded into something else…something that felt a little bit like adoration. "And maybe later when I get home, we can chat about a few things."

That sounded promising.

West felt the corner of his mouth tug into a grin. "Yeah?"

"Yeah. I think it's time." Her mouth was still just a whisper away from his.

If he hadn't had a baby in his arms, he might've buried his hands in her hair and given her a proper kiss goodbye.

But they weren't there yet, anyway. She still had his ring on her finger, but it had been placed there as part of a ruse. West longed to put it there himself, like he'd done all those years ago. To slide it in place with a promise.

It's time. Tonight things would change. They were finally ready to be a real family. She'd stopped waiting for him to bolt like a runaway horse. He could see it in her eyes.

"So do I, darlin'," he said, and then their sweet goodbye was interrupted by Zane emitting an earsplitting squeal.

Tabitha kissed the baby on the forehead then waved at Zach, and West managed to usher her out the door before she could change her mind and insist on staying.

"Okay, kiddos. It's just us," West said as he clicked the door shut behind her. "Boys' night."

Zach grinned and shoved one of his tiny fists into his mouth. Zane seemed a little less enthusiastic about the whole affair. He went stiff in the crook of West's elbow and started to fuss.

"Come on, buddy. It's okay. Daddy's here," West soothed.

"Dadadaddadada." Zach banged on the tray of his high-chair and kicked his legs.

"Dada," Zane said in a pitifully small voice.

"That's right. We're good, aren't we?"

West ran his hand over Zane's slender back, and for a second, he thought he'd managed to calm the baby down. But then Zane scrunched his face and began to cry in earnest—loud, wracking sobs that shook his entire body. Zach watched his brother, eyes as big as saucers, and then he joined in the chorus, screaming at the top of his little lungs.

Panic shot through West. What was happening? Tabitha probably hadn't even made it to the Chatelaine Bar and Grill yet, and already things were going off the rails.

It's just a few tears. Babies cry. No big deal. He'd certainly heard his sons cry before. Just not quite this loud. Or this urgently. And not both at the same time, as if they'd decided to gang up on him the second their mother had finally decided he could be trusted to look after them on his own.

"First things first. Let's get you out of that chair, Zach."

West put Zane down in his crib and then dashed back to the kitchen to get Zach. In the split second it took him to carry Zach to the nursery, Zane's cheeks had turned beet red, and his entire face was wet with some awful combination of tears and mucus.

He picked him up, held Zane close against his chest and took calm, slow breaths while he tried to remember what the parenting books said about crying babies. He ran through the list in his head—something about walking, rocking and singing. He couldn't remember, so he tried all three, but nothing worked. The baby's diaper was clean, but he was inconsolable.

Zach stood watching West's efforts from his crib, bouncing on his toes until he too, began to fuss. He still needed to be cleaned up from dinner. West had planned on bathing them together, getting them dressed in a pair of their cute, matching PJs and then reading them a bedtime story. It was a routine he'd practiced and perfected since he'd been living on Tabitha's sofa. But tonight, it just wasn't working.

Nothing was.

Breathe. Just breathe, he thought, but he wasn't sure if he was talking to the babies or himself.

You can do this. Tabitha has done it on her own for a year. You can handle two crying babies for a single evening.

West wasn't going to call her, either. He wanted to prove to himself that he was father material. If not now, when? He was just feeling a little out of his element, that's all, like a newborn colt trying to stand on wobbly legs. He'd simply stay calm, get the house cleaned up and stick to the routine. He'd figure out a way to mollify Zane, and when Tabitha came home later tonight, the boys would be as happy as two peas in a pod.

West took a deep breath and reminded himself how much he loved his family, how much he wanted this to work. How for nineteen long months he'd prayed every night for another chance to make things right with Tabitha. And when he'd finally made his way home, and found out he was a daddy, his very first thought was that it had all been worth it. All the days in the hot sun on the ranch. All the lonely nights. All the endless waiting…

He was home. He had a purpose beyond his wildest dreams. He'd overcome the lowest of lows, and at long last, he'd put the pain of his past behind him.

And then, just as West managed to talk himself back from the brink, things went from bad to worse.

TABITHA'S CHEEKS HURT from smiling so much as she sat in the red leather banquette at the Chatelaine Bar and Grill with her sisters. She couldn't remember the last time she'd laughed this hard. Or loud.

And she couldn't even blame it on the bottle of good red wine in the center of the table, which was steeply discounted for Ladies' Night. Tabitha, Haley and Lily had each consumed only half a glass by the time their entrees arrived. They'd been too busy talking to get through more than a third of the bottle between them.

It felt good to joke around with her sisters. This was the sort of camaraderie she'd longed for when she'd first found out she was a triplet. She wished she had more time to spend with Lily and Haley—time that didn't involve juggling, changing and feeding two babies while also trying to keep up with the conversation. Time was a precious commodity when you were a mom to twins, though, and Tabitha knew better than to waste it. So she did her best to ignore her phone and focus on her sisters. If the boys needed anything, West would call or text. Staring at the tiny screen wasn't going to do her any good.

"So how are things going at home?" Lily asked, eyes bright in the dimly lit restaurant.

Hands down the nicest dining establishment in town, Chatelaine Bar and Grill featured dark wood paneling and rich leather accents. The walls were covered with framed, sepia-toned photographs and old maps of the mines that dotted the town's landscape. Authentic retro pans that miners had used to search for gold hung in an artistic arrangement over the bar. Tabitha had always loved the way the town embraced its history. The way the mines were still incorporated into everyday life in Chatelaine ensured that the miners who'd lost their lives were never forgotten.

"'How are things going at home?'" Tabitha regarded Lily. "Is that code for asking me how things are going with West?"

"Perhaps." Her sister's mouth twitched into a grin. "Okay, yes. It was absolutely code."

Haley leaned forward on the leather seat of the booth. "Yeah, tell us everything."

"I'm afraid there's nothing official to tell." Tabitha smiled into her wineglass. "Yet."

"Yet?" Lily's left eyebrow quirked upward as she swiveled her gaze toward Haley. "Did she just say 'yet'?"

"One hundred percent," Haley said with a nod.

Then both of Tabitha's sisters squealed in unison.

"You love him. I knew it!" Lily punctuated her statement with a stab of her fork.

Haley spread her arms out wide. "We *all* knew it."

"Shhh." Tabitha laughed and pressed a finger to her lips. "West still doesn't know it, and I'd really like him to hear it from me first."

"When are you going to tell him?" Lily added a dollop of butter to her baked potato.

"I think I'm going to tell him tonight. It's time. You guys were right. Once I started trying to take things one day at a time, West and I sort of found our way." She toyed with the napkin in her lap. "He still hasn't said anything about the job at the sheriff's office, but maybe that shouldn't be a deal-breaker. He's so good with the boys. I'm genuinely starting to believe we have a shot at being a family. If we really love each other and if he really loves Zach and Zane, we should be able to figure out the rest. Right?"

It felt so odd saying these things out loud. Tabitha had been working so hard to keep her feelings in check and temper her expectations where West was concerned. After all, he'd let her down before. He'd shattered her heart into a million pieces, and it had been so tempting to think he could just swoop back in and put it back together.

But she had the boys to think about now. Like a mama

bear, she wouldn't let anyone or anything hurt them. The thought of their tender, innocent souls being rejected by a man who didn't believe he could ever be a father was too much to take.

West had changed, though. She'd seen it. It had happened right before her eyes, day by day. He'd committed himself to their little family, and she was tired of fighting the truth. Tired of waiting for the other shoe to drop, because what if it never did?

What then?

"Right," Lily said and pressed a hand to her heart. "Oh, sis. I'm so happy for you."

Haley nodded, but just as she was about to say something, the chime of a cell phone cut her off.

"Whose phone is that?" Lily fished around in her purse.

"It's mine." Tabitha glanced down at her device, where a notification from West lit up the small screen. "West is texting me."

"Aw, that's sweet." Haley reached for the breadbasket.

"I need to read it. He's alone with the boys for the first time. I'm sure things are fine…" Tabitha said, but no sooner had the words left her mouth than her heart stuttered to a stop.

West: I'm sorry. I don't know what to do. Zane won't stop crying. I've tried everything.

She frowned down at her phone. "He says Zane won't stop crying."

Her sisters exchanged a glance. Tabitha felt like she had cotton in her ears as the sounds of the restaurant faded into the background.

Haley reached over to rest a hand on Tabitha's forearm. "He's probably just feeling overwhelmed. He's not used to taking care of babies. My nephews are little angels, but they can be a handful every now and then."

"I'm sure you're right," Tabitha said, but the text message went blurry as her hand started to tremble.

West had been so insistent about wanting her to go out and have a good time. He wouldn't have texted her unless something was seriously wrong.

Don't panic. You can trust him. She knew she could. Wasn't that what she'd just been telling her sisters?

West knew how to comfort a crying baby. She'd watched him do it over and over again already, and it wasn't as if he didn't know how to keep calm in a crisis. Even when he'd been in the crosshairs of the Mexican drug cartel, he'd had the presence of mind to fake his own death.

Something is wrong.

Tabitha took a deep breath. If she called him and sounded anything but confident, she'd make things worse. Besides, Zane had been fussy earlier too. He was probably just getting a cold or an ear infection, either of which would throw West for a loop. The boys had been perfectly healthy the entire time he'd been back. But Tabitha remembered how helpless she'd felt the first time one of the twins had gotten sick. She'd been terrified. That had to be what was going on.

"I'm going to text him back," she said as she tapped out a message.

Tabitha: Try not to worry. He might be coming down with something. Does he seem warm?

West: His face is red, and he's burning up. I thought it was because of all the crying.

Now they were getting somewhere. The baby almost surely had a fever.

Tabitha: Take his temperature. The baby thermometer is in the bathroom cabinet.

"Is everything okay?" Lily asked, gaze fixed on Tabitha's phone.

"He's checking Zane for fever."

It was fine, though. Babies and small children got fevers all the time. A little Baby Tylenol would fix everything.

But then her phone chimed again, and the sound made Tabitha jump, as if she knew it wasn't going to be good news.

West: 104 degrees.

Things were most decidedly *not* fine.

TABITHA COULDN'T HAVE made it back to the cottage faster if she'd teleported, yet West still felt as if he lived and died a thousand deaths in the time between when he'd taken Zane's temperature and the breathless moment she flew through the door.

A fever.

How had he not known to take the baby's temperature? If he'd had the first clue what he was doing…if he had any natural parental instincts at all…he would've known to check. It seemed so obvious in retrospect. Zane had been so fussy, and the more he'd cried, the redder his face became. When West held him against his chest and tried to rock him to sleep, the baby had been hot as a fire poker. Still, he'd somehow forgotten that children got fevers.

And then it had been too late. The baby had started

shivering, and West knew he was in over his head. He'd been so sure he could handle things on his own, so eager to prove to himself that he was father material. Now Zane was burning up, and Tabitha would probably never trust him with the boys again.

Seriously? Acid churned in West's stomach. *That's what you're worried about right now?*

How selfish could he possibly be? Even now, when Zane should be first and foremost on his mind, West was thinking about himself. Bile rose to the back of his throat as the image of his dad's face swam in his mind.

Like father, like son.

The past had truly come home to roost. He knew all along it would only be a matter of time.

"West," Tabitha said, as she held a screaming Zane to her chest. Her voice barely registered in his consciousness. He scarcely remembered handing the baby over after she'd burst through the door a few moments earlier. *"West!"*

His head snapped up, and he realized Lily was there too. She had Zach cradled in one arm while she threw items into an overnight bag with her free hand.

"We need to take Zane to the hospital," Tabitha said in a startlingly calm voice. Her competency and ability to think straight in the middle of this crisis only made West feel worse. "Lily is going to take Zach home with her so she and Asa can watch him. Haley stayed back at the restaurant to pay the check."

"Good, good," West muttered as he raked a hand through his hair. Thank God. The actual adults were going to get everything under control so he couldn't ruin anything else. If she'd asked him to watch Zach while she took Zane to the ER, he wasn't sure he would've been able to say yes.

He shifted from one foot to the other while Tabitha

kept looking at him, as if expecting more of a response. He couldn't think with Zane screaming so loud. West felt each cry like a knife to the chest.

"Go get the keys. You're driving," Tabitha said, again in a serene tone that somehow seemed far more ominous than if she'd been hysterical.

West hoped she'd yell at him later. He deserved it. But now wasn't the time. They needed to get the baby to the hospital and get his fever down before...

Before what, exactly?

He grabbed the keys and squeezed them in his fist until the metal dug into his flesh. *Seizures? Unconsciousness? Brain damage?* Every terrible thing he'd read about fevers in the parenting books reared its ugly head as he rushed outside and held the back car door open for Tabitha.

She settled Zane into his car seat. He'd finally stopped screaming, which should've been a relief. But he was as listless as a wet rag, which terrified West right down to his core. Tabitha handled the baby quickly but tenderly, getting him safely strapped in for the short ride to South Texas County Hospital, located in the county seat near Chatelaine.

Then she slid in place next to the child in the backseat so she could be close to him on the way, and it wasn't until she was safely buckled in and West clicked the car door shut that her composure broke. If he hadn't turned his head for one last glimpse after he'd closed the door, he would've missed the quiver in Tabitha's chin and the way her eyes filled when she thought he wasn't looking.

In a night filled with regrets, that was the most shameful part of all.

West wasn't supposed to be making things harder. Tabitha shouldn't have to hide her feelings from him. A real father made things better, not worse. Then again, what did he really and truly know about being a dad?

Playing house...that's all you've been doing. You know that, right?

There was more to being a father than changing a few diapers and showing up at playgroup. Had he really thought that spending a few weeks on Tabitha's sofa would make them a family?

West tightened his grip on the steering wheel and steadfastly avoided looking at mother and child in the rearview mirror. He couldn't take it. He was an intruder in this scenario. He had been, all along.

Tabitha's heart was simply bigger than his. Always had been, always would be. She was a far better person than him, back before he'd disappeared, and that simple fact still held true. He'd endangered her life and left her pregnant, and when he'd swept back into Chatelaine on his proverbial white horse, the entire town called him a hero. They threw him a picnic in the park and offered him the keys to the freaking city. And West had bought into the spectacle, hook, line and sinker, when in reality, Tabitha had been the brave one.

She'd had no good reason to trust him anymore. She'd given herself to him, body and soul, and when the subject of children had come up, he'd all but used it as an excuse to cut and run. Yeah, he'd regretted it afterward, but the damage had been done. He'd broken their trust—not just damaged it, but set fire to it and watched it burn. And how had she responded when he'd strutted back into town?

By opening her home to him...and her bed.

And now West's only saving grace was that she'd stopped short of offering him her heart.

AFTER TABITHA CARRIED Zane into the emergency entrance of South Texas County Hospital, the hours that followed passed in a blur.

Upon their arrival, they were immediately whisked away to a bed in the ER, surrounded by a privacy curtain. Zane looked so helpless and tiny, surrounded by beeping monitors and medical equipment. There was barely room for Tabitha and West to squeeze beside him in two small chairs while the emergency nurse did a quick assessment.

Since West had been the one watching the baby, most of the nurse's questions were directed at him.

Is the child experiencing any confusion?

No.

Any vomiting?

No.

Any seizures, rash or trouble breathing?

No, no and no.

Tabitha began to breathe a little easier. Zane's IV drip already seemed to be working. He seemed calmer and less agitated than when they'd first administered the medication. Even his color was looking better.

She wasn't sure when exactly she'd first grabbed hold of West's hand, but she squeezed it tight, pressing as much reassurance into the gesture as she could.

See? Everything is going to be fine.

His palm was stiff in her grasp, though. He offered her no reaction whatsoever. The look in his eyes seemed almost haunted.

Even two hours later, when the emergency physician gave them the good news that Zane could go home, West still seemed rattled.

"Little Zane is going to be just fine. He's got a monster of an ear infection. That's what was causing the fever.

We've given him a big dose of intravenous antibiotics, plus a fever reducer and some fluids to ward off dehydration." The doctor ran a hand over Zane's head, smoothing back his wispy blond hair. "He's out like a light now. There's really no reason to admit him. I'm sure you'll all be much more comfortable at home."

West tensed beside Tabitha. "But what if his fever spikes again?"

"It shouldn't, now that we've got some medicine in him. I'm sending you home with some baby acetaminophen. For the next day or two, just follow the dosing schedule and it should stay under control. Cool washcloths on the forehead can help. Make sure to elevate his head while he's sleeping. That should decrease pressure on the ear and relieve some of the pain."

Tabitha nodded. "We can do that."

"I don't know." West pulled his hand away and crossed his arms. "Maybe he should at least spend the night. Just to be on the safe side."

"I know you're worried, but this is all completely normal and natural. Babies are prone to getting ear infections because their immune systems are still underdeveloped. Their eustachian tubes are very small and horizontal, which makes it difficult for fluid to drain out of their ears. This isn't Zane's first ear infection, is it?" The doctor's eyebrows lifted as he focused on West.

"I... I don't know, actually," he said quietly.

Tabitha shook her head. "It's not. He had one a few months ago. So did his twin brother, Zach."

"That's what I thought. This isn't his first, and it certainly won't be his last. Ear infections peak around this age, and they usually last until the child is eight years old or so. Most of the time, they start with a stuffy nose, but they can also come on quick like this one did tonight." The doctor rested a hand on Zane's chest, rising and falling as he slept. "Try not to worry. Just get this little one home so you can all get some rest. You should schedule a follow-up with your regular pediatrician a few weeks down the road. If possible, I'd keep Zane separated from his twin for two or three days. The colds that cause ear infections can be mighty contagious."

Tabitha glanced up at West. "I'll see if Zach can stay with Lily for a couple more nights."

He nodded without meeting her gaze. "That's a good idea."

It took another hour to complete the discharge paperwork and get Zane home. Tabitha changed him into fresh pajamas, and he settled down in his crib right away, exhausted by the entire ordeal. She'd called Lily and Asa on the way back to the cottage, and they'd promised they were happy to take care of Zach. Haley had checked in too, and she said she'd pop over to pick up more of Zach's things the following day and take them over to the ranch where Lily and Asa lived.

Tabitha was dead on her feet by the time she dressed for bed. She and West obviously wouldn't be able to have that chat tonight. A discussion about their future shouldn't be rushed, especially when he was so clearly rattled by Zane's illness. He looked so drained as he sank onto the sofa and pulled off his boots, bowed by the weight of the world. His left shoulder sagged. Most of the time, the lingering effects of West's gunshot wound were all but invisible. But tonight, the man before her was battle-weary and broken down.

"I'm sorry, Tabs," he said in a voice as soft as the velvety darkness. "So sorry. This was all my fault."

"No, it wasn't. You heard what the doctor said. Babies get sick. It happens all the time." She moved closer, but there seemed to be an invisible, impenetrable force around him that stopped her, just out of arm's reach.

"He was in the *hospital*."

He was beginning to scare her a little. Obviously, it was upsetting to see Zane so sick, but their son was going to be fine. The ear infection had come on so quickly. It happened, as Tabitha knew all too well.

"West, we're home now. And we're fine." She wrapped her arms around herself, but what she really wanted to do was wrap them around West.

Why did it feel like he was slipping away?

"Come to bed." She held out her hand.

He lifted his gaze to hers but didn't move a muscle. "What?"

"I don't want to sleep alone tonight. Come to bed." She wiggled her fingertips, feeling altogether too vulnerable in this moment. Earlier tonight, she'd been able to see their future so clearly. But now it kept slipping out of focus, like she was waking up from a deep, delicious dream.

Back to reality.

She could feel her heart beating in the center of her throat. Her head spun a little. If he didn't take her hand and follow her to the bedroom, she wasn't sure what she was going to do. She just needed to be held, to feel him again, skin to skin. Because then she'd know for certain that this was real—as real as the silver that had brought the miners to Chatelaine back before the search for gold had sent everything tragically tumbling down, down, down.

The moment stretched out between them until West finally rose to his feet, placed his hand in hers and let her lead him to the bedroom where he undressed her in the light of the silvery moon.

Then he made love to her, slow and sweet. Like the tenderest goodbye.

CHAPTER THIRTEEN

CHATELAINE TURNED UP on Tabitha's doorstep the following morning in full force.

She wasn't sure exactly how word of Zane's trip to the emergency room had spread around town so quickly, but first up was Betty Lawford from across the street, bearing a bouquet of roses from her garden and a batch of homemade peach jam. Then, the casseroles started rolling in, one right after another. Even Courtney stopped by with a mini-batch of her homemade ice pops. West spent the majority of the morning answering the doorbell and re-arranging things in the refrigerator, while Tabitha fussed over Zane.

The baby's temperature was down—not quite back to normal, but to a mild, low-grade fever that kept him sleepy throughout much of the day. Tabitha gave him plenty of fluids, held warm compresses to his ear and made sure his blanket stayed tucked around him while he rested in his crib. Between taking care of him and the constant flow of well-wishers, she didn't have a spare second to talk to West about the night before.

She'd wanted him...*needed* him...and she had no regrets. Making love with him again had been like finally allowing herself to take a full inhale after holding her breath for a very long time. In the light of morning, everything seemed good and right and perfect. Just the way it was supposed to be.

Of course West had been upset the night before. It had been his first experience dealing with a sick child. Tabitha still remembered how panicked she'd been when the twins had come down with their first upper respiratory infection. They were so tiny and helpless. Every cough had made her go all panicky inside.

Things were fine, though. Surely West could see that. Once they had a minute or two to themselves, they'd sit down and talk about their future. They were a family now, through thick or thin. In sickness and in health.

"Tabs." West poked his head in the doorway of the nursery and rapped his knuckles gently on the door. "Look who's here. She brought lasagna."

Bea Fortune appeared beside him, waving exaggeratedly and emitting a silent squeal at the sight of Zane asleep on Tabitha's chest in the rocking chair.

"Hi, Bea. It's so great to see you." Tabitha shifted the baby in her arms and stood. Zane's tiny rosebud mouth puckered in his sleep.

"I hope I'm not disturbing you, but I wanted to help. Also…" Bea ran her hand over the small swell of her baby bump. "I might have just wanted to soak up a little bit of motherhood. This pregnancy is giving me major baby fever."

"You can come hang out with the twins anytime, and you don't need to bring anything from the Cowgirl Café with you. Although, I've never turned down lasagna in my life." Tabitha laughed, and Zane stirred.

"Oops." Bea dropped her voice to a whisper. "Can I hold him if I'm really quiet and gentle?"

"Of course you can." Tabitha transferred Zane to the other woman's waiting arms, while West grabbed a blanket to drape over the baby.

Bea's entire face lit up as soon as she got her hands

on Zane. Back when Tabitha had been pregnant with the twins, she'd never once felt like she had the infamous pregnancy "glow." Grief over losing West had taken its toll, and she spent most days fighting off nausea with a sleeve of saltines while working from home in her comfiest sweatpants. Glowing, she was not.

But Bea was *luminous*. Tabitha was one of the first people she'd confided in after she'd found out she was pregnant. It had been a surprise, and it had come at a time when Bea wondered if she'd ever have children. Sometimes the most unexpected gifts really were the best ones of all. Bea and Devin's baby was going to be so loved.

"How are you feeling? Is everything going okay with the pregnancy?" Tabitha asked a little while later after Zane had gone back down for a nap in his crib.

The table was all set and the lasagna had just come out of the oven, along with a loaf of crunchy garlic bread.

"It's great, believe it or not. I feel amazing." Bea took a slice of bread from the breadbasket and then paused to take a second piece before passing the loaf to West. "I'm eating for two."

He gave Bea a crooked smile. "Indeed you are."

It was good to see him acting more like himself. They'd had a whirlwind twenty-four hours, but they'd made it. And now here they were, having dinner with family just like Tabitha had always wanted.

"How was your experience at the hospital last night? I know the emergency room isn't the same as labor and delivery, but I'd still love to hear a positive review," Bea said.

"Everyone there was great." Tabitha nodded, fork poised over her lasagna. "You've been there before, though, right?"

"Yes. Actually, I was just there recently visiting Wendell. He's been so frail lately, especially since his fall."

West frowned at his cousin. "I didn't realize Wendell was still in the hospital."

"I know. I've been meaning to talk to you about it, but you've had plenty to catch up on since you've been back," Bea said.

West sat back in his chair. "How is our granduncle doing? I can't imagine he's enjoying being in the hospital for so long."

Bea sighed. "Honestly, I'm concerned. When I was with him, he wasn't really himself. He seemed out of it."

Tabitha felt herself flinch. That didn't sound good.

"Do you think he was on some sort of medication that might have made him drowsy or confused?" she asked. It seemed like a feasible explanation.

"I don't know." Bea shook her head and absently pushed her food around her plate with her fork. Clearly she was worried. "It was so bizarre. He started talking like he was in a daze, which I guess could have been a side effect of something they'd given him. But the things he was saying were oddly specific."

West's frown deepened. "Such as?"

"He said he'd had a child out of wedlock."

Tabitha nearly dropped her silverware. "You're right. That's *super specific* and doesn't sound at all like something he'd say just because he was drowsy."

"Oh, there's more." Bea leveled her gaze at West. Whatever was coming next must be big. "Wendell said he'd secretly acknowledged this daughter. They had a relationship, apparently, and at some point, he'd forbidden her to date a man who he didn't think was good enough for her. The boyfriend was destitute, and—here's the real kicker—"

Tabitha was riveted. So was West, judging by the expectant glint in his eyes.

Bea took a deep breath and spilled the rest. "The desti-tute beau apparently worked in the Fortune family silver mine here in Chatelaine."

"Oh my gosh." A million questions swirled in Tabitha's head. "What happened to him? Was he killed in the mine collapse?"

West drummed his fingers on the table. His wheels were obviously spinning just as quickly as Tabitha's were. "And what happened to the daughter?"

Bea shrugged. "I don't know. Wendell wasn't in a state to answer any questions. I just caught those bits and pieces. Do you think all of that could be true?"

"I don't see why not." West gave a mirthless laugh. "It certainly wouldn't be the first Fortune family secret."

Bea rolled her eyes. "Good point."

"It sure would be interesting to find out, though," he mused.

"I feel like we're all missing something. There are a lot of strange things going on in Chatelaine, and I can't shake the feeling that they're all somehow connected." Bea pushed her plate away and rested her forearms on the table. "Last month someone left a note on the community bulletin board that said fifty-one people had died in the mine, not fifty. The note also mentioned Gwenyth Wells, the widow of the foreman who died. No one seems to know what happened to her. And now we've got Wendell talk-ing about a secret daughter."

"Freya has said some strange things too lately," Tabitha added, remembering their conversation outside the book-store.

West nodded. "We ran into her the other day, and she was shaken up about the new maid at her hotel—Mor-gana Mills. Freya said the young woman had been fol-

lowing her and asking questions around town about the
mine collapse."

Bea bobbed her head. "See? That's what I mean. All of
this *has* to be connected, right?"

"It's certainly possible but off the top of my head, I can't
see how," West said.

Tabitha waited for a beat, half expecting the old prosecutor in him to vow to get to the bottom of things.

Instead, he offered his cousin his apologies. "I'm sorry,
Bea. It's been a long time since I investigated things as
part of my job. I'm not really up for it anymore. For now,
I'm trying to focus on being a dad."

For now. Tabitha tried not to read too much into that
phrase.

"Oh, I understand. That's why I waited to even bring
this up." The corner of Bea's mouth lifted. "I'm just so
happy for you two. It's good seeing you together again,
just like old times."

Tabitha glanced at West. Were they together in every
sense of the word? She certainly thought so. They still
hadn't defined things, but he had just said he needed to
focus on family and that told her pretty much everything
she wanted to know.

When West met her gaze, he smiled, but she could still
see traces of the haunted look she'd spied in his eyes last
night. Then she blinked, and it was gone.

She was worrying too much. The man she loved was
still right here, and Zane was doing great. Their little family was just fine.

"You know, Bea. I have an idea." Tabitha stood and
started to clear the table. "If you want to do some digging
into all of this, you might want to talk to my sister, Haley."

"Oh, that's right. She's a journalist. That's a good idea,"

Bea replied. "Is she working on something to do with the mine collapse?"

Tabitha wished she knew. Haley was still keeping a tight lid on things. They hadn't talked about her work at all last night at the restaurant. "I'm not sure. Whatever she's working on right now is top secret. She won't even talk about it. I think it's a really big story or maybe even a book."

"I'll talk to her. Thanks for the suggestion." Bea started piling their dinner dishes in the dishwasher. "I'm going to talk to the other Fortunes too—my brothers and sisters, the other cousins and definitely Freya."

"You might try Wendell again too," West said.

"For sure." Bea nodded. "Like I said, he's still in the hospital but I heard he's doing a bit better. I need to visit him soon."

"Hopefully, you can figure out what's going on," Tabitha said.

West tossed a dish towel over his shoulder and gave them both a pointed glance. "Just remember—sometimes once you start pulling at threads, the whole mess unravels, and you end up with a much bigger problem than you anticipated."

"And sometimes you end up with a whole new understanding of your family history," Bea countered.

She simply wanted answers. Tabitha knew how West's cousin felt. Her own curiosity about her birth family was endless.

She glanced at the photo her sisters had given her for Mother's Day. It sat in its new place of honor on the mantel alongside baby pictures of the twins and a photo of West she'd clipped from the *Chatelaine Daily News* the day after the picnic in the park.

Maybe someday soon they'd add a wedding picture to the collection.

Maybe...

But for now, Tabitha tucked that thought away, like a treasured secret. Or a sparkly diamond tucked out of sight on a golden chain.

The ring felt more at home on her finger now, though. She'd gotten used to it there. If she took it off now, she still would've felt the weight of it on her hand, like a phantom limb. Just like West's absence had taken its own shape when he'd been away. Sometimes it felt like his ghost had sucked up all the oxygen in the room, leaving her gasping for air.

Tabitha's chest ached at the memory, and she reminded herself that those days were over. She and West were standing right at the brink of a happy ending. All they had to do was hold on tight and take that final leap.

But when she looked at West while he dried the dishes, she swayed a little on her feet, as if the ground beneath her was ever so slowly slipping away.

THE TWINS' BIRTHDAY party was scheduled for just a week after Zane's hospital scare, and West woke up every single one of those days with a crushing weight pressing down on his chest.

At first, he'd thought it would get better. He'd thought that if he just tried harder to be a better dad, he could make the feeling go away. But it didn't. If anything, it grew more intense, amplified by the fact that he was now sleeping in Tabitha's bed, which made him the very worst sort of imposter.

They hadn't been intimate since the night Zane came home from the hospital. He hadn't dared go there again. That night, he'd hoped the terrible feeling inside him was only temporary. West had wanted so badly to believe that he and Tabitha belonged together that he'd ignored the warning bells going off in his head and tried to love her the way she deserved. He'd savored every breathless moment and tried to kiss away the doubt that kept pressing its way in from the outside.

However, in the cold light of morning, he realized he'd made a grave mistake. Nothing had changed. He was still his father's son, and Tabitha and the boys still deserved better. In the days since, he'd been doing his best to pretend that they were one big, happy family, as if going through the motions could make it true. And now, the night before the birthday party, in the great tradition of dads everywhere, he was up late assembling toys for the big day.

"Now *that's* a ball pit." Tabitha swished into the living room from the kitchen, where she'd been icing the homemade cake she'd baked for the party. She smelled like sweet vanilla and warm sugar, and she had a dab of buttercream frosting stuck to her forehead.

West had never seen a more beautiful woman in his entire life. His heart squeezed just looking at her.

"What do you think?" He stood up to survey his handiwork.

The pool of the ball pit was made from soft foam, secure enough to support the babies sitting in an upright position, but at the same time soft enough to prevent bumps and bruises while they played. Two hundred crush-proof, candy-colored balls filled the interior. The twins were going to have a blast.

And poor Tabitha was probably going to be chasing down stray balls until they left for college.

"I think the boys are going to love it." She surveyed the rest of the room, which had been completely taken over by wrapped packages and party decorations. "And I also think that our guests are going to be sitting on top of each other."

West took a look around. She had a point. "Maybe I should move the ball pit someplace else..."

But where?

"I have another idea." Tabitha cleared her throat, and suddenly her expression turned hesitant—bashful, almost.

And West knew without a doubt that he was once again going to let her down. He knew it before the words had even left her mouth. This was it—the moment he'd been railing against all week. He'd hoped something might change before it came. He'd hoped *he* would change.

But people rarely did.

West's parents sure hadn't. Neither had the majority of the criminals he'd put away over the course of his career.

"Tell me," he said, as if he wasn't a mere breath away from breaking her heart all over again.

It's for the best.

He should've stayed away when he'd come back to Chatelaine. The second he'd spotted those two little boys, he should've done the right thing and left Tabitha alone. Instead, he'd let himself believe in a fantasy, and he'd turned all their lives upside down in the process.

"I think we should look for a bigger house." Tabitha swallowed. "Together."

"Together," West echoed, stalling for time.

He didn't want to do this, but he couldn't keep postponing the inevitable. It wasn't fair.

"Yes." She nodded, and the hopeful smile on her face wobbled, ever so slightly. "This house is just so tiny. It was already a bit small for just me and the boys, but now that we're all a family, we could really use more space. You think so too, right?"

"About the house?"

"I meant the family part, actually." Tabitha's face fell. She knew, and he hadn't even said the words yet.

But of course she knew. He'd let her down once before. Why wouldn't she expect him to do it again?

"West." She lifted her chin, eyes blazing. Her only telltale sign of vulnerability was the slight quiver of her bottom lip, which would surely be West's undoing. A tight band was beginning to form around his chest, making it impossible to breathe. "We *are* a family now, aren't we?"

Something inside West died for real right then. If it hadn't, he would've never been able to go through with it. He would've gone on pretending that he was enough, all the while knowing that he would never be the type of man that Tabitha and the twins needed.

But he couldn't do that to her. As much as it killed him to let her go, it was the right thing.

It was the *only* thing.

So he gave himself up again, just like he'd done on the riverbank. Only this time, there'd be no coming back.

TABITHA HAD KNOWN the end was coming.

She'd tried to tell herself that this had just been a crazy week. They'd all been shaken by Zane's trip to the emergency room. Then they'd been inundated with well-wishers while the baby was healing. Zach had only come home from Lily and Asa's house two days ago, and now she and West were neck-deep in preparations for the birthday party tomorrow.

They'd been too overwhelmed to really connect over the past few days. Too busy.

But deep down, Tabitha had known. She'd felt West slipping away from her since the night they'd taken Zane to the hospital. She just hadn't wanted to believe it.

Sometimes she wanted to squeeze her eyes closed and shut out the entire world. To pretend she'd never noticed the way West had seemed so shell-shocked as he'd answered the nurse's questions at the hospital. If she could just forget…if she could wipe her mind clean like an eraser, she wouldn't have to face the awful truth.

Because the truth was so much harder to take the second time around.

He point-blank told you he never wanted children. Why on earth would you believe that had changed?

She glared at West, all but daring him to answer the question she'd finally uttered out loud. When he refused, she asked it again for good measure—softer this time, with a rasping ache that made West wince.

"We *are* a family now, aren't we?"

Tabitha should've forced this conversation days ago, because putting off the inevitable had felt like a slow, lingering death. So much worse than a sudden gunshot wound or a fall from a riverbank. West's gradual withdrawal had been a death by a thousand paper cuts, and Tabitha had finally had enough of the pretense. If she was imagining things, he needed to tell her. Right now.

Please. She silently implored him as tears pricked the backs of her eyes. *Please tell me I'm imagining things.*

"Tabs." His gaze dropped to the floor. He couldn't even seem to look at her. "I'm sorry."

Sorry for what, exactly? For coming back to Chatelaine just when she'd been on the verge of putting the past behind her? For making her believe that he'd changed his mind about children and he wanted to get to know his sons? For making her fall for him all over again?

Tabitha truly wanted to know. But she didn't ask any of those questions because the only thing she could manage to say was the last thing he wanted to hear.

"I love you, West."

He shook his head. "No, you don't."

"But I do, and the twins love you too." She wrapped

her arms around herself, as if that could somehow keep her from fully falling apart.

"Well, you shouldn't. And neither should the boys." He let out a pained sigh. "I'm not what you need, sweetheart. I'm not what the boys need. For a little while, I thought that I could be, but I'm just not."

"This is about Zane's fever, isn't it?" Of course it was. Tabitha shook her head, incredulous. "West, I tried to tell you that babies get sick. The doctor said it too. Stop being so hard on yourself."

"It's not just about the fever. It's about everything. I wasn't here, Tabs. While you were pregnant, I was off playing cowboy."

"Because you had to fake your own death to protect me."

"Exactly. That's prime father material right there," he spat. "I never should've put you in that position to begin with."

"It wasn't your fault," she countered. Why on earth was she defending him? The man was obviously trying to break up with her.

Tabitha knew why, though. She was trying to make West see himself more clearly. It was on her to defend him because he'd never really had anyone in his corner growing up. He and his brothers had never had any sort of emotional stability. Their parents had been too wrapped up in their own drama to pay attention to their children. If Tabitha didn't defend West Fortune, who would?

"I'm just not ready for kids, and I'm not sure if I ever will be. I can't commit to the family thing right now," West said hoarsely.

It was almost word for word what he'd told her back when she'd ended their engagement. The only difference was that now there were two little boys who called him daddy.

"So what do you suggest you do instead?" Tabitha asked. It was getting harder and harder to maintain her composure when her heart felt like it was being put through a paper shredder.

"Maybe we should go back to concentrating on just being co-parents." His gaze flitted to the sofa. "I think I should go back to sleeping on the couch."

Had he completely lost his mind? This wasn't how breakups worked. It wasn't even how co-parents operated.

"And *I* think you should leave," she managed to say.

West's face crumpled for a beat before he quickly rearranged his features into a neutral expression, which made her soul shatter even more.

She slid his ring off her finger—the simple gold band and diamond solitaire that had meant so much to her while he'd been gone. Tabitha couldn't remember the last time she'd gone to sleep at night without the comforting weight of it on a chain around her neck or placed on her ring finger, just so.

Now, she placed it in the palm of his hand. Fortune family gold, returned to its rightful owner.

"I waited for you a long time, West." Forcing back the tears, she looked up at the man who'd given her the greatest gift in the world—her boys. And even though the resemblance was still unmistakable, she wasn't sure she recognized him anymore. He was just a ghost of the West Fortune she'd fallen in love with. "I can't do it anymore."

CHAPTER FOURTEEN

"WE BROUGHT REINFORCEMENTS." Haley held up a bag from GreatStore weighed down by what looked like a gallon of ice cream. "Cookies 'n Cream."

"Mint chocolate chip." Lily held up another bag. "And of course it's Blue Bell, because this is Texas, and our sister deserves only the best."

It had been less than half an hour since West had packed what little belongings he had and left. Tabitha wasn't even sure where he'd gone and, as she'd been reminding herself every five or ten minutes, she didn't care.

After he'd left, she'd realized she had two choices. She could either fall apart all by herself like she'd done the last time West had ridden off into the sunset without her, or she could call her sisters and let them help.

Tabitha wasn't accustomed to asking for help. She usually just powered through and handled things on her own. It was the Buckingham way, much like tennis on Saturday mornings and the country club for special holidays. But then Tabitha remembered that in Chatelaine, she wasn't a Buckingham. She was a Perry, and the Perry sisters stuck together. So she'd sent out a tearful group text to Lily and Haley, and now here they were, with enough premium Texas ice cream to choke a horse.

Sisters were the best. Tabitha wondered how she'd lasted without them for as long as she had.

"Come on in." She waved them inside. "I'll get the spoons."

They didn't bother with bowls. That seemed to go against the unwritten rules of breakups. Consolation ice cream was best eaten straight from the carton, so Tabitha and her sisters sprawled on the sofa together with their feet on the coffee table and dug right in.

"I can't believe he just up and left." Haley shoveled a comically huge spoonful of Cookies 'n Cream into her mouth.

Lily gave her a sideways glance, eyebrows raised.

"What?" Haley shrugged. "I didn't have dinner. I was working."

Lily wagged her spoon at her. "You shouldn't skip meals."

"Please," Haley said with an eye roll. "I eat ice cream for dinner on a semi-regular basis. When I'm on a deadline, I'm practically feral. Not all of us are all coupled up and living in perfect domestic bliss."

"That's right." Tabitha pointed her spoon at Lily. "Only one of us is."

"For now." Lily looked around the room, gaze flitting from the twins' wrapped birthday gifts to the ball pit still sitting in the middle of the floor where West had left it. "Look at all this. It looks pretty blissful to me. You and West really went all out. There's no way he's not showing up for the party tomorrow. Maybe tonight was just a big misunderstanding."

Tabitha's stomach churned. She hadn't considered that West might still come to the party, but surely he would. He'd rejected *her*, not the twins. Even though he felt like a failure as a dad, he still wanted to "co-parent," whatever that meant.

If he showed up tomorrow, she'd just have to put on her big girl panties and deal with it. The boys came first. West was their father, and she'd never prevent them from seeing him on their birthday.

Still, tomorrow night might require another gallon of Blue Bell.

"Unless there's a way to misinterpret the phrase 'I can't commit to the family thing right now,' it wasn't a misunderstanding," she said.

Haley pulled a face. "Ouch. He actually said that? I'm going to tell Sheriff Cooper. He needs to take back the key to the city, pronto."

"West qualified it, though. He said he couldn't commit *right now*," Lily said, ever the optimist. "He'll come back around. I know he will. He loves you, Tabitha. And he adores the boys."

The saddest part of all was that Tabitha agreed with her. She knew West loved them. She'd just always believed that love was enough.

Well, apparently it wasn't.

"I can't wait for him forever." She shook her head. "I shouldn't have to, and neither should Zach or Zane. I could never walk away from them. *Never.* If West can do it so easily, then maybe he's right. Maybe he really isn't father material."

"Something tells me he didn't find it easy. If what West really wanted was to get his old life back, he could've done that weeks ago. The sheriff all but handed it to him on a silver platter." Lily gave Tabitha a gentle shoulder bump. "He chose you instead."

"Temporarily," Tabitha reminded her.

"Was keeping things temporary West's decision, or was

it yours?" Lily asked as she dipped her spoon into the carton for another bite.

"West's, obviously," she said automatically, but then she realized it wasn't quite the truth.

One day at a time. Wasn't that what she and her sisters had talked about the last time they'd had a heart-to-heart about West? Tabitha hadn't been ready to jump in with both feet. She needed time to trust West again with her heart. He'd been the one who'd seemed ready to grab life with both hands and build a new future together. As soon as he learned he was a father, he'd been all in. Tabitha had been the one who couldn't commit.

Oh, how the tables had turned.

"He's just scared, hon." Lily gave Tabitha a sad smile. "He's scared he's not enough for Zach and Zane. All those things he said tonight were just fear talking. You know that, right?"

Of course she did. She just hadn't paused long enough to put it in perspective. When West had first come back to town, she'd been scared too. She'd been terrified to her core, and instead of pushing her to commit to a whole new life, West had given her exactly what she needed.

He'd given her space. And time. He'd shown up—at home with the twins, at her parents' country club, even at playgroup. In fact, he'd been there every single day, happy to take whatever she could give him without asking or pushing for more. And the minute he'd stumbled and he'd needed her to show up for him and love him in the same unconditional way, she'd refused. She'd drawn a line in the sand, and now there was no turning back.

Oh God. What have I done?

Tabitha stared at the ball pit sitting in the center of the floor and imagined a lifetime of birthday parties where

West would be nothing but a guest in her home. In his own children's hearts.

Had she rushed things? What was the time limit on waiting for someone to come back to life?

"I don't think I can eat any more of this." Tabitha placed a hand on her stomach. She felt sickeningly full and empty, all at the same time. "And can we talk about something else, please?"

Anything but West.

Haley nodded. "Sure. What do you want to talk about?"

"I know." Lily pointed her spoon at Haley. "Let's talk about *you*, and this mysterious secret project of yours."

"I like that idea." Tabitha sat up a little straighter.

Haley shook her head. "No. I can't, y'all. There's still too much to unravel."

Tabitha's mind snagged on the word *unravel*. It was the same exact term West had used when he'd been talking to Bea about investigating all the mysterious things going around Chatelaine. Probably just a coincidence, but Bea had asked if Haley was researching the mine collapse. Maybe she was.

But if so, why all the secrecy?

"Are you working on a story about the Fortunes and the mine collapse?" Tabitha asked before she could stop herself.

Haley went quiet.

Lily gasped.

"You *are*, aren't you?" Tabitha said.

"Yes, I am." Haley took a measured inhale and finally put down her spoon. "But honestly, we should just leave it at that, okay?"

Tabitha had pushed, just like she'd pushed with West. And once again, she'd gotten an answer that didn't make her feel any better.

"Okay." She bit her lip and wondered how Bea might feel about a full-fledged investigation into the mines.

Freya, too. She'd been beside herself at the thought of Morgana asking questions. The rest of the Fortunes probably wouldn't be any happier about it either. And West? What would he think when he found out?

But as the conversation moved on to other things and Tabitha talked long into the night with her sisters, she remembered that the Fortunes weren't her concern anymore. Neither was West or his thoughts about the mine collapse.

She'd made that crystal clear when she'd given him back his ring.

WEST SAT ON the back porch of Camden's ranch house and turned Tabitha's engagement ring over in his palm.

After all this time, she'd given it back. West had been shell-shocked when she handed it to him. Even when she'd broken off their engagement two years ago, she hadn't returned the ring.

Not that he would've let her. The ring belonged to Tabitha. It would've been less painful if she'd reached into his chest, yanked out his heart and placed it in his hand instead.

"You feel like telling me what happened?" Camden asked.

They were seated side by side, facing the pasture, where horses grazed in the moonlight. The night was painfully quiet. There wasn't a cricket to be heard, just the occasional swish of the horses' tails and their hooves moving gently over the damp ground.

West loved Texas. He couldn't imagine living anyplace else. The wide-open spaces always had a way of soothing his soul. Even when he'd been on the run, gazing up at the vast blue sky had made his problems seem smaller and more manageable. He'd just *known* deep in the pit of his soul that no matter what it took he'd go home some-day. Sometimes he'd choose a star—the one that shined the biggest and brightest—and he'd vow on that star that when he made it back to Chatelaine, he'd make things right with Tabitha. If fate gave him a second chance, he wouldn't waste it. Everything would be different. Perfect. Real.

Because his time away from Chatelaine hadn't felt like real life at all. It had felt like falling into a deep, dark sleep—the kind where you couldn't wake up, no matter how hard you kicked and thrashed. It was like being able to hear real life going on around him, muffled and far away. Forever out of reach.

But those days were over. West was home now, and he'd managed to mess everything up in a matter of weeks.

"I hurt Tabitha and the boys. I told her I didn't think I could be a father." He swallowed hard. "That's what hap-pened."

He could feel his brother's gaze on him, as hot and un-forgiving as a branding iron.

"Are you going to say something?" West turned to look at him.

Camden just shook his head. "You're going to have to explain, because all anyone has heard from you since you've been back is that you wanted to get to know your sons. You promised to make Tabitha and the boys your priority. They're the entire reason you still haven't given Sheriff Cooper an answer about the job offer, right?"

"Yeah." West stared down at his hands and balled Tabitha's ring into his fist. "I gave him my answer last week. I told him no."

"Well, that just makes things as clear as mud," Cam-den said.

"Tabitha doesn't know. I was going to tell her, and then

Zane got sick." West took a ragged inhale. "And then everything sort of spiraled from there."

"'Everything' spiraled?" Camden made annoying air quotes around the word. "Or *you* spiraled?"

West sighed. Had his younger sibling always been so adept at cutting straight to the chase? "Both, but mostly the latter."

"I don't get it, brother. I thought you said that Zane was feeling better. Aren't the boys having a big birthday party at Tabitha's house tomorrow with cake and ice cream and all that jazz?"

"Yes, and he's feeling much better. But that's not the point," West insisted.

"Then why *is* Zane getting sick such a big deal? Don't little kids get sick all the time?" Camden let out a laugh. "The three of us sure did when we were growing up. Remember when we all had the chicken pox?"

"That was—" West started.

And then they both finished the sentence in unison. "Bear's fault."

Bear's second-grade girlfriend had stayed home from school for a week with the childhood virus, and his poor lovestruck heart couldn't take her absence. He'd snuck over to her house after school and climbed through her bedroom window, like one of the heroes in the adventure stories he loved so much.

All three brothers had paid the price for that little escapade. West still had a chicken pox scar behind one of his ears.

"We survived," Camden said with a shrug.

West gave him a meaningful look. "Did we?"

He marveled at his brother's ability to put the past behind him. Camden had jumped into a relationship with both feet a while back, seemingly unfazed by their unhappy childhood. Of course that hadn't panned out, either, although West wasn't entirely sure what went wrong.

"It's my fault that Zane ended up in the emergency room," he gritted out.

"Maybe." Again, Cameron shrugged. "Maybe not."

His nonchalance was really beginning to tick West off.

"It was. If I'd known to take his temperature, the trip to the hospital could've been avoided altogether."

"Debatable. You don't have a crystal ball. No one knows what might've happened." Camden held up a hand to ward off the argument that West was ready to unleash. "But let's assume you're right. Would the outcome have been any different in the long run? Zane is *fine*. And knowing you, you now know more about baby ear infections than all the doctors at County Hospital put together."

Guilty as charged.

"I may have done some research," West admitted.

Camden rolled his eyes.

"What? A good prosecutor is always fully prepared."

"But you're not a prosecutor," Camden reminded him.

He was right. West wasn't the county prosecutor anymore, and he didn't miss it a bit.

"Old habits and all that," he muttered.

"West, you've got to let it go, man. Mom and Dad were awful parents, but that doesn't mean you're destined to follow in their footsteps. The longer you let the past mess with your head, the more you're missing out on. Zane and Zach are turning one year old tomorrow."

West gave a terse nod. "I'm aware."

He was also aware that he was probably the last person that Tabitha wanted at their birthday party. But was he really going to willingly miss it? What had happened to the man who'd once been so eager to sacrifice anything for a second chance at life? Where had *that* guy gone? West really wished he knew.

"Look, I get it. You had no idea you were a dad. The twins were the surprise of a lifetime." Camden looked at him like he wanted to give him a good, hard shake. "But everything you put yourself through for the past two years was because you love Tabitha. Why would you walk away from that now? It doesn't matter if you never wanted to be a father before. Ever since you set foot back in Chatelaine a few weeks ago, all you've done is pour your heart into those boys. You don't need to worry about learning how to be a dad. You already *are* one."

West went still and let his brother's words wash over him. But Camden wasn't finished. Just when West was about to offer a counterargument—because every trial lawyer was fully adept in the fine art of crafting a rebuttal—his sibling planted his hands on his shoulders and looked him straight in the eyes, as if doing so could sear what he said next directly onto his heart.

"And you're a *great* one." Camden's green eyes flashed, and after a tense beat, his gaze softened. "Trust me when I say this, brother. I would've given anything to have a dad like you when I was a kid."

They were just the right words at just the right time. Coming from anyone else, West wouldn't have believed them. But this was Camden. Only West knew the real meaning behind that statement. Bear would've too, if he'd been there.

West missed his other brother fiercely in that moment. It felt incomplete without all three of them.

"Thanks, man," West said quietly. He took a deep inhale and, miracle of miracles, the weight on his chest eased. Just a little bit...just enough to breathe again.

"Anytime." Camden gave his shoulder another firm pat

before sitting back in his chair. "Now that we've solved that crisis, shall we fix your unemployment situation? Because I was dead serious about giving you a job. I'm neck-deep in insurance paperwork and legal documents. I want to get this camp up and running as soon as possible."

West felt the corner of his mouth tug into a half grin. Camden was getting ahead of himself, as usual. Just because West might feel slightly better about the kind of father he could be didn't mean Tabitha would be willing to give him another chance. He wouldn't blame her if she never wanted to see him again.

But he had to try. He'd never forgive himself if he didn't.

As West opened his fist and he looked at Tabitha's ring in his hand, something stirred deep inside him. He was coming back to life—and he'd do whatever it took to prove to her and his sons that this time, it was for good. It was for better, for worse. For richer, for poorer.

For all the days of his life.

"So what do you say?" Camden reached over and flicked the brim of West's Stetson. "Do you want to leave that cowboy hat on and come work with me here at the ranch?"

West flashed his brother a smile and nodded. He was tired of standing still, letting his new life pass him by. Or waiting to feel like he deserved his good fortune. Tabitha and the twins weren't a prize he could ever earn. They were a gift—the most priceless gift of all, and all he could do was treasure them.

Gratitude burrowed deep. He needed to make some decisions, starting right now.

It was time to really start living again.

CHAPTER FIFTEEN

ZACH AND ZANE woke up with the dawn.

In her head, Tabitha knew her sons were only a year old and couldn't possibly understand the concept of a birthday party, but in her heart, she was seriously beginning to wonder. It was as if they knew that today was special. They were like two giddy kids on Christmas morning, happily babbling to each other from their respective cribs before Tabitha had yet to open her eyes.

She cracked an eyelid and checked the time on the clock on her bedside table. Just as she suspected, the hour was obscenely early. It might not have felt quite so obscene if she hadn't stayed up so late gabbing with Lily and Haley the night before.

Had they really eaten two full gallons of ice cream? Yes. Yes, they had. And Tabitha refused to feel a single drop of remorse about it. *Self-care.* Wasn't that what the internet called it? Everyone knew that there were five steps to surviving a breakup and the first step involved ice cream.

Or maybe she was getting things confused with the five stages of grief. Tabitha certainly knew a thing or two about that as well. She'd been ping-ponging between all fives stages for the better part of two years. Just when she thought she'd reached the fifth and final stage—*acceptance*—she plunged right back down to the start again. It was like being permanently strapped inside the world's most depressing roller-coaster ride.

Would it ever end?

Not today, it won't. With a resigned sigh, she climbed out of bed, slipped into her favorite fuzzy pink bathrobe and headed toward the nursery. Maybe she should've taken Lily and Haley up on their offer to stay the night. Just the thought of getting through the day seemed nothing short of exhausting. The party was set to start in a few short hours, and she needed to get the boys up, fed and ready before the guests arrived, all while navigating her way back to stage number one: *denial.*

Had last night really happened? Tabitha tried to tell herself it had only been a bad dream, but no amount of denial could hide the fact that West was gone. Her head hadn't been resting on his broad shoulder when she'd opened her eyes. His long legs weren't stretched out on her sofa. And to make matters worse, the ball pit he'd been so proud of was still sitting in the middle of the living room, mocking her in all of its cheery, candy-hued glory.

She'd really done it. She'd given him his ring back and told him to leave.

He'd hurt her, and this time, the wound had cut her to the quick. There was a limit to how many times a heart could break and then somehow manage to stitch itself back together. As far as Tabitha could tell, that limit was three times.

Third time's the charm. She pressed the heel of her hand against the raw ache in her chest as she paused near the nursery door. *Once, when we called off the engagement. Twice, when West "died." And again, last night, when all my hopes and dreams perished for good...*

Yes, the number was definitely three. Although, so far, the healing part hadn't even started. She still had to get through all five lovely stages first, and so far, her heart had planted its flag firmly in *denial* and refused to move.

If only he'd fight for me this time. Fight for us...

Tabitha gave her head a good, hard shake. She'd given West his ring back. She couldn't have given him a clearer signal if she'd tried. They were over. Period. He had probably already moved into the county prosecutor's office with a sleeping bag by now. And Sheriff Cooper was no doubt planning another over-the-top party.

Fine. Tabitha had her own party to worry about today, and the twins would never have another first birthday. She needed to pull herself together, paste on a smile and do what good mothers had been doing since the dawn of time: put her children first. She could fall apart later after the candles had been blown out and the floor was littered with crumpled wrapping paper.

"Mama." Zach peered at her over the rails of his crib. "Mama, mama, mama."

Zane joined in, pulling himself up to standing and calling out to her in a singsong voice. "Mamamamama."

"Good morning, my sweeties," she said in a gentle whisper. "Happy birthday."

And against all odds, she smiled. The three of them were going to be okay. They really were. They'd made their way through this storm before, and they could do it again. So long as Tabitha had her boys, she'd be all right.

She got the twins changed and decided to feed them breakfast in their pajamas so their new Western-themed birthday outfits wouldn't get messy before the party. It had been a while since she'd handled the morning routine completely on her own. Like most cowboys, West was an early riser. He'd thrived with the boys in the early morning hours when he'd been living there.

But Tabitha fell back into her single-mom routine with ease—on the outside, anyway. *Denial, denial, denial.*

She'd just put the boys in their matching highchairs and

begun gathering the ingredients for pancakes when Zach and Zane started babbling again. She smiled to herself. She needed this today. Nothing warmed her heart quite like the sound of her babies saying *mama*.

"Dada?" Zane said.

Tabitha froze. She'd been completely unprepared for the twins to ask for West. She'd thought they could go right back to the way they'd been before—back to a time when the boys had never known their father at all.

How could she have been so foolishly naive?

"Honey, Daddy's not here right now," she said, voice trembling.

"Dada," Zane said again, kicking his legs in his high-chair.

Zach immediately started parroting his brother. "Dada."

"I'm sorry, boys, but Daddy isn't here," Tabitha whispered. She could barely get the words out.

He's not here because I told him I wouldn't wait for him anymore. I told him to leave, even though that's the very last thing I wanted.

Tabitha's throat closed up tight. She couldn't do this. She couldn't pretend that West's presence in their lives, even for a short time, had never made a difference. Zach and Zane would never be the same after knowing their father, and that was a good thing. They deserved all the love in the world—more love than Tabitha could give them all on her own. Whatever West could offer his sons, she'd take it.

Seeing him again would hurt. There was no doubt about that, but the boys needed him. They *loved* him, and whether West realized it or not yet, he loved them, too.

"Dada," Zane said again.

Tabitha took a deep breath and turned toward her son, willing herself not to cry. "Daddy's not here right now," she repeated, "but we'll see him again soon. I'm going to make sure he knows that you want him to come to your birthday party."

Zane's little forehead scrunched and then his gaze shifted, so he was looking over her shoulder. "Dada." He pointed toward the window overlooking the front porch.

A shiver coursed through Tabitha as she turned around. *No*, she told herself. *It can't be.* West had already given her the surprise of her life when he'd been waiting for her on the front steps after playgroup a few weeks ago. He wasn't going to just keep turning up again until she decided to give him another chance.

He didn't *want* another chance.

But there he was, sitting on the top step, right where he'd been before. Just like last time, his black Stetson was pulled down low over his eyes.

Tabitha's heart nearly leapt straight out of her chest.

"Dada," Zane said in his singsong voice.

"That's right, baby. Daddy's home." Tabitha's hands trembled as she lifted him from the highchair and then did the same for Zach.

She put the boys on the floor and led them by their little hands to the front door. When she opened it and stepped outside, West didn't budge. The poor guy was sound asleep, sitting straight up and leaning against the porch railing. A massive bouquet of yellow roses sat beside him, tied with a white satin ribbon.

Tabitha could hardly believe it. He was back, and he'd *slept* there.

He must've shown up sometime after Lily and Haley had gone home the night before. All the while she'd been missing him, he'd been right there, keeping the promise he'd made her when he'd first come home.

I'm not going anywhere. You have my word.

How could Tabitha have forgotten that West Fortune's word was as good as gold?

"Dada!" Zane cried.

West's eyes drifted open. He squinted against the morning sun, and then blinked as his gaze homed in on Tabitha and the boys.

"Good morning, cowboy." She nodded toward the house across the street, where Betty Lawford's profile was clearly visible peeking out from behind a lace curtain in her front window. "You're really determined to keep the neighbors around here talking, aren't you?"

West looked up at her with eyes full of questions, and Tabitha's unspoken answer to every single one of them was an unqualified yes. She nodded, and when he stood to gather her in his arms, he held onto her so tight that she thought he'd never let go.

"I'm so sorry," he whispered into her hair. "Of course we're a family. Always have been, always will be."

"Always," she said through tears.

"I love you, sweetheart. Don't cry. Please don't. Today's a day to celebrate." He handed her the roses and then bent to scoop a twin into each of his arms. "Happy birthday, boys."

Zane tipped his head back and laughed.

"Buday," Zach said.

Tabitha gasped. "Did he just say birthday?"

Zach squealed, utterly pleased with himself. "Buday."

"That's right, son. It's your birthday." West beamed at him. "But why don't we take this little pre-party inside? Betty has probably had enough excitement for one day."

WEST DIDN'T WANT to leave anything unsaid.

He'd made that mistake before, and he had no intention of doing it again. Life was precious. Everything could change in a blink of an eye. He needed Tabitha to know he was all in this time. So later, once the party was in full swing and the boys were busy playing in their ball pit for an audience of all their loved ones, West slipped his hand in Tabitha's and tugged her into the only quiet corner of the house.

"Hi, there," he said once they were alone in Tabitha's bedroom.

She grinned up at him. "Hi, yourself. Is everything okay?"

"Everything is better than okay. Everything's perfect." He held up a finger. "With just one exception."

Her brow furrowed, and before she could ask him to elaborate, he dropped to one knee.

"West!" Tabitha gasped softly. "You really don't need to do this…"

"On the contrary. It's very necessary." He took her ring from his pocket and slid it back onto her finger where it belonged. "I know we've already said we're a family, but I want us to make things official. I want to marry you, Tabs—preferably as soon as possible. But if you want a big, fancy wedding, I'll wait."

"You mean at my parents' country club?" She winked at him.

West pretended to consider the suggestion. Not that she was at all serious. "I don't know. I'm just a small-town lawyer with a part-time private practice. I don't think I rank high enough for a wedding at someplace that fancy."

Tabitha's eyes went wide. "You're…*what*? You're not going back to work as the county prosecutor?"

He shook his head and said simply, "Nope."

"Nope? Just like that?" A burst of laughter escaped her, and she clamped her hand over her mouth.

"Just like that. I actually turned the job down last week

and hadn't found the right time to tell you. Camden has asked me to help him with some legal matters at the ranch. I'm going to be working with him for a while, and I thought maybe I'd open a part-time practice in town. Folks around here need legal help sometimes, and I might be the right man for the job. It probably won't be enough work to keep me busy full-time, so you might have to get used to having me around the house." He flashed her a grin. "Correct me if I'm wrong, but you seem okay with that decision."

"I'm over the moon. This is the best news I've heard all day." She glanced down at her ring and wiggled her finger. "Correction—second best."

"So the answer is yes? You'll marry me?"

"I love you. Try and stop me, cowboy." She gave his hand a tug. "Now stand up and kiss me."

"So bossy," West said as he rose to his feet. Then he dipped his head and brushed a featherlight kiss to her lips, but it was just a prelude.

"One last thing," he murmured against her warm, sweet mouth.

Nothing left unsaid.

"It had better be important," she whispered as she wound her arms around his neck.

"This house. You're right...it's far too small. I vote we start looking for something bigger right away." He pulled back, just far enough so he could meet her gaze. "And since we'll be moving, we should probably find someplace big enough for a third baby. Zane and Zach would make great big brothers to a new little one, don't you think?"

Tabitha beamed at him. When she smiled like that, with her whole, beautiful face, West felt warm all over. "Are you serious right now, West Fortune?"

"I've never been more serious about anything in my

life." Life was for living, and West had wasted enough time. Never again. "I'm all in, beautiful."

"So am I. Let's do it. Let's have another baby," Tabitha whispered, as if they were sharing their own special secret.

They'd share their good fortune with their friends and family soon enough, but for now, these promises were theirs and theirs alone. West and Tabitha had finally found their new beginning, and it started with a happy-ever-after.

Sealed with a kiss.

* * * * *

Don't miss the stories in this mini series!

THE FORTUNES OF TEXAS: DIGGING FOR SECRETS

Follow the lives and loves of a complex family with a rich history and deep ties in the Lone Star State.

Fortune's Lone Star Twins
TERI WILSON
April 2024

Worth A Fortune
NANCY ROBARDS THOMPSON
May 2024

Fortune's Convenient Cinderella
MAKENNA LEE
June 2024

MILLS & BOON

Her Temporary Cowboy
Tanya Agler

MILLS & BOON

Tanya Agler remembers the first set of Harlequin books her grandmother gifted her, and she's been in love with romance novels ever since. An award-winning author, Tanya makes her home in Georgia with her wonderful husband, their four children and a lovable basset, who really rules the roost. When she's not writing, Tanya loves classic movies and a good cup of tea. Visit her at tanyaagler.com or email her at tanyaagler@gmail.com.

Dear Reader,

Welcome to Violet Ridge! Wedding bells are ringing. For Lizzie, her father's nuptials are everyone's focus until she, thanks to an innocent mistake, winds up engaged to Lucky, a cowboy who's determined to keep to his bachelor ways. Fortunately for the unlikely pair, thinking of ways to break their fake engagement and sadly disappoint their families leads to finding out how much they have in common. And the love of a lifetime.

This story brought back memories of my wedding. My car didn't start, and my family helped me transfer the dress and other regalia to another vehicle. I made it to the venue at the same time as my groom. With my family holding on to superstitions, everyone was guiding me away from him and covering my eyes so I wouldn't see him before the ceremony. I hope this book stirs fun memories of your own.

I love to connect with my readers through my website and social media.

Happy reading!

Tanya

DEDICATION

There are family members whom we know from birth, and then there are people who become part of our families through time, shared experiences and loyalty.

This book is dedicated to my "brother" Matt. He and his family have become a part of my life, and I'm honored to be his little "sister."

CHAPTER ONE

"YOU'RE LIVING UP to your name, Lucky. You must not have a care in the world driving around in this." Lucky Harper's best friend, Sabrina MacGrath Darling, let out a long whistle as he ran his hand over the aluminum exterior of his combination horse trailer and RV.

Lucky almost pinched himself so he could make sure this was his home before following Sabrina into the living quarters. All the fourth-place finishes might never have landed him in the year-end rodeo finals, but they added up to a pretty penny, enough to pay off the trailer. Pretty good for a foster kid from upstate New York.

"Butterscotch likes it." His horse's comfort counted for something. Last winter, he'd helped a friend in Texas, not expecting anything in return, let alone the magnificent American quarter horse that knew a thing or two about tie-down roping. This year, he found himself collecting champion belt buckles, rather than landing smack-dab in the middle of the standings, like usual.

Sabrina explored the cabin's interior, where the small kitchen backed up to the tiny dining nook. Good thing he'd cleaned up, not that he skewed toward leaving messes around. That wasn't his nature. Neither was having too many possessions that might weigh him down. Except for Cherry's ring in his small safe. Even though they'd broken up the day before he'd been set to propose over a year ago, he still thought of it as her ring. Guess he shouldn't, as she was now married with a little one on the way.

"Then your horse has excellent taste." She settled herself on the black leather dinette seat and rubbed the granite tabletop that matched the counter near the sink. "Elizabeth Irwin said you can board Butterscotch here at the Double I Ranch. Even with my mother's upcoming wedding to her father, you don't have to worry about whether she'll take good care of him. When I quit my job, Elizabeth rolled my barn-manager position into the rest of her duties. She runs that stable with her usual efficiency."

Lucky shifted on his feet, the hardest part of today's visit upon him. "I'll make some coffee."

He gathered the filter and beans, his nerves getting the best of him. He'd put off telling her he wasn't attending the wedding as long as he could. The next rodeo beckoned, with its earthy smells and camaraderie among the crowd and contestants. He belonged there, in that exhilarating moment in the chute when adrenaline met nerves and anything could happen, spurring him to new arenas.

For a long time, he'd believed his best friends, people he considered his family, felt the same. During his first year on the circuit, he'd met Will Sullivan and they'd bonded over Will's border collie, who traveled with him, and the two became inseparable. A couple of seasons later, rodeo clown Sabrina completed their trio. Together, they'd celebrated their victories and nursed each other through sore muscles and broken bones. They prided themselves on one-upping each other on their birthdays with who could find the most unusual souvenir as a gift from their travels. Sabrina claimed the permanent title when she'd gifted them both tacky ceramic armadillos.

He thought the three of them would continue on their journeys indefinitely. But then Will's parents died, leaving him the Silver Horseshoe and a mound of debt. Will didn't look back—he'd left the rodeo to save his ranch and fallen in love with an energetic whirlwind in the process.

Months later, Sabrina had mysteriously accepted a job at the Double I before she revealed she was pregnant. Last winter, she and rodeo champion Ty Darling rekindled their romance before welcoming their daughter, Genie, and forming plans for a rodeo academy here in Violet Ridge.

Now he counted himself as the lone remaining rider, surprising since he hadn't grown up around horses like Will and Sabrina. But here he was, having his best season to date. Still, he wasn't fooling himself. The rodeo was merely a convenient excuse for turning down Sabrina's kind offer. Witnessing another wedding celebrating love and forever, after things had gone south with Cherry? No, thank you.

Hitting the road with Butterscotch was his chance to continue doing something he loved, somewhere he belonged. Maybe his next cobbled-together family would stick.

He fixed two cups of coffee and handed one to Sabrina. Then he sat across from her, breathing in the rich aroma. He never stinted on good beans. "About that."

Sabrina nodded her thanks. "Would you feel more comfortable boarding Butterscotch at the Silver Horseshoe? Will's been asking about you."

Lucky had spent many a relaxing day at his other best friend's neighboring ranch, but he didn't intend on visiting Will this time around. He shifted in his seat, already counting the minutes until this conversation would be over, and he'd be traveling to the next rodeo in Pueblo, a good three-hour drive from Violet Ridge. This time of year, the marigolds and other late-summer wildflowers would be blooming, although the aspens wouldn't change color for another month. While he wanted to lend his support to Sabrina, seeing as it was her mother getting married and all, this ranch was overwhelming with its rarefied air and all of its affluence. His childhood had been spent moving from foster home to foster home, never knowing where he'd be living the next day. As it was, all his worldly possessions fit into this trailer/RV, a throwback to the days when he had to be ready to shove his belongings into a black trash bag and head to the new family at a second's notice.

"Not really." Especially considering Butterscotch already had a home for tonight, an assigned stall in the rodeo stock pen. The organizers knew they could always count on Lucky to lend a helping hand wherever needed. A jack-of-all-trades, he was as adept at repairing fences as he was at wiring temporary structures.

Sabrina finished her cup of coffee and placed it in the stainless-steel sink. "Good. Then it's settled. Find Elizabeth Irwin. You know her, right? Auburn hair, green eyes and very pretty. Let her know you're ready to unload Butterscotch."

"We've never been formally introduced." That admission came easily. Admitting he wasn't staying for the wedding? That was hard. Disappointing someone he loved like a sister was rougher than eating dirt in the rodeo arena.

"What?" Sabrina laughed before she realized he was serious. "Then today's your lucky day."

Hardly, as he'd be hurting Sabrina. And, for the record, the luckiest days of his life were the days he'd bought a bus ticket for Steamboat Springs, Colorado, and landed at the Cattle Crown Ranch. Little did he know the owner was a hall-of-fame rodeo competitor who'd ended up taking Lucky under his wing and preparing him for the circuit.

Sabrina opened the door and exited, and light flooded into the small space. The August heat was rather stifling, and Lucky tugged at the edge of his T-shirt. He picked up his weathered brown cowboy hat and placed it on his head. She was at the horse trailer part of the RV by the time he caught up with her. "You're going too fast."

She shrugged and introduced herself to his gelding. "That's because there's so much to do." She cooed soft words to Butterscotch, who nudged her as if they'd known each other for years. "As soon as we find out whether Elizabeth wants you in the paddock or a stall, we'll be back for you."

"I'm mighty thankful for the invitation." Lucky fought for control of the situation. The longer he took, the hotter the water he'd find himself treading in.

"I'm the thankful one since you supported me through this. I can't believe my mother's back in my life, let alone marrying the owner of the ranch where I used to work." Sabrina had interrupted him before he could make his excuses. "Evie and Gordon mesh well together. Best of all, Elizabeth will be my stepsister and Genie's aunt. A new family, so to speak. Follow me."

The water went from warm to scalding. *A new family.* He'd give anything for an old family. "It's mighty kind of you to invite me to the rehearsal dinner." Especially since he'd never met the bride before. He'd been taken aback when he'd discovered his friend, who couldn't sing a note, was the daughter of one of the most recognizable singers in the world, Evalynne, known to her friends as Evie. He'd hummed along to Evalynne's hit "Misty Mountain" on the bus ride from New York to Steamboat Springs at least twelve times, if not more.

"Evie's excited to meet you, and Genie loves her uncle Lucky. You have the magic touch with her. I can't believe my daughter is already eight months old."

Sabrina was making his announcement more difficult

by the second, but she was happy with her new husband, Ty. He'd kept waiting for an offer to teach at their rodeo academy, but she never broached the subject. Instead, she congratulated Lucky on his season, telling him he still had his best rides ahead of him. She didn't need her old friend anymore, and neither did Will, who'd connected with the love of his life, Kelsea, last May. It wasn't their fault they'd found love. He just wished there was a place for him here in Violet Ridge, one of the prettiest places he'd ever had the fortune of visiting. Staying longer would only make him feel like a third wheel and remind him of what he lost when Cherry chose someone else.

He followed Sabrina past a field where a bull snorted and pawed the ground. "Speaking of the rodeo…"

"What about it?" Sabrina stopped and faced Lucky.

He'd known Sabrina too long to keep up the pretense any longer. "I'm not staying for the wedding."

She searched his face, and her jaw dropped. "You're serious."

He nodded and tipped his hat. "It's a family affair."

As hard as it was to admit it, Will and Sabrina were no longer his family. They'd moved on without him. His heart ached once again at losing the people who'd come to mean everything to him, but he was used to it. He survived before, and he'd carry on.

"You're like the brother I never had and always wanted, Lucky." Sabrina came over and laid her hand on his arm, her engagement-and-wedding-ring set digging into his skin. "You're my family."

Those brown eyes gazed at him with care and concern. Somehow, he had to let her down gently. Ty would more than make up for Lucky's absence. Hadn't she made it clear last Christmas when she and Ty separated themselves at the Mile of Lights holiday display that she was ready to move on without Lucky? At the time, Lucky thought he'd be helping Sabrina, lending his support during the last stages of her pregnancy by surprising her at the apple orchard where the Mile of Lights was being held. Instead of a happy reunion, though, Sabrina had gone off with Ty, leaving Lucky with Will and Kelsea until Lucky found an excuse to head out of town. It was a good thing Ty was the perfect fit for the woman he cared for like a sister. That helped soften the blow.

"You know I'd do anything for you." And he would, except he couldn't stay for the wedding. Anything but that after he thought he and Cherry were destined for each other, only to be dumped without a backward glance. No wedding bells for him, then or ever. "But this might be my only chance to make the finals. Every rodeo counts."

"Of course, you'd bring up the one reason I can't stay mad at you. As it is, I'm taking a three-week leave of absence from my rodeo-clown position to support Evie and Gordon." She released his arm and pushed on the sliding doors of the stable. "At least you'll stay for the prewedding festivities, right?"

"I just came to give Genie the rocking horse." The one he'd carved and then painted in his off-hours. "Hold on a second."

He went back to the trailer's storage compartment and returned with his gift for Genie.

"Lucky, it's beautiful. You made this?" Sabrina gasped and ran her hand across the sturdy oak that formed the horse's body with connecting wooden legs. He'd painted Genie's name on the strong base. "The craftsmanship is breathtaking. Look at that saddle and the tiny pink heart on each side."

Tears welled in the corners of her eyes, and she hugged him. He'd carved it for Sabrina as much as Genie.

Separating from his friend was almost impossible, but he'd manage. "I'm better with smaller pieces of wood. Whittling's more soothing, but this came out well. Since I delivered it, I'm heading out."

"Already? Lucky Harper, you can stay in one place for longer than ten minutes. Mold won't grow on you." Sabrina popped her hands on her hips and stared at him while something outside the stable caught his eye.

More like a someone. A little someone, probably five or six, by the way she held her teddy bear with tears running down her face. Was she looking for Sabrina? His heart went out to the little girl, those pink cheeks tugging at his heartstrings even though he'd never set eyes on her before. A few feet away from the stable, she stopped on the gravel path and sniffled. Her eyeglasses fell to the ground. She bent over for them and released her grip on her teddy.

Out of nowhere, a UTV barreled toward her. Horror gripped his chest when he noticed the driver was talking to the passenger and probably couldn't see the child. There was only one thing to do and no time to waste.

He sprinted away from the stable and scooped the girl up under his arm. Rolling, he landed on the other side of the path, the UTV missing them by mere inches. Shouts from the vehicle reached him while it parked on the nearby grass. Pain jolted through his shoulder, but the little girl was fine. That was what counted.

At least he thought she was until she burst out crying and wailing at the top of her lungs.

It seemed as though this wasn't his lucky day after all.

IN THE SMALL office next to the tack room, Elizabeth Irwin studied the blueprints for the row of four modern, updated bunkhouses she wanted to build behind the stable.

Anything to keep busy and away from the bustle of her father's wedding.

The current bunkhouse needed too much work with the upgrades costing more than new construction. Ten minutes ago, the architect had finally sent her the plans, and she opened each rendering on her tablet. The elevation view gave her a better sense of what they'd look like from the side and back. Constructing these would allow the Double I Ranch to retain long-term employees who wanted to live on site and hire more temporary workers for seasonal work. Female cowhands could have their own facility, and there'd also be ways to accommodate families. The best place for these bunkhouses was her father's favorite riding trail, and he always shut down any discussion of more utilitarian uses for the land. Sometime before the wedding, Elizabeth needed to find a minute alone with her father so she could convince him to approve the architect plans for the bunkhouses.

The Double I was the best ranch around, and these improvements would only make it that much better. While she loved every day riding herd with Andromeda and overseeing the stable, her favorite time of year was upon them, only days away from one of the three annual roundups when she and the cowhands moved the cattle to the autumn field. Preparations for that gave her a reason to hide out here in her stable office, far from the rest of her family.

A commotion arose outside the stable, and the horses whinnied their discontent at the sudden uproar. Elizabeth was unsure of whether to calm them or check on the cause, and it wasn't often she was unsure of anything.

After jamming on her red cowboy hat, she passed the stalls, taking care to keep a calm presence for the horses' benefit. There hadn't been this kind of noisy disruption since that camera crew finished filming the commercial ad last Christmas. She found her beloved Appaloosa, Andromeda, and murmured some sweet words until her mare's agitation settled. Then she quickened her pace and found bedlam outside. Her good friend and future stepsister, Sabrina, was on her knees next to Elizabeth's niece, Audrey, who was practically inconsolable. Two of the newest ranch workers were arguing with each other next to a parked UTV, and a man she didn't know sat on the ground, rubbing his left shoulder.

She hurried over and kneeled beside Audrey, brushing her niece's long auburn hair, which matched her own, away from her face. "Sweetheart, are you okay?"

Audrey sniffled and bit her lip. "Aunt Elizabeth, I want to go home." She threw her arms around Elizabeth, her tears wet and warm against the thin fabric of her tank top under her unbuttoned plaid flannel shirt. "My glasses are dirty, my knee is scraped and Zack says I'm gonna mess up the wedding."

Her chest tightened at her nephew Zack's comment to his younger sister. That sounded like something her brothers would have said to her twenty-five years ago when she was six, the same as Audrey now, although thankfully they'd grown up since then. If anything, she didn't see them enough with Audrey's father, Jeff, working as an attorney in Boston, and Ben stationed in Germany with his United States Air Force unit. Jeff was already here for the wedding, and Ben would arrive late tomorrow night. Elizabeth squeezed her niece tight before reaching for the bandanna she always kept in her rear pocket.

She located Audrey's purple frames on the lush green grass and wiped the dirt from them. With care, she placed them back on the bridge of Audrey's nose. "One problem solved."

Then she removed her hat and plopped it on her niece's

head. *Way too big.* Those sniffles turned to giggles, followed by a lone hiccup, since it covered her forehead and
most of the frames.

"I like you." Audrey grinned.

Something stirred within Elizabeth, and she wanted to
protect her niece, but first she intended to get to the bottom of what had just transpired. "What happened?"

Before Audrey could answer, her father marched over
with Evie MacGrath keeping pace beside him. America's
favorite bluegrass singer was a perfect match for her father.
In sync with their steps, the two also meshed in other ways.
They both strived to be the best in their chosen professions
while emphasizing their relationships with their adult children. More than anything, though, Evie made Dad happy
with her vibrant personality and positivity. He beamed
whenever she was around, and they interacted like they'd
known each other for decades rather than mere months.

Evie reached Audrey first, and her niece left Elizabeth's side for the older woman who was set to become
her grandmother and the new Mrs. Irwin on Saturday, a
mere two days away.

"Audrey, sweetheart. Are you okay?" Evie asked.

A second hiccup was Audrey's answer, and Dad pulled
the workers aside, the intensity in his dark eyes reflecting
his feelings about the matter. The fact that their conversation was too muted for Elizabeth to hear only confirmed
how upset her father was. He was using his quiet voice
of steel that cut to a person's core. She was watching the
workers departing, heads down and shame-faced, when
she spotted someone hiding behind an aspen in the distance. She stood and crooked her finger. "Zack, please
come here."

Now Elizabeth would get some answers. Her eight-
year-old nephew merely gulped and hung his head, but

did as ordered. Sweat dripped off his forehead, probably due to the sweltering August day as much as his nerves. He lifted his head in time to catch the tail end of one of his grandfather's patented Irwin glares. "Sorry, Audrey." Zack kicked at the dirt with his new boots. "You're not gonna ruin the wedding."

"Zachary Gordon Irwin, we're going to find your father and have a talk about being a gentleman," Gordon said. "I had several such discussions with your father and your uncle. Somewhere along the line, they received the message."

With a nod in Evie's direction, he reached for his grandson's hand and headed toward the main house.

So much for finding some time to talk to her father this afternoon. The down payment for those new bunkhouses was coming due soon if they were going to get a head start before winter. She'd have to get his approval some time before he left on his and Evie's honeymoon.

Evie oohed when she saw Audrey's knee. "Shall we get that cleaned up?" She scooped up the little girl with the same care and loving tenderness as she did whenever she reached for her beloved guitar. "A couple of my crew members like colorful bandages, so I have extra."

"I need Teddy." Elizabeth handed her niece her special bear.

Evie smiled as Audrey cleaned the dirt off her bear. "And if your teddy has a boo-boo, too, we'll kiss his knee and make it better," Evie said.

In no time, the crowd thinned to only her, Sabrina and the man sitting on the grass observing everyone, and everything, like a hawk. Unlike those birds of prey, however, the man seemed as though he didn't have a care in the world, but was just watching the world go by.

Sabrina walked over to the man and offered him her

arm, making Elizabeth feel rather guilty for not thinking of that sooner. "And that, Lucky, is my mother and future stepfather." She helped him rise and glanced at the main house before tugging on her long brown braid. "Would you mind if I check on Genie and Ty while you talk to Elizabeth about Butterscotch? Something must have happened for Ty to lose track of Audrey and Zack like that."

Without waiting for a response, Sabrina trailed in Evie's footsteps, calling for them to wait for her. That left Elizabeth alone with someone named Lucky. He dusted the grass and dirt off his T-shirt, the color of which matched the electric blue of his eyes. Wincing, he stretched his shoulder, bringing attention to the muscles under the shirt. Then he noticed her and grinned. "You must be Sabrina's friend Elizabeth. It's supposed to be my lucky day meeting you."

"Lucky day? Hardly." Even if he had a grin that would melt ice cream. Elizabeth bristled at Sabrina matchmaking before Evie and Dad's wedding. She'd have a little talk with her friend, and ask her to cease and desist any further efforts to pair Elizabeth with anyone. Just because Sabrina found her true love with Ty Darling didn't mean everyone wanted a relationship. The ranch was enough for her. That, and getting her father to accept her contributions to the family's legacy. All she wanted was a chance to prove to him she could run the ranch.

Then she saw a flicker of pain cross Lucky's face. He wasn't good at hiding secrets, if that look was any indication. "Now that everyone has scattered, can you fill me in on what I missed?"

"Uh, um, the important thing is that little girl is okay…" Lucky averted his gaze and searched the ground until he picked up a battered brown cowboy hat, grimacing as he raised his shoulder. "Congratulations on the upcoming wedding. Couldn't happen to a nicer family."

Taken aback at his sentiment, she concentrated on how he was flexing his biceps. Something had happened to this man on her land, and she'd find out what and fix whatever was wrong. "What happened to your shoulder?"

"Must have landed on it funny." So he knew more about the incident than he was letting on. She bristled at the fact some outsider had inside knowledge about her ranch that she didn't. He covered his longish, dirty blond hair with his hat. "I'll be on my way so your family can enjoy the festivities."

"I'll enjoy them better once you get that shoulder examined. I won't take no for an answer." With a glance toward the stable, she saw one of the grooms bringing out Margarita, her father's favorite mare, for exercise. She needed to deliver some instructions before she accompanied Lucky to urgent care. "Wait here."

In no time, she was back, but Lucky wasn't where she'd left him. She searched the area and came up empty. Where'd he go? He'd injured himself on her ranch and, although she still wasn't clear on the sequence of events, that made him her responsibility.

She passed the field where the wedding would occur in two days. The wildflowers were in full bloom, providing the perfect backdrop for the ceremony, along with the most spectacular view of the Rocky Mountains anywhere. Tomorrow, the arch would be constructed and the chairs assembled for the guests, one hundred of the bride and groom's closest friends and family. As of now, the weather promised a Saturday of sunshine, so the event should be the special day her father deserved.

Glancing this way and that, she found no sign of Lucky and headed to the guesthouse, where Sabrina and her husband were staying. In the driveway sat a behemoth of a horse trailer, and Elizabeth found Lucky at the rear of the vehicle. She stopped at the sight of a gorgeous American quarter horse, and her estimation of the man before her rose considerably. "Beautiful horse. Does she follow instructions better than her owner?"

"His owner. His name's Butterscotch," Lucky corrected her and patted the horse before pulling the door closed. "Thank you for the offer about my shoulder, but I'm due in Pueblo later today."

He retrieved the keys and winced, rubbing that same left shoulder. "You should reconsider. It won't take long to have someone examine you, and it would set my mind at ease."

"This here's nothing. I've hurt myself worse at the rodeo," Lucky insisted and headed toward the driver's door.

By his own admission, he was well enough to leave. That ought to be enough to satisfy her, but she was convinced he was underplaying the injury for some unknown reason. This close to the wedding, however, she wouldn't press him. "Then have a good day."

Unsure of why he caused such a powerful reaction in her, Elizabeth headed to the stable with a firm intent on checking on Andromeda and the other nine horses, all of whom didn't care for sudden, loud noises. She didn't have time to dwell on cowboys who refused a little attention, not with her ranch chores calling her name, followed by a final fitting for her bridesmaid dress before dinner.

She halted in her boots when she heard her name. Turning, she faced Lucky heading her way. "I changed my mind. Could you keep an eye on Butterscotch while I find the closest urgent-care clinic?"

His earnest face held her gaze. He placed the needs of his horse above his welfare, and that was an admirable trait. Good thing he had plans to compete in this weekend's rodeo. Someone with those eyes and a love of horses could disrupt her schedule in a hurry if she wanted that kind of disturbance. Which she didn't. The best way of ensuring Lucky's quick departure from her life was to get him cleared for the rodeo so he could move on before nightfall.

"Better yet, I'll unload him and get him settled in the stable. Then I'll take you myself."

CHAPTER TWO

THE PUEBLO RODEO would commence tomorrow night, but Lucky wouldn't be a part of it. The physician's assistant had cleared him with a warning. The shoulder was only bruised, yet one wrong fall could leave Lucky sidelined for the rest of the season, if not longer. Rest was recommended, and he'd done the math in his head. Sitting out this weekend shouldn't impact his current position in the standings, and he wasn't scheduled to participate in another rodeo for two weeks after that. Missing the rest of the season, however, would end any chance of heading to Vegas in December for the finals and instead have him searching for a cowhand position to see him through the fall and winter.

Emerging from Elizabeth's new truck at her ranch, and impressed at all the bells and whistles, Lucky considered the road ahead. Will and Sabrina had moved on, and he'd best do the same. He'd drive to Pueblo tonight and offer his help to the rodeo director. Even without competing, there had to be some way Lucky could make himself useful. Wherever he landed, he always met a friend who needed a hand. He slammed the door and gave her a nod. "Thanks for the ride. Appreciate it."

She came around the front of the vehicle and halted some distance from him. "What about dinner? Can I get our cook, Tammy, to prepare you a meal while I see to Butterscotch?"

How had he forgotten his gelding was in Elizabeth's paddock rather than in his trailer? It would take some time to transfer him and get him settled before they hit the road. With dusk approaching, he should really turn down Elizabeth's offer for a bite of supper. "Thanks, but I'd best be loading him so I can be on my way."

It was a shame he had to leave so soon, what with his earlier glimpse at Elizabeth's family. Three generations together at one ranch, looking out for one another. He'd have given anything for a chance to get to know them better. Then again, leaving now was for the best before something happened and he became too attached. Families had a way of closing their ranks inward, leaving him to look in from the outside.

"Did I hear you correctly? You're going to Pueblo tonight? I thought you weren't attending this week's rodeo to let your shoulder heal. My brother Ben isn't arriving until tomorrow. You can sleep in his room, unless you'd be more comfortable in your RV." Elizabeth gave him a once-over and shook her head as if exasperated. "You already decided, didn't you? At least wait until morning and have a good dinner first. Then you can set out bright and early. The deliveries for the wedding will commence shortly after dawn. We're on a tight schedule with the florist, the caterers and the bakers. I usually arrive at the stable around five a.m., and I can help you load Butterscotch then."

More proof of what a special family occasion this was. "Thanks, but it'd be a sight better waking up in Pueblo. I'll gather Butterscotch and be out of your hair within the hour."

"It's your decision, but surely you can stay long enough for dinner. Tonight's the last night Tammy is cooking until after the wedding. She's the best cook west of the Mississippi, and she and her husband, JR, he's our foreman, have worked at the Double I for nearly thirty years. They will be guests, like most of the ranch staff. Dad said, 'Tammy knows me better than most of Violet Ridge. She's family.' The newest hires and a few temporary workers are in charge of the cattle on Saturday. I'll check on them early that morning. I have it down to the minute how long it will take me to get ready."

If he were fortunate enough to be part of her family, one that incorporated its staff into its ranks, he'd lap up every minute with them rather than spending it in the stable. "Why are you spending so much time away from the festivities and your niece and nephew? Aren't you happy about the wedding?"

Elizabeth had already started toward the horses. She stopped and turned toward him, a scowl on her very attractive face. "Of course I am. Evie makes Dad happy. It's just that I'm more comfortable wearing these clothes." She plucked at her jeans and plaid shirt layered over a tank top. "And I'd rather not twist my ankle in the strappy high heels I have to wear in the meadow. I've been told to leave my favorite red cowboy hat in the tack room, too."

She tipped her red hat over her long auburn hair, which was tied back in a ponytail. The dark red highlights were more like the sky at sunrise than the deep orange and pink hues of the setting sun off in the distance. Her fresh heart-shaped face, with its wide apple cheeks and green eyes, had a timeless appeal.

So she was pretty. She was also practically in charge of this ranch and way out of his league.

With no warning, his stomach rumbled, reminding him that Pueblo was three hours away. He'd counted on restocking his RV refrigerator this afternoon after making sure Butterscotch was settled nicely in the stock quarters. With this delay, he hadn't had the chance, and taking up

Elizabeth on her offer of a meal would only set him back thirty minutes or so. There weren't that many fast-food places to stop on the highway.

Maybe he could convince Elizabeth to eat dinner with him. He'd love any advice or recommendations she could give for soft-shoe boots for Butterscotch during their long hauls to rodeos. In the waiting room, they'd talked about farriers, and she seemed knowledgeable about the subject, as well as easy to talk to.

Unless she had plans with her family. He blinked. She might even have a boyfriend or husband, for all he knew. Many cowgirls wore their wedding rings on a necklace or took them off for the day, donning them again after ranch chores were completed.

"Elizabeth." His stomach growled again, and she turned and faced him. His sheepish grin summed up everything right now. "I'd be mighty obliged to accept your dinner offer on one condition."

She placed her arms over her chest and arched an eyebrow in that same imperious manner her father had done earlier. If only he'd had an adult give him that type of glare growing up. While there was a hint of rebuke in such a look, someone had to care to stop everything and deliver their two cents.

"Really? We don't know each other well enough to make any conditions on each other." She tapped her dusty red boot and then grimaced. "Then again, you hurt your shoulder on my ranch. Name it."

"I'd like you to eat with me."

She checked her watch and considered his offer. Then she nodded. "Dinner makes sense. I have a long night ahead of me. This wedding is playing havoc with everyone's routine, and the animals don't know the difference between Saturday and any other day." Then her stomach delivered a long growl, and she looked embarrassed. "You're right. Dinner sounds pretty good right about now."

"See, that wasn't too hard to admit, was it?" he asked.

"You already got one concession out of me. Don't press your luck." She laughed, and he knew she was teasing him. She hooked her arm through his right one, almost eye level with him since she was taller than average, and he was a couple inches shy of six feet. "I know a shortcut."

"It's mighty kind of you to accept my invitation." He dipped his head in her direction. Then again, he shouldn't be too surprised. Any future stepsister of Sabrina was bound to be nice.

"I have an ulterior motive. I'm going to observe your shoulder and make sure you can drive." Elizabeth kept her arm entangled in his. "You must have landed on it pretty hard, considering they ordered X-rays."

"I've had worse falls, and there was no calf struggling to get free." Like in his event of tie-down roping.

Besides, Lucky would throw himself in front of that UTV all over again for this moment with the pretty cowgirl, not to mention that little girl, Audrey.

Elizabeth guided him toward the path leading to the main ranch house, and Lucky's mouth dropped. Never had he seen such an impressive mansion in the mountains. A circular pathway, full of SUVs and newer model trucks, led to an expansive front porch. Huge flagstones lined the facade, and the length of the house went as far as the eye could see. To the right, he spotted a pair of Adirondack rocking chairs on the long wraparound porch. Wisps of smoke curled out of the stone chimneys, rising higher than the golden aspens surrounding the area. This was a far cry from the houses he was shuttled between as a foster child.

She opened the front door, her arm still hooked through

his. "What's your preference? Chili? Stuffed jalapeños? Steak? I'm sure Tammy will have something to suit your fancy."

"Steak would sure hit the spot."

Out of nowhere, something latched on to his legs with the force of a stampeding bull. "You're back." Lucky glanced down and found Audrey attached to him.

Someone flicked on the lights in a nearby room. "Surprise!"

Elizabeth released his arm, and his jaw dropped. She led him toward a massive living room filled with people. Over a stone fireplace that extended to the ceiling was a sprawled banner with the words *Thank you, Lucky* drawn with every imaginable shade of crayon. Gordon strode toward him, his hand outstretched.

"Lucky, how's that shoulder?" He whapped him on the back, and Lucky feared his right one now might be worse off than the one he'd injured earlier. "Audrey told us the entire story. You saved her life."

Evie approached and hugged Gordon's arm. "Audrey and her teddy bear told us. It was the cutest thing. We both owe you a world of thanks for saving her and threw this together while Elizabeth and you were spending time together."

Two more adults came over. The man gave Lucky a hard whack on his bad shoulder, and it was all he could do not to cry out in pain. "I'm Jeff Irwin, Audrey's father. My wife, Nicole, and I—" he tilted his head in the woman's direction "—were on a conference call with our law firm back home in Boston. The call went on longer than we expected, and we didn't realize Zack and Audrey went outside to explore the ranch. Thank you for looking out for our little girl."

Elizabeth turned to him, her green eyes clouded with

surprise. "We've been together all this time and whenever I asked, you changed the subject. Now I know why."

He caught Audrey staring at him with stars in her young eyes and waved away the praise. "The UTV was slowing down. I'm sure of it."

Jeff and Nicole talked with him for some time, asking all sorts of questions about what he did and where he was from. At the first break in the conversation, Elizabeth passed a plate of food to Lucky. He salivated at the steak and roasted potatoes.

"Sorry, it might be cold," she said. "It's been thirty minutes."

That long? It seemed like five minutes, but it sure was nice feeling like he was part of the family all this time. He accepted it with pleasure. "Thank you."

"Steak and potatoes, along with some appetizers. Your favorite, right?"

"You know it." Always grateful for his favorite fixings, he delivered a wide smile for her thoughtfulness. It might be stereotypical for a rodeo rider to favor steak, but there'd been nights he went to bed with an empty stomach so he never took anything like this for granted.

"That's Elizabeth. Efficient to the core. Most of our friends wanted skis or a new saddle growing up. She asked for a computer," Jeff said, smiling.

Lucky looked Elizabeth's way and saw her smile tighten.

"We already owned the top saddles, and I prefer riding to skiing. To me, it was an easy decision. Lots you could do or find out with a computer," Elizabeth said. "Come on, Jeff. You've called me worse things than efficient, but we're older now and should be past that."

"True, and I'm sorry for sounding like an obnoxious brother." Jeff reached out and brought his wife close. "It's hard not to fall into the same habits now that I'm back. You turned out okay for a little sister."

"Now I see who Zack and Audrey take after with their quibbles. You two make me happy Evie's an only child." An older woman with short silver hair and a metal cane headed their way, her chin held high. Wrinkles lined her sun-beaten face. She stopped and stared at Lucky before giving a swift nod. "I've heard many stories about you from my granddaughter, Sabrina, all good. I'm the mother of the bride, and you can call me Grandma Eloise."

Her eyes twinkled, and Lucky liked her on the spot. What he would have given to have met an honorary grandmother years ago. As it was, he'd take this one in a heartbeat. "Nice to meet you, Grandma Eloise. I thought you and your husband couldn't attend." Sabrina had mentioned their health ailments.

"Bob's waiting for me in Texas." She crooked a finger, and he moved a few steps closer. "Just between us, he's having the time of his life without me looking over his shoulder all the time."

Lucky doubted that and held out his plate. "Care for a stuffed mushroom?"

"I never turn down sharing food with an attractive man." She accepted the one closest to the edge. Eloise's tone was light, and he found her delightful. Her face grew more pensive. "Speaking of attractive men, Bob is beside himself for missing his daughter's wedding."

"I can't attend, either," he said between mouthfuls of food. "I'm leaving tonight."

Audrey let out a gasp. "You can't go yet. My teddy hasn't thanked you."

Evie gave Gordon a firm look. Gordon approached him, his eyes piercing Lucky with the same glare he'd given Zack earlier. "What's this about missing the wedding?"

Lucky placed the plate on the hearth. "I'm heading out for the Pueblo rodeo."

"I should have known you were competing there." Gordon nodded with appreciation in his gaze. He was a long-time supporter of the sport and the primary drive behind the Violet Ridge Rodeo Roundup, the first event of the year. "You're having quite the season. Congratulations."

"We've kept Lucky long enough. Now that you've finished your dinner, I'll help you load Butterscotch into the trailer," Elizabeth said.

"Slow down, Elizabeth," Gordon admonished his daughter. "We need to show Lucky some hospitality, considering he saved Audrey's life."

This close to Elizabeth, he heard her breath hitch. "I thought I was being hospitable, offering to help with his horse. Gorgeous American quarter horse. Calm temperament and a large eye. One of the finest I've ever seen."

Gordon faced him, his lips drawn in a straight line. "My daughter gets caught up with horses naturally. Now, since Sabrina's one of your best friends, and Evie's happy when Sabrina's happy, I insist you attend the wedding as my personal guest, especially considering you saved Audrey. It won't be any trouble adding an extra seat since Elizabeth's not bringing anyone to the wedding."

By his side, Elizabeth blanched at her father's observation, while Jeff burst out laughing. Lucky tugged at his T-shirt. It was getting harder by the second to find some graceful way out of staying. While he'd do anything for Sabrina and already thought the world of her grandmother, he didn't belong at such a fancy event. He appealed to Elizabeth by reaching out and squeezing her hand. "Elizabeth? I could really use your help."

What was he doing, expecting someone he'd only

known for a few hours to read his mind and come up with a convenient excuse for his departure?

"He can't be your personal guest…"

Lucky let out the breath he didn't realize he'd been holding. Color flooded back into Elizabeth's cheeks, and relief flowed through him. This wedding was a family event, and he didn't belong here. As it was, being thanked this much for being in the right place at the right time was downright uncomfortable, and he counted the minutes until he was on the road.

"Because he's already my plus-one."

ELIZABETH GROANED AND rubbed her head before donning her work gloves in the stable. A good hour of mucking out stalls would clear her mind. The horses depended on her and, whether or not her father recognized her contributions, the ranch needed her.

What had she been thinking earlier this evening, announcing to her entire family that Lucky was her date for Dad's wedding? No sooner had she made the biggest mistake she'd made since dating Jared, than her brother scoffed at her declaration. Only after Nicole pointed out that Elizabeth and Lucky had walked into the living room arm in arm, and she knew what his favorite meal was, did Jeff let the matter drop.

Pride, pure and simple, had sucked her into a tight vise. It would serve her right if Lucky loaded Butterscotch into the trailer in the middle of the night and went on his merry way.

"I don't even know his last name." She exerted extra force in shoveling the hay from Andromeda's stall.

"Harper."

Her heart nearly exploded out of her chest at the sudden sound of his voice. She glanced backward, only to find him picking hay off his jeans. "Oh, I'm sorry." For everything, starting with asking him to stay for dinner and then putting him on the spot like she had. Now she only compounded her error by accidentally pelting him with discarded hay. "Let me get you a towel."

He brushed off his jeans and his T-shirt. "I'm good."

Why did he go along with her? What was in it for him? She was about to ask when her father entered the stable. Normally, Dad left the horses to her care, his entrepreneurial enterprises extending beyond the ranch to the arena named after her family in town. He managed all that while she coordinated management of the extensive stable, the hiring and firing of cowhands and everyone's schedule. While the upcoming wedding and cattle drive had knocked everyone's schedule out of whack, horses didn't care about orange blossoms or cake flavors. Instead, they went about their business, which was comforting in and of itself.

"Lucky, I'm glad you're here. Since the two of you are dating, it figures you'd follow Elizabeth when she left abruptly like that. That's real nice."

Elizabeth bristled at the implication she'd run from the impromptu celebration. She never ran from anything. She had merely waited for what she thought was a reasonable amount of time before making her excuses, namely the horses.

Lucky looked away. "Well, yes, I suppose so…but I also came out here to check on Butterscotch."

Dad murmured some words to his favorite mustang, Margarita. Then he reached into his pocket and brought out apple slices. The mare nuzzled his hand and neighed her thanks. "You're modest. I like that about you, and it's good to meet a man who values a horse. You can tell a lot about a person by how they treat animals. Elizabeth, this one's a keeper. You should have brought your boyfriend to the ranch sooner."

She considered correcting her father's misperception about Lucky, but she'd start with the easier subject first. "Dad, speaking of people and animals, those two temporary cowhands won't work out." She leaned the shovel against the closest stall door. "They didn't show up for their shift. I tried calling their cell phones, but no answer."

If they were this unreliable now, how would they measure up next week at the annual cattle roundup?

"Didn't you get my message?" Dad folded his arms across his chest. "Those were the men who almost ran over Audrey. Jeff and I discussed the matter with them, and they agreed a future here was out of the question. We cut their final paychecks and sent them on their way."

"Why Jeff? Is there something I should know?" Elizabeth reached for the shovel and gripped the handle so much it hurt. She was always in charge of personnel matters, rather than her brother, who didn't even live in Colorado.

Dad's chest puffed out. "I told Jeff that he and Nicole would be more than welcome to come home to the ranch and offered them a position as my personal attorneys. Or the guesthouse if they practice law in Violet Ridge. I'd regret it someday if I didn't ask them to move back, especially seeing how fast my grandchildren are growing up. It would be great for Audrey and Zack to know how to ride. When I was their age, I collected the eggs and helped with the hay harvest." The same chores she, Jeff and Ben could do before they entered elementary school.

Her jaw slack, Elizabeth couldn't believe what she was hearing. She'd been the child who'd stayed behind and sweated over vaccinations, roundups and every facet of ranch life. Now her father wanted Jeff to return just like that and, most likely, take over what was mostly her role. Once again, her father underestimated her.

"What did Jeff say?" Elizabeth sounded as numb as she felt inside.

"You and Lucky walked into the room before he answered me. There was no time to follow up on the matter." Dad faced Lucky with a smile. "We're being rude to your boyfriend. I don't know why you didn't tell me about your relationship before now."

Elizabeth's stomach tightened. This was the moment. She should come clean and admit the truth. She opened her mouth, but no words tumbled forth.

"You know, it's funny how these things start." Lucky shrugged as if sensing her distress. "Turns out we care about the same people, and you've heard so much about them you feel like you know them. That's the case with us. I'm getting to know the real Lizzie, and she's giving me a test run, so to speak, but the minute I met her it was as if I'd been run over by something stronger than both of us."

How did Lucky do it? Everything he said was true, while glossing over the fact they'd just met. Dad nodded, and Elizabeth squinted. It was as if there were stars in Dad's eyes. "I like that. That's a lot like Evie and me. Evalynne is part of her, but Evie's the whole package." He blinked and cleared his throat. "I trust you'll be at the wedding rehearsal, then?"

"Um…" Lucky tugged at the collar of his blue T-shirt. "That's a family affair."

"Nonsense. You're Elizabeth's plus-one, so you're coming tomorrow night. I insist." Dad patted Lucky on the back. "The dinner will be at Mama Rosa's in Violet Ridge since everything for the wedding is being set up at the ranch tomorrow."

Elizabeth wouldn't let her father drop the other matter

so fast. "So you and Jeff fired the two workers who were driving the UTV without consulting me?"

"They were negligent, Elizabeth. A little girl, my grand-daughter, could have been injured or worse." Dad stroked Margarita's muzzle. "It was the right thing to do in the moment."

His cool tone made it clear he was acting as the ranch owner in this moment, not her father.

"Probably so, but who will take over their responsibilities during the wedding and for the roundup?" Elizabeth bristled on the inside, but tried not to show it.

"I'm sure you'll find someone. You always do."

So the employee decisions were his to make when it suited, yet she was the one who was expected to produce cowhands out of thin air with the wedding now less than thirty-six hours away and the roundup starting on Tuesday? It would be a sight easier to employ quality staff with extra benefits, including onsite housing.

"Speaking of our cowhands, I'd like to show you something regarding our future prospective employees. It'll only take a few minutes." With more amenities and benefits, the newly hired ranch hands might stick around longer.

"Maybe tomorrow. I don't have time right now. Evie's expecting me, and we're going downtown to pick up the wedding rings. The jeweler is staying late, just for us." Dad tipped his hat in Lucky's direction. "See you at the rehearsal."

Disappointed, she watched her father leave the stable. How would she get everything done before the wedding and hire extra hands for the roundup? It wasn't like Jeff or Ben had handled ranch chores in the past fifteen years, so they'd be more of a hindrance than a help.

She blew out a deep breath and started cleaning the nearest stall.

"Want to talk about it?" She'd almost forgotten Lucky was still here.

"Not really." She was determined the stable would never look better than when she left tonight. At least she had control over that. Efficient Elizabeth to the rescue, like always.

"You know you already cleaned that stall, right?" Lucky pointed out what should have been obvious, but in her state, she had managed to overlook that.

"My horses deserve the best." And that included employees who knew what they were doing.

Lucky laughed. "Can't fault that line of thought."

There was something genuinely nice about this man, and here she'd used him to make herself look good to her family, her father in particular. "I *can* fault myself for using you the way I did tonight. Now you're on the hook for the wedding rehearsal, too, when you wanted to get to Pueblo."

He shrugged and glanced around the stable. "Got another one of those shovels?"

"I'm giving you a chance to leave when no one's looking. Or is there something about you I should know? Are you a glutton for punishment?" She leveled a look at him. "After all, you're supposed to be my date to my father's rehearsal dinner and wedding."

"Maybe I'm a sucker for wedding cake and dancing." He grinned and held out his right hand. "Besides, now that I'm staying longer, Butterscotch will need an extended stay in your stable. He can't be in the trailer that long. Helping with the chores is the least I can do to earn his keep."

"How's your shoulder?" The last thing she wanted was to have him injure himself further on her watch.

"Ibuprofen wore off a couple of hours ago, and I'm fine." That was the first trace of exasperation she'd heard out of him. Guess he was like her and would rather be useful than sitting around doing nothing.

She returned in no time with extra supplies, including a pair of work gloves and another shovel. "Don't suppose you know any cowhands who are looking for temporary work? I have two openings for Saturday and for our annual cattle roundup, which begins on Tuesday. We pay well."

"I'd offer, but apparently I already have plans for Saturday." He winked. "I'll make some calls and get back to you."

Elizabeth had no doubt he would, either. They fell into a companionable silence, getting the horses fresh hay and water. After they finished, he murmured sweet words to his quarter horse, their bond clear.

"How long have the two of you been a team?" she asked.

Butterscotch nickered, and Lucky produced a peppermint from the pocket of his jeans, which looked the worse for wear, the rip near the knee a product from the earlier accident. "A little over six months."

She was impressed. It had taken Andromeda a while to accept her, yet Butterscotch delivered a look of pure devotion to his owner. Probably on account of Lucky being laid-back, yet sweet and kind. It was no secret that some in town called her imperious and thought she was snobbish. That wasn't the case, as her friends knew. She was just more comfortable around animals.

"Thanks for your help." And for bailing her out earlier and not embarrassing her in front of her family. He'd done more than his fair share to help her, and now it was time to return the favor. "Look, I was out of line. Jeff had me on edge, and then I panicked. You don't have to go to the wedding as my plus-one."

"Breaking up with me before our first date?" He crossed his palms over his heart and pretended to stagger backward. "I'm devastated."

Despite everything, she laughed. "There could be worse dates, except I roped you into it because of my pride."

"Then let's make it right." He hung his hat on a nearby hook and then removed his gloves. He reached for her hands and clasped them firmly. She liked his callused palms, a sign he wasn't afraid of hard work. "Ms. Irwin, er, Elizabeth, you don't know me, but my best friends Will and Sabrina will vouch for my character. I've heard there's a little shindig taking place this weekend in Violet Ridge. Would you do me the honors of being my date?"

She giggled and nudged the straw on the ground with the tip of her boot. "I do have the perfect dress."

"I happen to clean up pretty well myself." He released her hands and scrubbed his jaw, his stubble more attractive than it should be. "Then it's a date that's not a date."

Who could argue with logic like that? And why was she suddenly looking forward to the wedding more now than when she'd entered the stable?

CHAPTER THREE

THE NEXT AFTERNOON, Lucky stepped out of Harold's Barbershop in downtown Violet Ridge, feeling a pound lighter with a couple of inches of his shaggy, dark blond hair left behind on the faded linoleum floor. Last night, he told Elizabeth he cleaned up well, and he went for the whole shebang, treating himself to a close shave and haircut. A promise was a promise, and keeping his word led to a good night's sleep. He was proud to say he hadn't lost out on too many nights.

He rubbed his jaw, the smoothness unusual and a little disconcerting. Was it too obvious, though, that he was trying hard to impress Elizabeth and her family? He still wasn't sure how he felt about last night. He was fine with Elizabeth claiming him as her plus-one. If anything, he was still blown away by her snap decision, trusting him with that kind of privilege.

What was troubling, though, was her family proclaiming him a hero. He was no hero. Far from it. Still, it was nice to have Zack and Audrey claiming his attention for one night. Almost as nice as helping Elizabeth in the stable, working side by side, tending to the horses. Butterscotch seemed most content with his surroundings, and who could blame him? Posh didn't even begin to describe the Double I Ranch. He'd even taken up Elizabeth on the offer of staying in Ben's room. While he'd never thought a ranch could be elegant, what with the cattle, interesting

smells and noise, this one was definitely more sophisti-
cated than Cale's down-home Cattle Crown Ranch, where
he'd landed on his feet years ago.

He stepped out of the barbershop, a block away from
the primary group of shops and parking deck. Sabrina had
lent him her SUV so he wouldn't have to drive his large
horse trailer/RV.

With only a couple of hours until he was due to escort
Elizabeth to the wedding rehearsal and dinner, he'd best
pick up his pace. Still, he spared the time and stared at the
window display in front of the Reichert Supply Company,
an assortment of candles and homeware on one side and
toys on the other. Was he supposed to purchase a wedding
gift for the happy couple? What did a rodeo competitor buy
for a successful ranch owner who was marrying a famous
singer? Silver candlesticks? A crystal decanter? A kite?

Sighing, he turned and found Sabrina exiting the Think
Pink Salon, along with her mother and grandmother. Hur-
rying toward them, he called out Sabrina's name, and she
let out a squeal.

"Lucky!" Sabrina ran over and hugged him. "I almost
didn't recognize you with a haircut and a shave."

She elbowed him while Evie and Grandma Eloise
caught up to them. He reached for his cowboy hat, forgetting he'd left it back at the ranch, and then moved his hand
to hide his mistake. "Ma'am."

He nodded at both and then searched behind them for
Elizabeth, but she was nowhere to be found. Evie smiled.
"Your girlfriend is back at the ranch. Gordon told me what
you said to him last night. That was so romantic." Lucky
blinked until he realized Evie was talking about Elizabeth. "We invited her, but she insisted she was too busy.
Now we know why. She's working hard while you're in
town so the two of you can spend time with each other

later. You'll have to pry yourselves away from each other tomorrow when my personal makeup artist and hairstylist arrive early. They'll be staying as guests for the wedding after they finish getting the bridal party ready, too."

Was Elizabeth hiding behind the horses? With a family like this? Either way, he was glad she'd be part of this loving group tomorrow. Families should stick together, and she was gaining a loving stepsister in Sabrina.

"Elizabeth will look beautiful, no matter what." And that was the truth. Elizabeth's inner radiance stood out last night, impressing him more than he should have let it.

"Good answer." Grandma Eloise tapped her cane on the sidewalk. "Elizabeth is smart to keep you around. I hope the two of you can separate yourselves from each other long enough for you to save this old lady a dance tomorrow."

"I'll be the lucky one if we light up the dance floor together." Lucky grinned.

"You have a silver tongue." Grandma Eloise chuckled and placed both hands on her cane. "The price for that is two dances."

"You're a real taskmaster, Grandma Eloise." He winked his approval.

"We still have to pick up Ben's tuxedo at the alteration shop." Evie patted her watch. "He's missing the rehearsal, but Jeff can fill him in on his usher duties when he arrives late tonight. See you later, Lucky."

Sabrina delivered an extra hug. "I'm keeping my fingers crossed about you and Elizabeth. Evie told me everything. I should have known you were playing with words when you said you'd never been formally introduced. It's obvious you two didn't need a formal introduction and found each other just fine. You're her lucky match."

Hardly, and guilt over not correcting everyone's im-

pression of him and Elizabeth as a couple glued him to
the sidewalk, the summer sun beating down on him. What
would Will and Sabrina say when they found out the two
weren't dating? If he hadn't lost them already, he'd have
lost their respect when everything came to light. Families
didn't come along every day, and he already missed them.
Maybe he should try to confide in them now?

Passing more of the local shops, he considered other options for a wedding present. Maybe Elizabeth would know
if Gordon and Evie had announced a charitable foundation for donations instead of gifts. Then a beautiful arrangement in the window of Forever Violets Floral Shop
caught his eye. Four huge tissue paper peonies roughly
Audrey's size were surrounded at the edge of the display
by real bouquets of daisies and violets, arranged in a way
that combined whimsy with beauty. Maybe flowers would
be a nice thank-you gift.

Lucky entered the shop, and the light wind chimes
greeted him along with a cool blast of air-conditioning.
He didn't see anyone behind the counter. A minute later,
a harried worker in her late fifties hurried over and wiped
her forehead with the back of her hand. "Sorry about that.
I'm getting ready for a weekend wedding. How can I help
you?"

Good question, as he wasn't quite sure himself, but he
didn't want to appear at Elizabeth's door empty-handed before the rehearsal dinner. He glanced at the double refrigerator unit with glass doors beside the counter. Corsages
dotted the upper level. He'd never given anyone a corsage,
since he'd worked on prom night, busing the tables of his
classmates at an upscale restaurant.

"I'd like to buy a corsage." He could write a book about
training colts or how to lasso a steer, but what he knew

about flowers wouldn't fill a paragraph. "Do you have any suggestions?"

"What color is her dress?" The woman was all business as she pulled out an order pad.

"Um, I don't know. Does that matter?"

"It's a general starting point." She reached under the desk and produced a card. "When you ask her for the details, see if she's willing to give you a picture of the dress. Then I can also match the ribbon to the hue and style of the cut."

Even something as simple as flowers was anything but, the same as everything else on this trip to Violet Ridge. "I need one for tonight." Grandma Eloise seemed as though she'd appreciate one as well. "Actually, two of them. What about those?" He pointed to the top shelf of the refrigerator. "Are any of them for sale?"

She winced and shook her head. "I'm sorry, but those are for the Irwin wedding tomorrow. The co-owner of the shop is at the location, setting up and finishing the prep work."

"Thanks for your help. Mighty obliged." He dipped his head and went to leave.

Sabrina sailed in and stopped next to Lucky without looking at him. "I'm here to make sure the last of the flowers for the Irwin wedding are ready." Then she whipped her head back and laughed. "Lucky Harper. You're everywhere."

"Guilty as charged." Lucky stepped back and reached up, missing his cowboy hat once more. "See you tonight at the rehearsal dinner."

"Wait!" The store owner rolled her eyes. "You know the Irwin family?"

"He's Elizabeth's plus-one." Sabrina hugged Lucky's

arm. "Of course, I should have guessed you'd also be at the rehearsal dinner."

"You're Ms. Irwin's date?" The owner's gaze wandered over him, and he couldn't help but feel as though he was lacking the panache of someone worthy of Elizabeth.

"They're perfect for each other." Sabrina let go of his arm. "I knew the two of you would get along."

Uh-oh. He also wasn't sure how Elizabeth would like the news about their date becoming fodder for gossip in Violet Ridge. One date that wasn't a date was one thing; people talking in her hometown about the two of them was another.

"I'll whip up an extra two corsages in no time for you tonight, sir." The owner glanced at Lucky and smiled. "You didn't tell me one of the corsages was for Ms. Irwin. I'll be right back with the best I've got left."

The owner disappeared behind the curtain, and Lucky wasn't sure he liked receiving this type of preferential treatment. If this was the impact of having money and influence, where people treated you differently, he'd rest better at the next rodeo having nothing but a modest sum in his bank account after paying cash for the trailer this year and for the engagement ring last year.

Sabrina leaned on the counter and nodded at him. "I know you too well so I know what you're thinking. Between you and me, I prefer being Sabrina and wearing my rodeo-clown outfit." She squeezed his hand. "Folks living in this area respect the Irwins and how they've always supported not just their home and business, but Violet Ridge, too. This kind of thoughtfulness, at times, is part and parcel of dating an Irwin."

He kept from frowning. His experience centered on the opposite treatment when it came to people judging him based on his family, or lack thereof. Some of his friends' parents had treated him with disdain once they found out he was a foster kid. One even locked her purse in a cabinet right in front of him. Ever since, he'd tried to treat everyone with the same level of respect, whether they were rich or poor, were a foster kid or had a loving family.

Problem was, he wasn't dating an Irwin.

"I'm not…"

Before he could elaborate, the owner reappeared with a large box with a smaller one nestled on top. She handed them to Lucky. "The colors for the wedding are dusty rose and moss green. So I prepared one large and one small corsage with that as my guide. The rest of the flowers are well in hand."

Sabrina shook her head. "You didn't have to get me anything."

His cheeks grew hot. "Actually, the other corsage is for your grandmother. I thought your grandpa Bob would have bought her one."

She rose on her tiptoes and kissed his cheek. "Elizabeth better not break your heart, or she'll answer to me. Grandma will be tickled pink—" she flashed her hands "—which will match our nails. Gotta run and check on my daughter before the wedding rehearsal. See you there."

Sabrina departed the shop, and Lucky paid for the corsages. An hour later, he rang the doorbell near the ranch house's massive mahogany front door, and Elizabeth answered.

His breath whooshed out of him. She'd been attractive yesterday in her jeans and boots, but tonight she was stunning in a sage-green sundress dotted with dusty pink flowers. The color brought out her emerald eyes, and her auburn hair was swept up, showcasing her long neck. He wobbled in his crisp gray trousers, paired with a white dress shirt and tie. Speechless, he thrust the boxes toward her.

She opened the larger one and gasped. "The corsage is beautiful, but there are two boxes."

The sound of a cane hitting the hardwood reached him before he spotted Evie and Grandma Eloise heading their way. "The second one is for Grandma Eloise." He reached into the box and presented the orchid to the older woman. "I thought Bob wouldn't want me to forget you."

Evie smiled and patted his arm. "I should have thought of that. Thank you, Lucky." She grinned and faced Elizabeth. "This one's a keeper, just like your father."

He thought he saw a tear in Grandma Eloise's eye. She tapped her cane twice on the hardwood floor and nodded. "Bob would approve, and so do I." She then placed her hand over her heart. "Nothing like a corsage to make a woman's heart pitter-patter, right, Elizabeth?"

"When it's the right person, absolutely." Elizabeth snapped the corsage on her wrist. "We're running late to the rehearsal. We better hurry to the meadow since we have to drive into Violet Ridge for the dinner at Mama Rosa's immediately afterward."

She led the group to the outdoor area, where a field had been transformed into a wedding wonderland. Overhead, twinkling lights lit the rows of white chairs that faced an arch decorated with dusty pink roses and sage greenery. The Rocky Mountains rose majestically behind the arch, as if overseeing the wedding itself. Even tomorrow's weather was custom-made for a once-in-a-lifetime day, with the forecast predicting sun and perfect August temperatures.

Gordon separated himself from the group and handed Evie one of the crystal goblets he had been holding. He kissed his future bride on the cheek, his ruddy cheeks deepening to red, his love for her evident in his eyes. "You look lovely, Evie. The best thing I ever did in my life was ask you out."

Beside him, Lucky heard Elizabeth gasp softly and saw her face flame into a deep red before her breathing grew regular again. He leaned in and, soft enough for her ears only, whispered, "One of the best things. I'm sure that's what he meant to say."

Her smile didn't reach her eyes. "My father always says what he means."

"The officiant is here." Gordon's gaze shifted to a man in a solemn gray suit. "Before we start, has anyone received a text from Ben? His plane should have landed by now."

Members of the Irwin family reached into purses or pockets for their phones. Jeff shook his head, but Elizabeth paled. "Excuse me for a minute."

Walking away from Lucky, she pulled her father aside, and Gordon's face turned beet-red. Evie came over to Lucky. "What did the text say?" she asked.

"I don't know."

Gordon proceeded to the archway where the officiant would perform the ceremony while Elizabeth moved to the rear, joining Lucky and Evie. "Attention, everyone."

The small crowd gathered around Gordon. Lucky kept his distance, away from the family, while Evie joined Gordon by his side.

"What's wrong?" Evie asked, placing her arm around her fiancé.

"Ben texted Elizabeth. He missed his flight because of a last-minute emergency. Military business. He isn't coming." Regret and sadness came through in his voice. Gordon dipped his cowboy hat before taking it off and fiddling with it. "We're an usher short."

"Jeff can walk Elizabeth up the aisle, and then go back for Nicole," Evie suggested.

"Or I could escort one on each arm." Jeff held out his elbows as if proving his point.

"I can walk down the aisle by myself," Elizabeth said, with conviction.

With no place for him in this circle, Lucky backed away. In his experience, this type of family dilemma was always settled better with less of a presence from outsiders. He glanced around for something to do, someone to help.

"Lucky!" Evie called out, and he stopped in his tracks. "You look like you're the same size as Ben."

His hands grew clammy. "Nah. I'm shorter than Gordon and Jeff."

"So's Ben." Gordon sized him up and nodded. "You'll fit into his tuxedo with no problem. Congratulations, Lucky. You're promoted to usher, and you'll walk Elizabeth down the aisle."

THE PRIVATE ROOM at Mama Rosa's always promised a special evening, and this night was no exception. Candlelight bathed the walls in a soft glow, highlighting the one covered with pictures of Gordon and Evie. In the background, Evalynne's greatest hits serenaded the small group, but not too loud as to get in the way of good conversation.

With the remnants of her eggplant parmigiana on her plate, Elizabeth motioned for Lucky to lean into her. A whiff of his lime aftershave mixed with a faint scent of horses and sunshine was more calming than she'd have liked. A few days ago, she didn't know him, only what she'd heard about him from Will Sullivan or Sabrina, yet now she found that scent combination was just like him: earthy with a twist of something invigorating.

"I had no idea what your father was planning." Lucky kept his voice low so only Elizabeth could hear him, just as he had several other times throughout the evening. "I couldn't think of a way to bow out gracefully."

Welcome to her world. At least he didn't fault her for this conundrum, although she wouldn't have blamed him if he had. "Believe me, I've been there, but we need a plan for after the wedding. A reason for us to break up." Especially since everyone now believed they'd been carrying on in secret all this time.

"Hmm. I can fill you in on all of my bad traits, and you can pick the worst. Sometimes I'm in a hurry and don't clean out the sink after I shave."

Elizabeth laughed. "I don't think anyone would believe I broke up with you over that."

The server brought dessert—tiramisu for Lucky and cheesecake with strawberries drizzled with chocolate for her. This time Lucky motioned for her to come close to him. "Anyone who doesn't choose raspberries over strawberries? That's a deal breaker for me."

She burst out laughing. "Good thing they didn't offer me a choice."

"Then we'll just have to stick to the truth. That's always for the best, anyway." Lucky was so close she felt his breath tickling her ear, a quite pleasant way to end the perfect meal.

"Look at the lovebirds." Evie's pronouncement sent her back to her seat as her future stepmother approached with Sabrina at her side. "Whispering to each other as if they're the only two in the room. They've been doing this all night."

"I love seeing you happy, Lucky." Sabrina beamed at the pair of them. "You deserve all this, and more."

And she had tied this nice guy into her crazy scheme. Elizabeth transferred the mossy green napkin from her lap to her plate. She needed time to think and plan. The nighttime stable duties with the familiarity of the horses and her routine would provide just that. "Can you drive Lucky back to the ranch, Sabrina? Then I can finish the instructions for the crew for the weekend."

"No problem. It'll give me time to get the full scoop." Sabrina winked at Lucky.

Elizabeth rose and ignored the slight flutters when Lucky stood at the same time, his gaze earnest and insightful. "I'll be on my way, then."

Back at the ranch in her bathroom, Elizabeth sent a lingering look at the corsage on her wrist before taking it off and placing it on the counter. Lucky shouldn't have gone to such trouble, but she had the feeling remembering little details like this were part of his personality. Why hadn't she told him how much this unexpected and thoughtful gesture meant to her?

Any other time, under any other circumstances, she'd love to get to know Lucky better. And yet this was the worst time for emotions to get in her way. She'd been preparing to take over management of the ranch her entire life, and now her father wanted to pull her oldest brother back into the fold?

Hardly a ringing endorsement of her abilities as manager. What would Dad say if he found out her pride had goaded her into claiming Lucky as her plus-one? That might make him push for Jeff, and possibly even Ben, to return and run the ranch. Worse still, Lucky had been roped into being part of the wedding party.

What the laid-back rodeo star must think of her now, she didn't want to know.

She hastily scrubbed off her makeup and changed out of the beautiful dress into her favorite jeans and threadworn flannel shirt. Then she donned her boots and headed for the stable. After a quick check of the notes left by the lead groom, she sent a longing glance toward Andromeda's stall. What she'd give for a nighttime ride under the stars with the cattle lowing nearby. Next week would deliver moments like that with the roundup. Once that was over, her father and Evie would leave on their honeymoon while Elizabeth tended the ranch and monitored the corn being cut up for silage. The resulting product, with its high-energy content, would feed the cattle long into the cold Colorado winter.

Somehow, during the cattle drive, she'd have to get her father on board with her plan for the new bunkhouses. When he returned from his honeymoon, she planned on implementing yet another change that would shore them up for the long term. While the Double I was residence to one thousand head of Angus cattle, she'd been reading up on another popular breed in Colorado: Simmentals. Introducing that breed to the other side of the ten-thousand-acre ranch could reap benefits down the line. She counted on her father being in a good mood for that discussion.

On her way to the tack room for the fly spray she needed to apply to each horse, the stable cat's purrs reached Elizabeth. She rolled up the sleeves of her flannel shirt and climbed the ladder. Once at loft level, she checked on the cat. Content and relaxed, the cat raised its head. She must have been satisfied Elizabeth didn't constitute any kind of threat because she curled up and went to sleep. That type of personality must be nice. In a way, the cat reminded her of Lucky, who seemed to take life in stride.

With reluctance, she gathered her supplies and applied fly spray to each horse, except Butterscotch, texting Lucky that she'd apply it if the gelding had no problems with the brand she favored. As always, she saved Andromeda for last. That way, she could spend extra time with her mare. She placed the spray bottle on the ledge.

"Oh, Drommie." She rested her head against her horse's flank. "What a night!"

"A good one, I hope." Lucky's voice came from behind, and her heart raced.

A glance at him with his white dress shirt stretched across his broad shoulders, the top button unbuttoned, only made her heart beat that much faster. She took a deep breath and pushed aside her reaction to him. It was surprise, that was all. "You scared me. You could have just texted me back."

"I was already on my way." He jerked his thumb toward Butterscotch. "I wanted to check on him before bed. Appeared we had the same idea."

The best idea, in her opinion. She liked how his mind operated almost as much as she liked his droll sense of humor. Still, guilt flooded her about how her pride was causing him all this extra trouble. She grabbed the fly spray and went over to him. After exhaling a deep breath, she said in a rush, "I didn't mean for you to get caught up in my family's issues."

He laughed and then shoved his hands in his pockets. "I don't mind at all, and that's a bit of an exaggeration, isn't it? You're making everything sound so serious. This wedding is a joyous occasion."

"One you weren't going to attend, and now you're in the wedding party."

"A promotion. Who can argue with that?" His gaze held bemusement, and she wondered if anything ever bothered him. "And that dinner tonight more than made up for any inconvenience. Good food, great company, a beautiful woman at my side."

She thrust the bottle of fly spray into his chest. "You seem too good to be true."

Lucky applied it to Butterscotch's legs. "On the contrary. I've just seen too much in my life to get upset over something that's not worth it."

For some reason, she wanted to know more about him. "Like what? Tell me about yourself."

He squirted some of the spray on Butterscotch's flank. "It's too late at night for that, and we have a wedding to attend tomorrow."

Avoidance, pure and simple. Or perhaps he didn't feel comfortable around her. The conversation at the rehearsal dinner had been light and simple, the casual chat of acquaintances who'd never see each other again.

"Another time," she said. Not that there would be one. After the reception, he'd head to the next rodeo, and she had the roundup on the horizon. If anyone asked why they weren't dating anymore, she'd tell the truth. They'd agreed to the one date, and nothing more.

Somehow, though, not getting to know him better or even seeing him again caused a ripple of sadness to run through her.

After he finished, he returned the bottle, and she returned to Andromeda. He followed her and murmured sweet words to her mare. Was he a horse whisperer, or did he make everyone feel special, allowing them to open up to him?

"What do you get for a rancher and a singer as a wedding gift, anyway?"

"They specifically asked for no gifts. Guests can make a charitable donation to a local horse shelter or causes Evalynne supports in her professional capacity, but it's not like anyone's going to check for a receipt at the door." She rubbed the spray into Andromeda's coat, taking care there was a fine sheen afterward.

"I like that idea. I don't think Cherry would have gone for anything like that, but I would."

"Cherry?" All this time she thought he was single and unattached, but she must have figured wrong. "Is she your girlfriend?"

Her voice sounded too high-pitched and garbled for her liking.

"My ex-girlfriend." That revelation shouldn't have made her as happy as it did. "She's married to someone else now."

She had no idea if Jared had ever married, nor did she care enough to find out if he did. "That must have been rough." Elizabeth set down the spray bottle and reached into her pocket for some apple slices for Andromeda.

"I've handled worse." He reached for a slice and fed one to her mare, who nuzzled his hand searching for more.

"Breakups are never easy." She should know, although losing Jared ended up being a blessing in disguise. He'd been interested in signing a lucrative contract with her father rather than pursuing her out of sheer love. Even though that was a while ago, it still left an unpleasant taste in her mouth. She reached for the fly spray and held up her right index finger. "If you have a minute, I'll walk with you back to the house. I need to put this away first."

"Thanks. I'm meeting Evie and Grandma Eloise to try on that tuxedo, and I appreciate the company." Lucky followed her into the tack room.

In no time, everything was in its proper place for the night. She found a supply of peppermints and raised one. "I remember Butterscotch likes these. Can he have the special treat tonight?"

"He *loves* them, so, yes." They walked together to the gelding's temporary stall. "Thanks for boarding him. Maybe Sabrina was right after all. I guess it was lucky for me you didn't have a date for the wedding."

"Guess you're living up to your nickname." She smiled and reached into her pocket for the peppermint.

He stared at her, squinting those electric blue eyes that observed far more than he let on. "The men of Violet Ridge's loss is my gain."

She met his gaze, and something stirred within her. His calmness seemed to balance out her constant need for activity. Too bad they had to meet like this. Too bad that he'd be heading to the next rodeo and out of her life by nightfall tomorrow. "I'll take your word for it."

"It's the truth." He reached out and stroked Butterscotch's muzzle.

"Cherry seems to be the one who missed out on something." The air crackled around them, but there was a wedding taking place on the ranch tomorrow. That, along with the balmy summer night, explained everything.

"At the time I wasn't happy about it, but now I'm relieved I never asked her to marry me." He shrugged and shook his head. "It must be that glass of wine at dinner. I don't like to talk about myself."

Was this his first flaw? Or was it refreshing to find someone who didn't spend every minute talking about himself the way Jared had? "Well, for the record, no one's ever asked me."

She reached into her pocket, and the peppermint fell to the hay. About to bend down, he beat her to a kneeling position. "Allow me." He picked up the peppermint and held it up to her, a smile lighting up that friendly face. "I can't believe you've never heard the words *will you marry me* before."

She laughed and reached for the peppermint so he could rise more gracefully without crushing the candy. "Yes—"

Shrieks came from behind her. Her blood chilled, and

her eyes grew wide. Lucky rose to a standing position, and they both turned to find Zack and Audrey standing there.

"A proposal. Yuck." Zack scrunched up his nose and made a face. "Mom and Dad were wrong, and you were right, Audrey."

"I get to tell them." Audrey ran out of the stable toward the house. "They're engaged!"

Elizabeth stood rooted to the spot, her legs too heavy to move. Her mouth dropped as she glanced at the peppermint in her hand. How could anyone mistake a peppermint for a ring?

Worse yet, the date that wasn't a date might just have turned into the engagement that wasn't an engagement.

CHAPTER FOUR

LUCKY DUSTED BITS of straw off his good gray dress pants. A glance at Elizabeth confirmed she was as shell-shocked as he felt inside. Seemed as if he wasn't living up to his nickname after all.

Then again, there was a simple explanation for this misunderstanding, and everyone would laugh afterward. "If anyone else comes, we'll show them the peppermint." Lucky held out the candy, and Butterscotch whinnied for the treat. Before Lucky could move his hand out of the way, he felt the gelding's tongue and mouth tickling his palm as Butterscotch lapped up the peppermint.

"The peppermint you just fed to your horse?" Elizabeth's wry voice was a stark reminder about the real reason they were in the stable.

"Yeah, that one." He wiped his hands on his pants and kept from sighing. Who was he kidding? Once Gordon and Evie heard the entire story and he became a laughingstock the night before their wedding, they'd probably rescind Lucky's invitation as acting usher. That would be the end of his time here, period.

Elizabeth leaned her ear toward the stable entrance, and her face softened. Then a peal of nervous laughter swept over her. "Nothing. No one's coming, so they're either busy, or Zack and Audrey got sidetracked. Thank goodness no one believes we're really engaged."

A brief pang of regret over how relieved she sounded

flitted through him. He couldn't blame her, though. Who'd believe someone as beautiful and accomplished as her would end up with this kid from upstate New York who only had two nickels to rub together?

"Well, then, I have a tuxedo to try on." If it didn't fit, that would be another sign he shouldn't be in the wedding party and might be able to leave town with some grace. "Unless you want me to go, Elizabeth. Just say the word and I'm out of here."

Even though he hadn't known her long, he enjoyed her company and liked what he'd seen, but if his absence would help her, he'd follow through on his offer in a heartbeat. His gaze met hers in the dim lighting of the stable. Her emerald eyes glistened with uncertainty. Somehow, he knew that scared her more than anything. He understood that kind of fear.

Before she could answer, shouts and exclamations came from the direction of the house. Elizabeth reached for his hand and pulled him outside. "Uh-oh. This kind of excitement's not good for the horses."

And, by association, for her, either, but he stayed silent, as a throng of Elizabeth's family members headed for them with Audrey and Zack leading the pack. Lucky squeezed Elizabeth's hand for courage.

"See, Mommy. They are happy. They're holding hands just like you and Daddy," Audrey insisted as everyone stopped a decent distance from him and Elizabeth. "I told you she said yes."

From the opposite direction, Sabrina and Ty arrived with baby Genie quiet and content in her mother's arms. "What's going on?" Sabrina was out of breath. "We were changing Genie when we got a text to come to the stable at once."

Jeff huffed. "Really, Elizabeth and Lucky? You couldn't

let Evie and Dad have the spotlight to themselves?" He shook his head and let go of Zack's hand. "This weekend is about them, not the both of you."

All the wind left Lucky's sails. He had been so happy to be included in the Irwin family wedding, but Jeff was right. This disruption was taking the focus away from Gordon and Evie. He glanced at Gordon, who wiped a tear from the corner of his eye. It appeared as if he'd overstayed his welcome at yet another home.

"I'm sorry, sir," Lucky said, releasing Elizabeth's hand.

"Wait a minute, Jeff," Sabrina said. She handed Genie to Ty, who didn't miss a beat and tickled Genie's nose, the baby's giggle a sweet sound in a sea of disapproving faces. Then she marched over to her future stepbrother and popped her hands on her hips. "Lucky Harper is one of the most selfless people I've ever met."

He appreciated Sabrina coming to his defense. "Thanks, but…" Lucky began, but bedlam was breaking out with everyone talking at once. Jeff and Nicole were arguing with Sabrina, and Elizabeth was saying something to Gordon and Evie.

What had he done, bringing dissension into this wonderful family who'd opened their home to him?

Something, or someone, tugged at his pants. He glanced down at Audrey, whose smile was almost as wide as the frames of her purple glasses. "I'm glad you'll be my uncle."

Lucky's chest expanded with something warm and fuzzy filling his heart. Thank goodness, he'd been in the right place at the right time, so she wasn't hurt. At that moment, a whistle pierced the air. Everyone stilled.

Evie held her head high and smiled once she had everyone's full attention. "Good." She fanned her face. "This was getting too heated for my comfort. Gordon has something to say."

"Thank you, darlin'. That was perfect." Mr. Irwin hugged his fiancée. "I never knew you could whistle like that."

"There's a lot you don't know about me yet." She winked, her eyes holding a hint of mystery and humor. "Still want to marry me?"

"Wouldn't miss it for all the acres in Colorado." Gordon grinned, a look of admiration spreading across his face. Then he cleared his throat, and that serious glare returned. "Now, there seems to be some misapprehension that Lucky and Elizabeth are stealing our thunder. Evie and I are more than capable of speaking for ourselves, and she just showed how she's capable of getting anyone's attention when she wants it."

"And don't you forget it." She nudged him and brought forth a burst of laughter.

Gordon grew serious once more. "Having Evie by my side, supporting me, loving me, is something beyond my wildest dreams." He wound his arm around her slighter frame. "If you're lucky enough to have a whirlwind of love in your path, sometimes you have to ride into the storm rather than get out of its path."

"You're adding to our celebration." Evie leaned into Gordon's solid frame. "And you have our blessing."

Gordon nodded. "You'll make an excellent addition to our family, Lucky. I can already tell you and Elizabeth are a perfect match."

Sabrina extended her hand toward Jeff. "You'll come to love Lucky as much as Ty and I do. I promise."

Jeff accepted her offer of a truce while his wife Nicole stepped forward. "Let me see the ring."

Nicole's gaze shifted to Elizabeth's bare left hand. The light from the full moon shone brightly enough for him to see Elizabeth blanch. "Well, you see, this is all a big…"

She glanced at Lucky as if appealing to him to bail her out of the situation.

Gordon looked at him with anticipation, and Lucky gulped. "The ring's still in my trailer."

"Really?" Jeff asked. "How did you propose to her? With a horse bit? Elizabeth, this is Dad's special occasion."

Elizabeth stood there like a statue, hurt on her face. Lucky had to say something. "It might have been on the spur of the moment, but Zack and Audrey witnessed it. She said yes, and the ring is waiting for her."

"This cold air and all this excitement is too much for me tonight." Grandma Eloise double tapped her cane into the soft grass. "I need my beauty sleep, so I look gorgeous in the wedding pictures. Besides, the lovebirds need some time alone. And I mean all the sets of lovebirds."

Zack scrunched up his face. "Ew, gross. Come on, Audrey. I'll race you inside."

Gordon and Evie escorted the older woman along the path with everyone else dispersing in different directions. In no time, he was alone with Elizabeth.

"Thank you for defending me to Jeff, but a ring in your trailer? That's a little far-fetched. I'll explain everything to my father." She groaned and placed her face in her palms, her chest falling and rising with a deep breath. With a shiver, she rubbed at her arms. "Dad looked so happy. Bursting his bubble before the wedding—"

Guilt over the position he'd put Elizabeth in gnawed at his insides. He couldn't leave her in the lurch any more than he could stand by while that UTV barreled toward Audrey.

"Come on, Lizzie. I really have a ring in my RV. We have a fake engagement to plan." He reached for her hand and squeezed it. "And a fake breakup, too."

LIZZIE? HE'D CALLED her Lizzie out in the courtyard. Where did that come from? Why that and not Beth or Bessie? Everyone had stuck with Elizabeth since her mother, who always called her Lizzie, had died. Elizabeth set her red cowboy hat on Lucky's dinette table and bit back a laugh. Of all the problems from tonight, she was dwelling on a nickname? She had to get her head out of the clouds and her boots planted on brown Colorado soil again.

Collapsing into the plush black leather seat, she rested her head next to her hat. She needed time to think. What she'd give for a long ride on Andromeda right about now.

Plunk! Something plopped next to her, and she raised her head and found a small black velvet jeweler's box. "What's this?" she asked.

"It's an engagement ring." Lucky settled across from her and clicked on the lamp on the wall, illuminating her surroundings.

She liked what she saw, an efficient setup that would allow him to go anywhere at any time. Perfect for him, and while she craved that type of freedom this second, this ranch was her home, her livelihood, her first love. She'd do anything for the Double I and her father, including letting her family believe she was engaged to a rodeo star on the eve of Dad's wedding. She wouldn't place a damper on the proceedings, especially now that her father had finally approved of something she'd done. Or didn't do, as the case may be.

Her gaze locked on the box and she picked it up.

"You happen to drive around with an engagement ring?" She pushed the case back toward him. "Just one or more than one? I'm not sure this isn't a little creepy."

"Just the one." He nudged it back in her direction. "I intended on proposing to Cherry and never did."

She snapped the case open. Unlike the clean, classic

lines of her surroundings, the ring, an oval diamond of at least two carats surrounded by little diamond chips, was rather ostentatious and over-the-top. Not her style at all, but it didn't look like a genuine diamond, and for that she was thankful. "This is quite a ring."

He shrugged. "I know it's flashy, but it's available." He reached for the box and pulled out the ring. "Try it on."

While she summoned the nerve to see if it fit, skepticism bubbled inside her. Why had Lucky gone along with this? Jared's duplicity popped into mind. That experience had ended badly. Her ex-boyfriend claimed to love her, but he'd only been after her father's signature on a lucrative contract that would have lined Jared's pockets for life. He wanted the Irwin name, not her. Her first impression of Lucky had been different, especially with Sabrina vouching for him, but only time would tell if he was different from Jared. She brushed aside the unpleasant memory, but she had to dig further and find out what Lucky was after.

"I don't get it. What's in this for you?"

He flinched. "Why does there have to be anything in it for me?"

"Everyone always wants something." That was why she liked horses.

"Maybe I'm not most people." He leaned back on his side of the dinette, raising his arms until they rested on the top of the cushions. "You go first. What do you want out of our fake engagement?"

Guilt churned in her stomach. She'd stood rooted in the spot, unable to defend herself. It was just that Jeff's attitude had rankled almost as much as Dad's immediate acceptance of Lucky. Her father was known for his quick judgments, which usually proved correct. With all his business acuity, why couldn't Dad recognize she was a genuine asset to the Irwin family? "I insist you start." Then she might read him better.

"I like to think I'm a gentleman. Ladies first." He dipped his head in her direction.

"Do you make everything difficult?" She fidgeted with the box, unable to keep her hands from fluttering around, the same as she couldn't control the flutters in her stomach every time she looked at him.

"Just fake engagements." He chuckled, a low sound that also played havoc with her insides.

"How do we end this without anyone getting hurt?" She hadn't known him long, but she valued his feelings. Hurting him was the last thing she wanted to do.

"Same way as I tie the calves in the rodeo, fast and careful."

"Not tomorrow, though. This wedding should be a joyous occasion. Dad deserves it." She wouldn't do anything to ruin tomorrow for Dad and Evie.

"Agreed." He moved his arms and leaned forward. "So why didn't you speak up?"

While she'd have thought her *why* was as obvious as that diamond, she owed him an explanation. She continued fiddling with the case, turning it this way and that, until he rested his hands on hers, the callused fingers calm and steadfast, good qualities in anyone. Maybe she could trust him. There was only one way to find out. "Growing up an Irwin is not as easy as it looks. Growing up the remaining Irwin on the ranch is even harder."

"I'll take your word for that." Lucky's stiff posture was different from his usual laid-back stance. She didn't know much about the man she was supposedly engaged to. This could be a good time to get to know him better.

But there was a wedding tomorrow, and they still had to

figure out how to foil an engagement: namely, their own. "We need a good cover story for our breakup."

"I'd think that would be the easiest part." He leaned back again as if attempting to put distance between them. So much for believing there was an attraction brewing, as it was obviously one-sided with her imagination working overtime. Who could blame him for not wanting to get involved with someone who should have spoken up and admitted this was a big misunderstanding?

She nodded and reached for the simplest explanation. "After you leave for the rodeo, I'll explain we had too many differences to make it work. You wanted your freedom, and I agreed." After all, she'd lived in one place her whole life, but he must love to travel. Even his home was on wheels.

"Except I'll come back to see Will and Sabrina. We have to think of an excuse that won't paint me in a poor light." A shadow fell over him, and he shook his head. "Never mind. That'll work. We just have to get through the wedding and afterward I'll leave as planned."

"Wait. You're right." She hadn't considered how her refusal to speak up in the courtyard would impact his relationship with Will and Sabrina. She might not know much about her fake fiancé, but she knew Sabrina counted him and Will Sullivan as her best friends.

"How about we concern ourselves with the breakup down the road? No sense inviting trouble yet where there's none." He tapped his watch. "And I really need to go try on that tuxedo."

A rather cavalier approach, but it was late, and she had a lot to do before tomorrow's wedding as well. There was her nightly discussion with the head groom, followed by a quick check on Andromeda to make sure she hadn't been spooked by the commotion.

"Lizzie?" Lucky broke into her thoughts.

That was at least the third time he'd called her that. "I prefer Elizabeth."

"Okay." He scrutinized her face. "Elizabeth, are you thinking about the stable?"

"Always. The ranch comes first. It's everything to me."

"And you have a competent staff who will perform their jobs so you can enjoy the wedding." He pointed at the ring. "Does it fit?"

She removed the gaudy gold ring, heavier than she'd anticipated, from its slot. Whenever she'd envisioned this minute in her life, she always thought her fiancé would always be the one sliding the ring onto her finger, yet this wasn't a real engagement, so she did the honors.

To her surprise, it fit as if it was made for her. For some reason, relief flooded her at one problem solved. The fact that it presented a host of others wasn't lost on her.

"Yes, it fits." She twisted it and found her first impression was wrong. It was a little loose, but nothing a bit of clear tape couldn't handle.

Then again, maybe that was a sign she should let Lucky keep the fake ring, and she should march to the house and explain that this was a big misunderstanding before anyone's feelings could be hurt.

"Thank you for sharing your family with me."

What did he mean by that?

Before she could ask, he rose from the table and headed to the door. "I'll walk you back. I have that tuxedo fitting."

She'd almost forgotten that, even though he'd just told her. He was distracting her. She usually prided herself on being the observant Irwin who remembered details and kept the family organized. That was her role, and she usually filled those boots well.

"On Sunday, once the wedding is over, we'll nail down the ending to this charade."

With that note of certainty, she brushed past him. Electricity traveled down her spine more than that time she'd been jolted by some live barbed wire. Somehow, she wondered if her feelings were already involved. Looking at her left hand, she'd just have to play the part for a few days before she'd return this rhinestone ring, and that would be that. No one would be the wiser, and everyone would get on with their lives.

One look at him, and she wasn't sure if it would be that simple.

CHAPTER FIVE

LUCKY STRAIGHTENED HIS bow tie, but no matter how many times he positioned it, he just didn't look like himself in this custom-tailored tuxedo made for someone else. He fingered the fine silk of the lapel. While he possessed the same measurements as Ben Irwin, he'd never fill his boots in the family. He resisted the urge to untie the bow tie and head for Casper.

Someone knocked, and Will Sullivan entered the guest room where Lucky was staying so as not to exhaust his RV's electric reserves. Actually, it was Ben's room, but Lucky had to remember staying here and wearing the middle brother's clothes didn't make him part of the Irwin family.

"I miss one rehearsal dinner and have to find out from Sabrina that you're engaged?" Will folded his arms from his stance at the doorjamb.

With the late-night fitting followed by a long talk with Butterscotch in the stable, Lucky knew he'd forgotten something. Namely, to let his best friend in on what was happening at the Double I Ranch.

"Surprise?" Lucky tried to laugh it off, but one look at Will confirmed that wouldn't work. He had assumed he'd be able to keep his story simple, including the breakup, but maybe that was a little naïve. Someone had to take the fall and Elizabeth lived here. The Sullivan ranch bordered the Double I. Long-term neighbors supported each other. It made far more sense for him to position himself as the heartbreaker.

"That's putting it mildly. Don't keep anything this important from me again." Will frowned before he embraced Lucky, patting him on the back for a second before separating.

"Don't worry. I won't." A swift pang of guilt brought a shudder through him, and he tamped it down the best he could.

Here he was keeping a huge secret from his best friends, especially Will, who'd taken him into his fold when Lucky was a greenhorn. The three of them had celebrated countless holidays together on the circuit. Definitely more than he'd ever celebrated with any one foster family. They'd taken side trips, too. The three of them had visited Yellowstone and the Grand Canyon and every barbecue joint in between seeking out the best brisket in the West. Sabrina always sampled whatever cobbler Lucky ordered and usually ate more of his dessert than he did.

Will and Sabrina were like family, but there was a hidden layer of vulnerability to Elizabeth underneath that efficient exterior. How she talked to the horses appealed to something deep inside him, something that recognized a common kinship with animals.

Will shook his head and pointed at Lucky's attempt at tying the bow tie. "Before he passed, my father taught me how to do that. Do you mind?"

"It would be my honor." Lucky appreciated Will's discretion of delicately handling the matter of Lucky's past, including stints in countless foster homes, each one progressively worse. There were many great foster families out there, and someday he would love nothing more than to be a foster father to a child in need, but his experience wasn't one of the positive ones. It didn't stop him from hoping that one day, though, he'd be part of a loving family.

Too bad it couldn't be the Irwins.

Will unknotted the tuxedo tie and held the long black strip in his hands. "It's an honor for Kelsea and me to be invited."

"Your ranch borders the Double I." Lucky breathed more easily once his bow tie wasn't constricting his throat. "And you and Kelsea are Sabrina and Ty's best friends."

Kelsea and Will had met a little over a year ago, but Lucky credited her with bringing out the best in his friend's personality. Marriage suited Will.

"The Sullivans and Irwins have been friends for years. Evie and Gordon's wedding will only cement the bond between all of us. One thing bothers me, though."

"Only one thing?" Not much slipped past Will's notice.

Will quirked one eyebrow, and he gestured to Lucky to raise the lapels of his shirt collar. "It's actually a pretty big thing. Sabrina said you just met Elizabeth the other day."

"She said that, huh?" With Sabrina and Ty building their rodeo academy near Will's ranch, she and Will would have many more conversations in the future and remain close. This was extra proof they'd be just fine without him. He could return to the circuit any time. "Her mother's getting married today. I'm sure she has a lot on her mind."

"The first step when you tie a bow tie is to make sure the right side is shorter than the left." Will looped the tie around Lucky's neck, and Lucky felt the tight fit.

"Got it." Lucky made mental notes but gave up. He understood the calves who were darting out of the chute looking for a safe place to hide a sight better at this moment. Besides, it wasn't like he'd have another occasion anytime soon to wear a tuxedo and bow tie. In the rodeo, a bolo tie suited formal events just fine.

"Then you put the longer side over the shorter end and loop it under," said Will, demonstrating the procedure. "Getting back to Sabrina. You know she's sharp and doesn't miss much."

Countering Sabrina's strengths with Elizabeth's seemed the best way out at this point. "Elizabeth also has a mind of her own, and she's pretty strong-willed."

Will pinched the fold of the looped end and pushed it through the small opening. He pulled on the folded parts and tightened the bow. "You know her better than I thought." Will adjusted the bow tie until it was balanced and straight. "You know Gordon tried to matchmake the two of us a long time ago? Something about the Silver Horseshoe and the Double I being stronger if they were merged."

Something tore at Lucky's chest at Elizabeth getting together with Will. "You seem a little too intense for each other." Besides, he couldn't see Will with anyone other than his wife, Kelsea.

"That's true, but Elizabeth says it's because I knew her when she wore braces."

"I'd like to have seen that." Lucky laughed at the image of a serious yet gangly teenage Elizabeth with braces and her red cowboy hat.

Will stepped back and examined his handiwork. "Sabrina and Elizabeth are important to me."

Lucky met his gaze, and the laughter faded from his lips. "Not denying that."

"So why are you and Elizabeth pretending to be engaged?" Will flicked a piece of lint off Lucky's coat and then crossed his arms.

"Who said we're pretending?" Lucky would tread carefully, toeing the line as closely as he could. He wouldn't do anything to hurt Elizabeth, or ruin Gordon and Evie's wedding day. He and Elizabeth had agreed to stage a breakup after the wedding so her father could marry Evie with his happiness intact.

Protecting Elizabeth through this experience was the best and only wedding present he could give the Irwin family.

Someone knocked at the door. Jeff stuck his head through the crack. "Wedding pictures are taking place at the meadow in ten minutes. Dad and Evie want to get them done before the guests trample the grass."

"Lucky will be there," Will confirmed. As soon as Jeff left, he held up his hands. "Whenever you're ready to tell me everything, I'll listen. No judgments."

Will left Lucky behind without a backward glance. Lucky picked up a high school half-marathon trophy from Ben's bookcase and wished he'd left Violet Ridge when he'd had the chance. But that didn't seem true, either. He'd enjoyed being with Elizabeth every moment they'd had together, so far. The best he could do was enjoy the wedding and hold on to what he had a little longer.

Grabbing his new cowboy hat, a present from Gordon to all the ushers and the best man, he was determined to do just that. Then he'd walk away, exactly as planned.

WHILE THE PHOTOGRAPHER snapped pictures of the bridal party in the meadow, Elizabeth's cheeks hurt from all the smiling. After a new set of instructions from the photographer, she held the bouquet of roses close to her chest and tried not to glance in the direction of the stable. The ranch animals would be fine without her for one day, just like Lucky said. Concentrating at the task on hand, she drank in the beauty of the day that couldn't have been any more perfect if it had been made to order.

"Everyone except Evie, hold up your bouquet and

pretend you're about to throw them." The photographer snapped more pictures. "Have fun. The joy will reflect on your face."

As Elizabeth raised her arm, the morning sunlight glinted off the engagement ring on her left finger. Rather than joy, guilt over what she'd done to Lucky and her family made her stomach clench. She should just come clean so they could get on with the important day.

Except one look at her father stopped her in her dusty pink calf-high cowboy boots. Dad radiated happiness, something he'd done every day since meeting Evie, but he'd never looked as happy as he did today. As it was, Elizabeth would disappoint him all too soon when her and Lucky's fake engagement came to an end, but today she couldn't—and wouldn't—do anything to spoil this happy occasion.

Dad's gaze didn't leave Evie, who was flanked by three on each side. Elizabeth stood to her immediate right, with Nicole and Audrey beside her. To her future stepmother's left were Grandma Eloise, Sabrina and Evie's best friend, Robyn, her longtime drummer.

"Time for something different!" The photographer set her camera in a safe spot and handed out the new dusty rose cowboy hats Evie and Gordon had given the bridesmaids and flower girl.

"This is one gorgeous Stetson." Robyn placed her hat on her head and whistled. "Evie, you and Gordon sure know how to throw a party."

"This will ruin my hair." Nicole cringed with disdain and smoothed her moss-green tea-length dress, which was a twin of Sabrina's.

"Stuff and nonsense. There's nothing like a cowboy hat at a ranch wedding." Grandma Eloise grinned and placed hers on her head at an angle, the pink nicely accenting her silver lace dress, which matched her hair. The older woman glowed with the attention of being the mother of the bride. "Besides, that's what a brush is for."

Along with the can of hair spray Evie's hairdresser had insisted on using this morning, Elizabeth mused. Her hair would stay in place like this for the rest of the year. Elizabeth accepted the hat and helped Audrey with hers. Both she and her niece, along with Robyn, wore dusty rose dresses, which matched their hats.

Something was wrong, though, as her cowboy hat didn't fit right. Elizabeth looked inside at the inner lining near the sweatband, where their names were embroidered. "I have your hat, Nicole."

They traded, and the photographer encouraged them to hold them high over their heads, adjusting the group until the Rockies provided the perfect backdrop. More clicks and more smiles.

Evie faced Elizabeth, who admired the bride's champagne-colored wedding dress embroidered with tiny dusty pink roses, her trademark color, along with moss-green leaves. "Your wedding will be here before you know it. Are you holding the ceremony here or in town?"

Considering she and Lucky had no intention of getting married, she hadn't thought of an answer. While she and Jared were dating, she'd dreamed of having the ceremony at the ranch. This site would still be her preferred venue, but she'd need a groom for that. "I don't know."

"Do you have a date yet?" Nicole left the line and picked up her moss-green clutch from the front row of chairs. She returned with her phone and swiped on the screen. "Jeff and I have a packed schedule over the next few months between Zack and Audrey and work, but I know he won't want to miss his sister's wedding."

Audrey tugged at Elizabeth's skirt. "Can I be your flower girl?"

"When I get married, you can be my flower girl." Elizabeth was purposefully vague, disliking this hole she was digging for herself.

Audrey touched her glasses and straightened them on her face. "I like bright purple. It's my favorite color." She twirled around in her flower girl dress, the skirt made for dancing. "I love this dress, Grandma Evie. It's so pretty."

"Thank you, sweetheart. Just hearing you say 'Grandma Evie' made my day." She bent down and hugged Audrey before standing and facing Elizabeth again. "There's a good chance Lucky will make the year-end finals. If so, he'll be busy until December. What about a Christmas wedding?"

Elizabeth's heart thundered, and she was surprised everyone didn't hear it almost pounding out of her chest. To make matters worse, Dad appeared out of nowhere. "This conversation seems serious. You're not getting cold feet, are you, Evie?" His voice held a note of frantic worry with just enough humor inserted so he could sound nonchalant. A fine sheen of sweat broke out on his forehead despite this being one of the prettiest August days in Elizabeth's memory—crisp and clear, with nary a cloud in the cerulean sky.

"Never." Evie hugged Gordon. "You and the Double I are a part of my life now."

As it was a part of Elizabeth's life. Once Dad realized Elizabeth loved it with the same devotion as him, he might finally listen to her about her plans for its future.

"This day, and you, mean everything to me, Evie. The only thing that made it even better is Elizabeth's engagement."

Evie beamed and slipped her arm around Dad. "We were just talking about Elizabeth's wedding. Nicole asked if she and Lucky had set a date. Nicole, will you and Jeff fly here for the holidays if it's a Christmas wedding?" She smiled at Elizabeth. "Having your family around makes the big day even more special."

"My parents are hosting a New Year's party, but I'll talk to Jeff about Christmas." Nicole swiped the screen. "We'd have to arrange the time off with our law firm, and we won't stay as long."

Dad faced the photographer. "How far ahead are you booked? Are you available either the weekend before or after Christmas? Add their wedding deposit to our balance." Then he turned to Evie. "We can also talk to the other vendors when we pay the bills. I'm sure they'll accommodate another wedding at the Double I."

"I'm available the weekend after Christmas." The photographer started texting. "I'm engaged to the caterer, and I'm checking with him about his schedule."

This was getting out of hand fast.

"I haven't checked with Lucky," she protested, trying to figure out how to stop this madness from escaping her control. "He should have a say in this."

Evie winked at her. "He's in love and will go along with any date you choose. That is, unless you two want to get married even sooner than that?"

Elizabeth wasn't planning on getting married at all.

She grasped at anything to draw the attention away from plans for a ceremony that would never happen and back to the one that would. "Your wedding is in two hours. Shouldn't we finish this?"

The photographer took back control and called for Elizabeth, Nicole and Audrey to surround Gordon. She assumed her place before the photographer lowered her camera and stared right at her. "Elizabeth, your expression went wonky. Smile this time, okay?"

In the distance, Lucky and Will walked toward the picture area. Her stomach did a funny flip, and she took a deep breath. It wasn't anticipation about Lucky's presence that caused that inner dance. Embarrassment did funny things to a person, and that's all it was. She'd roped him into this mess on her behalf. If the photographer's down payment was nonrefundable, Elizabeth would repay her father the fee, but that was the least of her quandaries. How was she going to explain to Lucky that they now had a date for the wedding?

Sabrina spotted the group walking toward them. "That's what happens when your fiancé heads this way." Laughing, she lowered her bouquet and faced Elizabeth. "But one thing bothers me."

Grandma Eloise started coughing and everyone crowded around her. Will rushed over while Lucky diverted in the other direction. Evie patted her mother's hand. "Sit down. All this excitement must be affecting you more than I realized…"

"Here's some water, Grandma Eloise." Lucky appeared with a glass, the liquid sloshing over the top.

"That's just what I needed, Lucky. Thank you." Grandma Eloise accepted the drink with a smile.

"Maybe you should lie down until it's time for the wedding." Concern laced Evie's tone, and she appealed to Gordon with her eyes.

"Stuff and nonsense." Grandma Eloise drank a few long sips and reached for her cane. "Sabrina will help me freshen up. Afterward, I'd like the photographer to take a picture of me and Genie together."

"Of course, Grandma." Sabrina reached for her grandmother's arm and led her away.

While Sabrina ushered Grandma Eloise toward the main house, Gordon pulled aside the photographer, and the two had a private discussion. As much as she wanted to interrupt them and confide that her wedding to Lucky was off because it was never on to begin with, she couldn't ruin her father's important day.

A minute later, her father reappeared with a big grin. "Before the guests arrive, the photographer is going to take Lucky and Elizabeth's engagement pictures." He patted Lucky on the back. "Congratulations! Elizabeth and Evie talked, and the Saturday after Christmas works well for everyone. You and Elizabeth can talk about it before the reception and finalize the date. With this much notice, we might even get Ben to come home for the holidays. Welcome to the family."

The photographer came over and led Elizabeth and Lucky away from the crowd.

Lucky mouthed "Christmas" at her, a shocked expression spread over his face. She grimaced and nodded. Somehow, a wedding date, engagement photos and deposits made the disaster of this more real.

Then his gaze swept over her, and his mouth dropped open. Wonder lit his eyes, and she looked around her, expecting a reason for the change in his reaction. Her head stilled, and she sent him a questioning glance. He smiled, pointed at her and mouthed "beautiful." Somehow, amid the impending storm, his presence calmed the roiling emotions inside her.

Suddenly, she didn't know which was worse—his presence growing on her to the point where she felt lighter when he was around, or facing the inevitable music when their ruse was discovered.

Falling in love was too real and too painful. Keeping her wits about her and heart out of this arrangement was the only way she'd be able to get through the fallout when this facade ended.

CHAPTER SIX

LUCKY RETURNED TO the rear, having seated the final guests, friends of the groom. Before today, he'd only attended two other weddings: Will and Kelsea's, followed by Sabrina and Ty's, both times in clothes that belonged to him. He tugged at the tuxedo shirt collar, the stiff fabric unfamiliar and chafing, until he spotted Elizabeth kneeling in front of Audrey. Suddenly his discomfort faded as he concentrated on the pair. Elizabeth straightened her niece's purple frames and tipped the cowboy hat upward so Audrey's face was more visible. Elizabeth winked at her niece and hugged her before rising and handing her the basket of pink rose flower petals.

Lucky swallowed, the intimate moment between the two family members not lost on him. Elizabeth cared more than she let on to others. He understood that too well, but maybe it was time to change all that. Maybe it was time to express his appreciation in words as well as deeds.

Then, Elizabeth donned her hat and approached him, sunlight bathing her in a golden glow. She held out her elbow for him, and his heart raced at the woman by his side. It didn't matter whether she wore flannel or silk. Her inner radiance set her apart from every other woman he'd known.

"Ready to walk me down the aisle?" Her cheeks grew as pink as her hat. "You've done so much for me and my family today. Thank you for staying." She hesitated and switched her bouquet to her other hand. "There's something else you should know."

"Tomorrow. Today is a day for happiness." He was the one who should be thanking her, and he recalled his new promise to himself. "Elizabeth, thank you. There's nowhere else I'd rather be."

Someone tapped them, and they proceeded down the aisle, where she took her place next to Nicole and he stood beside Jeff before the string quartet ceased the processional music. Then everyone rose to their feet as the musicians launched into the wedding march. Evie appeared and glided down the aisle, smiling at some guests who were dotting at the corners of their eyes with tissue.

Gordon and Evie exchanged vows they'd written themselves, and Lucky snuck another glance at Elizabeth, her gaze locked on his as if they were the only ones here. No matter what else happened after today, this shared moment would stay with him.

The wedding ended without a hitch, and Lucky walked into the reception tent. Someone he didn't know came up and patted him on the back. "Welcome to Violet Ridge. The Irwins are a fine family."

Others followed, their congratulations sincere yet foreboding. It would be a total disaster when they learned his engagement to Elizabeth was a sham. Instead of finding a place to belong, this was merely another rest stop on his way to his ultimate destination, wherever that may be.

This wasn't the time or place, though, for those kinds of thoughts. Gordon and Evie had spared no expense with the festivities, and he, along with everyone else, settled back and enjoyed the dinner. He'd never tasted a meal this exquisite, and he'd never seen anyone as beautiful as Elizabeth, who was whispering something to Sabrina.

The band was now warming up, and Grandma Eloise

tapped her silver boot tip against the wooden floor under the reception tent.

Someone clinked their crystal goblet, and the guests turned their attention to Jeff, who was rising to his feet a few seats away from Lucky at the head table. It must be time for the toasts. Lucky listened while stealing glances at Elizabeth, who didn't realize the vision she was in that dark pink dress with her burnished auburn hair cascading in curls over her shoulders.

More people spoke until Gordon finally rose, with Evie joining him at his side. She spoke first, expressed her thanks and then turned over the microphone to her new husband.

"Tonight, I look out and see so many colleagues and friends who've come here to celebrate with me. Thank you for spending your evening with us and for your friendship, which has enriched my life." Gordon dipped his head and waited for the applause to fade away before he continued. "A special thanks to Evie's family for bringing me and mine into your fold. To my family, a special thank-you for the love you've extended to my new wife, and just when I thought my happiness bucket was so full, it now runneth over with the addition of Lucky Harper, who's engaged to my daughter, Elizabeth. Save the weekend after Christmas for a return trip to the Double I, as that's the Saturday they're getting married. A toast to my daughter and future son-in-law."

Gordon raised his glass, and the crowd chimed in with their congratulations. Elizabeth's cheeks turned a brighter shade of red than her hair, and Lucky barely kept from falling off his seat. How had this engagement gotten so far out of hand so fast?

Grandma Eloise scrambled to her feet, reaching for her cane and standing steady. "Gordon, I speak for Bob and myself when I welcome you to the MacGrath family. Lucky and Elizabeth, I hold both of you in my heart and am always here for you as your honorary grandmother. As the mother of the bride, I think I've earned the privilege of announcing the first dance between Gordon and Evie. Then, it's every person for themselves as I am a mean line dancer. Watch out that my cane doesn't stub your toe."

Laughter filled the room as the band began the familiar chords of "Misty Mountain," Evie's signature song, which Lucky figured was now hers and Gordon's as well. Evie nodded at Gordon, who escorted her to the middle of the dance floor. Lucky darted a look at Elizabeth, still bright red from the announcement, as guests came over and congratulated her. Her tight smile didn't waver, and she twisted her engagement ring. She glanced down and must have realized what she was doing as her blush deepened.

In his rush to become accepted by her family, he'd placed Elizabeth in quite a predicament. Why he'd thought the news would only stay among her family until they ended it, he wasn't sure. Somehow, he had to make this right for her before he left town.

Or should he sneak out and leave her to handle the aftermath? No, that was wrong, and Cale had taught him a sight better at the Cattle Crown Ranch in Steamboat Springs all those years ago.

He fiddled with his fork while guests began congratulating him. After the tenth or so, he lost track of how many, he needed a minute to himself, as the well-wishers' good intentions were biting at his conscience. With a smile he didn't feel on the inside, he left the reception tent for a breath of fresh mountain air.

Walking a short distance away from the tent, he heard sniffles. That halted him in his tracks. Was someone crying? And why? Had he made Elizabeth cry on her father's wedding day? His breath caught, and he peeked behind the closest aspen. His heart skipped a beat at the sad sight. Audrey Irwin sat under the tree, crying. What was the girl doing outside by herself?

"Audrey?" He went over and sat by her side.

She glanced up and blinked. "Uncle Lucky!" She threw her arms around him and hugged him. "Whatcha doing out here?"

"I could ask you the same thing." Lucky reached into his pocket and pulled out the linen square. "Did you tell anyone where you were going?"

She started nodding before she met his gaze and slowly shook her head. "Mommy and Daddy are dancing, and so are Grandma Evie and Grandpa Gordon. Zack is busy with his video-game player. There's nothing for me to do."

He handed her the cloth and motioned for her to wipe her eyes. "I know what it's like to feel left out. It's not fun." Growing up, though, he hadn't had anyone who'd be upset about him disappearing, like she had now. "You know, though, you have to tell an adult before you go anywhere. When people care about you and love you, they want to make sure you're okay."

She sniffled and removed her glasses. After she blotted her eyes, she handed him back the square, but he folded her hand over it and told her to keep it. She gave him a slight smile before she winced. "Am I in trouble?"

He didn't want to think about the irony of her question, as he'd be in far worse trouble if the residents of Violet Ridge discovered he had no intention of marrying Elizabeth. Not that he didn't want to get married someday, and not that Elizabeth wasn't the most beautiful, intelligent, kind woman he'd ever met. He'd be, well, lucky to have someone like her in his life.

Any other time, he'd have loved to be friends with

someone like her, if not more than friends. But he was out of his league here with all the surrounding opulence.

Audrey's face looked expectantly at him, and at least he could solve this problem. "Not if we both get back to the reception tent, where we belong." He used the aspen for leverage as he rose. "And I might be able to help you with your boredom."

He reached for her hand and helped her off the ground. "It's all icky adult stuff in there." She wrinkled her nose and her purple-rimmed glasses fell a few inches.

"Depends on your perspective." He raised his chin and grinned. "You're speaking to someone who's a big kid at heart. I'll bet you your piece of wedding cake we'll have fun."

"Cake? There'll be cake?" Audrey looked skeptical. "I don't believe you."

"I'm wounded to the core." He clasped his hands over his chest. "Of course there's cake. You saw it. The pretty one with the pink flowers."

"We get to eat that? It's not just a decoration?" Her big green eyes lit up behind those frames. "Let's go."

She grabbed his hand and pulled him toward the tent, but not before he caught sight of Elizabeth standing behind an aspen, relief all over her face as she pointed toward Audrey. How much of that exchange had she witnessed? Still, she'd noticed Audrey was missing and had searched for her.

The Irwins did stick together, an enviable trait indeed.

ELIZABETH TAPPED HER toe under the table. She watched Lucky demonstrating to Audrey how to move her feet for the line dance.

Grandma Eloise sat next to Elizabeth and huffed out a

breath. "That was fun." She tapped her cane before placing it between them. "Why aren't you out there?"

Elizabeth pointed to her cowboy boots. "Two left feet."

"Maybe you just haven't danced with the right person." Grandma Eloise pointed toward the dance floor. "Lucky saved two dances for me. Your fiancé has some moves."

Elizabeth reached for her water and downed the last drop. "He's having fun with Audrey."

Grandma Eloise clucked her tongue. "I think he wants to dance with his fiancée."

At that moment, Lucky glanced their way and wiggled his finger at Elizabeth to join them. Not only did that tuxedo show off rather broad shoulders, but Lucky was also a genuinely nice person. She'd gone looking for Audrey earlier, only to duck behind an aspen tree so she wouldn't interrupt their conversation. The way he'd coaxed Audrey back had pulled at her heartstrings. If only they'd met under other circumstances…

Who was she kidding? The time still wouldn't have been right. Not with those architect plans waiting to come to fruition and possibly introducing a new breed of cattle to the ranch. A question about Simmentals came to mind, and she grabbed her phone. Her fingers flew across the screen.

A boot stopping inches from her led her gaze to Lucky, who shook his head. "I know that look. Even your father is taking today off, and deservedly so." Lucky pointed toward Dad, who was laughing as he stumbled and bumped into Evie. His new wife righted Dad, and they resumed their dance. "Ranch business can wait until tomorrow."

Grandma Eloise rose and reached out for Audrey's hand. "Come with me. You can help me with something before we tell Evie it's time to cut the cake."

The pair left, the older leading the younger, and Elizabeth never realized you could be alone with someone in a crowded room before. Lucky tilted his head toward the dance floor. "You need more fun in your life."

"I need two working feet in my life." She laughed away her nervousness, not sure whether the offer to dance or Lucky's presence was the culprit. Either way, her stomach was doing backflips at the sight of him, so handsome in his tuxedo.

"One dance, and if I hurt your feet, I'll rub the soreness out myself." He flexed his hands and cracked his knuckles.

"That isn't a rousing endorsement of your skills."

"It's best to show you, anyway. Telling you isn't half as fun." He waggled his eyebrows until she stood and threw her napkin on the table.

"You're incorrigible."

"Thank you. May I have this line dance?" Lucky bowed at the waist.

"Be careful with my feet. They're tender."

Her breath caught as she met his gaze. Without further ado, she grabbed his hand and led him to the back of the dance floor. "What do I do first?" she asked.

The song ended, and the singer announced there'd be one slow song before Evie threw the bouquet and cut the cake. Elizabeth headed for the table, but Lucky tapped her arm. "Afraid of a little dance?"

She raised her chin. "You should be afraid for your feet."

"I take my chances inside a rodeo arena. I can manage this." He reached for her, and she dipped her head.

"You can't say you weren't warned."

Without another word, she slipped into his waiting arms, and he placed his arm around her waist. Her breath hitched at the close contact, and he stepped back, obviously thinking she didn't want him so close when his presence was actually throwing her for a loop. "I was surprised, that's all."

At feelings she shouldn't be feeling for her fake fiancé who was getting under her skin more than she wanted to admit.

"I promise. You're in safe hands for the next few minutes."

The band started playing a ballad, and other couples swayed to the sweet music. Enjoying one dance with Lucky wouldn't harm anything, or anyone. She met his gaze and regretted her last thought. This dance could irreparably harm her heart.

He pulled her closer, and they began dancing. She laid her head next to his chin, his skin warm. "I'm sorry about earlier."

"Why? You were looking for Audrey, weren't you?"

Yes, but that was beside the point. "You were so sweet with her, but that's not why I'm apologizing. The whole Christmas wedding date happened so fast."

"Elizabeth, there will be time for that later." He waited until she met his gaze, still sweet but with a note of warning. "I have a beautiful woman in my arms at a wedding I'd never imagined anyone like me would ever be invited to. When was the last time you enjoyed something for the sheer fun of it without worrying about the future?"

Her insides felt light and carefree. He thought she was beautiful. Maybe she should let go of worrying about how they were going to end this with no one getting hurt and go with the flow for tonight at least. The animals and plans could wait a little longer as the ranch hands were taking good care of the former, and the latter weren't going anywhere today, anyway. She snuggled close to him and let the song's rhythm seep into her.

But it ended too fast, and everyone was gathering around the cake table. Audrey approached Lucky and gestured for him to pick her up. He obliged and swept her into his arms. She hid her face in his shoulder. "I don't think I can watch Grandma Evie cut the cake," Audrey said.

Lucky tapped her until she looked at him. "Why not?"

"It's so pretty." She resumed her earlier position as he cracked a smile that showed he was doing his best not to laugh and hurt Audrey's feelings.

While the crowd watched her father and Evie, Elizabeth couldn't keep her eyes off Lucky. He'd make someone a very happy spouse someday. An image of him with another woman sent a shock through her system.

Was that a twinge of jealousy that zapped her? It couldn't be. This wasn't real. What her father and Evie had was real. Her gaze floated to Sabrina, the back of her head resting against Ty's chest, their love also genuine and inspiring. Her and Lucky's relationship was as fake as the ring on her finger.

Applause greeted the couple, and an attendant started handing out slices of cake to the crowd. Elizabeth accepted hers, the raspberry mousse filling complementing the buttery richness of the vanilla cake. She couldn't help but miss her brother Ben. Raspberries were his favorite.

The energy of the crowd, though, was electric with everyone buzzing about the wedding and the delicious cake. No sooner had she finished her slice and set down her plate than someone tapped at the microphone. "It's time for Evie Irwin to throw the bouquet."

More applause and Elizabeth started to walk toward the sidelines. At least her engagement to Lucky would get her out of this part of the reception. She approached the crowd off to the side, only to see Grandma Eloise shake her head and point her cane toward Audrey, Robyn and the others, waiting for Evie to toss the flowers. "You're still eligible to catch the bouquet."

Sabrina and Nicole nodded and pushed a protesting

Elizabeth back toward the dance floor. *Fine*. She'd go out there, but she'd stand at the back, where she'd have no chance of drawing any more attention toward her.

After an announcement asking if anyone else wanted to join in the fun, Evie glanced over her shoulder. "Where's my stepdaughter? I hope you catch this, because you're next. I can't wait for Christmas now."

Elizabeth hid behind Violet Ridge's favorite identical twins, one of whom was widowed, while the other was divorced. If Evie aimed for the rear, one of them would surely snag the floral arrangement.

Squeals accompanied the toss, and the flowers were batted from person to person like a hot potato until they finally hit Elizabeth in the head and fell into her hands. Her cheeks burned hot as everyone turned to congratulate her on catching the bouquet and her December wedding.

CHAPTER SEVEN

IT WAS SO early on this Sunday morning that it was actually the middle of the night. Lucky listened to the crickets chirp and the lowing of the cattle before he slid open the stable door as quietly as possible. Growing still, he searched the area in case any ranch hands might raise an alarm about his presence. One of the outside dogs, an alert border collie, ran over and sniffed him.

"It's okay, Moose." Audrey had laughed upon learning the dog's name, and Lucky kept his voice low as a barn owl screeched in the distance. "It's just me."

Fortunately for him, Moose wagged his tail before returning to his guard post. With this first hurdle cleared, Lucky patted his jacket, the letter he'd written to Elizabeth secure in his pocket. He'd leave the note on her office desk, load Butterscotch in his trailer and be on his merry way to Casper for the next rodeo.

Yesterday's wedding had been a real barn buster, and so much more. The Irwin family had included him in everything, and for that, he'd always be grateful. For one day, he'd had a grandmother and so much more. Others may take that for granted, but he never would.

Once inside, he noticed Butterscotch at the front of his stall, awake and alert, a slight whinny his greeting for Lucky.

"Shh. I'll be right back, and we'll move on to other pastures." Maybe not as green as those here at the Double I, but something good always waited on the horizon.

He made his way to Elizabeth's tiny office and entered, flicking on the light.

"Going somewhere?" Elizabeth's voice startled him, and he turned.

He waited a few seconds until his breathing returned to a normal, steady rhythm. "What are you doing here?"

"It's my office. I was in the tack room about to start my morning routine when I heard someone in here and came to investigate." Passing him, he noticed she was already dressed in a flannel shirt layered over a red tank top paired with blue jeans and red boots. She looked just as beautiful in the fluorescent light and her cowgirl clothes as she had in the bridesmaid dress. A brief flicker of hurt crossed her face. "Were you really going to sneak out without saying goodbye?"

He reached into his pocket and pulled out the letter he'd spent so much time composing last night. "I was going to leave this behind."

She stepped forward and reached for it. "May I?"

"No need." He crumpled it and replaced it in his pocket. "You can simply tell your family it didn't work out because you were caught up in the whirlwind of Evie and Gordon's wedding."

Her wry chuckle filled the air. "You must have me mixed up with someone else if you think my family would ever believe that excuse."

She stood so close it was hard not to reach out and smooth her hair. Touching her, though, might cross the invisible line.

"You have some hay in your hair," he said, wincing at how ridiculous he sounded. She reached up and the lone straw fell to the ground while he leaned against the door post. "You'll think of something. You're intelligent and perceptive."

Conflict warred in those expressive eyes, and she put a gentle hand on his flannel shirtsleeve. "I'm sorry I put you in a tight spot. I'll take the blame, so Will and Sabrina won't be upset with you."

His jaw clenched. Will and Sabrina had each found love. They didn't need him anymore, and he accepted that. Somewhere out there, someone needed him. "I'm not worried about that."

"Then think of my taking the blame as a way of thanking you for yesterday."

"Thanking me?" Her statement was almost as much of a surprise as her presence in her office this early in the day. "I'm the one who gained everything yesterday. I should be the one expressing my gratitude."

"You encouraged me to live in the moment and enjoy myself, which I did. That'll make the aftermath more than worth it." Elizabeth delivered a winsome smile, one he could find himself wanting to see often. "But why don't you take your own advice and stay one more day? It's recovery day, and we can both use that. Tomorrow's the preparation for the cattle roundup, which starts bright and early Tuesday and goes through Friday. It makes more sense to leave in the morning when you're well rested."

He hesitated. If he left now, he wouldn't get attached to this family and Elizabeth. Who was he kidding? He already cared about her. Look at how often he thought of her when she wasn't around. No matter how he looked at it, he'd need time over the following weeks to bounce back from once again being so close to a family and having it yanked away.

She was right. He needed time to regain his bearings. Could one day really make his departure worse?

She must have sensed his hesitancy. "Tammy is making dinner with all the fixings tonight. You'll love her huckleberry pie with homemade ice cream."

"I've never had huckleberry pie before." He hadn't texted his friend that he'd arrive in Casper today, leaving his arrival time vague and open-ended.

"And you've never seen a sunrise at the Double I on horseback. How about we take Andromeda and Butterscotch for an early morning ride? We can discuss the best way to end this charade. As I see it, we can break up after dinner, or you can take your leave while I'm away on the cattle roundup. While this is fake, I'm sure you want your ring back." She held up her finger and twisted it so he could see the clear tape on the back. "I'm worth more than a mere letter. Let me be in on the details, okay?"

Saying goodbye to Audrey and Grandma Eloise were added bonuses. And one more day with Elizabeth? That was priceless. "I've seen some mighty pretty sunrises in my life. You think this one can compare?"

She grabbed her red cowboy hat and plopped it on her head. "Once you see one on the Double I, it'll ruin you for all others."

That was exactly what he was afraid of.

ELIZABETH REINED IN Andromeda and gasped at the ribbons of orange on the horizon meeting the lush green landscape. No longer was the mountainside bathed in shadow, but there was a glow that promised a full day ahead. Was it only the scenery that catapulted this sunrise into the magnificent category?

Or did Lucky astride Butterscotch add something to the fullness of this moment?

"You're right. That sunrise is unlike any other." Lucky

pulled up beside her, his eyes soaking in the beauty of the day.

That made what she had to say all that much harder. "Well, so is our engagement." The early rays caught the diamond, and a rainbow prism seemed to bounce on the saddle's pommel. "We need a plan to get out of it."

"I like pineapple on my pizza. You could say that was the ultimate dealbreaker."

She laughed. "Except everyone knows I order it the same way."

"Then that won't work." He shrugged and flicked the reins so Butterscotch proceeded at a slow trot. "How do you like your French fries?"

Andromeda kept pace with Butterscotch. "I dunk mine in my puddle of ketchup."

Lucky shook his head. "While barbecue sauce is better, I drizzle ketchup over fries. That way it's even."

"They get soggy like that. My way's much better." How was he making something so serious as staging a fake breakup so much fun?

He brought Butterscotch to a stop and searched the mountainside, his smile fading like the colors on the horizon. "Why now? This sunrise is something special."

And just like that, the day was upon them. "The sooner we end it, the less likely anyone will discover how everything spiraled out of control."

He stared at her a long time, and she held her head high. So he didn't eat his French fries the same way she did. He liked pineapple pizza and horses and made dreaded family occasions into something special. She had to break up with him now, or else…?

She could fall for him.

"Tonight, then. We'll stage a pretend fight, and then I'll leave for the rodeo." There was a slight movement near his jawline, enough for her to want to reach out and reassure him that his presence at the wedding had changed everything for her.

But then she'd never know if he could fall for her, just her, and not the whole Irwin family, who'd been on their best behavior during the wedding. "I think it needs to be convincing."

"Elizabeth, you leave your imprint on everything. They'll believe you." This was sounding too real, too fast. Nothing came this quickly and lasted.

"For good measure, I'll talk about the ranch and how much it means to me." She remembered his earlier advice about sticking as close to the truth as possible.

"And I can't imagine any other life than going from rodeo to rodeo. We simply couldn't make it work."

They practiced their mock argument, and the light faded from his eyes. She couldn't let it end like this.

The sunrise moment, that was. "I'll race you across the meadow. You haven't lived until you feel the morning breeze kissing your cheeks with sunflowers all around you."

A hint of a smile curled up his lips. "You're on, in three. One, two..." He spurred on Butterscotch before he said *three*, his laughter the real cue to resume their fun.

Her laughter met his as she joined him for one last horseback ride.

Hours later, with the down payment for the construction of the bunkhouses due a week from tomorrow, Elizabeth stilled her hand on the doorknob to her father's study. No doubt she'd find him here, as he and Evie were waiting until the end of the cattle roundup to leave for their Hawaiian honeymoon. The day after the wedding should be the perfect time to broach business, just as tonight should be the perfect time to end the sham of an engagement.

If Dad agreed to the construction and everything proceeded as planned with Lucky, Tuesday would be the beginning of the best roundup yet.

Not that her days with Lucky hadn't been special. And
this morning was the most special time of all with her and
Andromeda keeping pace once he and Butterscotch gal-
loped across the meadow.

Now, though, she had to return to reality and leave the
splendor of Lucky's company in the past. Otherwise, one
of them might get hurt, and she didn't want him to get so
involved that there might be any heartache on his part as
well as on hers. Once the line was crossed on either side,
it was impossible to keep emotion at bay.

"It's an afternoon made for riding." Her father's booming voice could be heard down the hall.

Dad wasn't in the study. Instead, she found him in the
living room with Zack. "Fresh air and horses are more fun
than any video game."

"No way. I'm almost leveling up." Zack's gaze didn't
leave his handheld game unit. "Then I can get more stuff
and be faster."

Dad turned toward Jeff and Nicole, who were involved
in a deep conversation that made them oblivious to what
was happening around them. Dad tapped Jeff's shoulder.
"What about a family horseback excursion? Then I can
gauge how long Zack and Audrey can ride on Tuesday.
They've been doing really well in our riding lessons. Audrey's a natural."

That was high praise from her father.

Nicole glared at Jeff and nudged his side. "Go on, tell
him."

"Tell me what?" Dad crossed his arms as Lucky approached the living room from the opposite direction from

Elizabeth. "Ah, here are Elizabeth and Lucky. Perfect. Now I won't have to repeat myself."

Elizabeth let out a long, slow breath, knowing improved housing was a necessity to attract long-term workers. "I have something I need to talk to you about before the roundup."

"I thought we weren't bringing this up until after dinner." Lucky paled under his tan.

"I have some plans I want to run by you," Elizabeth said to her father, before widening her eyes in Lucky's direction, hoping he would realize she wasn't referring to their breakup before he said anything more.

Nicole crossed her arms over her chest, a frown marring her face. "I can't go on the roundup. There's an important deposition this week that I must attend. Fortunately, it's virtual."

Dad shrugged. "We'll miss you, but we'll keep Audrey and Zack so busy they won't even notice you're gone." He waved away Nicole's concern like it was nothing and faced Lucky and Elizabeth. "Now, you two don't have to worry about a thing to do with your wedding. Evie and I paid the caterer last night and placed the deposit for your reception with him. Same with the photographer and florist."

Elizabeth couldn't seem to catch her breath. Her father was a force of nature. While her father and Evie had employed the best in Violet Ridge, the same as she most likely would have hired, that was beside the point. When she married someone, she wanted to plan everything and hire everyone herself. "Thank you, but that's not what I wanted to talk to you about…" Her mouth went dry. She knew exactly what she wanted to say about the bunkhouses. Why was it harder now when there was an audience?

"What Elizabeth is trying to say is—"

Lucky was interrupted when Evie burst into the room,

waving her phone in the air, a huge smile gracing her face. "You'll never believe it!" She ran over and hugged Gordon, then Zack, then Audrey. "I have the best news."

"Nicole's not going on the roundup. She has legal matters," Dad began before he blinked, as if Evie's words had penetrated his senses. "Sorry, darlin'. What's your news?"

"Oh, the roundup." Evie gulped and shook her head. "For a minute, I forgot about it. Never mind."

Dad placed his hands on her shoulders. "What's your news, darlin'?"

She held her phone up to his face. "The producers asked me to be a guest host on *Your Next Favorite Song.*"

Dad's face lit up, and he hugged his new wife. "That's wonderful. I know how much you've wanted to appear on that television show."

"I'd have to be in California tomorrow night. The show films this week." Evie's smile wobbled, and then her shoulders slumped. "I grew up on a ranch and remember how important this cattle roundup is. I'll see if they'll have me a month from now."

"This is important to you. I promised you yesterday I'd be there for better or worse, and this qualifies for the better part of my vows. You're going to be the prettiest, most talented guest host ever." Dad faced Lucky. "You'll be riding along with Elizabeth, right? And Jeff's an old hand, too. You rode on these for what, ten years, before leaving for college if my memory is right."

Elizabeth struggled to maintain her composure. What was going on here? He was turning to Lucky and Jeff when she'd been the one accompanying him for the past twenty years. "Dad, I can do this in my sleep. Our cowhands are the best." At last, an opening appeared for her to bring up the bunkhouses. "And speaking of our staff—"

"You're right, Elizabeth. Our staff, along with Jeff and

Lucky, can handle this." A wide grin broadened across Dad's face. "Evie, you text your acceptance, and we'll start our honeymoon early. I'll go with you to California, and then we'll head to Hawaii as planned."

Once again, her father had undermined her, bringing Jeff and Lucky into the equation. This only seemed to confirm those fears. Was this the best time and place, though, to confront him about it?

"I'm sorry, sir." Lucky leaned against the wall. "But my horse isn't outfitted for the roundup. It was one thing to ride with Elizabeth this morning, but his shoes aren't right for the terrain."

"Not a problem." Gordon dismissed his concern, too. "You can use Margarita."

She winced. Dad never let anyone ride Margarita on the trail.

"Thank you, but the rodeo—"

"Doesn't start for another week and a half. This is only a four-day event. Besides, this will give you time together. Plus, you can decide where you want to honeymoon, our treat, now that all the deposits have been paid." Gordon nodded and reached for Evie's hand. "Elizabeth, Lucky and Jeff have everything in hand. That takes a load off my mind, so I can sit back and bask in everyone adoring my talented wife. We can leave whenever you're ready."

Evie smiled, and the two left the room, oblivious to the rising tension. There went a chance to get Dad's approval for the bunkhouses. Worse yet, this only confirmed her fears it was an uphill battle to get his approval at all.

Lucky joined her and rubbed her shoulders, her tension melting under his fingers. She soaked in his presence. His sense of calm and his down-home common sense were rare qualities indeed. She could use a little of that in her life, even if it was just temporary. To her surprise, she wouldn't mind if he made Violet Ridge his permanent home base.

Stop it, Elizabeth. He wasn't her actual boyfriend any more than the ring on her finger was made of genuine diamonds. This was a fake engagement, but the feelings she was beginning to feel for him weren't fake.

Her father's pronouncement added a new wrinkle to this dilemma. Her father wanted Jeff and Lucky on the trail with her. She was more than capable of handling everything herself, but her father wanted them by her side. For the sake of his happiness and well-being, she'd go along with it for now.

Maybe this was a blessing in disguise. The trail might provide the perfect place for her and Lucky's so-called breakup. Without her father's disruptive presence, she and Lucky could end this charade, once and for all.

Then she'd also find a way to close the door on the jumbled emotions his presence caused whenever he entered the room.

CHAPTER EIGHT

LATE MONDAY AFTERNOON, Elizabeth entered the grocery store and selected a cart. With Tammy's list in hand, as well as requests from several of the cowhands and her brother's family, she headed for the produce stand. Even though she rarely ran ranch errands, she'd jumped at the chance to head into town and get away from the constant scrutiny of the engagement. Even the grooms had been asking questions about her wedding, and she longed for a respite from the constant barrage.

"Elizabeth Irwin, one of my favorite students." Mrs. Sanderson, her fifth-grade teacher, hailed her from a spot near the peaches. "A little birdie told me you're engaged!"

So much for keeping the engagement under wraps. Elizabeth propelled her cart toward the nectarines and stopped near one of her favorite teachers. She twisted the ring on her finger, the tape a temporary fix, but then again, this was a temporary engagement. "You heard about it already?"

"I just had my hair done." She fluffed her blue-gray pageboy and smiled. "It was all the talk at the Think Pink Salon."

Of course it was.

"You know, a lot can happen between now and December." Maybe laying the groundwork now for the broken engagement would help her escape scrutiny down the line, although that seemed unlikely in a town the size of Violet Ridge.

"Does that mean you might move up the date?" Mrs. Sanderson clapped her hands. "I'm so happy for you."

Elizabeth sent her the woman a wobbly smile while Mrs. Sanderson pulled her into an embrace. After she escaped, Elizabeth gathered the items on her list while even more town residents stopped her and congratulated her on the news. Distracted, she threw anything in the cart and blinked at the register. Cookies, processed cupcakes and kettle potato chips weren't part of her regular diet, and she never purchased them. Yet that and every other form of junk food had made its way into her cart.

The cashier greeted her and made a big deal about the ring on Elizabeth's finger, leaving no chance to ask for the food to be returned to the shelves.

Was there any graceful way of getting out of this?

SUMMER IN VIOLET RIDGE was crowded with tourists taking pictures of the metal buffalo in front of a restaurant that served bison burgers. While crossing Main Street from the parking area to the shops, Lucky held on to Zack's and Audrey's hands. This town had always been one of his favorite stops on the rodeo tour, with its picturesque downtown, the pastel facades showcasing some fun stores and delicious food. Today, he had one destination in mind: Reichert Trading Company, where he'd seen children's fishing poles next to those bright and colorful kites. Earlier, Jeff had pulled him aside and asked him if he wanted to spend some time getting to know his future niece and nephew. There was no way Lucky could turn down such an offer, his happiness overflowing at making it onto the list of approved caretakers for these two.

"I have a fun afternoon planned." Lucky released their

hands and warned them to stay by his side. "What do you say to a horse ride to the meadow with the duck pond? We'll go fishing and have a great time." Audrey pulled him over to Rocky Mountain Chocolatiers. "Can we have a treat, too?"

It was next to impossible to say no to that elfin face framed with those big purple glasses. A customer opened the door and delicious smells of chocolate and sugar filled the air. "All that fresh air and exercise calls for something special."

Even Zack's face lit up when they entered the shop. They waited in line, and Lucky laughed at hearing the siblings change their mind umpteen times about what they'd choose for their treat. He'd never had a day like this when he'd shuttled from foster home to foster home, and he'd savor every moment as much as he'd enjoy a chocolate turtle the size of his hand, his favorite chocolate confection with pecans and caramel.

When it was their turn to deliver their orders, Zack asked Lucky's permission for an apple covered with caramel and nuts while Audrey's eyes grew wide at the sheer number of varieties of fudge. The attendant laughed and pointed at the second row. "My daughter's a little younger than you are. The strawberry tuxedo fudge is her favorite. It's white chocolate fudge with chocolate chips and swirls of strawberry flavoring."

"Yes, please." Audrey looked at Lucky for approval, and he nodded at both children.

"Aren't you Elizabeth's fiancé?" The attendant boxed up the order. "She's a sweetheart."

Lucky nodded, and Audrey jumped on her toes. "You know my aunt Elizabeth?"

"You must be Jeff's son and daughter." The woman, who appeared to be about the same age as Lucky's thirty-one, smiled at the pair and gave them each a tiny plastic spoon with a sample of the fudge. "I attended school with your aunt, and she's really smart. She helped me with my business plan, and she knows everything about horses."

That was quite a compliment. Then again, Elizabeth was quite a woman.

"I'm Zack, and this is my sister, Audrey." Zack placed his hands on Audrey's shoulders in a protective way.

"Nice to meet you. Tell Elizabeth that Emma said hello." Emma gave them a big smile.

They finished the transaction, and Lucky dipped his cowboy hat at Emma. When they stepped out the door, bright sunshine flooded their eyes, and it took a minute to adjust. Then they made their way to Reichert Supply Company. What should have been a two-minute walk turned into a half hour as nearly everybody they met told him a story about Elizabeth, all of them positive.

The townspeople loved her, and he couldn't blame them.

Lucky headed for the sporting goods section and studied the display for the best equipment.

Zack tugged at Lucky's sleeve. "We don't know how to fish." Then the young boy picked up the longest pole and swung it around.

"I can teach you." Lucky stopped the pole before it hit Audrey. "But these are more your size."

He gestured to some smaller poles, then selected ones that would work. Audrey looked with longing at the bright kites. "Can we fly a kite, too?"

"Why not?" He had them all day, thanks to Jeff and Nicole's afternoon and evening with phone conference meetings. "More fun stuff to tell your parents."

After a great deal of back and forth between a dragon or a unicorn kite, Lucky suggested a compromise. He paid for the sunflower kite, and they found themselves back at the ranch a short time later.

Never one to stand on formality, Lucky entered through the kitchen rather than the more impressive front door. He found Elizabeth helping Tammy unload groceries.

Tammy clicked her tongue. "It must be love," she said as she reached in for the fourth package of chocolate sandwich cookies. "You never buy junk food."

"Aunt Elizabeth." Zack reached her first and began telling her about the trip to Violet Ridge.

"Emma says hello," Lucky added at the end.

Elizabeth reached for her red cowboy hat on a nearby hook. "Sounds like a great day. I'll be at the stable if anyone needs me."

"Why don't you go for a horse ride with us?" Lucky offered. "I'll wager you have everything ready for the cattle roundup."

She scoffed. "Of course, but I can't leave all of my work for the grooms."

"They're looking after the stable, right?" He waited for her acknowledgment. "Then I'll sweeten the deal. I bought two turtles, but you can have one."

She narrowed her eyes, and yet that didn't hide the twinkle in them. "You drive a hard bargain. Emma makes really good turtles."

"I'll be the judge of that." He'd be getting more out of this day than she realized. "Come with us."

Within minutes, the four of them were riding out to the field of sunflowers, the long green stalks bending in the strong breeze. Nearby the sun glistened along the ripples of water where a mother duck swam with her ducklings following behind. They tethered the ponies, and Audrey ran over to the lake's edge.

"One, two, three, four duckies! Aunt Elizabeth, come see them," Audrey said.

Elizabeth hurried over and talked to Audrey while Lucky extracted his portable fishing pole and gear from Butterscotch's saddle. He demonstrated how to hook the fly and cast off. Elizabeth pulled Lucky aside.

"Audrey wants to pick some flowers for her mom, and then we're going to go in search of more ducks." Elizabeth leaned into Lucky, close enough for her soft hair to brush his cheek. "I think she just wants to observe everything, and she's too sweet to resist."

The females waved goodbye, and Lucky was patient with Zack, giving him pointers on staying quiet and observing everything around them. Still, the fish weren't biting this afternoon. Elizabeth and Audrey returned with a bouquet of wildflowers and the kite, and Lucky stowed the fishing gear.

Sunlight reflected off Elizabeth's auburn hair, revealing spun-gold highlights. The day was perfect for kite flying. He extracted the kite from its packaging and stood with his back to the wind. He held it aloft and let out the string line. The kite sailed upward, and he ran the length of the field until it gained enough altitude for it to stay in the air.

"Can I hold it?" Audrey and Zack said in unison.

"How about Aunt Elizabeth gets a turn first?" Lucky waved away her protests until she stood close enough for him to smell the light scent of her perfume.

Elizabeth held up the line and kept the kite steady in the air. "You're good at this. You must have done a lot of kite flying with your parents."

"Never." This wasn't the time for her to hear his life story, although there was no one he wanted to share it with more, and that included Cherry, the woman he'd almost asked to marry him.

Elizabeth handed the kite to Zack, and he and his sister alternated turns while Lucky spread a blanket on the grass. Then he checked on the horses, making sure they had water and everything they needed. Afterward, he relaxed on a blanket and patted the open spot next to him. She hesitated and remained standing. "Maybe I should get back to work now?"

"All work and no play make Elizabeth a tired person." He opened the box of turtles, using his hand so the aroma of the chocolate would entice her to stay.

She settled next to him and kept her gaze on her niece and nephew. "You're great with kids. You'll make a good father."

Whether that was true had entered his mind hundreds of times over the years. Without a father figure or even a father, period, he'd struggled with the idea of bringing a child into the world. Would he make a good dad? That was one reason it had taken him so long to cozy up to the idea of a serious relationship. Cale and Will gave him hope, though, that he'd rise to the task.

He bit into his turtle, the pecan salty and crisp, the caramel oozing out of the sweet chocolate shell. "This is the life for now."

He watched her enjoy her treat, and he relished the time in the sweet summer sunshine to do the same.

BEFORE DAWN ON this dry Tuesday morning, Elizabeth yawned and approached the stable, yesterday's afternoon of relaxation and fun behind her. Time for hard work and getting the second of the ranch's three annual cattle roundups on the trail underway. The roundup involved quite a bit of labor as she and the crew checked on the cattle before moving them to their fall field, but there was also time for fun. Tammy's chuckwagon cooking, nighttime campfires and a singalong. Not much about it had changed since she started accompanying her father when she was eleven, and she wouldn't have it any other way. She stopped and let her eyes acclimate to the dim surroundings. The shadows of the mountains rising majestically in the background hid the muted colors she loved so much. Far away, the distant howl of a coyote sent a shiver through her. On the horse ride out to the summer pasture, she'd keep a close eye on the fences. The ranch didn't need to lose any cattle to a nocturnal visitor.

Moose, the outside border collie she'd known since he was a pup, ran over as if he also felt the excitement and energy in the air. He ran circles around her, and she laughed. "Yes, you're coming along. I couldn't do this without you."

"That sure is a pretty way to start the day." Lucky's smooth voice could melt butter, but it still startled her.

She caught her breath. "You scared me."

"Didn't mean to. I just wanted to thank you kindly for letting me go on the roundup with your family." Moose increased the radius of his circles until he herded the two of them together. In close proximity to Lucky, she felt those cartwheels in her stomach twist more rapidly than ever. "How can I help you this morning? Fun is fun, but there's also a time for hard work."

Elizabeth slid open the stable doors and greeted a groom coming from the opposite direction. Then she faced Lucky. "You can stay out of the way while we work."

He shook his head. "I have to earn my keep. I've worked on many a ranch over the past thirteen years."

Those blue eyes were pleading his case. His pride was at stake, and she recognized that emotion all too well. "Okay. You can check the saddlebags." She listed everything she expected in each, except for Zack's and Audrey's, since their packs would be lighter.

She was concerned about her niece and nephew coming along, but Tammy had assured her she'd look after them while the others checked on the cattle's welfare. The promise of campfires and no showers had cinched the deal for Zack, and Audrey was looking forward to sleeping in Aunt Elizabeth's tent.

In no time, they readied all the equipment and animals as sunrise greeted them. Elizabeth glanced at her watch and tapped her cowboy boot on the brown dirt outside the stable. Where was everyone?

Lucky must have noticed her agitation. "They're coming. So much has happened over the past few days, and not everyone's used to this schedule, but they're coming."

He was right, but that coyote howl had her on edge. Okay, so did Lucky, who had no more intention of staying in one place than she did about leaving the Double I Ranch. She was letting her heart cloud her better judgement. Hadn't she learned anything from the debacle that was her relationship with Jared?

For the umpteenth time, she reminded herself this situation was different. Once they ended their "engagement," though, she wasn't sure whether she could call Lucky for a pep talk or ask his advice on the new watering post she'd read about. Sabrina said Lucky dropped everything at a minute's notice for a close friend, and yet when this was over, would they consider themselves friends? She knew one thing for certain. Lucky Harper's friendship was a treasure beyond compare.

As if on cue, a line of people headed toward the stable with Grandma Eloise leading the group. Something was different about the older woman, but Elizabeth couldn't discern what it was. Still, it was sweet that Evie's mother wanted to send them on their way. Most likely, the older lady would say her goodbyes now and return to Texas while they were gone. It was a shame she and Bob lived so far away. Sabrina glowed whenever her grandmother was in the room, and Elizabeth wasn't surprised. Grandma Eloise had a resiliency and strength about her that brought out the best in people.

Jeff held Audrey's hand while Zack followed, his fingers flying across his handheld video game. Elizabeth considered asking him for the unit and giving it back to him tonight, if for no other reason than his safety around the horses, but decided against calling him out in front of an audience. She'd make sure it was safely ensconced at the bottom of his saddlebag. Who needed a game console when there was this beautiful scenery and excitement all around?

Grandma Eloise came over, and Elizabeth finally put her finger on what was different. Her cane was nowhere in sight. "Do you have room for one more?"

"One more what?" Elizabeth blinked as Grandma Eloise pointed to herself.

Elizabeth blew out a long, deep breath. She disliked having to turn down the sweet woman, who was now as dear as a grandmother to her, but she'd already have to slow the pace with Jeff, Zack and Audrey coming along. At least Tammy was helping with the younger pair so that they'd be out of the way once everyone arrived at the campsite. Elizabeth, a good four decades younger, sometimes returned from the roundups happier for the experience but drained, both physically and mentally, from the activity. How could Grandma Eloise keep up with everyone? Letting her down gently seemed the best approach. "It's going to be rugged out there. We'll be in tents and riding for four days."

She looked toward Lucky, who approached Grandma

Eloise, his face calm and kind. "Elizabeth's worried about you."

Grandma Eloise raised her head and pointed toward her cowboy boots. "I've been on more roundups than your ages combined."

"Horseback riding requires a certain amount of agility." Elizabeth was hoping against hope the woman would take the hint. The ranch was her responsibility, as were the health and welfare of those on the roundup.

"Horseback riding is one of the most therapeutic activities." Grandma Eloise delivered a curt nod. "There's increased range of motion, and it helps develop muscle strength. I won't beg, but I'd be a real help with Audrey and Zack."

Elizabeth inhaled a deep breath. Grandma Eloise was right, especially with Nicole staying behind to work on the deposition. Tammy could only do so much with Zack and Audrey while cooking. With the coyote making his presence known this morning, she'd have to keep a close eye on the fences, making Grandma Eloise's presence a necessity. She asked the groom to prepare Maisy, a gentle mare able to make the trip, then turned to the older woman. "We'll try it out this morning. If you feel like you need to return to the ranch, just say the word at lunchtime. Tammy's riding out with the catering chuck wagon and joining us after that. You can go back this afternoon, if necessary. After that, it'll be harder for anyone to reach us because of the rocky terrain. Promise you'll come back if you're exhausted?" She looked at Jeff and the children. "If it's too much on them, I want you to make the same promise."

Jeff nodded, and then Elizabeth turned to Grandma Eloise.

"Of course. Thanks, I won't be a bother. Be back in a

jiffy." Grandma Eloise's eyes glinted in the dim lights of the stable.

"We'll wait for you," Elizabeth said while adding fifteen minutes to the departure time.

"No need." Grandma Eloise ducked into the stable and returned a minute later with her sleeping roll. "Had my gear in the tack room."

Elizabeth called everyone together. "This is a long trek, but there's nothing else like it. Is everyone ready for a great time?"

"Can I stay with Mom?" Zack kept his gaze glued to his game player. "I can play my game and be really quiet while she works."

Jeff reached out his hand for the console. "I'll take that for now. You can have it back tonight when we break camp. It will be good for you to spend some of your summer vacation outside."

With reluctance, Zack handed it over and trudged over to the horse he'd been riding during his lessons. Elizabeth approached Jeff. "Nice job with Zack."

"Thanks. He's a good kid, and I don't get to spend enough time with him or Audrey." Jeff glanced at the cowhands. "Time to load up and head on the trail."

Bristling at Jeff's taking hold of authority, she felt better when JR, the foreman, looked at her for confirmation. She gave a slight nod, and each member of their group checked their saddlebags and cinches. As casually as possible, Elizabeth monitored Grandma Eloise while she adjusted her gear and climbed into the saddle.

Elizabeth sensed Lucky's presence by recognizing the spicy scent of his aftershave. "She's a wonder, isn't she?" he asked.

She faced him and nodded. "I hope I'm like her someday."

"You'll be just as feisty at her age." Admiration lurked in Lucky's gaze. "I'll watch out for her and the kids."

He mounted Margarita with a smooth motion. Everyone set off, and Elizabeth rode next to JR. He and his wife, Tammy, had been employed at the Double I since before she was born. "Tammy's meeting us with the chuck wagon, right?"

"Yep. She's looking forward to riding with us to the summer pasture after that." JR nodded and reined in his American quarter horse, Copper. "We should be there by nightfall."

"I'm looking forward to Tammy's flapjacks tomorrow morning." Elizabeth's mouth watered. "There's nothing like her campfire pancakes."

"Pancakes?" Zack turned around, his smile evident at the mention of food. "Those are my favorite."

Elizabeth returned his smile while checking on the fences. So far, no signs of any disrepair or coyote tracks, either. The morning passed by quickly as the group made their way to the checkpoint, where Tammy greeted them with a veritable feast. Elizabeth cared for the horses and then checked on Grandma Eloise, who insisted she was having the time of her life, before heading for food.

"Turkey or ham with fresh-baked buns." Tammy ushered everyone through the line, scooping out mashed potatoes and green beans on plates, along with biscuits the size of Elizabeth's hand. "Brownies for dessert."

Elizabeth sidled next to Jeff, determined to bond with her brother over these next four days. With Ben stationed a thousand miles away and unable to come home on a regular basis, maybe it was time to gauge Jeff's interest in Dad's offer. "Hi, Jeff."

Jeff nodded at Tammy. "No gravy for me. As it is, Nicole is already discussing how soon we need to resume our diets." Jeff patted his flat stomach and then faced Elizabeth. "I'd have thought you'd have wanted to eat lunch with your fiancé."

"I thought I'd spend some time with my brother. Get to know you again."

Jeff thanked Tammy. "I'd like that. Nicole told me I owe you an apology for accusing you of trying to steal Dad and Evie's thunder. Now that I've seen you and Lucky over the past few days, I'm just surprised you didn't announce your engagement sooner."

Why did people keep saying that?

She glanced at Lucky with a day's stubble gracing his face, a good look on him. Whatever story he was recounting to Grandma Eloise, Zack and Audrey must be captivating, as they seemed to be hanging on his every word.

Despite everything, she couldn't take her eyes off Lucky. She caught some of what he was saying, namely his preparations for the Casper rodeo. Another reminder he would be on the road soon enough. She'd relied on him too much this morning, and there was no use getting attached to someone who intended to leave.

Too late. She already liked having him around. Best to raise her guard and protect her heart.

She led Jeff over to one of the makeshift tables. "I thought we could talk about the ranch." Maybe she'd been approaching the discussion of the architect plans with the wrong person. If the past few days were any indication of Jeff's continued sway over Dad, getting Jeff on her side would maybe help gain Dad's approval. That would make it easier, and then he'd authorize the down payment and the project in general. "Did you know JR and Tammy live in Violet Ridge instead of on the ranch?"

The foreman and the cook would have their pick of the bunkhouses if this went through, or even work with the architect on a home of their own. That was, if they wanted to live on the ranch. Jeff slathered his biscuit with Tammy's homemade huckleberry preserve. "If I did, I'd forgotten." He took a big bite and moaned. "I'd also forgotten how much I love Tammy's cooking."

"Does that mean you're considering Dad's offer to move here?" How could he choose Boston when he could have the open range and spend every day on the ranch?

"I thought that was settled."

Yes, but which way? She watched her brother closely as he swallowed the last bite of his biscuit. Her father was a hard customer to resist, and it was better to have Jeff as an ally if he moved here. "According to Dad, you're moving here." While she'd started out with mixed feelings about it, Jeff was family. "He's counting on you, and JR told me you've been asking the cowhands about water rights and discussing property issues. I have a couple of ideas to run by you about how to better guarantee employment retention along with some cattle-breed improvements."

"Hold up." Jeff's cell phone rang, and he startled. "I didn't think I'd be able to get reception out here."

"After Sabrina and Ty were caught in a blizzard, Dad invested in top-of-the-line signal boosters." For a few days last winter, everyone in the Irwin household was on edge when Sabrina, who'd been pregnant and the barn manager at the time, had found herself stranded at the family cabin with Ty. That same blizzard had trapped Evie at the Double I and had been the catalyst for her and Dad to find out how much they had in common, and they'd ended up falling in love.

"I have to take this. Excuse me." Jeff walked away while Moose approached.

She threw the border collie some of her green beans. Moose gobbled them and then proceeded to run in circles around the group, narrowing the distance each time as if he was herding them instead of cattle. With a casual glance toward Lucky, she marveled at how he still had Grandma Eloise and Audrey eating out of the palm of his hand.

Jeff muttered something, and she focused on her brother again. He wrung the back of his neck and then transferred his phone from one ear to the other. Something was bothering him as he swiped on the screen. He sent a longing glance toward Zack and Audrey. Then his lips narrowed into a thin line.

"That was Nicole. There's been a development in one of my cases, and the junior associate can't handle it." There was an edge to her brother's voice she'd never heard before. "I should have known this was a bad idea."

"What? Getting away from work or spending time with Zack and Audrey?" She echoed his tone, unclear of his meaning, just as she was unsure whether she knew Jeff anymore. As it was, the ten-year age difference had caused a chasm between them growing up, when she'd trailed him everywhere while he sought solitude.

"This action-oriented business demeanor is a new side of you. I wish we could have spent more time getting reacquainted." He sighed and ate his last bite of mashed potatoes. "Then you might not be thinking the worst about me. For the record, Nicole wanted all of us to fly back this morning, but I wanted Zack and Audrey to spend some time on the ranch. See if they liked it here more than I did growing up. It was a bad idea allowing them to start something I had a feeling we wouldn't be able to finish."

"I never realized you didn't like growing up on the ranch." What wasn't to love? These were ten thousand of the prettiest acres anywhere in the world, and there was always something new in terms of cattle management or in the stable. As far as Elizabeth was concerned, there was no other place she ever wanted to live. Did that mean Jeff wasn't moving back? He still hadn't answered her directly.

"I might look like Dad, but I take after Mom. You're our father to the core. Ben's the only one whose personality combines the both of them." Jeff stood and motioned for her to follow him to the trash receptacle. "I'll take Zack and Audrey back to the stable with me."

She finally had new insight concerning Jeff's feelings regarding the ranch, but the verdict was still out about Audrey and Zack's perception of life out west. "Why not let them finish what they started? Grandma Eloise is here, and Audrey loves Lucky."

As if on cue, Lucky hefted Audrey onto his back, her giggles echoing in the mountain air. "Faster, Lucky!"

Lucky sped up and darted around the area. Then he made a beeline for Elizabeth and Jeff. With a slight grimace, Lucky lowered Audrey to the ground and dipped his cowboy hat. "Sorry that I've been monopolizing your daughter."

"No more than I was monopolizing Elizabeth, but I'm happy Audrey enjoyed her lunch. I need to talk to her and her brother. Zack!" Jeff's gaze traveled to Zack, who stood next to Grandma Eloise and their horses. He acknowledged his dad, and Jeff motioned for them to join the group. Grandma Eloise walked over with Zack, and they laughed along the way.

Jeff updated Zack and Audrey on the change of plans, and her niece and nephew let out groans. Audrey's eyes filled with tears behind her purple glasses, and Zack stomped the ground. "I want to stay."

Elizabeth blinked. A few hours ago, her nephew had wanted to stay at the ranch house, so Elizabeth took Zack's outburst as a win for the great outdoors. Over the years, she'd grown apart from Jeff, and perhaps this time on the trail was important for her to bond with her niece and nephew. "My offer stands," Elizabeth said. "That is, if Zack and Audrey would feel comfortable riding without you, and vice versa."

"Can we, Dad?" Zack's large blue eyes pleaded with his father.

"I want to stay, too." Audrey wiggled her front tooth. "You might not even recognize me if I lose my tooth."

She grinned as if reassuring Jeff that would clinch the deal instead of the opposite. Her brother looked conflicted, but nodded. "You'll have more fun here. School starts next month, and you'll be cooped up in the classroom then."

"You bet your briefcase, they will," Grandma Eloise said, her eyes twinkling.

They made arrangements, and Jeff kissed them both before heading back to the stable on Rocky. Elizabeth smiled at Audrey and Zack, who'd finish what they'd started here. Best yet, they'd act as a buffer between her and Lucky.

Her niece and nephew crowded around Lucky, who obliged them by showing them some lasso tricks. Despite the myriad tasks on her shoulders, Elizabeth let herself get lost in his mastery and clapped with the cowhands, Zack and Audrey. Realizing everyone had stopped and watched him, Lucky blushed to the roots of his dirty blond hair. That type of modesty was a rarity.

With moves like that, guarding her heart just became that much more imperative, so Lucky wouldn't break it when he left, as he inevitably would.

"TAMMY, I DIDN'T know how you were going to top this afternoon's lunch, but you certainly did with this dinner." Lucky patted his stomach and paid his compliments to the chef.

Tammy's husband, JR, chimed in his appreciation

and then delivered a kiss to her cheek, and the older lady blushed. "Get on with you. Neither of you are on cleanup duty tonight."

JR sneaked in one more kiss before Tammy shooed them away. He tipped his hat, then excused himself for the campfire preparations.

Dusk was approaching, and more shadows dotted the Rockies. Lucky went toward the campsite, only to find everyone was still finishing dinner. With some time on his hands, he retrieved his whittling knife and latest project, a set of miniature animals for Sabrina's birthday. His stomach wobbled. After he and Elizabeth broke up and he moved on from Violet Ridge, Sabrina would have ties to Elizabeth and her family through her mother's marriage to Elizabeth's father. Of course, she'd have to support Elizabeth. More than ever, the realization of damaging his close friendship with Sabrina and Will, something he thought he'd accepted, sank into him.

Returning to the rodeo as soon as this roundup ended became that much more necessary. A clean break and distractions had always helped him whenever he moved to a new foster home. Remaining here was only prolonging the agony.

He found a seat some distance away from everyone. Holding the basswood that would become a miniature version of Butterscotch with his left hand, he picked up his whittling knife with his right hand. Humming under his breath, he braced his thumb against the wood and used short strokes to whittle the legs.

"Whatcha doin'?" He'd been so engrossed with the wood he hadn't seen Audrey appear. She wrinkled her nose and her glasses slid slightly. "Why are you cutting that piece of wood?"

"It's called whittling. I'm carving Butterscotch."

Zack joined them and whistled. "Is that a real knife?" Zack asked. "How do you carve the wood so that you don't get splinters? Are you afraid you're going to cut yourself?"

That was the most he'd ever heard out of Zack at one time. "Yes, this is a real carbon-steel whittling knife. I use basswood although pine and cedar work well. Basswood doesn't splinter easily, and my friend and mentor, Cale, went over the safety rules for using a knife before he taught me. I've been doing this for quite a while now." Lucky showed them two other figures he'd carved. "These are my friend Will's goats, Snow and Flake."

Then he handed one to Zack and one to Audrey, who jumped up and down. "Can you make doggies?" She tapped her chin. "Or a unicorn?"

"I'll see what I can do," Lucky promised.

"I like horses now. Blaze is amazing. He likes me a lot." Zack puffed out his chest before his stomach and posture deflated. "Then again, you might not have time for us. Dad was supposed to be here, and he has to work."

Lucky's heart went out to the pair, who went from excited to forlorn in the space of a second. He'd never known his father, but that wasn't the case with them. And he knew Jeff was trying. After all, he'd seen the longing and love in Jeff's face as he rode away earlier. "Your parents love you."

"I guess." Zack kicked at the dirt.

Elizabeth joined them and cringed, a pained expression on her face, as if she was the bearer of bad news. "Hey, Zack," she said. Lucky braced himself. "I guess you're upset about your console. I forgot to ask your father for it before he left."

"I forgot, too. It'll be there when I get back." Zack shrugged and then held up one of the carved goats. "Could you teach me how to make something like this?"

"And me?" Audrey clearly didn't want to be left out.

"Did you make these?" Elizabeth sounded impressed, and Audrey handed her goat to Elizabeth. She studied it and smiled before returning it to Lucky. "It's beautiful."

"I'm not as good as Cale, but it's relaxing, and it keeps my fingers nimble." His mentor had carved a chess set and had taught Lucky how to play. That set had gotten plenty of use, as he'd spent many evenings playing chess with Sabrina while Will read a book in the same room.

"Nonsense. You're very talented with woodworking," Grandma Eloise said as she came over and popped her hands on her hips. "You made Genie's rocking horse."

"I remember now." Elizabeth whistled. "It's gorgeous."

JR called out from the campfire and motioned at Lucky. "Hey, Lucky. Could you give me a hand?"

Thankful for the interruption, Lucky excused himself after collecting the figurines. He helped JR with the preparations by laying hickory logs in the center of a circle of stones well away from a grove of aspens to the east and the meadow with the cattle a good distance off in the north. Dusk fell upon the site. Grandma Eloise excused herself, choosing to turn in early, while JR lit the fire. Smoke plumed in the balmy summer air, and the heat felt good now with the temperature quickly cooling this high in the mountains.

In no time, JR handed out long metal skewers while Tammy trailed behind with a package of marshmallows and gave them to everyone. Zack ate his without toasting it while Audrey held up her skewer. "What's this for?"

"S'mores." Elizabeth followed and opened a box of graham crackers. She handed two to Zack. "I'll show you how to toast your marshmallow so it'll melt the chocolate on your graham cracker."

Elizabeth aided Zack while Lucky helped Audrey.

"Do you like your marshmallows burnt on the outside

or lightly toasted?" Lucky asked while twirling the stick over the fire.

Audrey licked her lips. "I don't know. I've never done this before."

He caught his marshmallow on fire and then blew it out, the exterior all brown and charred. "I like them toasty."

She looked skeptical and then her lower lip went all quivery. "It caught on fire."

He ruffled her hair. "I promise it's delicious." He presented the skewer to her. "Try this one and then we'll make a s'more."

She scrunched her nose and accepted it, and then bounced up and down on the log, excited for more. They chatted and laughed while eating the treats. He glanced over at Elizabeth, the fire's glow bathing her in soft light and highlighting her natural beauty. She caught him staring at her, and he grasped for a reason to have been looking her way. "You have a dot of chocolate on your nose."

"I'm not sure I believe you." She raised her chin. "I'm usually meticulous."

He reached out his hand and wiped some of the brown smear, holding it out for her to see. Their gazes met, and something between them changed in that moment. The racing of his heart and these escalating feelings were very much real. No longer did this seem like a fake romance.

"Good grief. Just kiss her. It's not like Audrey and Zack have never seen adults kiss before." Grandma Eloise emerged from her tent and reached for a skewer, making a s'more of her own. "It smelled too enticing out here to sleep."

Elizabeth's wide green eyes connected with his, and he hadn't thought about this part of their fake engagement. Of course people would expect them to kiss. Somehow, they'd fooled everyone at the reception, with no one expressing any doubt, at least not to their faces. Apparently they'd been so convincing they now had a wedding date. She braced herself and nodded.

No matter that it was just for show, he didn't want their first kiss to be in front of everyone like this. When he kissed someone, he wanted it to be special. So he kissed her nose and stepped back. "Mmm, chocolate. That was too good to go to waste."

She opened her eyes, and relief seemed to lurk there, as well as gratitude. "My hero."

JR unlocked a guitar case and pulled out the instrument. "It's time for some music," the foreman said. "I'm not in Evie's league, but I can carry a tune."

With the awkward moment passed, everyone started singing familiar favorites. Above, the stars twinkled bright, extending as far as the eye could see. The fire popped, and an ember escaped, landing on his arm. He brushed away the spark and made sure everyone else was far enough away so no harm would come to any of them.

Elizabeth expressed her concern and checked his arm. He reassured her he was fine. The ember hadn't burned him, but he'd been scorched in the past when families took him into their fold and then rejected him. The last chords of the song lingered for a few seconds before fading away in the night. Nothing lasted forever, and Lucky would do well to remember that before this relationship seared him and branded him for life.

CHAPTER NINE

WITH THE SECOND day of the roundup almost over and quite successful, they'd be moving the cattle to the fall pasture tomorrow morning. So far, the medical checks on the cattle had progressed faster than expected, with no major issues. Still, something wasn't right. Then Elizabeth heard the sound again. She tracked the plaintive mooing until she found the young weaner on the side of the mountain, stuck in a ravine. There was always one stray on these roundups. Soon, this cow would be reunited with the rest of the herd.

She dismounted from Andromeda and tied her Appaloosa to a nearby aspen. Maybe she should contact JR on her two-way radio for assistance, she thought, then scoffed at the idea. Why bother her foreman when this weaner wasn't that big, only around six months old? Rolling up her sleeves, she approached the animal, still mooing, a sign she hadn't been standing here too long. It simply needed incentive to leave its cool shady spot in the creek and return to the pasture.

Wading into the creek, she spotted the problem. The weaner's hoof was trapped between two rocks. The poor thing was stuck and couldn't free itself. Even if this had started as a way to beat the summer heat, it could have ended badly if Elizabeth hadn't arrived in time. She exerted some force, but the cow didn't budge, its hoof wedged in tight. Another angle might work better, and she waded into the stream until she was ankle deep.

Grunting, she attempted to move the rocks so she could dislodge the young cow. Instead, her arms flailed, and she lost her balance.

She fell backward on her bottom. Frustrated, she sat in the creek, droplets dripping off her brow, the water flowing past her with the sun beating down overhead. Then she laughed. Truth be told, the cool creek felt good. It was just her ego that was bruised. At least no one was around to witness her fall.

She tilted her head and tried to figure out how to free the weaner.

An exclamation came from the western ridge, and hooves thundered toward her. She struggled to her feet, but the slippery rocks had other plans for her. She landed in the creek once more. So much for a graceful move. Lucky dismounted and tied Margarita near Andromeda. "Elizabeth!"

He hurried over and reached out his hand. With a murmured word of thanks, she accepted his help and made it to the water's edge. "Her hoof is caught in the rocks."

"You should have called me. I know a thing or two about calves' hooves." He crouched into position and gauged the water's depth. Then he searched the area. "Do you see anything we can use as a lever?"

She spotted a long, sturdy oak branch on the opposite side of the bank. "Over there."

"I'll get it." Lucky forded the stream and returned with the branch. "I'll wedge this under the rock while you help the weaner."

"The rocks are more slippery than they look. Be careful," Elizabeth said.

"Thanks for the concern. There's nothing like a cool, refreshing swim in summer, but I prefer my swim trunks." He winked, and her stomach did a funny flip.

The weaner's moos were getting weaker, and they turned their attention to the animal. On the count of three, Lucky pushed against the rock while she helped the weaner. In no time, the young cow was free, and she scrambled out of the creek, bleating her happiness at being on firm ground again. The cow shook the excess water off her coat and proceeded in the herd's direction, not needing any encouragement from Elizabeth or Lucky.

She glanced in his direction, his smile and expression a sign of his relief. Then his grin faded.

"Why didn't you call me on your two-way radio?" Lucky cautiously moved to the creek bed, still holding the branch.

Elizabeth kept a careful eye on the cow, making sure it headed in the right direction. Moose appeared and took the lead. Only when the weaner and dog were out of sight did she address Lucky. "At first, I thought she was enjoying the water on a hot day. She obviously wanted to escape the heat, but she didn't count on the rocks trapping her. It wasn't until I fell into the water that I realized the severity of the situation."

Her words hit her hard. She'd also wanted to escape— from being the unattached member of the wedding party— but hadn't counted on circumstances tying her to Lucky. Now, the weaner might have gotten away without any injuries—but would she be as fortunate?

"You could have been hurt." He leaned the branch against a nearby aspen and then wiped the water off her face. His callused fingers brushed against her soft cheek, and she leaned into his touch. Suddenly, she knew without a doubt that getting out of this without injury was impossible. She had fallen too hard, too quickly, and Lucky meant too much to her now.

"I'm tough." Her whispered and warbled words hung in the air, and their gazes met.

His electric blue eyes had anything but a calming effect on her as she sniffed, his spicy aftershave lingering in the air.

"I know, but relying on others isn't a sign you're weak." He reached into his pocket and pulled out a dry cloth, blotting the moisture from the other side of her face. "Having people in your life who will stand by you is everything."

Electricity sparked the charged air around them. Everything surrounding her stilled. The nearby lowing of the cattle blurred into a silence that captivated her. She nodded, and he leaned toward her, his lips nearing hers for their first kiss.

"Aunt Elizabeth! Lucky!" Zack's shouts of glee reached them, and Elizabeth scooted away from Lucky.

She glanced around until she found Zack at the top of the ridge. "Grandma Eloise is giving me and Audrey more pointers about how to fish." He held up a good-size trout. "She says I caught dinner!"

Elizabeth and Lucky mounted their horses and met Zack, then rode back to the campsite, where she heard sniffles. Elizabeth dismounted and handed her reins to Lucky. She ran over to Audrey. "What's wrong, sweetheart?"

Her niece's bottom lip quivered. "We don't get to keep the fishies to take home." She pointed at Grandma Eloise. "*She* said we're eating them for dinner."

Elizabeth embraced her niece. Grandma Eloise came over. "I'm sorry, Elizabeth. Living on a ranch for so long…"

Elizabeth raised her head and nodded at Grandma Eloise over Audrey's shoulder. "I think she misses her parents." She leaned back but slipped her hand into Audrey's and gave it a light squeeze. "Hey, Audrey, darling. This is a ranch—"

That lip kept quivering, and Audrey sniffled. "Daddy wouldn't have hurt the fishie."

"Why don't we take a walk and watch Moose herd the cattle until dinner is ready," Elizabeth offered.

More sniffles came before Audrey gave a little nod. After a brief word with JR and Sweeney, the longtime cowhand who was also on the trip, Elizabeth spent time with her niece, whose tears dried in no time, until Tammy called them all together for dinner. Audrey bounced into the chow line, her resilience remarkable. Irwin females took everything in stride. Elizabeth filed that away for reference for when Lucky left the ranch for good.

Tammy offered Audrey a turkey drumstick instead of grilled fish, and Elizabeth mouthed "thank you" to the wise cook. Everyone settled at the campsite, and Audrey situated herself between Elizabeth and Lucky. At least that move prevented any awkwardness that might have resulted from that near kiss.

What would it be like to kiss Lucky? Would his kisses be soft and gentle like his everyday personality? Or would his rodeo persona, full of energy and charisma, make for a kiss of flashing fireworks?

Elizabeth pushed aside that thought, same as she pushed around the pieces of fish on her plate. She had just raised her fork to her mouth when Audrey jumped in the air.

"My tooth! It's out." She held up a small pearly tooth and went around showing it off to everyone in the circle, finishing at Elizabeth. "See, Aunt Elith, Elith…"

Lucky had called her Lizzie a couple of times, the same nickname her mother had used before she died when Elizabeth was Audrey's age. Elizabeth sounded formal and stiff, and she wanted Zack and Audrey to feel comfortable around her. "How about you call me Aunt Lizzie? That might be easier to say."

Audrey grinned, that gap-toothed smile as endearing as Andromeda's nuzzles. "Aunt Lizzie, look at my tooth." Then the grin disappeared. "Will the tooth fairy visit me? How does she know where I am?"

Zack scoffed. "Aw, Audrey, everyone knows." He stopped and looked around. Grandma Eloise and Lucky both sent him unspoken warnings. He rolled his eyes. "Everyone knows the tooth fairy keeps track of where the teeth are."

Lucky rose and placed his hands on Audrey's shoulders. "Don't worry. The tooth fairy will love it. Looks like a perfect addition to her collection."

Lucky must have a wonderful family to understand kids so well. Suddenly, Elizabeth had an overwhelming urge to know everything about his childhood and family. His parents must be pretty special people to produce such a loving son.

Audrey came over and hugged Elizabeth, her purple glasses digging into her shoulder. "Thank you, Aunt Lizzie."

Then Lizzie it was. She choked back the emotion and held the embrace for a bit longer, soaking in her niece's joy. If Jeff did move to Violet Ridge, she'd be a bigger part of Zack's and Audrey's lives. For the first time, the thought of Jeff rejoining the ranch family didn't seem so bad.

LUCKY TAPPED ON the side of Elizabeth's tent. "Hey, are we still taking the first shift together?"

Elizabeth murmured something that sounded like "come in," and he opened the flap only to find Elizabeth with one index finger on her lips while the other pointed to a sleeping Audrey, who was sprawled over Elizabeth's sleeping bag. "She misses her mom."

"Is the tooth fairy here?" Audrey flew into a sitting position and reached for her glasses. "Oh, hi, Lucky."

"Audrey wants to stay awake all night for the tooth fairy." Elizabeth hugged her niece, conflict written all over her expressive face. "Sweetheart, I have to help make sure the cattle are safe and protected."

"I can do that," Lucky volunteered. There was no way he wanted Audrey disappointed this young in life, as he'd been even younger than she was now when he'd entered the foster system and was confronted with reality.

"But you don't have to," Elizabeth protested.

"I want to." Lucky sent a smile in their direction, both Irwin females appealing in different ways.

"Audrey, sweetie, I need to give Lucky some instructions, and I'll be right back." Elizabeth finagled her way out of the tent and joined him.

"JR and I can work together," Lucky said. "If you have any directions, tell me now."

"Hold on a second."

She sent a thumbs-up toward Audrey and closed the flap behind her when she caught sight of Grandma Eloise coming toward them. The older woman tightened the shawl around her shoulders. "Good. You two lovebirds get to spend some time under the stars."

"Actually, Elizabeth and Audrey are setting a tooth-fairy trap," said Lucky. "She's giving me some orders for my night shift watching over the cattle."

Elizabeth ran a hand over her hair. "Grandma Eloise, can you keep an eye on Audrey for a minute? Lucky and I have something important to discuss."

"Of course I'll stay with Audrey, dear." The older woman smiled and neared Elizabeth. "You know the best things all have a little magic in them and take on a life of their own."

Elizabeth tugged on her boots while Grandma Eloise entered the tent and situated herself next to Audrey. The young girl snuggled against the older woman, showing her the tooth. Together, they radiated contentment.

Elizabeth neared him, and her cheek brushed his. Her soft skin was still warm from the tent. "I need your help."

There was a nip in the air, the higher mountain altitude bringing a nighttime chill. He led her over to the campfire, and he couldn't help but notice how she was wringing her hands. "What's wrong?"

She pulled her flannel shirt closer until it hugged her chest. "I don't have a dollar."

"Excuse me." He blinked and tapped his ear. "The fire crackled as you spoke."

"I never carry money with me on the roundups." She sent a nervous glance toward the tent. "The tooth fairy."

He excused himself for a few moments, then returned with a dollar. She stood on her tiptoes and kissed his cheek, her lips burning an imprint on his cool skin. "Thanks! You saved me." She stepped back and pocketed the bill. "We make a good team."

With that, she outlined some instructions for him and JR and then returned to the tent. They did make a good team. Was there any way to explore a possibility of that teamwork turning into a real friendship and then possibly more?

Or had this fake engagement already doomed any chance of a future for them?

CHAPTER TEN

THE NEXT AFTERNOON, Lizzie admired Moose's tenacity while the border collie pursued a stray head of cattle and brought it back to the herd. Moose's innate ability was a sight to behold.

At last, they reached the autumn pasture, the green fields stretching as far as the eye could see with only clumps of silver aspens dotting the hillside. The end of the summer months had brought little in terms of precipitation, but that would change with the fall rains. Moose watched over the herd as the cattle filed into the new spacious grazing fields.

JR reined in his horse near Lizzie. "Right on schedule." He sounded shocked, and she couldn't blame him. With the extra riders, she hadn't been sure they'd arrive here on time, but life surprised her sometimes. One look at Lucky cemented that.

Her gaze returned to the cattle. "And they're all accounted for. They're safe and ready for autumn. That's what's important."

"Your father will be proud of how well you handled the drive. Of course, he wouldn't have gone to California if he didn't think you'd manage everything."

Lizzie started at the foreman's praise. She wished her father would take a page from JR's playbook. "He thought Jeff would be along for the ride."

JR shook his head. "He knows you're more than capable."

Why was it easier for JR to see that? But was he on to something? Did her father appreciate her efforts more than she acknowledged? "Thanks for the vote of confidence, JR."

"Your father will come around, especially now that he's found love with Evie. He's pleased as punch that you've found that same type of happiness with Lucky," JR said.

This line of talk cut too deep. This engagement was a sham she'd gone along with so as not to further disrupt her father's wedding day. Now that he was on his honeymoon, this thing with Lucky had to end so it wouldn't be hanging over them any longer.

But there was one topic she could broach with the foreman right now. Since JR was proving more amenable to her leadership, she decided to confide in him and start making her own imprint. "What do you think of adding some Simmentals to our ranch? They're more docile and resistant to stress."

JR's gaze narrowed, and his head waffled to the point she could see the gears turning in his mind. "Their large frames sometimes make the calving process more difficult. Mastitis is a real problem with that breed."

"I've heard that's better with some of the black Simmentals, and they're also known for their milk production and a high yield of flavorful beef." After pleading her case, the foreman seemed swayed by her arguments.

He rubbed his chin. "Hmm. We could start with a small sample group for a few seasons. Slow and steady, and see if we get good results," he said.

Getting JR on her side would help her when she presented the same idea to her father. She spotted a problem with the fence at the far western end of the pasture and eased up on the reins. "We need to check out that hole. Ride that way with me."

As they neared the problem area, JR pulled up on the reins and squinted. "Uh-oh. I see the problem." They both dismounted, and JR followed her to the damaged portion of the fence, a big hole near the bottom. He studied some nearby tracks. "Looks like a pronghorn crawled under it."

"And ripped the bottom out," she said, finishing for him. "I don't want any of the cattle escaping. It shouldn't take me too long to fix this. Tell Tammy to save me a plate."

She rolled up the sleeves of her flannel shirt and rummaged through her saddlebag for the tools she'd need for taking out the damaged section.

"Will do, boss." JR tipped his cowboy hat and rode toward the rest of the group.

A little hard work was just what she needed so she wouldn't dwell on Lucky, especially seeing how she'd been thinking of him far too much on this roundup.

LUCKY RODE MARGARITA over to the section where Elizabeth was fixing the fence. He unloaded the new wire and brought it over to her, along with some water.

"Thought you might need this." He handed her the drink, and she removed her cream-colored leather-and-canvas work gloves before accepting the reusable bottle.

"Thanks." She stood and swigged a big sip, the sunlight reflecting off the diamonds in the engagement ring, and then wiped her mouth with the back of her arm. "You didn't have to do this."

"Maybe I wanted to." He was getting the feeling he'd like to do more for her with each passing day. "Teamwork, remember?"

Her smile brightened his day, already memorable from the moment Audrey had awakened the entire camp with the news the tooth fairy had come, then waved the dollar bill around as if it was a golden belt buckle.

"As if I could forget." She set the bottle on the ground next to the post.

"How can I help?"

"You brought the supplies I need. That's more than plenty for now." She kneeled and donned her gloves before picking up the electric fencing pliers.

He tapped her on her shoulder. "I'm more than a pretty face."

He scrunched up his nose and crossed his eyes, bringing forth a laugh, the prettiest sound in Colorado as far as he was concerned.

"Have a pair of work gloves?" she asked.

"Sure do." He extracted them from the back pocket of his jeans.

"Good. Can you use the fence stretcher to pull the broken sides back together?"

In his sleep, but he merely nodded. Over the next few hours, they worked together, laughing at times, a pleasant silence at others. Then she slid the pieces of wire together through a crimping sleeve while he bound the sleeve in place. They stood and checked out their handiwork. "Clear of debris and safe for the cattle. Good work, partner," he said.

He extended his hand until they shook in a firm handshake, shivers running through him at the contact. He kept that to himself.

"Thanks, Lucky." It was her turn to scrunch up her nose. "Some fiancée I am. I don't even know your real name."

He removed his cowboy hat and dipped his head. "Lucas Harper at your disposal."

She laughed. "Nice to meet you, Lucas Harper."

He joined in the laughter. There was something about Elizabeth that put him at ease. While she had a slightly formal manner about her, fitting for the future owner of the Double I, she wasn't pretentious or fussy. He'd never felt this comfortable around anyone, not even Cale, Will or Sabrina. "And I'd say Audrey's on to something. You seem more like a Lizzie than an Elizabeth to me."

Her slight sigh was almost lost in the breeze, but he noticed everything about her. "I have a feeling my nickname might be one thing that endures after this trip."

Too bad their relationship couldn't have had that same lasting power. He'd like it if her last name was Harper someday, but he roped calves and she owned them. "Would that be a bad thing?"

She shrugged. "My mother called me Lizzie."

Her use of the past tense also didn't go unnoticed. "What happened to her?"

"My mother died of cancer when I was Audrey's age. I always think of her when the gardenias bloom. It reminds me of her perfume." She removed her gloves and averted her eyes, as if she didn't want him to see her weakness, although her sharing this with him was anything but weak. It was a sign she was starting to trust him.

"And after she passed away, you insisted on going by Elizabeth again." He waited for her confirmation.

"I always preferred Lizzie, though. What about you? Did your parents nickname you Lucky when you were a baby or was it from a cute incident in your childhood?" She added a light note to her question, enough for him to go with the flow and focus the attention on him, something he didn't like around others. Around her, talking about himself didn't seem so bad.

He packed the tools in her saddlebag. "I barely knew my parents. I was raised in the New York foster-care system. When I landed on Cale Padilla's doorstep a week after I graduated high school, I stuttered over my name. He put me at ease by telling me to slow down. Arriving at his ranch was the best thing that happened to me up to that point, so I told him to call me Lucky."

Her mouth dropped open. "I didn't know you were raised in foster care."

"Why would you?" He snapped the bag closed. "It's not a first-date kind of discussion. More like a third."

He grinned so she wouldn't see the hurt inside him. She must have picked up on his discomfort, and that mask of pity was replaced by a far more impish look. "This might be stretching it, but the rehearsal dinner could be called our first date. Then the wedding was our second, and dinner last night was our third."

"If that's your idea of dating," he laughed.

"No, but this isn't my idea of an engagement, either." She giggled, and the absurdity of the situation seemed to overtake both of them. Her giggles turned into full-blown gales of laughter until she doubled over. "I haven't laughed like that in forever."

"Well, if we can't laugh at ourselves…" He stopped and let one last chuckle escape. Then he wiped a tear from the side of her eye, the softness of her skin a balm to his calluses.

"You're a good man, Lucas Harper."

She neared him, and he removed his cowboy hat, resting it next to his leg. The scent of wildflowers drifted toward him, and he knew he'd always associate the smell of them with his Lizzie. He stepped toward her, but the sound of hooves in the background caused her to jump away from him.

JR approached, and he directed his gaze at the fence, repaired and good as new. "Tammy sent me to tell you your dinner's getting cold, but I should've known better than to volunteer to check on the engaged couple." A twinkle sparked in his eye, and he busted out laughing. "When you're done here, it's spooky story night." He made ghost noises and then clucked his tongue, leading his horse away from them. "Don't worry. I'll keep it tame for the kiddos."

The moment for kissing her had already passed. Without a word, Lucky mounted his horse and headed back to the campsite.

SPOOKY STORY NIGHT was always Lizzie's favorite part of the roundups. With the cattle grazing in their fall pasture, JR popped popcorn over the campfire before tomorrow's ride led them home. The rhythmic sound of the kernels exploding should have lightened her mood, but one glance at Lucky sent her spirits plummeting again.

He hadn't said a word after JR had interrupted them earlier that evening. Who could blame him? Here he'd told her something deeply personal about growing up in the foster-care system, and she'd ended up in tears from laughing. What he must think of her and her manners. She was mortified at her treating anybody with anything less than the utmost respect. In just a week, Lucky's perception of her mattered a great deal.

Instead of getting comfortable, she found she couldn't enjoy herself while knowing he thought less of her for her reaction to his childhood. Resolved, she rose and tapped his shoulder. "Have you seen the different flavors Tammy brought along with her for sprinkling on the popcorn? There's butter, cheddar cheese, cinnamon sugar and more."

"Plain works for me." Lucky kept his gaze on the fire.

From across the way, JR laughed. "Son, she's trying to get you alone."

Even in the dim light, she noted that Lucky's cheeks blushed to a deep red under that tan of his. "Right."

Everyone's gazes seemed to be on them as she led him

toward the supply wagon. Satisfied no one could hear them, she reached for his hand. "I'm sorry..."

"For what, Lizzie?" He shoved his hands in his pockets. "I'm the one who went along with this."

That was another thing. For the life of her, she didn't understand why he didn't call her out at the beginning, when everyone congratulated them at the stable. "Why haven't you said anything?" She drew in a deep breath and exhaled. "That's not why I dragged you over here. I have to say this, or I won't be able to enjoy tonight. Please let me finish and don't distract me."

"I'm distracting?" His wicked grin kicked her in the gut. He leaned against the supply wagon. "That's nice to know."

Did the man not understand his appeal with that cowboy hat hung low, shading his eyes? And that didn't even take into account the flannel shirt stretched tight across his shoulders...

She pulled herself together. "I'm sorry for laughing earlier."

He frowned. "Why? You weren't laughing at me. Sometimes a good laugh is exactly what the body needs."

"Then why did you leave so suddenly after JR told us dinner was ready?"

He raised his eyebrows. "Guess we both find each other a tad distracting." His low but steady tone sent a thrill through her. Despite everything, she stood there, grinning like she'd already eaten the bucket of popcorn. He continued, "And considering I have a full rodeo slate ahead of me, one of us had to dial it back. Tomorrow, I leave for Casper."

Cold creek water couldn't have put more of a damper on her.

He just confirmed that he had no intention of settling here, no intentions with her.

"Aunt Lizzie! Lucky?" Audrey's voice reached them.

"Over here." Lucky responded faster than she could, and Audrey headed their way.

"Zack said he's gonna eat all your popcorn." Audrey pushed up her purple glasses. "I won't let him."

Lizzie hid her smile at her niece's concern. She walked over and scooped her into her arms, thankful for the interruption that came before she did something foolish, like ask Lucky to reconsider his plans and stay at the ranch. He was a rodeo cowboy with his own life to lead, just as she had hers. "JR makes enough for everyone in Violet Ridge. That's probably just Zack's way of saying he's tired of waiting for us."

Audrey indicated she wanted down. Once her feet were back on the ground, a good place for them rather than hovering in the air, as hers had been just a few minutes earlier, she ran over to Lucky.

"Zack said the stories are gonna be scary." She bit her lip and squished her nose. "I don't like scary stories."

Lizzie kept a straight face. "I'll tell JR to tell some funny ones, too."

Audrey grinned and then yawned. "Good, because I'm tired from waiting for the tooth fairy. I still can't believe she got away."

"You have the dollar, though," Lucky said, as he hefted Audrey into his arms and carried her back to the campsite.

Even with the smoke and the light, the firmament of stars winked at her as if letting her know that even for one night, all was right with the world. Lucky's nearby presence added to that, but she couldn't commit to anything knowing he wasn't staying in Violet Ridge. Her chest constricted at the very thought of leaving the ranch to follow him.

After whispering to JR to take it easy with the stories, she settled next to Lucky. He smiled and held up his bucket of popcorn, offering to share with her. "The cattle are lowing and are just fine. Go with the flow and lose yourself in the story."

Audrey tucked into Lucky's side, and Zack sidled up next to Lizzie. "I'll share my popcorn with you, Aunt Lizzie."

He held out his bowl, and Lizzie smiled. "I'd be honored to share your popcorn, Zack."

Lucky leaned his head in her direction. "Aunt Lizzie suits you. So does the glow from the fire."

Her insides warmed, and she settled in her spot, intent on staying in the moment. JR began weaving words together in spellbinding fashion, keeping them all on the edge of their seats. Zack snuggled up to her, and his soft, downy hair brushed against her flannel shirtsleeve. He shoveled popcorn into his mouth without taking his eyes off JR, hanging on the foreman's description of the stinky sneakers that could walk on their own.

She glanced over at Audrey, concerned about whether the story was too intense, but she needn't have worried. Audrey wore a content look and her eyes were half-closed. Every few seconds, her head would jerk up, and she gazed at JR like she was trying to piece together what she'd missed.

Lizzie transferred her gaze to Lucky, the tenderness in his eyes striking. He'd be wonderful with his own children someday. That was, if he ever settled in one place long enough. The man lived in a combination RV and horse trailer while she lived and breathed the happenings of the Double I Ranch. There was no future for them, even if everyone else was convinced their future was as bright as the glow of the fire.

For now, though, she let herself be lulled by the snap and crackle of the flickering flames.

"DO I KNOW how to put everyone to sleep, or do I?" JR looked pleased with his pronouncement and then excused himself.

Lucky remained behind. It was hard to move considering Audrey was splayed across him, her deep breaths proof she was sound asleep. These types of memories were precious, and he should know. Growing up in foster care, he never knew where he'd be sleeping the following week.

There was that one month he'd stayed in three different foster homes. He'd never forget the couple who'd barged into his current foster home and accused him of planting a six-pack of beer in their son's room. The man, who was the best friend of Lucky's foster father, had railed at him, his face mere inches away from Lucky's own, each sentence louder than the last, while the man's son stood behind him, out of sight, sneering at Lucky. That night, the state worker had arrived at the foster home and accused him of underage possession while removing him from the house, unwilling to give Lucky the benefit of the doubt. Fortunately, he'd turned eighteen and graduated high school soon thereafter. For one of his last projects, he'd written a report about cowboys and had been enthralled by the photos of majestic sunsets and mountains hinting at natural wonders unlike any he'd ever seen.

That had spurred him to buying a one-way ticket out west, where he stumbled onto Cale's ranch. Cale and Vivi had brought him into their fold and taught him the ways of cowboy and rodeo life. After Cale and Vivi had welcomed their fourth grandchild into their family, Lucky had moved on to the rodeo circuit and responded to anyone who sent out a plea for help. During his second season, he'd met

Will and then they'd added Sabrina to their little family a couple of years later.

Moving on had always served him well. A sharp stabbing pain went through him at having to do the same once more.

How he'd extricate himself from Audrey without waking her up was as baffling as how he'd leave Violet Ridge without his heart breaking. Lizzie Irwin had no idea of how appealing she was. With her head bent in slumber against Zack's, she was even more beautiful.

A coyote's howl cut through the night, and everyone bolted to an upright position. Lizzie's gaze was immediately focused, and Grandma Eloise and Tammy both popped out of their respective tents. They hustled Zack and Audrey away, and Lizzie joined JR, their heads huddled in deep conversation. Lucky hurried to join them as Moose rushed over from his area of slumber by the fire.

"How can I help?" Lucky offered, unwilling to wait around for any interlopers to harm anyone at the campsite or any of the cattle.

Lizzie glanced his way. "Guard the camp."

While he loved those kids like they were his own niece and nephew, he wanted to ride the range. "Tammy and Grandma Eloise can do that." Lucky decided to plead his case. "I've been on plenty of night watches."

JR nodded. "We always pair up if we're riding horses around the perimeter at night. He would round out the search party."

She seemed to absorb the advice of her foreman and nodded. "Okay, then. JR, you and Sweeney ride south with Moose while Lucky and I head north. We'll meet you on the other side of the pasture."

In no time, he and Lizzie were riding the open range, side by side. The smoky smell of the campfire dissipated the farther they traveled. Only the soft lowing of the cattle and the light sound of the horses' hooves trotting along the grassy plain broke the silence of the night. He glanced at her, alert and on guard, her spine straight as she and Andromeda created an impressive sight. Another memory to file and cherish after he moved on to the next rodeo.

"Thanks for recruiting me on your team," Lucky said.

She pulled up on the reins and searched the area, vigilant for any signs of wildlife or other disturbances. "That's not even a dent in all I owe you for what you're doing for me."

She still didn't get it. She thought he was doing this for her when the pull of her family was everything. His chest tightened, the sharp pain forcing him to confront the truth. That was why he'd gone along with the setup, but that wasn't why he continued the farce any longer. Lizzie was a strong, independent woman, a force to be reckoned with, and he'd also seen glimpses of her caring nature. Her layers reflected a yearning for someone to see past the polish and let her be Lizzie, efficient to the core with the added bonuses of laughter and affection.

"You let me into your family for a week. That's enough for me." He couldn't be greedy and expect someone like her to want him as a permanent fixture in her life.

"You deserve more than a week, Lucky Harper. Don't cut yourself short." Her voice grew deep. Another howl cut through the mountainside, and she dug her heels into Andromeda's side, sending the Appaloosa into a gallop.

Lucky did likewise to Margarita until he caught up to her. They kept pace with each other, riding to protect the cattle and the loved ones as much as for the pure enjoyment of a midnight gallop under the stars. Finally, she transitioned from galloping to a brisk trot, and he kept up with her, Margarita more than capable of doing whatever he asked of her. The trot turned into a canter, and she led Andromeda over to the fence they'd repaired earlier. There was no sign of any predator. She dismounted, then reached into her saddlebag and pulled out a handful of oats, taking care of her horse before turning her attention to the cattle and then, at last, him. He'd already followed her lead and was looking after Margarita, a pure joy to ride.

"Not many could have kept up with me."

"I had to learn how to adapt." Especially helpful when he always had to be ready to leave at a second's notice.

"I couldn't." Her voice cracked like her admission wrenched something deep inside of her, a perceived weakness that was anything but. "Adapt, that is. When I was six."

"When your mother died?" He moved closer to her and away from Margarita. She gave a brief nod, and his heart ached for that little girl. "You were so young."

She turned her back to him under the guise of watching over the cattle, but he understood why. Sometimes it was easier to talk with no one's eyes on you—people could make rush judgments on something they didn't understand or want to fathom. "And I had the ranch to sustain me, along with Jeff, Ben and Dad. I had everything I could ever want at my fingertips."

Wants and needs were different. He knew that better than anyone. He held her, her back pressed against his front, willing to be a part of her world and listen for a little while. "Kids need a parent or a caring adult looking out for them. What happened to your mother?"

"The doctors discovered her stage-four cancer right after she and Dad separated. They reconciled after that, but the end came quickly." Lizzie didn't glance his way, but he listened with a stillness that equaled the surrounding night. "Then Dad threw himself into his work. For so long, all he did was work, and his distance put up a wall between him and my brothers. I think he was devastated when Jeff came home from college and announced he was going to law school, following Ben's decision to join the military a year before."

"And you stepped into the void." He could see Lizzie with a stiff upper lip, so efficient in her tasks that even those close to her forgot about her caring heart and need for approval.

"It wasn't hard. I love this ranch." At last she turned to him, her face showing how conflicted she was. "I feel like I'm letting everyone down by keeping up with this sham of an engagement."

Now he understood her better. A father, caught up in his grief, projected responsibility onto a young girl's shoulders, a girl too young for such a large load, and he should know. That kind of responsibility before you were ready for it was overwhelming. Even the strongest shoulders needed rest and recovery, or, at the very least, another person to lighten the load.

"People love you, Lizzie." She arched an eyebrow as if she expected him to still call her Elizabeth. He brushed his finger against her smooth cheek. "You're always going to be Lizzie to me. Elizabeth is the more formal side you present to the world, but I saw you a bit ago with Zack snuggled up against you. You love being Aunt Lizzie. It's just another side of you, one you shouldn't be afraid to let everyone see."

"Does that mean I get to call you Lucas?"

He chuckled at the challenge in her voice. "I chose Lucky, and it's your choice from here of whether you prefer Lizzie or Elizabeth. You have wonderful memories of being Lizzie to your mom." It was his turn to watch the cattle and search the area for any signs of anything in their midst that could sneak up and attack at a second's notice. "You're reconnecting with that side of you, and the good that comes with it. But I'll respect your decision about your name."

"So Lucas brings back bad memories." She fixed him with a curious stare until he had no choice but to look at her.

He shrugged. "Let's just say it doesn't evoke any good ones." She was bright and light, and he didn't want to ruin this moment with bringing up his past. He stepped back, before those dark moments threatened to take away everything again.

"And yet you didn't lose your innate optimism." She reached for the sides of his flannel shirt and pulled him back toward her. "I think it's time for you to have one good memory of someone saying your real name, Lucas."

He didn't object when she brought him so close he could feel her breath on his neck. She kept her long fingers curled around his shirt, the knuckles brushing against the cotton of his T-shirt. Her green gaze met his own, and he nodded. "Are you always right, Elizabeth?"

"Just about the important things, and that's Lizzie to you." An impish gleam he'd never seen before twinkled in those bright emeralds.

He lowered his lips to hers, and shivers cascaded to his toes. She kept her hands between them as he curled his arms around her waist. The kiss deepened, and it was like the stars sparkled even brighter in this moment. The sweet scent of wildflowers tickled his nose along with the salty goodness of the popcorn, and he lost track of time and everything around them until a single solitary howl brought him to his senses.

They backed away, and the sound of hooves barreling toward them sent them to their respective horses. She mounted Andromeda with an ease he envied and pulled up on the reins. While JR and Sweeney were still specks in the distance with Moose trotting alongside, she clucked her tongue for Andromeda to hold up.

"You know, maybe we've been approaching this all wrong," she said, hesitating before licking her lips. "We're both intelligent people. It's time for us to find a way to move forward and begin something instead of ending it outright."

Hope flickered in him and then exploded out of the chute while he steadied Margarita with a firm grip on the reins. She found him, Lucky Harper, intelligent, and this could be the start of a real family. He nodded. "Beginnings herald promise. I've always looked forward to whatever life holds on the horizon."

Then JR and Sweeney crystallized into view, no longer silhouettes, with their features defined, their gazes on full alert about whatever might threaten the well-being of this ranch.

Lizzie's home and place of employment, where people looked up to her and counted on her sound judgment.

"Then it's settled." She smiled, the moonlight creating a soft glow around her that he'd never forget. Same as he'd never forget her, but he couldn't accept what she was offering.

"Lizzie, the rodeo is my new beginning this year."

And just like that, her posture stiffened in the saddle. "I see."

JR and Sweeney approached, and they all conferred together. Lizzie and JR headed toward the sound, while Sweeney and Lucky agreed to take the first shift guarding the pasture perimeter.

Thankful for one memory where someone called him by his given name, he regretted it would be the last kiss he and Lizzie would ever share together. He saw the level of respect Sweeney and JR afforded her as the owner's daughter, who'd eventually take over the care of the ranch. That type of respect had been hard-earned over a number of years. If anyone found out that this engagement wasn't real, she could lose that respect, no matter that she'd started this as a way of protecting her father on his special day. He wouldn't let that happen.

The same bittersweet feeling clenched his chest now. He and Butterscotch would leave after the roundup with the memory of that kiss sustaining him while his heart once again shattered into a thousand pieces.

CHAPTER ELEVEN

WITH LAST WEEK'S cattle roundup in the rearview mirror, Lizzie had business in town at the architect's office that couldn't wait any longer. Running behind this afternoon, she arrived with only a minute to spare. She listened as Mr. Krakowski elaborated on why they'd have to delay the construction until next spring. In order to proceed, he needed the down payment now for the cost of the materials. With Dad and Evie in Hawaii, she had no choice but to cut the check from her personal account. Once they'd returned, she'd have to come clean to her father about everything and get reimbursed then.

What would she do if Dad wasn't on board with the new construction? This was a sizable amount of money. She didn't hesitate to sign her name. Her father always looked out for the employees. She just needed to be open with him and confide in him the reasons behind her decision.

Thanking the head architect, she left the building and stopped short on the sidewalk. Was that Jeff leaving Wayne Coltrane Realty?

Maybe her brother and Nicole had changed their minds during the roundup and decided to move to Violet Ridge after all. Instead of managing the Double I by herself, it would become a family enterprise. For the past ten years, she believed she'd be her father's successor, having toiled in the stable and out in the pastures, birthing and vaccinating calves and taking over the barn management after

Sabrina and Ty married and rejoined the rodeo circuit on a part-time basis.

The topsy-turvy nature of it all brought back the mixed emotions, but Dad would be even happier when he returned, if that was even possible, at this latest development. While it wasn't her ideal choice, she couldn't blame her father for wanting his family around and working together. Besides, it would be fun watching Audrey and Zack grow up, something she wouldn't have been able to do if they had continued living in Boston.

Jeff was busy talking on his cell and must not have seen her. She yelled out his name, and he glanced around and acknowledged her. "I didn't expect to see you in Violet Ridge this afternoon."

"I could say the same." She pointed toward the window, with its display of posted available properties in the area.

His breath hitched, and he pocketed his phone. "It's not what it looks like."

She laughed. If anyone could appreciate appearances not being what they seemed, it was her, but the evidence here was as striking as the fake diamond in the engagement ring still ensconced on her left hand. "If you're worried about my reaction to your moving back to Violet Ridge, don't be. I loved spending time with Audrey and Zack last week on the roundup. They're delightful, but I don't understand why you and Nicole don't just move into the guesthouse instead of approaching a real-estate agent for your own place." Even though she had set her sights on the guesthouse for her own use. She was getting too old to live in her father's house any longer.

Jeff shook his head. "Have time for a cup of coffee before you head back to the Double I?"

Whatever he had to talk about must be something he wanted to tell her away from the prying ears of everyone at the ranch. "Blue Skies is only a block from here. They're open for another hour."

Lizzie led her brother along Canyon Drive until it intersected with Main Street, and there was the Blue Skies Coffee House. Jeff held the door open for her, and she entered, removing her sunglasses. The cooler interior air was a pleasant change from the summer heat. Before she could make her way to the counter, a friend from high school waylaid her and exclaimed over the ring. By the time she finished their conversation, Jeff had grabbed a table, and she joined him.

He pushed a beverage toward her. "Plain black with two sugars." That was exactly how she preferred it.

"Thanks. Good powers of observation about how I drink my coffee. I'm impressed." She opened the plastic lid and let the steam and aroma waft out.

"In my profession, you have to be observant."

She kept from stating the obvious about his biggest miss, namely her and Lucky's engagement. "Well, I observed you coming out of the realtor's office. Even though I wouldn't have felt happy about it a month ago, I'm glad you and Nicole will be moving here."

Jeff held up his hand. "Slow down. We have no intention of moving to Violet Ridge."

She blew on her beverage, confused for a second before realizing she had jumped to conclusions the same way as everyone else had about her and Lucky. "Then why were you at the realtors'?" She pieced together his other actions of the past few weeks. "Does it have anything to do with why you've been asking my cowhands questions about property rights?"

"They told you. The staff is loyal to you." He used a wooden stirrer and then placed it out of reach. "My questions relate to a big case Nicole and I are working on. That was why we agreed to come to Dad's wedding."

She leaned back against the cold black metal of the iron chair. Apparently, she'd given him too much credit for choosing family over work commitments. Then she stopped herself, as she'd done the same when she hid out in the stable. "You weren't going to come otherwise?"

Jeff huffed out a breath before his shoulders fell, a sheepish look breaking out on his face. "Well, our nanny is also on vacation."

She leveled her brother a look to let him know he was treading on even thinner ice. Not coming home for his own father's wedding? She'd talked to Ben last night, his genuine regret about not coming home for the wedding evident. Ben would have been there if his military service hadn't prevented it.

In the end, though, did it matter why Jeff came to Colorado? She felt as though this was her last chance to bond. If she let it slip away...

He was family. "Maybe Zack and Audrey could visit every summer. Then you and Nicole could spend a weekend here when they're ready to fly home."

"I could talk to Nicole about that," he said, building on her effort, "but I need your help with something."

Her older brother needed her help? That was a change from the teenager who'd always shooed away his younger sister. "There's a first time for everything. Is this about your legal case or something else?"

"Actually, you're the person who can convince Dad I'm not moving back. No matter how many times I try to correct him about Nicole and myself staying in Boston, he's still holding out hope I'm going to cave." Jeff's green gaze, so like her own, met hers.

Maybe Jeff was her ace in the hole. This very situation

might help him understand how everything had snow-balled. If so, he might be able to assist her and Lucky in finding a graceful avenue of escape. "Dad has a forceful personality."

"Tell me about it. Zack reminds me of him while I see some of Mom in Audrey." Jeff looked wistful for a minute before he gripped his coffee again. "You were in kindergarten when Mom and Dad's differences caused some intense arguments. Then Mom was diagnosed with cancer and they agreed to reconcile to make her last month easier for her and us. It took Dad a long time to recover from all of that. Evie and Dad are so suited for each other. I'm glad he's happy, but my life is in Boston. I talked to Nicole, and we're flying here for Christmas with Audrey and Zack. Audrey is ecstatic about your wedding. Nicole will get in touch with you about bridal studios in Boston and coordinating dresses and tuxes on our end."

Without a reason to return in December, Lizzie had a feeling it would be a while before she saw her niece and nephew again. She had to get him to agree to visit regardless of the wedding. "Are those reservations confirmed?"

"Yes." He laughed and then sobered. "If you're worried there are too many differences between you and Lucky, like there were with Mom and Dad, don't be. I see how Lucky looks at you. That man would lasso the moon for you if you asked."

For her family, yes. For her? Not so much. The rodeo was too much of a lure for him, and she'd never leave the ranch. That thought was like a direct hit to her heart. "I'm glad you like him. He loves the Irwin family, especially Audrey and Zack."

"What's important is he loves our family for who we are, not what we own or represent." He leaned across the table. "I never understood what you saw in Jared."

She waited for those old feelings that always surfaced whenever she defended her ex in the past. Nothing. "Jared was charming when he wanted to be, but it didn't take long for him to show his true self to me."

For a long time, she thought she'd fallen in love with Jared, a man who showed one front to the world while only wanting what was best for him, but she hadn't. Time had finally helped put that relationship into perspective. She'd fallen for his smooth lines and his polished exterior until that fateful day when she discovered his true intent of using her as the means to a promotion that depended on her father's signature on a contract. He'd figured out the best way to get close to Dad was to cozy up to her. When she'd confronted him, he'd defended himself until he ran out of excuses and turned on her, calling her cold and stiff. He'd been a wolf in an expensive suit and cowboy boots. Lucky, though? He was the same inside and out, a true gentleman to the core.

She twisted the engagement ring on her finger, the adhesive tape a little looser. Some of it must have fallen off during the roundup. She'd best fix that when she arrived home. Then she realized if this was a real engagement, she wouldn't care what size of ring it was. It was the thought that counted.

"You've come a long way since then. I see it in the eyes of all the cowhands. They hold you in high esteem. So does Dad." He smiled. "So will you talk to Dad for me?"

Starting off with Jeff's news would put her father in a bad mood, and then she'd have to compound it with the status of her and Lucky's relationship. Still, it had to be done. Jeff put his finger on it. She was the barn manager and working heir to one of the largest ranches in southwest Colorado. Only by telling her father the whole truth could she then work on earning back the trust she'd lose when everything came to light.

With a nod, she agreed to Jeff's request.

WITH ONLY TWENTY-FOUR hours until Lucky had to head to Casper for the next rodeo, he'd tackle the deep-cleaning chores for the RV and trailer that he never had time for during the long traveling season. This late-morning sudden storm, perfect for this dreary Wednesday, prevented him from taking Butterscotch into the corral at the Silver Horseshoe and practicing ways to shave off milliseconds from the chute release. Besides, cleaning provided a perfect excuse for remaining at Will's ranch, an unexpected detour after the roundup. Will needed an extra cowhand for vaccinations, and Lucky was more than happy for an excuse to clear his head, something he couldn't do whenever Lizzie was around. Evening practice with Will and Ty provided a double win: an excuse to be at the Silver Horseshoe all day and night to prepare for the next rodeo.

He inserted a special attachment to his vacuum and began cleaning the RV's ceiling, taking care around the corners for the little cobwebs that had sprung up. A sudden loud noise caused him to turn off the vacuum. Someone was banging on his door, and it sounded like they meant business. Since the vacuum had given him away, Lucky had no choice but to open the door. For a second, Will stood on the step before sailing past Lucky, then he removed his raincoat and planted himself on the black leather couch opposite the kitchen sink.

"Make yourself comfortable," Lucky said in a wry voice, gesturing with his arm for Will to come inside. He looked around for Sabrina but didn't see her outside the RV, so he closed the door before turning to Will, whose stony face reminded Lucky of what Will had looked like before he met Kelsea. Lucky kept his tone light. "Do you need a towel to dry off? Would you like something to drink? I can make some coffee—"

"When are you going to call off the engagement, Lucky?" Will didn't mince words and leaned his elbows on his knees. "Someone's going to get hurt the longer this goes on."

"Or we can just talk and make the both of us uncomfortable," Lucky muttered while pushing aside the vacuum.

Leaning against the refrigerator, Lucky kept his feet on the carpeted floor and his tongue in check. Lizzie's future depended on how this conversation played out. He wouldn't do anything that might cause her pain or embarrassment.

"Tell me you met Elizabeth before a few weeks ago, and that you love her. I'll apologize and we'll never speak of this conversation again." Will's gaze never left Lucky, concern radiating out of his dark brown eyes.

"Where's Sabrina?" Lucky looked away from Will, still expecting the third member of their trio to walk in any minute.

"She and Ty just left for the rodeo, along with Genie. She mentioned something in passing, and it confirmed my suspicion that you and Elizabeth met recently." Will stood and walked over to the basket of cleaning supplies. "I've never seen someone who's in love and about to endure a brief separation lose themselves in cleaning."

Lucky raised his eyebrows, doing mental cartwheels about how to get Will off his case. Nothing came to mind. "I'd expect Kelsea to bring this up, but you?"

"You're my best friend. I don't want to see you hurt." Will didn't even blink. Instead, he just shrugged and picked up the multipurpose cleaner. "Do you want some help or are you insisting on doing everything by yourself?"

Only the pitter-patter of raindrops on the trailer's roof broke the silence that extended for a few minutes.

"If you want to start on the sink and counter, I'll clean out the refrigerator." Lucky reached for the fresh box of baking soda next to the other supplies. "So people in love can't clean their houses? I'd think wanting to impress that special person would allow for some minor chores here and there."

"You've been at the Silver Horseshoe since the roundup." Will sprayed some cleaner on the countertop. "Either you had a fight, or you were never engaged. Since you've been walking around muttering goodbye to everything when you think no one is listening with an expression that portends doom, I'm guessing the latter."

Lucky plucked a new trash bag off the roll and snapped it open. "I'm not following your reasoning, Detective Sherlock. If I look as if doomsday was upon me, wouldn't that imply Lizzie and I had a fight?"

"It's more like you're taking in every motion as if your world was about to turn on its axis, like you were never going to see us again." Will reached for a sponge, then wiped the surfaces and let out a wry chuckle. "Now that I'm saying all of this out loud, it does seem absurd."

Lucky opened the refrigerator door and began ditching all the old takeout containers into a trash bag. "Almost as much as underestimating Lizzie." He stopped what he was doing and wiped his hands with a towel. "I won't do anything to hurt her."

Will sighed and made circular motions with the sponge. "You're the most admirable person I know, Lucky. Considering what you endured growing up, that's pretty darn amazing. You could have been bitter or distrustful of people, yet you give your heart to your friends. I'm just worried whatever you two are doing is going to leave your heart shattered, same as it did when that family blamed you for the son's underage drinking."

Will was one of the few people who knew about the alcohol incident and how Lucky ended up taking the blame. At first, he believed he'd land in another foster home, but instead he'd aged out of the system and then boarded the bus to Colorado.

"Lizzie's not like that. I respect her."

Will's brow furrowed. "That's what's confusing me. Elizabeth Irwin is the most efficient, dependable neighbor around. I can't believe she'd go along with anything like this."

Which was another reason Lucky had already made up his mind to stay on the road after the next rodeo. The good part about the height of the rodeo season was that there was always one happening somewhere. With this trailer, transportation wasn't a problem.

"Just because someone's efficient doesn't mean there's not a beating heart under the surface." There was so much more to Lizzie than she let on to most people.

Will studied him. Lucky didn't squirm or budge. Then Will threw the sponge in the sink. "There's no one else around. While I don't like keeping secrets from Kelsea, I'll have your back. What's the genuine story between you and Elizabeth?"

"I won't lie to you, and I won't do anything to get between you and Kelsea." Lucky had been in town the day Will met Kelsea. Lucky had arranged to meet Will at the Violet Ridge Inn for a drink so they could catch up on what was happening in their lives, but Will had spotted the sales representative who'd come to his ranch earlier that day sleeping in the hotel lobby. When she woke up with the two of them standing there, the sparks had been evident between her and Will, and Lucky had rescheduled a time for him and Will to talk. Over the next few months, Lucky had been privileged to witness the two of them fall in love in between his various rodeo stints. "So if that means keeping my cards close to my chest for now, so be it."

Will's gaze narrowed on something to the left of Lucky, and his friend reached out his arm. He plucked a piece of paper off the refrigerator, and Lucky groaned. He'd forgotten about the itinerary he'd created for himself late last night. "Colorado, Arizona, Wyoming, Texas, Nevada." Will scanned the list. "You'll be doing a lot of traveling to qualify for the year-end finals. When will you have time to return to Violet Ridge? Plan a wedding? Spend time with your fiancée?"

Staying busy, so busy he'd collapse on his bed every night, was the only way Lucky could think of to keep from having his heart shatter into a million pieces. "Gordon already arranged everything for the wedding, and Lizzie knows what the rodeo means to me." So far, so good. Everything he said was the truth. "People without obligations travel pretty fast."

Using the same and only magnet, Will pinned the itinerary back on the refrigerator. "I might be grasping at straws, but I'd hate to think you thought of our friendship as an obligation. You and Sabrina? We're more than friends. We're family." His voice cracked, and he stilled. Then he wiped something from the corner of his eye. "You kicked up too much dust in here."

"Your friendship kept me going too many times," Lucky admitted, that same dust also lodging in his throat.

"Would it help if Kelsea and I engineered a situation so that you two could call everything off? We can host a dinner tonight for you and Elizabeth to do just that."

Lucky appreciated the offer. This was why he'd miss Will, but he had no intention of putting Will in the middle of all of this any more than he'd ask Will to keep a secret from Kelsea. "Thanks, but Lizzie and I have this under control."

Will's gaze went to the refrigerator and the itinerary. "You're not coming back, are you? At least, not for a really long time. Till the dust settles and then some."

Will knew him too well. Next year, he'd find another rodeo, one that didn't take place in Violet Ridge, to kick off his season. A clean break was always for the best, and goodbyes ranked down there with pumping out his trailer. "When Cale took me in, I found hard work and decent meals did wonders for my sleep schedule."

"We have plenty of that here at the Silver Horseshoe, and I expect you home for the holidays after you make your first appearance at the year-end finals." Will moved his arm as if he was about to hug Lucky and then thought the better of it. "I'll save this hug for then."

For Lucky, this trailer was his home, but the full impact of Will's words hit him in the gut. "Thanks for believing I'll get that far."

"You and Butterscotch are fluid in motion in the arena. You make a good team." Will reached for his raincoat, donned it and headed for the door. "Sabrina, you and I make a good team, too. Whatever you need from us, all you have to do is ask."

Will opened the door and glanced behind him. Lucky nodded as rain pelted the ground outside the trailer, and Will departed. A slow ache spread across his chest at the thought of losing the best friend he'd ever had. While he'd like nothing more than to load Butterscotch and sneak away to the Casper rodeo, he had to make one more stop before he left town. He might not say goodbye to Will, but there was one person for whom he'd set aside his dislike for goodbyes.

Somehow, he'd find the courage to speak to Lizzie one last time.

CHAPTER TWELVE

WITH HIS RV SHIPSHAPE, Lucky ran out of reasons to stall any longer. It was time to say goodbye to Lizzie and head to Casper. He left his raincoat in the mudroom of the ranch house and dried his hair before he entered the kitchen. A sugary aroma warmed him to his toes. He found Tammy sliding cookies off an aluminum sheet with Zack and Audrey on the other side of her, licking their lips.

Zack reached for one, and Tammy batted away his hand. "They have to cool off first."

Then Audrey glanced toward Lucky and launched herself at him. "You're back. Where have you been? I missed you."

Her glasses dug into his hip, but he didn't mind much. "I was at my friend Will's ranch, practicing for the next rodeo. I have to keep in shape."

"Does that mean you can't try one of my special homemade Double I Ranch cowboy cookies?" Tammy waved one under his nose before placing it back with the others. "They're JR's favorites, with cranberries, dried cherries, coconut and almonds."

His mouth watered, and he rubbed his stomach. "I always make room for your cookies, Tammy. If they taste half as good as they smell, I can see why they're JR's favorites." He grinned, glad he had plenty of time for the drive before sunset. While he technically could wait until tomorrow to leave, he didn't want to draw out the goodbye.

While he didn't like leaving Lizzie to fend off the questions about their failed engagement alone, he was so close to making the year-end finals. What other choice did he have? His dream was within reach.

"You can each eat one cookie now," Tammy said, holding up her index finger to Zack and Audrey. Then she pulled Lucky aside while untying her apron and hanging it on a nearby hook. "Can you watch them while I finish making the chicken and dumplings for the cowhands? Nicole asked if I'd watch Audrey and Zack today while she and Jeff worked in Mr. Gordon's office. Lizzie and JR rode out to check on the cattle, and Grandma Eloise is having lunch in Violet Ridge with some of the local ladies."

Lucky glanced at Audrey, who was taking small nibbles of her cookie while Zack had obviously crammed the whole cookie in his mouth. "Say no more." He knew what it was like to be passed from adult to adult, and he wouldn't let them feel unwanted. "As long as you save some for me, that is."

"As if you even had to ask. Besides, seeing you will raise Lizzie's spirits, considering how she's been moping since you've been gone." She walked over to Audrey and Zack and ruffled their hair. "Do you want to spend time with Lucky?"

Zack pulled his video-game console from his pocket and flipped open the lid. "I don't need anyone to watch me. I can keep myself occupied."

Lucky recognized Zack's defensive posture. The boy was smart, and he'd obviously figured out what was happening. "It's raining, so we can't visit the duck pond, but I seem to remember a promise from the roundup to teach you and Audrey how to whittle."

Zack's eyes lit up. "Really? With a real knife and everything?"

"I want to make a unicorn." Audrey's head nodded faster than a bucking bronc.

"It might take a few lessons before you work your way up to that." Lucky thought of what he'd need. Everything was in his trailer, which he'd parked near the stable. "Safety instructions first."

Audrey tugged on Lucky's sleeve. "I'm going to name my unicorn Lucky."

Touched at the gesture, Lucky was about to speak when Zack started first. "I guess it might pass the time. I'll go so I can keep an eye on Audrey."

Despite his grudging tone, Lucky understood too well how Zack was on the verge of a big leap, no longer a young kid but not quite a tween. With caring support around him, Zack would adapt to the changes.

"Big brother looks good on you, Zack. Wait here while I okay this with Jeff." Lucky had barely pressed send on his text when Jeff provided his approval. He placed his phone back in his pocket. "We need to make a quick stop at my trailer, and then we'll find a good, dry place for whittling."

In the mudroom, they found a stand with a host of blue-and-brown golf umbrellas, all sporting the ranch logo. Lucky borrowed one while Audrey and Zack shared one.

He opened the back door only to find gray skies continuing their deluge of rain. Gusty breezes whipped the tops of the trees, and the three rushed along the path to Lucky's trailer. He hurriedly ushered them inside.

"Wow! All of this is yours?" Audrey's eyes, magnified by the thick lenses of her purple glasses dotted thick with rain droplets, grew as wide as a rodeo champion's belt buckle.

Lucky handed her a tissue so she could dry her glasses. She thanked him while Zack climbed the two steps to Lucky's bed. "This is so cool! You can go anywhere you want. I'd drive to the Grand Canyon and sleep under the stars."

"No, you wouldn't. You'd go off somewhere and play your video game all the time." Audrey joined him and started bouncing on the bed.

"Would not," Zack argued as he mimicked her actions.

"Would, too."

"Stop!" Lucky took a deep breath. "I have to sleep on that bed, thank you very much, and I have responsibilities, too. Tonight I'm leaving for the Casper rodeo."

Audrey frowned. "You're leaving?" Her face crumpled, and she sniffled. "I thought you were marrying Aunt Lizzie."

If Lizzie was here, they might have been able to clear up the misunderstanding, once and for all. Without Lizzie, though? He gulped. "I travel for my work, Audrey."

"It's like when Joey's dad goes on trips for his job. He always comes back, and Joey says his mom takes a long bath while he and his dad go out for fast food." Lucky hid a smile at Zack's matter-of-fact tone in teaching Audrey about how the world worked.

Audrey jumped off the bed and tugged at Lucky's damp flannel shirt. "Mommy and Daddy are taking us to the Summer Send-off before we go home. Are you taking Aunt Lizzie?"

Lucky had seen signs for the festival in town, but it didn't start until this weekend during the Casper rodeo. He'd love to go with this family. Specifically, he'd love to see it through Lizzie's eyes. "I don't know."

"Dad says I can eat a corn dog. I've never had one before." Zack rubbed his stomach.

"And I've never been on a Ferris wheel before." Audrey made a circle with her index finger. "Will you be back from your rodeo in time to go with us? I won't be scared if you're on the Ferris wheel with me."

"Won't you want to go on it with your dad?" That seemed like a perfect father-daughter activity.

"I can go once with him, and once with you," Audrey pleaded, her hands clasped so tight her knuckles were turning white.

If he and Lizzie were engaged for real, he could see a little girl with Lizzie's serious expression and his curly hair, or a boy with her green eyes. They could even discuss the possibility of becoming foster parents. He dismissed the thought and contemplated Audrey's request. One return trip to Violet Ridge couldn't cause any additional permanent scarring to his heart, could it?

Zack's gaze burned into him. "We know you're busy." Zack's disappointment was clear.

Already, Zack had learned adults didn't always keep promises, a hard lesson for anyone but devastating for an eight-year-old. Lucky would already be letting down the Irwin family when they found out about him and Lizzie. He didn't want to let down Zack over this.

More time with Lizzie was a bonus. "I'll come back after the rodeo."

Audrey hugged Lucky's waist and then stepped back. "Promise?"

Lucky nodded. "Yep, and a cowboy promise is worth its weight in silver horseshoes." He glimpsed a hint of a smile on Zack's face. "And I promised to teach you how to whittle. Time's a wastin'."

The rain showed no sign of letting up, and Lucky bustled Audrey and Zack into the stable rather than getting mud all over the ranch house. Lizzie's office might be small, but that made it all the better for the first whittling lesson, as there'd be less chance of the two siblings wandering away and getting into trouble. They closed the umbrellas and said hello to the grooms.

Audrey peeked into a stall and turned toward Lucky. "What's her name?"

Lucky joined her and found the stable cat peering with one eye at them from her position of repose. "I don't know," Lucky admitted. "We'll ask Aunt Lizzie the next time we see her."

"She needs a good name." Audrey gave one nod, as if emphasizing her point.

They entered Lizzie's office and flicked on the light. Lucky placed the damp paper bag on Lizzie's desk before propping the door open with her boot scraper. A whiff of wildflowers hung in the air, and the small space seemed imprinted with traces of Lizzie: her day planner, a tube of ChapStick and a container of her preferred hand lotion. Lucky upended the bag, and the contents spilled out on the desk.

"What's with the potato peelers?" Zack grasped one and scowled. "I thought we were going to use real knives."

"In good time. Everyone starts somewhere." Cale had been patient with him when Lucky arrived on his ranch and coached him through everything step by step, and he'd do the same with Audrey and Zack. "And that somewhere is safety."

Zack looked bored, and Lucky saw Zack's hand moving toward his pocket, no doubt reaching for his ever-present video console. "Give me a chance before you reach for your game."

Zack rolled his eyes. "I thought you said this was gonna be fun."

"That depends on you." Lucky walked to the other side of the desk and sat in Lizzie's chair. "But it's no fun if you accidentally cut yourself."

Zack shrugged, but Lucky noticed he listened to the rules of how to handle a knife. "Remember, a dull knife is

more dangerous than a sharp one." Then Lucky unwrapped
the three bars of soap and handed one to Zack and one to
Audrey. "We're just going to practice on this today. If you
enjoy this hobby and if I have permission from your parents, I'll see if I can buy you beginner knives to keep here
on the ranch for your visits."

Zack's eyes lit up, and then he sighed. "Mom will never
go for that."

"That's why we're working with soap and then stripping bark from those three pieces of wood so you can prove
you're ready for the responsibility. That, and being open
and honest." Guilt at his failure to communicate the truth
to the Irwin family, who'd taken him into their house over
the past few weeks, gnawed at him.

"But soap? What can you do with soap?" Zack scoffed.

"Plenty." Lucky reached for his knife and one of the
pristine bars of soap. In a few minutes, he carved a turtle.
Zack relented once he saw the finished shape.

"Okay, maybe I'll try it." Zack strove for nonchalance,
but the way he leaned forward gave everything away. He
was hooked.

Lucky showed Audrey and Zack how to shave the soap
with the vegetable peeler. In no time, Zack proved himself
capable of handling a bigger challenge, and Lucky showed
him how to strip bark from sticks.

"Nice job, Zack," Lucky praised him, and the joy on
Zack's face was everything. "We have a little more time
until lunch will be ready, so why don't you try my knife
while I'm right here?"

"Really? Thanks. I remember everything you said. Only
use it with an adult present. Always sheath the knife when
not in use." Zack recounted the rest of Lucky's lecture, and
Lucky felt like a proud uncle.

Lucky waited while Zack donned the safety gloves, and

then he demonstrated how to use the pocketknife under careful supervision. Zack made his first few cuts and then folded the knife. He placed it on the desk before he jumped to his feet. "Aunt Lizzie! Come look."

Lizzie stood in the doorway, her red hair damp and tousled from the rain. "What do we have here?"

Zack held up his stick. "I'm making a wand so I can be a wizard."

Audrey jumped from her chair and hugged her aunt before producing a mottled block of white soap. The little girl placed hers next to Lucky's turtle. "My turtle doesn't look as good. Guess it's 'cause I have a peeler and not a knife." She shrugged and smiled. "It's fun, but Grandma Eloise taught me how to cast with knitting needles. I like making a blanket for Teddy better."

Lizzie's eyebrows raised a fraction of an inch, and she wiggled her finger at Lucky. "Can I see you alone for a minute?"

Lucky pocketed his knife and nodded. "Sure thing." He winked at the kids. "Guess she's jealous and wants her own whittling lesson." He followed Lizzie, who stopped near the archway of the stable. "I'm supposed to be taking care of Audrey and Zack while Tammy makes chicken and dumplings, and their parents work."

"And how is treating them differently taking care of them? Did you hear Audrey?" Lizzie tapped her red cowboy boot against the straw floor. "I can't blame her for not enjoying your whittling lesson seeing as how she's using a vegetable peeler while Zack's using a knife."

"Wait a second." Lucky bristled at Lizzie's implication. "I'd never be so unkind as to make one of them feel inferior."

He'd had enough of that growing up with some of his foster parents showing preferential treatment to their biological children. Not all foster parents were like that. There were good people out there caring for the children who came into their home, and Lucky hoped someday to be one of the good ones.

Lizzie kept tapping her boot in time with the rhythm of the rain. "It looked like you were favoring Zack."

"What I was doing was taking their individual personalities into account. Audrey is younger and has some depth-perception issues." Lucky stayed calm and continued, "Her fine motor skills aren't as advanced as Zack's. If she likes knitting and sticks with it, that will help with her hand-eye coordination. She also fidgeted a lot during my safety talk. On the other hand, Zack listened and recited every rule back to me. He's a couple of years older than Audrey, and he finished his task faster, so I let him use my pocketknife once. That's all."

"Sorry. I should have listened first." Lizzie stared at him, the left corner of her lips scrunching upward in a half smile. "We just had our first fight."

Their gazes met, a plum opportunity for him to finish what hadn't even started, but he wanted more time with her. The mere thought of wanting to have something meaningful with Lizzie—a family, where they'd go through life together left him a little dizzy.

The clean lines of the luxurious stable came into view, a reminder they were from two different worlds. His life was on the road, and this was his big year on the circuit. And if he didn't make the finals this go-around, there was always next season, or the one after that. Have RV, will travel.

"A fight like that could lead to a broken engagement quite easily, but Tammy's making chicken and dumplings. You can't expect me to miss that, could you?" He kept his tone light.

"That would be too mean. After all, Tammy's chicken

and dumplings are legendary and can't be missed." Her eyes started twinkling, and then she held out her hand. "Friends again?"

Friends. Could he deal with just that?

He slid his hand in hers, wanting more, specifically another kiss, so he could discover if his strong reaction to that first one was a fluke. As matters stood, he had no choice but to settle for this truce and her friendship. "It takes more than a little disagreement for me to break a friendship. I'm always there for my friends."

They heard the kids' voices before the pair appeared before them. "Aunt Lizzie, is it lunchtime?" Zack rubbed his tummy for emphasis. "I'm starving."

She laughed. "I'm sure Tammy's ready for us."

As they darted out of the stable under the umbrellas, Lucky caught sight of his RV through the misty rain. He should get in the trailer now and head for the next rodeo, and the next, and the next. Then, he remembered his promise to Audrey and Zack that he'd return from the rodeo for the Summer Send-off, and he groaned. Promises were forever, and this time at Violet Ridge was just temporary.

Lizzie glanced at him, and he longed to turn this friendship into a permanent relationship so he could share how beautiful she was with her hair wet from the rain, her cheeks kissed from the wind. He longed to take her aside and tell her how she made him feel inside—special and cared for and treasured. And yet he was a simple guy from upstate New York, a far cry from the man she deserved. So he only smiled and held the umbrella over Audrey.

"Last one to the chicken and dumplings is a wet blanket," he said while picking up the pace.

LIZZIE WALKED AN imaginary diagonal line along the pasture adjoining the stable. The ground was rather soft from yesterday's constant storms, but not so saturated as to cause trouble for any of the horses. While yesterday had been gray and dreary, today's dawn heralded blue skies, perfect for being on the range, checking on cattle and giving Andromeda free rein to gallop.

With the help of the youngest groom, Roy, she finished the morning chores and began turning out the horses. She paused at Butterscotch's stall. Should she allow Butterscotch some freedom in the pasture before the horse left for this weekend's rodeo? She pulled out her phone to text Lucky when a voice called out behind her.

"I saw the other horses going out to the pasture and realized it was time to load Butterscotch into the trailer. You made a good call yesterday asking me to stay for one more day because of the rain."

She swiveled and found Lucky there, wearing his old brown cowboy hat. "The flooding on the local interstate has cleared. Do you need some help putting him in his trailer?"

"Are you offering your services or Roy's?" His eyes held a hint of challenge.

"While Roy is most capable, I think you need my personal touch." Then she blushed, as that could easily be misconstrued. "Um—"

He chuckled. "I know what you meant." Then he leaned against the side of the stable wall and grinned. "A wanderer like me could get spoiled by your personal touch."

A wanderer. Even after a couple of weeks on the finest ranch in Colorado, he still couldn't wait to hit the road while she cherished every minute on the ranch.

The stable cat investigated the source of the voices and wound her lithe body around Lucky's legs. He bent and lavished affection on her while the independent cat lapped up the attention. "You're spoiling her."

"What's her name? Audrey asked me yesterday, and I didn't know it." Lucky gave the cat a pat and stood straight again.

"Name?" Lizzie racked her brain.

"Everyone, even a stable cat, should have a name," he said.

"Let me think. I'm trying to remember what Sabrina called her when she had kittens last year. Will took one, and so did his uncle Barry for Regina's feed-and-seed in town. Good stable cats are snapped up around here." The cat came over to Lizzie and she petted her. "I don't think we've ever named her, and this sounds personal for you. I'm open to suggestions."

He approached Butterscotch and pulled an apple slice from his pocket. "We should probably consult Audrey." Butterscotch nudged his shoulder as if asking for another slice. "She's really something. Last night when I told her and Zack goodbye for now, she reminded me about the Summer Send-off and showed me the app. She already knows what she wants to do, and she's only six. When I was her age…my mom took off. New York State couldn't track down my father, and so it began."

He'd been younger than Audrey when he entered the system, younger than she was when her mother died. He treated others with compassion, and her heart broke for the little boy who'd witnessed that.

The cat crossed back to him. Beyond the stable doors, Lizzie spotted a glimpse of Grandma Eloise, who'd come home yesterday from her lunch with a mouthful about how the town was still buzzing with news of hers and Lucky's engagement.

"How about Weezie? I think that's a nickname for Eloise."

"I like that." He scratched the cat behind her furry ear.

"Congratulations, Weezie. May you live long and guard the stable well."

In no time, Lizzie helped Lucky load Butterscotch into the trailer. The gelding acted almost giddy at the thought of a ride, as if it was an adventure of a lifetime. Lucky's eyes seemed brighter than usual as well, also as if he couldn't wait to get on the open road. Who could blame him? He must have such an exciting life on the road, whereas Lizzie was always content knowing she belonged here on the ranch.

He dipped his hat in her direction, and his gaze lingered on her, almost as if he was wondering whether he should kiss her goodbye. She'd like nothing better.

Grandma Eloise approached them, her cane sinking into the softer ground. "Tammy sent me with something to tide you over until you return next week, a care package of food. I personally baked the apple pie yesterday, and JR thought you might like that book you two discussed on the roundup." She handed Lucky a tote bag. "I'll be here until Evie gets back from her honeymoon, so I expect to see you sooner rather than later."

He leaned over and kissed her cheek. "Thank you kindly." When he stepped back, Lizzie thought she saw his eyes misting. He'd probably never had anyone give him a care package before. "This is really something."

"Don't stop kissing your fiancée on my account." Grandma Eloise tapped her cane on the ground twice as if for extra emphasis, and then started back toward the ranch house.

Lizzie caught the older woman glancing back their way.

"I don't want to disappoint her." She closed her eyes and puckered.

When nothing happened, she opened her eyes and found Lucky leaning against the trailer, a few steps away, definitely too far away to kiss her. Why? Didn't he find her attractive?

"Yes, I do, and I want to kiss you." Lucky approached, and she gasped as she realized she'd asked her last question aloud. "But for the right reasons. Not for anyone else. Just you."

She shuffled her boots, suddenly self-conscious. "Oh."

She fidgeted with the engagement ring, and it slipped off her finger and plopped on the dirt. He reached down and brushed it off. "Wouldn't want you to lose this." He slid it back on her finger, and goose bumps dotted her arms. "If you want to have it resized while I'm gone, go ahead."

She made a note to add an extra layer of adhesive tape to the back of the ring as soon as Lucky left. "No. Anyway, I'll be giving it back to you soon, and it's not like this is a real ring, right?"

"Huh?" He leaned back against the trailer once more. "It's real."

She chuckled. "Of course it is, but the stones are fake, right? I mean who carries around a genuine diamond ring in a trailer?" Her chuckles faded in the wind, and her cheeks grew warm as the silence stretched out. The diamond caught the sunlight, and the warmth expanded to her neck and chest as well. "These are genuine diamonds?"

He nodded. "I thought Cherry was ready to get married. She was, but to someone else. I'd been planning on asking Will to keep it in his safe, but I never did."

Butterscotch made his presence known, neighing and pawing the bottom of the trailer as if he wanted to get the show on the road.

"I'll wrap this again so I don't lose it." Her stomach was churning at his entrusting her with a valuable engagement ring.

He stepped toward her, taking her hands in his, sending shivers down her spine. Why did the worst person for her, a wanderer to her homebody self, elicit this type of reaction in her? "For the record, I wouldn't have bought you a diamond ring."

"You wouldn't?"

He shook his head. "I'd have bought you a ruby to match your hair and your fiery spirit. See you after the rodeo."

"Better yet, how about I kiss your cheek for luck? Just for us, and not for show."

She stood on her tiptoes, their hands still entwined. Her lips came in contact with the bristly stubble on his cheek, and his closeness erased everything but the happiness inside her.

He grinned, rubbing her kiss into his skin. "Now I'm sure to win."

She twisted the ring as he climbed into the front seat of the truck that hauled the trailer/RV unit and waved as he started up the engine. Rubies were her favorite, but she'd never told anyone else that.

Somehow, he knew her better than people who'd known her for her whole life. What would it be like to be with a special someone, sharing more roundups, more sunrise rides and, most of all, more magnetic kisses?

His trailer became a speck on the road and then disappeared altogether. Too bad the wanderer wasn't that special someone.

CHAPTER THIRTEEN

LIZZIE TAPPED HER ankle boots on the plush carpet in her father's office. This Sunday morning was almost over, and Jeff was still engrossed in his legal case, so much so he hadn't even noticed her approach. Or he wasn't acknowledging her. She held her composure together for Audrey and Zack, who'd been looking forward to the Summer Send-off all weekend. She was proud of how they'd completed all their chores yesterday and today in anticipation of the event. They were becoming real cowhands.

When her brother still didn't acknowledge her presence, she cleared her throat from the doorway. "Jeff? Audrey and Zack are ready and waiting."

He lowered his reading glasses and placed them next to his laptop. "For what? We aren't leaving for Boston until Friday."

"The Summer Send-off, remember? You promised to go with them, and I moved up the date since you said you had online appointments all day tomorrow. Are you always like this back home? They'll grow up before you know it and you'll have missed it." Lizzie couldn't believe her brother had already forgotten the Summer Send-off, if it ever was on his radar to begin with.

"We have an excellent nanny." Jeff picked up his glasses once more. "Nicole and I are putting in extra hours here since we're away from our paralegals and staff."

"Then next year we'll make arrangements to cover for

that, but this year, it would be nice if you spent time with Zack and Audrey and made some memories." Her point clear, Lizzie left the room and then placed her back against the wall, purposefully bringing her head in contact with the solid surface.

Why could she confront her brother about his life and not her father about hers? She'd do just that once Dad returned from Hawaii. Hopefully, she'd changed enough, become strong enough for that. Immediately, she thought of Lucky and how forthright he'd been with her about everything and wished for some of it to have rubbed off on her.

At least she spoke her mind to Jeff. The rest was up to him. She hurried to the living room, where Zack and Audrey were waiting. She clapped her hands and pasted on a smile. "It's Aunt Lizzie's turn to spoil you. What are we waiting for?"

"Hopefully me?" Her breath escaped as she recognized Lucky's voice from behind her. "I got your text about the day change and hurried back."

"Lucky!" Audrey ran to him and hugged him. "You won!"

Zack hurried over and gave an awkward shrug, although he looked like he really wanted to hug the rodeo cowboy. "Congratulations."

Lucky reached out his arm and included Zack in a quick group embrace before stepping back and showing everyone his new belt buckle. "I left the prize saddle in the trailer."

"I watched on television. You were amazing," Lizzie said, letting pride for his achievement wash over her.

Those blue eyes glinted, and he grinned. "It was your kiss that did it. You're my lucky charm."

Audrey tugged on his shirt. "Are you going with us to the Summer Send-off?" Then her eyes lit up behind her purple glasses. "Can I call you Uncle Lucky now?"

Lizzie reached for Audrey's hand at the same time Lucky did, and she backed away. She met Lucky's gaze, a misty film rising to the occasion. "How about you wait until after the wedding?" Lizzie asked.

Audrey seemed to take Lizzie's request in stride, but Lizzie saw an unfamiliar tic in Lucky's jaw as if she'd let him down. Being their uncle, anyone's uncle, was an honor Lucky would cherish.

THE AROMA OF grilled meat tempted Lucky's taste buds along with the sugary smell of funnel cakes. He waited outside the makeshift row of bathrooms for Audrey and Zack. Lizzie was a few yards away, lost in conversation with another rancher, something about the preferred method of branding cattle. She shook the rancher's hand and then strolled over to him, her head stuck in the paper map everyone received upon entrance. Her auburn hair was piled upon her head in a messy bun that complemented her summer outfit of a short-sleeve plaid shirt, jeans and ankle boots. She even made her casual clothes look smart.

Another reminder of how they were worlds apart.

When she reached his side, she didn't glance up from the pamphlet. "Where do you want to stage the breakup? At the Wild West show? On one of the rides?"

He placed his hand on the paper and lowered it until she met his gaze. "I appreciate the efficiency behind that statement, but look around you."

Crowds bustled about the fairgrounds on this beautiful Sunday afternoon. Vendors barked out their food options, and while the thought of trying fried jellybeans held an alluring appeal, what he really wanted was to get Lizzie alone and to himself.

"Exactly. Many people will witness our fight." Lizzie tapped her ankle boots on the cement sidewalk, a sure sign of how nervous she was. "It'll be the talk of Violet Ridge that our engagement is over."

"While it might be a sight more efficient to end this in public, I won't do it in front of Zack and Audrey." Many a night he'd heard adults fighting, sometimes over him, often over other issues in their lives.

"I didn't think of it like that. You're right, and thank you for thinking of them." She paused and then studied him closely. "You're speaking from experience, aren't you?"

He nodded. "There were nights when I'd lay awake after doors slammed."

"No child should have to go through that." She squeezed his arm. "You're an honorable man, Lucky. You're going to make someone a wonderful husband someday."

She leaned up and brushed his cheek with her soft lips. Sunshine glinted off the auburn highlights of her hair, and she seemed more relaxed. His promise to Audrey and Zack might have been the official reason he returned to Violet Ridge, but Lizzie held the real lasso encircling his heart. He was head over heels for her. While her family was a bonus, there were so many appealing qualities about her. Her polished exterior was part of her, as was her caring core. Everything she did was an act of love, from her tracking down a lost calf to being there for her niece and nephew.

He should have set forth for the next rodeo rather than detouring here, especially as she'd cautioned Audrey about calling him Uncle Lucky before the wedding. Perhaps it was a subtle hint not to get too attached to him. Yet he was already close, and he wanted more time by her side. More kisses, too.

Zack came out first, followed soon by Audrey, who wrinkled her nose. "I like inside bathrooms much better."

Lucky laughed and pushed her glasses back into place. "Pretend you're camping again."

Audrey perked up and smiled, the gap for her missing front tooth making her that much more adorable.

"What does everyone want to do first?" Lizzie held up the flier. "The merry-go-round? The Tilt-A-Whirl? The Ferris wheel?"

Lucky grinned, not surprised that she craved the thrill of the action. "So you like the rides?"

She blushed. "Who doesn't?"

He wouldn't know, as this was the first time he'd been to anything like this. He'd never had this sort of family outing with any of his foster parents, and once he started on the rodeo circuit, he'd been too busy learning the ropes or helping his new friends whenever Will mentioned this festival. "I'll take your word for it."

Her eyes widened. "It's your first time, isn't it?"

It was his turn for heat to spread across his face and down his neck. "I thought this would just be a small craft fair. The Summer Send-off is huge." He cricked his neck. "There are even hot-air balloons."

With scheduled shows, rides and food trucks, it would take the entire afternoon and evening to experience everything.

Audrey caught sight of something and pulled on Lucky's hand. "Ooh, there are games over there."

They walked in the direction of the carnival games, with the hawkers extolling the virtues of each. Lights flashed at the top of the brightly colored stalls, decked out with all sorts of prizes. Rows of stuffed animals decorated one booth while another featured various sports. Farther down the line, a row of rubber ducks in a plastic pool of water beckoned for preschoolers.

"Teddy wants a friend." Audrey dragged Lucky over to the booth with the ring toss. "So he won't forget this trip."

"You already have twenty stuffed animals back home. You don't need another one," Zack complained. "This is for kids."

"I'm a kid," Audrey protested.

Lucky extracted his wallet. "Memories are forever."

Lizzie scoffed. "No one ever wins at these." No sooner did those words escape her mouth than a man sank three basketballs and chose his prize. She sighed and shrugged. "I'll prove myself wrong and give it a go."

Audrey's little chin jutted up. "I'm a big girl. I can do it myself."

"Yeah, right." Zack chuckled before her glare silenced him and sent his lips into a straight line.

Lucky plunked down enough money for Audrey to take several turns. The attendant accepted the bill, then handed Audrey three plastic rings and explained she needed to sink all of them around the glass milk jugs in order to win a prize.

Audrey scrunched her nose in concentration and tossed the first, encircling one of the jugs.

"You did it, Audrey! Just two more." Lizzie cheered for her niece and grasped Lucky's hand. He didn't want to ever let go. She kept her hand in place, smiling at him.

The next one also reached its target, and Lucky felt like he was back at his first rodeo, his nerves on full alert. Audrey grinned and pushed up her glasses, her face determined. The third ring fell short and clattered on the floor. Disappointment flickered for a second before she smiled. "I tried."

Her plucky spirit endeared her to him even more. Lucky stepped toward her and rolled up his flannel shirtsleeves. "It's my turn."

Zack shook his head and inserted himself between Lucky and his sister. "I want to win one for her." He glanced at Lucky. "I'm her big brother."

He couldn't be prouder of his own son. Lucky smiled and nodded as the attendant placed three rings in front of the young boy. "Go for it."

Audrey hugged Zack, her eyes full of admiration. "I'll share if you win."

"Nah." Zack fingered a plastic ring and gauged the distance between him and the rings before he grinned back. "Just name him after me."

Lizzie gripped Lucky's hand, almost cutting off his circulation, but he wasn't about to complain or break Zack's concentration. One down, then two, and Lucky held his breath. The third flew across the distance and landed atop the others. Audrey selected a pink elk. "Meet Zacky."

Zack groaned. "I just had to say she could name it after me... I'll never live this down."

"A promise is a promise," Lucky said, laughing on the inside and the outside. Then he glanced at Lizzie and thought he glimpsed longing in those eyes. He released her hand and faced her. "Has anyone ever won a stuffed animal for you?"

She scuffed the ground with one of her ankle boots. "We're here for Zack and Audrey," she said.

He didn't miss her wistful glance at Audrey hugging her pink elk, though. Lucky rolled up his sleeves and dropped more money on the counter. He wanted Lizzie to have a permanent memento of this day. "I have all the time in the world."

"Glad to hear that." The attendant smiled as if rather confident of selling plenty of tickets to this group.

Lucky wasn't a calf-roping champion for nothing. The first landed around the milk jug, and his stomach clenched.

He wanted this as much as he'd wanted his first belt buckle as a rodeo champion. The second also met its mark, and he let out the breath he didn't realize he'd been holding. Before he picked up the third ring, Lizzie tapped his arm. He faced her, and she leaned up to him on her tiptoes. She brushed his cheek with her lips. "For luck."

If anything, though, her kiss was distracting. She had no idea how beautiful she was or how much he wished their engagement was real. Women like her, though, didn't fall for cowboys who'd spent their childhood in and out of foster care. Yet when he was around her, she made him believe in hope.

He concentrated and tossed the ring. It bounced off a milk jug, and his shoulders slumped. Then the ring landed on the one behind it. He'd done it! Lizzie threw her arms around him.

"That was magnificent." She faced the attendant and picked out a fuzzy brown elk, hugging it to her side.

He captured the memory as his memento from this experience.

Lizzie whispered something to Audrey, who nodded and accepted Lizzie's stuffed animal, introducing the two elks to each other.

Lizzie reached into her purse and extracted money from her wallet. She laid it on the counter. "Now it's my turn to win something for my nephew." "

She accepted the three rings from the attendant.

Then she faced Lucky and blew on her fingers. "I was the point guard on my high-school basketball team for a year when my father suggested I try something new, something that didn't involve the ranch."

She tossed the three rings with dexterity, all landing on their intended target. The attendant reached for another elk.

"Aunt Lizzie." Zack cleared his throat. "I'd like a baseball, not a stuffed animal."

The attendant placed it back on the shelf and handed Zack his prize. Then Lizzie plunked more money on the counter. "Three more rings, please."

What was she up to? Lucky didn't have to wait long to find out as once again, each ring landed around a different milk jug. She asked the attendant for the large tan-colored horse that resembled Butterscotch. After he used a long metal stick for the one Lizzie selected, she thanked him and then gave the stuffed animal to Lucky. "Everyone's first Summer Send-off needs something as special as they are."

Lucky felt like he could float higher than those hot-air balloons.

Zack tapped Lizzie's arm. "I'm hungry."

"Then it's time for food. We can all order something different and see what we like best." Lizzie ushered their group into the bustling crowd, her green eyes sparkling with happiness.

The four of them hustled away, but not before Lucky clutched the horse to his chest for a second, already a treasure he intended to keep. Today, he felt like this was his family, and any doubts he was falling for Lizzie were now gone. His feelings for the beautiful cowgirl were real. How would he ever get over her?

LIZZIE SAW COLORFUL hot-air balloons in the distance at the edge of the festival fairgrounds, which usually served as athletic fields. Violet Ridge prided itself on adding something new to each Summer Send-off, and this year was no different. From the middle of the makeshift picnic tables, she watched one soar into the sky, its orange and yellow colors bright and festive. That's how her heart felt whenever Lucky was around.

She snuck a glance at him. His thigh was pressed next to hers as they sat side by side on the bench across from Audrey and Zack. He dipped one end of his fried pickle into some sort of white sauce and then popped it in his mouth, contentment settling over his face.

Good. After his rodeo victory, he needed a day off, and she wanted to make it special. While he'd been competing in the rodeo, she'd taken time to think about the heartache and struggle he'd experienced while bouncing from one foster home to the next. Losing her mother at such an early age had weighed on her, but her father had loved her and her brothers as he'd coped with his grief and his broken marriage and the conflicting feelings about how it had ended so irrevocably. The ranch and stable provided plenty of room to explore and chores to keep her occupied.

Lucky had never had a place to call home.

Some might have grown jaded or aloof, but not Lucky. Instead, he was having the time of his life from the way he approached everything at the festival.

The balloon faded into the horizon, and guilt prickled at her about the whole situation. What had started as a way to not disappoint her father before his wedding was starting to cause anxiety. Somehow she'd started caring about Lucky, but she was putting him through too much by continuing this charade.

Lucky deserved more than a fleeting family. He deserved love.

Then she turned her attention to the remaining half of her barbecue beef sandwich and shoved the plate away from her. She wasn't hungry anymore.

She caught sight of Audrey's and Zack's faces, their cheeks stained with chocolate from the fried candy. Despite her heartache, she laughed and plucked two napkins from the pile.

"Audrey!" Lizzie exclaimed. "How did you get chocolate on your glasses?"

"I don't know." Her niece licked her lips. "I tried my best to get it all inside my tummy. That was so yummy. Mommy never lets us have anything like that."

That pronouncement made the barbecue sandwich sit even heavier in her stomach. Lizzie reached over the table and wiped Audrey's face. "You can tell your parents about Zack winning your new stuffed animal for you. I'll take full responsibility for the junk food."

Audrey faced Lucky, who was downing the last of his fried pickles. "You're sure Zacky is okay in the car?"

Lucky swallowed and then took a sip of his pop. "Zacky is sitting in your booster seat with a great view of the parking lot, watching everyone go home after a day of fun. He's also holding Zack's baseball so it doesn't get lost."

Hearing his tender and perceptive answers to Audrey's questions confirmed what Lizzie already knew. He had so much love inside him, waiting for a family of his own.

Zack wiped his hands on the bottom of his sky-blue T-shirt. "Can't you name it something else?" Zack wrinkled his nose.

"The elk will remind her that you cared enough to win it for her." Lizzie handed him a napkin. "What's next? The bumper cars?"

In the distance, another balloon, this one with alternating stripes of pink and red, soared beyond the horizon. Audrey pointed toward the field. "I'd like to go up in the sky."

"Junk food is one thing, but a hot-air-balloon ride? I can't do that without your parents' permission." There was no chance Lizzie would keep something like that from Jeff and Nicole, and she wasn't sure they'd say yes to this activity.

"I can text them. Can I borrow your phone, Aunt Lizzie?" Zack bounced in his seat. "That is probably so much fun."

Lucky already had his phone out and read his screen. "Sorry to disappoint you, but you have to be at least forty-eight inches to ride in one of them." He reached over and ruffled Audrey's hair. "You have a little more growing to do."

Audrey's lower lip quivered, and she glanced at Zack. "Do you want to go without me?"

Zack looked at the pink-and-red balloon with longing and then back at his sister. "Nah." Then his eyes grew round with mischief. "I'd rather see if you'd throw up if we rode the Tilt-A-Whirl."

Lucky held up his hand. "Hey, I found something. You can get a picture of you with your aunt Lizzie in one of the baskets."

Audrey's eyes lit up. She reached over and grasped Lizzie's arm. "Then next summer I'll be big enough to go up with you and Uncle Lucky."

Lizzie's head swirled. How was she going to explain the breakup to her niece and nephew?

She reached for her pamphlet. "What about those bumper cars instead? Audrey, you can ride with me. That sounds like a lot of fun."

Audrey shook her head. "I want a picture with you and Uncle Lucky. Then Mommy and Daddy will know I really want to do this next year because I'll sleep with the picture and Zacky every night."

Would Audrey be so excited to return when she and Lucky were no longer together, not that they were ever really together? Somehow, he'd become a fixture in her family, and it was her fault he wouldn't be here next summer. If Audrey found out the truth, Lizzie could lose the close bond with her she'd gained over the past month.

And she'd deserve that.

THE PHOTOGRAPHER GESTURED with his hands for the four of them to move closer together in the hot-air-balloon gondola. A wave of guilt swept over Lucky—he didn't think he should be in the picture. He moved away from Audrey, Zack and Lizzie. "You know what? This should be Aunt Lizzie with the two of you."

Audrey and Zack protested, and Lizzie implored him to stay. "This is your day, Lucky. I want you to be in the picture."

Her words struck him in the gut, and he moved back into the frame. The photographer told some cheesy jokes to try to elicit smiles, but all Lucky had to do was turn toward Lizzie, her auburn hair free from its usual ponytail, her face light and happy with her hands on Zack's shoulders. There was something about her that always made him smile.

Within minutes, the pictures were ready. While Lizzie spoke with yet another rancher, the respect Lizzie commanded in the community on full display, Lucky purchased a set for him and one for Audrey, who hugged him. He stared at them for a long, hard minute. Anyone might mistake them for a real family, except they weren't.

More so, he'd have to keep these away from Will or Sabrina. They'd see the truth in a second, as Lucky hadn't been able to keep his eyes off Lizzie. It was written all over his too expressive face. He had been swept off his feet by the attractive cowgirl.

Then Audrey wrinkled her nose. "I look funny without my tooth."

Zack opened his mouth, but one glance from Lucky and Zack quickly clammed up. Lucky kneeled down until Audrey met his gaze. "I see a happy little girl in that picture, and the tooth will grow in so fast I won't even recognize you the next time I see you."

"Promise?" Her face lit up, and Lucky's insides clenched.

He prided himself on not making promises he knew he wouldn't keep.

He rose and gripped her hand. "I promise you're cute, with or without that tooth."

Lizzie finished her conversation and joined them. "Who's ready for some rides? It's not a Summer Send-off without a turn on the Tilt-A-Whirl and the Ferris wheel."

Zack's arm shot into the air, and Lucky laughed and joined Zack, shooting his arm upward.

THE TILT-A-WHIRL WAS as wonderful as Lizzie remembered, a rush with the cars going around a circular track, the centrifugal force causing a dizzying effect. She glanced at Lucky, his head slightly swaying as his feet claimed solid ground again. Her adrenaline burst from the ride was nothing compared to the swirl of feelings he created in her.

No sooner had they reached the main path than Audrey ran off in the distance.

"Audrey!" Lucky started rushing forward, as did Lizzie.

What was her niece thinking, running away from them in such a crowd?

Then Zack gasped and dashed after his sister, and Lizzie blew out a breath. How would she ever explain losing their children to Jeff and Nicole?

"Mom! Dad!" Lizzie heard Zack's shouts of joy over the noise of the crowd.

When she spotted her brother and sister-in-law heading toward her and Lucky, that knot in her stomach unraveled.

Jeff scooped up Audrey, the joy clear on her expressive face while Nicole reached for Zack's hand, his body quivering with happiness.

Concern flitted through Lizzie. Had something happened at the ranch? Why else would they be here?

"Daddy, you should have seen Zack. He did something wonderful, and I can't wait for you to meet Zacky." Audrey grinned while Jeff seemed to hang on every word.

"Zacky?" Nicole blinked and shuddered. "It's not a goldfish or a pet pig or anything like that, right?"

"Zacky is an adorable pink elk," Lizzie said, and Nicole's eyes widened in alarm. "A stuffed pink elk."

Nicole exhaled before her gaze went to Zack's T-shirt. "What have you been eating?"

Jeff set Audrey back to a standing position and rested his arm around his wife's shoulder. "Nothing Lizzie wouldn't have eaten herself. We trusted them to her, and they're happy kids."

Trust. There was that word again. People trusted her, and she'd let everything with Lucky get out of control. As soon as her father was back, she'd clear the air and come clean about her pride over not having a plus-one for his wedding, which had escalated in no time.

"Thank you, both of you." Nicole brought Lizzie out of her reverie, and she found everyone looking at her.

"For what?" Lizzie didn't know what she'd missed.

"For reminding us they won't be this age forever." Jeff placed his free hand on Audrey's shoulder. "You and Lucky are off the hook. Enjoy the rest of the day, just the two of you."

In the blink of an eye, the foursome faded into the crowd, leaving Lizzie alone with Lucky. Without Zack and Audrey, she'd run out of reasons not to stage a scene to end this phony engagement once and for all. Just because she was starting to quiver whenever the lanky and attractive cowboy came into view didn't mean he felt the same way, and who could blame him, considering she'd acted before thinking too often in the past few weeks?

Her ankle boots became rooted to the sidewalk, and her mouth was drier than the ranch during a drought. The perfect opportunity was now upon them, but she was having so much fun. However, if they got everything into the open, this new friendship might develop into something deeper.

The sooner she acted, the sooner she'd know for sure. "This has been fun—"

"Lizzie, you won't deny me company on my first Ferris wheel ride, will you?" He held up a handful of tickets.

Sitting with him in such a confined area? Where the sky was as blue as his eyes and the wind swayed the bucket enough for a thrill without worry of the world collapsing under her? She shivered with anticipation. "It would give us a chance to talk…"

He came over and put his finger on her lips. "About us, but not like that. Just talk about who we are on the inside. Get to know each other. I don't have to head to my next rodeo for a couple of days, so why don't we have some fun and ride that Ferris wheel?"

Sharing who she was on the inside with him was almost as scary as admitting her newfound feelings for him. Maybe more so as she'd lost loved ones in the past, first her mother and then Jared, since he'd wanted to be a part of the influential Irwin family rather than loving her for herself.

And yet the man in front of her whose face radiated joy at the Ferris wheel looming large in the center of the festival grounds had been through far more in his life and hadn't lost his optimism.

She couldn't resist his positive attitude, wrapped nicely

with a ribbon of charm to pull him together. She only wished she were this handsome cowboy's lucky match. "You're impossible, do you know that?"

"I've been called worse." He grinned and held out the crook of his arm. "Are you game?"

She linked her arm through his and walked alongside him. One night of fun to cap off a perfect day seemed a little too good to be true—a lot like him, but she was more than willing to rise to the occasion.

UP CLOSE, the Ferris wheel loomed much larger than it looked from a distance. Lucky had no problem being in a closed arena with a two-hundred-and-fifty-pound calf, but this? This was a different story. At the front of the line, Lucky gulped as the attendant accepted two tickets.

"It's only fifty feet in the air." The attendant deposited the tickets while Lucky and Lizzie settled in the bucket seat. "It takes about eight minutes to reach the top with all the starts and stops. You picked the perfect time of day with sunset approaching."

The attendant closed the bar and moved the lever until they rose slightly to the next position. Lizzie reached over and patted his hand. "Are you okay? You're stark-white under your tan."

He didn't look down and instead practiced measured breathing. "Just dandy."

She rubbed his knuckles. "No, you're not. You're stressed, which is so unlike you."

It had taken one long bus ride to turn his life around and start afresh, and now one quick Ferris-wheel ride threatened to bring back his insecurities. "Cale taught me I can't control much, but I can control my feelings about how I approach my surroundings. He and his wife, Vivi, helped me learn how to survive on my own."

"They sound nice. It must have been a big change going from New York to Colorado." The Ferris wheel jerked into the next position, and their bucket swayed from the movement.

"It was nice being in control of where I went and when." He'd never admitted this to Will or Sabrina, even though he considered them his closest friends. "I guess I just like having the ground under my feet."

She chuckled before the smile left her lips. "Sorry. I wasn't laughing at your present predicament. It's ironic to me that you feel that way considering how often you ride a horse and how many times you've been in the air in the rodeo."

"Practice and training give me the confidence I need for the arena." He dared to peek over the edge and immediately moved back to the center. Instead of looking outward, he concentrated on Lizzie, cool and unflappable even with the evening breeze whipping through her hair. "Having Butterscotch in my corner this year helps."

Lizzie rubbed the back of his palm with her thumb, and suddenly he wanted the ride to go on forever. The warmth of her hand brought his racing pulse under control, and the engagement ring glinted in the rays of the setting sun. He wondered if a rough rodeo performer and a smooth ranch owner could make a success of a relationship. Cale had taught him nearly everything was possible with determination and hard work. And time spent with Lizzie was anything but hard. Taking this to the next level would have to wait until he finished this ride without having a panic attack.

"I know how you feel. When I'm riding Andromeda, it's like we're an unstoppable team."

Despite their differences, they had so much in common about what really mattered in life. That lifted his spirits.

"It's rare to find that kind of connection." Whether with an animal or a person, Lucky could attest to that. When something was right, could it be this effortless, this easy? His breathing steadied, and his usual calm flooded him and centered him in this moment.

She squeezed his hand. "Your resilience is inspiring."

"I learned from the best, Cale and Will." The Ferris wheel moved once more, and they were halfway to the top. "Cale told me something I believe with all my heart. Find a way to turn your biggest weakness into your biggest strength."

"You obviously succeeded. I admire how laid-back you are."

"Some of my foster families didn't see me that way." More than once, he'd been accused of being inattentive or uncaring. "It depends on your perspective."

Her green eyes glittered as brightly as the lights coming on around them. "From where I'm sitting, going with the flow and accepting others is a strength, and I think you feel more deeply than you let on. I understand that too well." She twisted the ring around her finger. "You must have loved her if you intended to propose to her. Remind me, what was her name?"

"Cherry." He shrugged and kept his focus on Lizzie so he wouldn't look down. "I thought I loved her, but she wanted someone different, someone more like her."

But whatever he'd felt for Cherry was nothing compared to the Tilt-A-Whirl of emotions he experienced whenever Lizzie was around, or even when she wasn't. He'd seen the beautiful cowgirl rise to her feet in the creek before they worked together and dislodged the calf's foot. Today, she'd proven she wouldn't judge him for his past, even going as far as winning him a stuffed horse. He'd keep that in his trailer, for sure.

"I thought I loved Jared until I found out he only wanted my father's signature on an important contract." Lizzie stared straight ahead. "It's hard when things don't work out as planned."

"But those are the times that mold us into who we are now." The Ferris wheel jerked in motion again, and they stopped one position away from the top.

"So you turned what you thought was a weakness into a strength. You accepted your resilience and used it to your advantage. How did you move on without looking backward?" Lizzie faced him, yearning in her eyes.

The evening breeze rustled her auburn hair, and her apple cheeks grew rosy pink, with a smattering of freckles obvious this close to her. Another memory for his permanent databank.

He stored it away and then considered her question. "It was that or stay bitter."

"I was rather bitter after I discovered Jared dated me so he could get close to my family. Afterward, I threw myself into the ranch. Somehow, I thrive best by staying in one place."

"I love seeing new places. That kept me going when Cherry broke up with me." His stomach clenched. He left Violet Ridge faster than a barrel racer when he'd seen Sabrina with Ty last Christmas, not that he'd felt anything for her beyond brotherly affection, but it was the impact of the family he'd formed with Will and Sabrina coming to an end that had overwhelmed him. He'd grasped the first excuse to leave so he wouldn't have to face harsh reality so close to the holidays.

Maybe he should thank Lizzie for everything that had transpired. He had intended on leaving, but she kept providing him with reasons to come back to Violet Ridge. All this time he thought he'd be able to walk away from everyone he cared about, even Will and Sabrina. That it would be easier to be the one who left rather than facing his fears of being left behind. Starting over was fine when he'd been eighteen. Now, though? Will and Sabrina were too important to him. They had made room for him, as had their respective spouses, Kelsea and Ty. He'd just been too afraid to accept their love. He wasn't afraid anymore.

It was nice having this town as a soft spot for landing amid the rough circumstances of life. New places were always on the horizon in his profession, but a home with someone there? He didn't realize until now how much he'd been missing having Lizzie to talk to, to hold her hand, to kiss.

The bucket lurched into the top position, and the breeze ruffled his hair. He'd never visit an amusement park without remembering this moment. From here, Violet Ridge seemed like a robin's egg nestled high in an oak tree. One thing was for certain—this moment was theirs and theirs alone with no outside influences dictating what they had to feel or do. Lizzie faced him, and that same knowledge gleamed in her eyes. He caressed her soft cheeks with his hands, and her lips met his in a kiss that sent him soaring even higher.

But it wasn't what was around them that made this moment so special, this kiss mesmerizing and real. It wasn't just a memory; he was living in the moment, seizing life by the horns. And he was kissing the most beautiful, action-oriented woman. Lizzie was so much more than the efficient facade she presented to the world, just as he was more than the laid-back rodeo cowboy. Her layers surprised and astounded him. He relished the moment—his first Ferris-wheel ride was both unforgettable and breathtaking.

The bucket jerked once more, and he broke the kiss, leaning his forehead on hers. He drank in the moment, heady for a kid who grew up never knowing where he'd be living from one week to the next.

"I'd say you made this day go from great to monumentally memorable," Lucky said.

"Hold on. The ride's about to get even better." She laced her hands through his and the wheel began to spin, gaining speed as it made its rotations, the world passing by in a blur.

Too soon, the attendant raised the bar that held them in the bucket, and he and Lizzie alit from the ride. He staggered for a second before regaining his equilibrium. And yet, he didn't want the dizziness he felt whenever she neared to end. He wanted to grasp this happiness with both hands and not let go. It might be time to take Cale's words to heart and change his biggest weakness into an undeniable strength. He didn't have any experience staying in one place, always moving on when the caseworker appeared or a friend called upon him. It was time to stop running when relationships took an unexpected turn. Growing up on the Double I, Lizzie was teaching him a thing or two about permanence, and he couldn't think of a better place than Violet Ridge for him to hang his lasso for good.

CHAPTER FOURTEEN

LIZZIE'S STABLE OFFICE was getting too crowded for her liking on this Wednesday. Over the past three days, she'd enjoyed Lucky's presence in the evenings after he spent the day with Ty and Will preparing for the next rodeo in Arizona, but he'd be leaving tomorrow night. Next Monday would herald his return, as well as that of the newlyweds. Would it also be the end of this friendship, or whatever it was that had been developing between her and Lucky?

She pushed that out of her mind as JR and Roy waited for her next move. A nervous gleam in his eye, Roy shifted in the doorway and switched the envelope from one hand to the other while her foreman frowned from his position in front of her desk. This past weekend at the Summer Send-off already seemed like it happened last year.

"JR…" Lizzie settled herself into her chair for the first time all morning. "You first."

"Our computers are down, and I can't access Cattle-Max." He referenced the program used for keeping track of the vaccinations and other records for the cattle. "I need another temporary cowhand to help with weighing the calves, except the bunkhouse is full."

"About that." Roy came forward and laid the envelope in front of Lizzie. "Maria and I set a date to get married. That there's my notice. In two weeks, I'll be working for her dad on their ranch."

Her headache was close to turning into a migraine.

Lizzie kept from reaching for the bottle of ibuprofen in the bottom desk drawer. "We've enjoyed having you work here, Roy. We'll miss you. You're a hard worker." She made a note to include a bonus in his last paycheck, a wedding gift of sorts, while mentally rearranging the work schedule. "If I find a replacement before the two weeks are up, you can leave even earlier. Until then, those calves are our priority. After that, JR and I have to get started on winterizing."

Roy removed his hat and held it close to his chest. "I was sort of hoping you'd let me go early. Maria's dad is slowing down, and we need to bring in the hay."

Lizzie exhaled and nodded. The Vasquez family's ranch bordered hers and Will's, and Esteban was always gracious and accommodating. "Of course. I know him, and he's been a good neighbor to us." She faced JR. "At least that solves the issue about the bunkhouse."

It sure would help to have those new bunkhouses, each with updated kitchens and new beds, as a selling point for employment. Dad was due back soon, and she'd talk to him then. No use interrupting his honeymoon with news about their employment issues. Next week would be soon enough to discuss that and her plan to introduce Simmentals to the western pasture.

JR nodded. "I'll start putting out feelers."

"And I'll cut you your last check, Roy, at the ranch house." Lizzie reached for her red cowboy hat and donned it before escorting Roy to Dad's office. The ranch would be working with a skeletal staff until at least two new hires came on board.

In her father's office, she settled accounts with Roy, adding a bonus despite the lack of notice. It was the right thing to do, especially given that they'd be neighbors.

His eyes widened as he checked the amount. "There must be a mistake."

"No, you earned that. If you know anyone looking for work at competitive pay, send them to us." Besides, she should have seen Roy's departure coming, especially given how he and Maria had been sweet on each other for some time.

A commotion in the front of the house led to a quick goodbye, and Lizzie investigated the cause of the noise only to find Audrey hugging her grandpa Gordon while Zack was on the receiving end of an Evie embrace. Her dad appeared relaxed, with a rugged tan and a hint of a smile on his face. She'd never seen a Hawaiian shirt paired with a Stetson before, but it worked on him.

Jeff and Nicole emerged from the library, holding hands and appearing happier than ever. Jeff blinked. "I thought you were on your honeymoon until Monday."

"I couldn't keep him away any longer." Evie also seemed more relaxed and radiant.

"Good thing, too, as we ran into JR on the way inside." In the blink of an eye, Dad transformed from glowing new-lywed back into the rancher everyone around here knew so well. "What's this about Roy?"

And just like that, she was back to square one in terms of ranch management. "I'm in charge of employment matters, especially the stable. I handled it and will continue to do so." She straightened her spine and took charge. "Once you and Evie get settled, I'll tell you about my plan to attract workers with a new perk."

Dad squeezed Audrey one more time before setting her near Jeff. "I'm settled now."

Evie reached for Audrey's and Zack's hands, one on each side of her. "How about we go see what good stuff Tammy baked while I was in Hawaii? Then later, before

I lunch with Sabrina and my mother at Miss Tilly's Steak House, I'll see whether we brought back any souvenirs for you."

Her laugh was the answer, and Dad's gaze didn't leave Evie until they disappeared from view. Lizzie pulled herself together and pointed to the living room. "Would it be easier if we were comfortable?"

"I've been sitting on an airplane too long, and I want to see my horse," Dad said. He opened the front door. "A long ride and a check of my cattle. That's my ideal afternoon."

Nicole kissed Jeff before squeezing his hand and heading in the direction of the kitchen. Something was going on between them. Had Violet Ridge's charms at the Summer Send-off finally entranced them into moving to the Double I? Lizzie wouldn't blame them one bit, especially given how Audrey and Zack had flourished over the past few weeks. No, she wouldn't be like her dad and presume otherwise. She trusted Jeff, and his family would be returning to their home.

Jeff gestured for Lizzie to exit first, and she hurried to catch up with her father, who was already halfway to the stable. "Hold on." She approached his side. "I know you love the trail on the other side of the stable, but it's the perfect place for a set of four new bunkhouses. Modern construction will help us attract and retain workers."

Wrinkles popped out on Gordon's forehead. "I built that trail myself."

This was one reason she'd been so hesitant to approach him. "I studied the plat maps and located another site for a riding trail, but I've consulted architects in town and placed our down payment. The current trail is the best and most economical choice for the construction. I've contracted renderings for the buildings, one of which will only house female cowhands."

They reached the stable, and Gordon's eyebrows raised. "You did all that without consulting me?"

She adjusted the cowboy hat on her head and met his stare. "Yes. You put me in charge of employment matters, and lodging and competitive salaries are part of that."

Gordon entered the stable and made a beeline for Margarita's stall. "Hmm, is she favoring her left leg? Is it swollen?"

"Not at all. Lucky took exceptional care of her during the roundup." He was a horse whisperer, and Margarita had connected with him. "And I walked her out to pasture at dawn and picked her hooves afterward."

"Lucky's a good man." That was high praise from her father, and the perfect opening as far as Lizzie was concerned.

"He is, but there's something you should know."

Gordon turned to her, his eyes discerning. "Springing the bunkhouses on me, the hour I return from my honeymoon, wasn't enough?"

She steeled herself as her father would have every right to be upset with her about her decision to spare his feelings on his wedding day by letting everyone believe something that wasn't real. Her pride aside, she'd have to accept whatever he decided about her future at the Double I. "This is much more important than the new construction."

"Thanks, Lizzie, but it's not fair for you to tell him what I should have been firm about all along." Jeff stepped forward. "I've been asking Lizzie to keep a secret until you returned from your honeymoon."

"Lizzie?" Gordon's throat bobbed. "I called you that before Heather died."

That was what he'd narrowed in on? Lizzie sighed. "I like it better than Elizabeth."

"Evie wants to travel more, let me trust the two of you

with extra duties. So many changes." Gordon's mouth clamped into a straight line. "Still, your initiative with the bunkhouses is sound. What do you think, Jeff?"

Jeff shook his head and held up his hands. "I don't have a say in this. The ranch is yours and Lizzie's domain. Nicole and I aren't moving back. We're staying in Boston."

His jaw firm, Dad glanced at Lizzie. "And you knew about this? For how long?"

"Dad!" Jeff placed his hand on Dad's shoulder. "Don't blame Lizzie. I told you we weren't moving several times. This isn't where I belong. The roundup confirmed that. Nicole and I are happy in Boston. We want Zack and Audrey to spend summers here with you, Evie, Lizzie and Lucky. That family bond is important."

Dad scrubbed his chin and reached out for Margarita, who nickered and approached as if sensing something was wrong. He rubbed her muzzle and nodded. "Sometimes we see what we want to see and hear what we want to hear." He patted Margarita and moved away from the mare, placing his arm around Jeff. "That's a lot to digest in a short time. Evie has some commitments in New York over the winter. Would you be up to a visit from us if we make the jaunt to Boston afterward? Elizabeth, er, Lizzie and Lucky will no doubt be taking good care of Margarita and the ranch for me."

"How about we go see if Tammy has any of those cowboy cookies left?" Jeff headed for the exit, and Lizzie watched them leave.

So close and yet so far.

LUCKY THANKED THE clerk for ringing up the horse bit and left the saddlery. Downtown Violet Ridge sure was pretty, with the sun flooding its golden light on the pastel storefronts. Its glow didn't compare with the way Lizzie's hair shone in the dusk. Somehow, the two of them had to find a solution so they could spend time with each other free of the expectations everyone placed on them.

Since when did he care so much what others thought of him? He'd left everything familiar and headed for Steamboat Springs, all those years ago, without a second thought. But then he'd met Cale, who'd taken him under his wing and taught him about ranching and the rodeo. Eking out a living at what he loved was second to the friendships and connections he'd made along the way.

Until now, it was always easy to go from town to town with fresh faces to meet and new stories to hear. However, Cale had taught him a thing or two about facing up to what he'd started and being brave. Staying here and facing the aftermath once his engagement to Lizzie ended was the only courageous route out of this mess.

He ducked into the Blue Skies Coffee House. He ordered plain black coffee, a perfect pick-me-up on a Wednesday afternoon, and waited at the counter. The cowbell above the door jangled, and in walked Grandma Eloise, the thump of her cane pounding the hardwood floor, followed by Evie. If Evie was back in town earlier than expected, so was Gordon.

If he and Lizzie talked to Gordon together, the older rancher might accept his and Lizzie's need to figure out what they meant to each other before rushing into anything. Following behind them was Sabrina. Closing the door behind her, she squealed and made a beeline in his direction. "Congratulations. That was some ride last weekend."

"I could say the same about Ty." Sabrina's husband also finished first in his respective event. He removed his hat and nodded at the group. "Could I order for you while you take a seat? My treat."

Grandma Eloise perked up at his request. "I never refuse an offer from a handsome fellow."

Evie placed her packages on the hardwood floor next to an empty table. "That would be lovely. Then we can talk about tonight."

What was happening tonight?

After he memorized and placed their orders, Lucky waited at the counter while the three women settled at the table. When the barista called his name, he carried over their beverages and found Evie rubbing her mother's hand. "I just arrived back in Violet Ridge, and I already have to say goodbye." Evie's throat bobbed, and she sat straighter in her chair. "If you and Dad moved here, you'd be able to see Genie more often."

Grandma Eloise's eyes misted. "I'll keep that in mind in the future." Lucky had never heard her voice so husky. "For now, Bob needs to stay put in Texas, and it's time I go home. He needs me."

Love glistened from every pore of Grandma Eloise, and Lucky was in awe of the depth of her emotion. More than anything, he wanted that kind of relationship with Lizzie. As of now, their foundation was too shaky, a literal house of cards that threatened to topple over at any minute.

Evie gave another squeeze and then stared at Lucky. "Before I forget, Gordon and I are hosting a little get-together at Mama Rosa's tonight. Of course, you and Elizabeth are invited."

"My mother's idea of little and mine are worlds apart," Sabrina said, stifling a giggle.

Then this was definitely the night. With the Irwin family in full attendance, he and Lizzie had the perfect opportunity to clear the air that they wouldn't be getting married in December. If he made the finals, and after this weekend, that was more likely than ever, he could reimburse Gordon and Evie for the canceled contracts.

Who was he kidding? If nothing else, he could sell the engagement ring. That would more than cover his share of the expenses. Down the line, if he ever asked Lizzie to marry him, he'd buy her a ring of her own. Something with rubies to match her inner fire.

"As long as it's an early night for me since Butterscotch and I have to head to Arizona for the next rodeo at the crack of dawn." And there wasn't any reason to believe he wouldn't be asked to leave early after he and Lizzie talked to Gordon.

Evie smiled. "Well, that's between you and Elizabeth." Then her gaze fell on her mother, and her smile faded. "I'll miss you."

"There's no reason you can't come visit. Our door is open, and everyone at the assisted-living complex loves you." Grandma Eloise tapped her cane near Sabrina's foot. "And you bring Genie often. Bob loves seeing her. Ty's not so bad, either."

The implication was clear: Bob wasn't the only one who loved Genie. That sweet baby was a ray of sunshine, like Sabrina.

Tonight was the night to ask Lizzie if she could look past his rough childhood and care for him, even though she deserved someone who could offer her so much more. His troubled past was behind him. It was time to look forward.

Would it be a new beginning for him and Lizzie?

Or the end?

EVEN THOUGH IT was only the last week of August, Lizzie grabbed a shawl for tonight's party. In the Colorado mountains, temperatures could take a tumble at a moment's notice. After a long Wednesday in the stable, she would have normally bowed out of a weeknight party, but she couldn't in this case. Goodbyes meant everything. They captured the moment and provided closure. She'd miss Grandma Eloise, and the older woman deserved to return to Texas after a family evening to share with her beloved Bob.

By the time she saw Zack and Audrey again, Audrey's adult tooth would have made its appearance. She'd miss her niece and nephew. Without a wedding in December, she wasn't sure whether Jeff and Nicole would make the trip to Violet Ridge even though they'd already purchased plane tickets.

The doorbell rang, and she found Lucky at her doorstep, right on schedule. His gaze wandered over her, and his eyes widened. That made the extra effort and time with a hair dryer and the mascara wand well worth it. He held out a bouquet of pink and yellow snapdragons. "For you. The florist said they represent grace and strength."

She blinked, the sentiment not lost on her, and then placed her shawl on the entryway table next to her clutch. With both hands, she accepted the flowers. "Thank you. They're beautiful. I'll be right back." In no time, she returned with a lovely crystal vase that had belonged to her mother. "I'll just put these somewhere safe."

They looked more beautiful on her dresser next to the framed print of her and Lucky and the kids in the hot-air balloon gondola. In no time, she returned to the foyer.

Lucky removed his cowboy hat and placed it over his heart. "That dress almost does you justice."

"Thank you." She swirled around, and the flouncy asymmetrical skirt of her light pink lace dress swooshed above her knees.

Then she admired his appearance. He looked particularly handsome in that crisp blue denim shirt paired with black dress pants. She moved toward him and reached for his bolo tie. "May I?"

He nodded, and she straightened the thin pieces of the leather cord held together with a beautiful silver medallion with a daisy on it. "This is beautiful," she said, tracing the flower's petals.

"Cale gave it to me to celebrate my first rodeo win."

"That makes it more special." She reached for her shawl and small clutch. When she faced him once more, he was almost ashen under his deep tan. "Lucky, are you okay?"

He winced and leaned back against the wall. "So you told Gordon and Evie?"

"Told them what? I tried telling Dad about us earlier today, but Jeff interrupted me and said he and Nicole are staying in Boston. Another missed opportunity."

"You're not wearing the ring."

She checked her left ring finger, and it was, indeed, bare. Her heart thudded until she realized it must still be in the bathroom. "After a day in the stable, I reeked." She waved her hand under her nose. "I must have forgotten to put it back on after my shower. I'm still getting used to wearing it."

No sooner would she get used to the feeling of it on her finger than she'd be returning it to him. She hurried upstairs, and he followed, the sound of his boots loud against the dark cherry hardwood. Panic set in when she couldn't find the ring on the white quartz bathroom counter.

Her breathing became shallow spurts. She racked her brain but couldn't remember taking it off before her shower. When was the last time she'd seen it? She'd definitely worn it this morning at breakfast, but after that? It was a mystery about where or when it fell off. She laid the clutch and shawl on the counter and brought her hands to her face.

The only part of this engagement that had been real was that ring, and she'd lost it.

She faced him, tears forming in her eyes. "I'm sorry, Lucky. I should have been more careful with your ring."

"Hey, no tears. We'll find it. You might ruin your makeup, and you look beautiful." He approached her and gave her a hug. She inhaled his spicy aftershave and soap, his presence more than comforting. Beyond dependable, he calmed that need inside her to fill every waking moment with action. Even now, when she wanted to overturn the ranch house and stable, she stayed still in his arms, letting his solidity soothe her ruffled self. He stepped away and rubbed the side of one eye, moisture dotting his finger.

From inside her clutch, her phone buzzed, and she checked the incoming texts.

"Everyone is wondering where we are." She cleared her throat and reached for a tissue, dotting away the last of her tears. "Should I send our regrets? We can change and start looking in the stable for the ring."

"Tomorrow is soon enough to find it and talk to Gordon together. Too often, I never say goodbye." He wrapped her shawl around her shoulders. "I'd like to send Grandma Eloise, Zack and Audrey away with a hug and a parting word of friendship."

A poignant reminder of how he'd grown up. He was right. This night was going to be a special family occasion, and she wanted him by her side. He reached for her hand, and they made their way downstairs.

The problem was, she wanted him by her side for the long run. Would he take her losing his ring as a sign that she was careless about his feelings?

And his heart?

CHAPTER FIFTEEN

LUCKY ESCORTED LIZZIE to the front door of Mama Rosa's and halted. Lizzie looked at her bare finger and pursed her lips together, obviously devastated about losing the ring. It was just a possession. Everything except relationships could be replaced.

He approached her and fingered her silky shawl. "We'll find the ring tomorrow. I'm sure of it. It has to be somewhere at the ranch. How about we enjoy tonight?"

"You are a man beyond compare, Lucky Harper." In her three-inch heels, she leaned over and kissed his cheek. "How do you do it? How do you make everyone feel better about themselves when you're the one who has every right to be hurt by my careless action?"

He savored the softness of her cheek with his fingers, the warm imprint from her skin lingering behind. "I had to learn how to be adaptable to survive, but that gave me an out, too. It was always easy to move on, to not make any emotional connections. I thought I didn't need them."

It turned out he needed them more than he'd known. Specifically, he wanted Lizzie in his life, but he needed more stability to become a part of her world.

Instead of leaving never to return, he now had an important reason to come back. Qualifying for the year-end finals would prove he belonged here in Lizzie's world.

Maybe if he made the finals, he'd also prove something to himself and be worthy of this magnificent woman. He wouldn't know, though, unless he gave it his all, something he couldn't do if he was distracted. And Lizzie was the biggest distraction to his head and his heart.

There was one other important factor in all of this. He had to prove to himself he could finish something he started.

More so, he could take the initiative with Sabrina. Instead of waiting for her to ask him for a position at her rodeo academy, he'd offer his services. A steady job in the area would give him a more constant base.

Lucky opened the door, and the maître d' nodded at them, coming around the tall reservation stand. "Please follow me. They're expecting you."

He and Lizzie entered the back room, and everyone yelled, "Surprise!"

A huge banner that read "Congratulations, Lizzie and Lucky!" was draped on the rear wall. This wasn't a farewell party; it was an engagement party. For them.

Lucky's mouth dropped open, the shock invading his system. Gordon came forward, laughing. "Leave it to the engaged couple to show up half an hour late to their own party." He reached into his pocket and handed a handkerchief to Lucky with a discreet *ahem*. "You have Lizzie's lipstick on your cheek."

Friends came rushing toward them, expressing their best wishes, while Lucky rubbed his cheek with Gordon's handkerchief. He was still too numb to do anything else. Will approached with Kelsea, who hugged Lizzie. He raised his glass to Lucky. "Congratulations. Never happier to be wrong about something."

Music started playing over the speakers, and people milled about with flutes of champagne. Audrey rushed over and held up her own goblet containing a golden, fizzy liquid. "I love ginger ale. It's so yummy." She pushed her purple glasses higher. "And Mommy says I can stay up past my bedtime."

Evie approached with a crown for him and a tiara for Lizzie. "You had no idea how hard it was not to ruin the surprise of your engagement party this afternoon. I'm so happy for the both of you. You're perfect for each other."

Before he knew it, Lizzie was swept away to a different side of the room, and Gordon kept talking to him about his future plans after the year-end finals.

"I never think that far ahead," Lucky said.

Gordon seemed taken aback at that answer, and Lucky excused himself. Suddenly, the crowd seemed to part, and luminous light fell on Lizzie. He captured yet another internal photo of how she looked in this moment, her auburn hair cascading over her shoulders, her apple cheeks pink from the attention. While she preferred spending time with the animals on the ranch, there wasn't anything she wouldn't do for anyone in this room. Whether she was riding Andromeda or spurring others into action, Lizzie glowed from within.

He was hopelessly in love with Lizzie.

What was he going to do about it?

He gathered his wits, recalling the foster family he'd lost when the husband's best friend claimed Lucky had corrupted his underage son with alcohol. Others may have thought the worst of him, but he'd known the truth. Honesty was the way to move forward. That was how he lived with himself and could live up to being the type of man Lizzie deserved. He inhaled a deep breath and wondered where to start. He moved toward Lizzie, when Gordon clanged the side of his champagne flute with his fork.

The crowd silenced, and Gordon turned on the microphone. A loud, high-pitched squeal echoed through the room, and everyone winced. The echo ended, and Gordon began by thanking everyone for attending on short notice. Then he gestured for Lizzie and Lucky to join him. Lucky grabbed a flute of champagne from the nearby tray while reaching for Lizzie's hand. Her presence would help him through this.

Gordon smiled at them and then spoke into the microphone. "When I met Evie, I thought nothing could make me happier. Then I married the most captivating woman in the world, and I convinced myself that was the pinnacle." He winked at Evie, who winked right back at him. "But I was wrong. Seeing my daughter in love with the man who's captured her heart, the man who has made her smile and laugh, the man who encouraged her to reconnect with her inner Lizzie—that has raised the bar once again. To Lucky and Lizzie."

Everyone raised their glasses and drank. Lizzie moved to take the microphone. "There's something I need to say."

"There's more." Gordon kept the microphone and moved it close to his chest. "Evie and I talked about it. We're giving you and Lucky the cabin. Well, actually, Lucky, it's our gift to you. That way, you always have some place to stay when you're not heading to the next rodeo."

Lucky's fingers went numb. The flute of champagne slipped to the floor and broke into a myriad of shards, liquid spilling everywhere.

What had he done?

THE BUBBLES IN her ginger ale fizzed to the top, and Lizzie stared at the liquid. She limited herself to pop so her head would remain clear. There was still time to salvage this mess of a situation brought about by her pride and good, but misguided, intentions about Dad's wedding. She started counting the bubbles, anything to stop her from counting the consequences of her ill-fated decision. Tonight proved, once and for all, that she had to step up and face the music. It was no longer only about deposits that she could afford to repay; it was about trust.

If she'd earned Dad's trust with hard work, this prolonged engagement might have broken that tenuous thread. Dad might even demote her or, even worse, fire her. No matter what, though, she'd admit how it started when she claimed Lucky as her plus-one. Then she'd shore up her courage and tell Will and Sabrina that Lucky went along with her out of pity, or some other unfathomable reason.

And there wasn't anyone else who would have brought such joy to this entire experience. Lucky teased out a softer side of her, one that sought experiences with people rather than hiding in the stable. No one else had ever challenged her how he did with his calm yet practical manner. The handsome rodeo cowboy was special.

And his kisses?

Unforgettable and earth-shattering, the same way he conducted himself in the arena, judging from the hour she'd watched this past weekend. The more hours she spent with him, the more that slow, radiant smile of his curled her toes. Many a time in the past few days she'd contrived excuses to see him and that grin. There was so much depth to him. He always provided her with a fresh perspective about one of the horses or something else on the ranch.

She glanced over the rim of the flute and observed Lucky, who looked forlorn. Anyone with eyes would sense there was something wrong between them. No one had yet commented on the fact she wasn't wearing his ring. After she cleared the air with her father, regardless of what happened with her job on the ranch, she'd head to the stable and comb through every stall and every inch of the place until she found the ring.

The servers were whisking away the dinner plates, and

music began playing over the speakers. Couples moved to the makeshift dance floor, and Dad headed toward Lizzie while she saw Evie approaching Lucky.

"May I have this dance with the future bride?" Her father held out his arm, and Lizzie could hardly refuse such an offer, especially as she hadn't thanked him for the party.

Dad led her to the center of the floor, and they began their father-daughter dance. "Thank you for this, but…"

"I'm the one who should be thanking you. I reviewed the bunkhouse plans with Tammy and JR. They agree the updated living quarters are long overdue." He let out a blustery laugh. "This isn't a time for business. Evie's been a good influence on me. She's made me confront my life and my mistakes. I wanted to get you to myself because I owe you an apology. I wasn't a better father when you missed Heather, and I was dealing with how badly it ended between us. Audrey reminds me so much of you at that age, and I hope to be a better grandfather for her and Zack, and any other future grandchildren."

Never before had she seen his sentimental side. He claimed Evie was behind the change. She liked to think it was part Evie and part passage of time. She swallowed the big lump in her throat. "I never expected an apology. I understand the ranch is an enormous responsibility."

Slightly uncomfortable at the turn of events, she glanced at Lucky. His past gave her the wherewithal to confront her past. She didn't miss the longing look Lucky sent in her direction. For a split second, it almost seemed as though he wanted to dance with her and her alone, which was wishful thinking on her part. They weren't really a couple, and this was all staged for Dad's benefit.

Evie maneuvered herself and Lucky over to where she was dancing with Dad. "I believe I haven't danced with my husband yet." Her eyes sparkled as brightly as the sequins on her dress.

"The newlywed stage." Gordon's smile was as wide as his face. "There's nothing like it. You'll see later this year."

Lucky held out his arm, but he had to do so with everyone's gaze upon them. She relied on her instincts and rested her head near his cheek. They swayed in time to the sweet and slow love song.

The music came to an abrupt stop, and gasps echoed throughout the room. Lizzie wondered what was going on until goose bumps dotted her arm. She turned and found a solitary figure standing in the doorway, his uniform and regulation haircut bringing immediate recognition of her brother's arrival. She cheered and rushed over to him. "Ben!"

Lizzie reached her brother at the same time as the rest of her family. She waited her turn for her hug, and she grasped Ben's solid frame before stepping back and searching for Lucky. "You have to meet Lucky." She pulled Ben over to where the handsome rodeo cowboy was standing in the shadows, as if allowing the rest of her family to have a moment without him.

Didn't he know he was part of the family?

No, he didn't because none of this was supposed to be real, but somewhere over the past several weeks, reality blurred as Lucky reconnected her with feelings she'd repressed deep after the death of her mother. And the way he made her feel inside?

His calm optimism, despite all he'd endured, soothed and excited her at the same time. Her chest constricted as the truth slammed into her with more force than the Tilt-A-Whirl they had ridden at the Summer Send-off. He was a man beyond compare, and she was in love with Lucky Harper.

Now, what was she going to do to get them through this mess? She almost gasped, as the answer was so obvious. By herself, she couldn't do anything. With him by her side, though? Together, they made a formidable team.

However, it took two to make a team, and the crestfallen look on his face made it all too clear he didn't have the same feelings for her.

"I've heard so much about you." Ben's voice broke through Lizzie's thoughts, and she looked up in time to see Ben shake Lucky's hand. "No one else has ever made my sister look so happy."

How could someone look so happy on the outside and yet be so miserable on the inside?

Gordon came over and patted the backs of Ben and Lucky at the same time. "Will you be able to take time off at Christmas and return for their wedding?"

Ben laughed. "I haven't been back for five minutes and you're already asking when I'm coming home again. Guess you've finally noticed I haven't been around after all."

Gordon's chest fell and rose. "I deserve that. I hope we can take some time while you're home and resolve the issues between us."

Evie joined the group and hugged Ben. "You're here. I'm so happy to see you."

"The base is still talking about your concert. It's always a pleasure." Ben dipped his head in Evie's direction while Lucky kept backing away until he hit the wall.

At the sound of the thud, everyone turned in Lucky's direction. He blushed a deep red. "This is a family moment. I'll call it a night, especially since I have to leave tomorrow to head to the rodeo in Arizona."

"Any way you can stay the whole day?" Ben asked, removing his hat and placing it on a nearby table. "I'd like to spend some time getting to know my sister's fiancé."

Sabrina joined the group. "At last I get to meet my other stepbrother." She extended her hand and smiled. "I'm Sabrina Darling, Evie's daughter."

"You're the rodeo clown, and your husband's also in the rodeo. And you have a daughter, right?" Ben smiled but sounded like he was reciting information from an index card.

"Yes." Sabrina pulled out her phone and showed him a picture. "And I hope you get to meet Genie tomorrow. We'll be leaving early the day after next for the next rodeo."

Everyone's gaze fell on Lucky, and he shrugged. "Guess if Ty and Sabrina are staying, I can, too."

Evie grinned, and then she whispered something in Dad's ear. "Evie, you're absolutely right. I don't know why I didn't think of that sooner." His booming voice caused chills to cascade down Lizzie's spine.

Lizzie reached for Lucky's hand and spoke before Dad could make any more announcements. "Since we have all day tomorrow to catch up, Lucky and I are going to call it a night."

"What if tomorrow's your wedding day?" Gordon might have used the microphone as the guests in the room seemed to still and take note of his words. Then a buzz swept over the crowd, and everyone started clapping.

The metallic taste of fear coated her mouth, and sweat broke out on her forehead. This couldn't be happening. How had everything escalated so fast? Again. Her throat grew so dry she couldn't speak.

"We don't have a license." Lucky's calm tone was a match for his unruffled self.

Why wasn't he panicking along with her?

"There's no waiting period in Colorado, and you can get one tomorrow morning." Gordon waved away Lucky's concern. "Ben's here, and he just said he can't guarantee he'd be here at Christmas. It's obvious you and Lizzie are in love. You can get married and Lizzie can go with you to the rodeo. Then you can leave for your honeymoon from there."

Lizzie's breaths came fast and shallow. "No cake." Her voice came out more like a croak, and she found the strength to swallow. "And no dress."

Small details, and ones she didn't really care about, but she'd latch on to them if it postponed this wedding long enough for her and Lucky to end this once and for all.

Audrey wiggled her body into the middle of the circle. "Aunt Lizzie, you looked beautiful at Grandpa's wedding. That dress was so pretty."

Evie nodded. "You can wear your bridesmaid dress unless you want to try on my wedding gown for the something borrowed."

Zack joined her and pointed to the table in the corner. "And Tammy made that today. Isn't that a cake?"

Out of the mouths of babes. Lizzie entered full panic mode, and Ben reached over and rubbed her arm. "I missed Jeff's and Dad's weddings." Regret coated Ben's words. "I'd like to make it to one family event."

Gordon called out, "All of you are invited to our ranch tomorrow at three for the wedding. Plenty of time for morning ranch chores, followed by the afternoon ceremony."

Lizzie's cheeks went as numb as the rest of her, and she grasped at straws. "We don't have an officiant."

"I'm available." Zelda Baker stepped forward from the crowd. "I'm not only the former mayor, I'm also the justice of the peace."

How would she get herself and Lucky out of this mess? While everything was in place for an impromptu wedding, there was one thing missing: a groom in love with the bride. Somehow, they'd gone from having several months to end the engagement to less than eighteen hours. If Lucky didn't despise her before, he surely did now that she'd trapped them both in a situation that seemed destined to hurt too many people.

CHAPTER SIXTEEN

LATER THAT NIGHT, in the privacy of Will's stable, Lucky patted Butterscotch's muzzle and then reached into his coat pocket for an apple slice. "How did everything snowball so fast?"

One minute he was single and unattached, and the next he was single and attached. All this time, he thought he'd been craving time with Lizzie's family, when the truth was he'd fallen in love with her. Now she must loathe him. He could have put an end to this sooner, but belonging in Violet Ridge as part of the Irwin family had been like a dream come true.

Almost as much as his yearning to qualify for the finals. But even with that accomplishment close and within his grasp, victory would be hollow without Lizzie to share his joy.

Butterscotch whinnied as he could smell the apple Lucky still grasped. He held it out, and the gelding accepted it with gusto, the brush of his muzzle preceding the scratchy feel of the tongue against Lucky's callused hand. "We'll get through the breakup together, right? You and me?"

"Of course. Family sticks together." Will's firm voice came from behind, and Lucky's legs buckled as he realized what he'd muttered to his horse was loud enough for Will to overhear.

He waited for his breath to return as his friend emerged

from the shadows. "You should have made yourself known earlier," Lucky said.

"Seems like that's my line," Will said. "Why don't you tell me the whole truth from the beginning?"

The moment he'd dreaded for so long was here. Once again, he was the kid piling his meager belongings into a trash bag with the caseworker standing by, waiting to take him to another temporary home. Leaving now would keep from putting Will in a bad spot when this fell apart. The Sullivan family had been ranching next to the Double I for some fifty years. More than neighbors, Will and Lizzie had grown up together, and Lucky had seen the interaction between the ranches over the past few weeks. Of course, Will would have to maintain good relations with his closest neighbor, leaving Lucky on the outside. What he intended to do all along was upon him, ripping his insides to shreds, and now it was irrevocable.

"You don't have to worry. The wedding's not going to happen, and this will all be over." In more ways than one, but it had been a good ride. Better than good. It had been nearly perfect.

That this was a fake engagement, where his heart became attached, kept it from being perfect. This time, he had no one to blame for what happened. He was an adult, and he was responsible for his actions.

"You don't get it, do you?" Will's gaze narrowed, and he moved closer. Out of nowhere, Will's dependable and trusty border collie, Rocket, circled him and Will until Lucky stood a few feet away from his friend.

"Get what?" Rocket and Will were working together, but Lucky didn't know their plan.

"You're family." Will's eyes showed the concern and care behind those simple words. "You, me and Sabrina. I will always be here for you."

Lucky considered his choices. When he began on the rodeo circuit, he hadn't had a family, and Will had taken him under his wing. Then Sabrina had joined their family when they had found themselves at the same bar one Saturday night. They'd bonded over comparing whose ride had been worse, Lucky's or Will's. Since Will had been nursing a broken nose, he'd won. Then there was the night when Will and Sabrina waited in the hospital ER room while he received stitches. He almost laughed at the memory of Will eating a bucket of edible cookie dough while Sabrina applied their facial masks on her birthday.

Lucky stopped strolling down memory lane, especially with Will's direct gaze shooting lasers at him. "We had some pretty good times, but everything comes to an end."

"Kelsea's taught me a thing or two about beginnings. Why is this the end and not the beginning?"

Lucky gulped and told Will everything.

"Why didn't you tell me the truth sooner?" Will folded his arms and leaned against the unpainted wood of the nearest stall. "You used to trust me."

"At first it was because of the Irwins. They made me feel like I was part of their family, and you know why I couldn't resist that. But it's because of Lizzie." The mental picture of her atop the Ferris wheel with the wind mussing her auburn hair flashed in front of him. "I meant it when I said I wouldn't embarrass her. She's special, and original, and, well…" Lucky rolled his neck and sighed.

Will reached up to the wall behind him and handed Lucky a currycomb before taking one for himself and tending to his stallion, Domino. "Sabrina and I will always have your back, same as you've always had ours."

He had found his family after all. That should have meant everything, yet without Lizzie? It was bittersweet indeed.

Together they cared for the horses, falling into the

same familiar pattern as the past couple of years whenever Lucky visited the Silver Horseshoe. The rhythmic strokes of combing Butterscotch soothed him, but try as he might, he still couldn't come up with answers to his problems. There wasn't an easy way out that wouldn't hurt Lizzie.

"How did you keep it together when Kelsea left the ranch?" Lucky's throat clogged as he had to figure out how he'd find the strength to hit the road for the next rodeo tomorrow, alone, like always. He wanted to stay and comfort Lizzie rather than just walk away, but her family would be there for her.

The sound of the stable door sliding open gave Lucky time to pull himself together. Kelsea entered the stable with a plate of sandwiches and cookies. "You should have asked for a better bachelor party. Even though dinner was delicious and filling, I thought you could use some nourishment." She set the dish on a stool and glanced at Lucky, then Will. "I'll tend to the goats before I call it a night."

She hugged Lucky and kissed Will before taking her leave. Will reached for the top sandwich. "I didn't keep it together. My uncle Barry told me I was a bear before I booked my flight to Atlanta."

Will and Kelsea had gone through a rough patch after they met. While it had been obvious to everyone around them they were in love, a forced separation had finally caused them to confront their feelings.

It would be nice if he knew the same outcome was waiting for him and Lizzie. Better than nice, but a happy ending depended on two people feeling the same way.

"I can't guarantee I'll take it that well."

Will swallowed the bite of his sandwich. "You're the calmest, steadiest person I've ever met, but sometimes you have to take action and fight for what's right." Then his smile faded as he kept his gaze on Lucky. "You're in love with her."

It wasn't a question, but a statement. He owed Will, and himself, the truth about this. "Yeah."

"If you don't cancel the wedding before she walks down the aisle, I'll object," Will said.

That was one reason Lucky cared so much about Will and Sabrina. Either would do anything for him.

Even though Will had Kelsea and Sabrina had Ty, they still had his back and always would.

No matter how hard the next few days would be, he had to stand up and do the right thing.

"Thank you, but Lizzie and I got ourselves into this, and we have to get ourselves out of it." Before the wedding, though, Lucky had to do something important, something he should have done a long time ago. He glanced at his watch. He still had fifteen hours until the wedding. More than enough time for something too important to wait any longer. "Can I borrow your truck?"

Will reached into his pocket and threw Lucky a set of keys. "Return it with a full tank of gas."

Lucky caught them and raised his eyebrows. "No questions asked?"

"For the record, I don't let my uncle Barry borrow it." Will grinned. "But I trust you, Lucky."

It was time he trusted himself. Lucky reached for a couple of sandwiches and added a cookie the size of his hand for good measure. "See you at the wedding."

WITH ONLY THE faint ray of morning light on the horizon that heralded her wedding day, a ceremony she had to stop, Lizzie steered the UTV around the pothole. JR grasped the sides of his passenger seat, and Lizzie lifted her foot ever so slightly off the gas. Arriving at the field in one piece took priority over speed, same as the animals took priority over solving her dilemma without Lucky. Moose barked from the rear, a reassuring sound that he'd find any stragglers who might have wandered away from the herd. They approached the field where the cowhand waited for them with the plaintive sound of lowing cows growing louder.

Lizzie parked the UTV. JR and Moose hurried toward Sweeney, the reliable night cowhand who notified them a mere forty-five minutes ago at the first signs of bloat, a potentially serious issue this time of year for cattle. She grabbed the medical kit from the rear of the UTV and joined them.

Sweeney had already treated the worst case, and the cow was now recovering. In no time, she and JR checked the rest of the herd and found five more displaying the classic signs of bloat. With their stomachs protruding and lack of movement, there was no time to lose. The three of them worked in tandem and alleviated the symptoms of the cow who appeared to have the worst case.

"Should we call the vet?" Sweeney asked.

"Go ahead, while JR and I keep treating the cows." Lizzie reached for her bag and assembled the tube for the procedure to fight the bloat. "I don't think any of them are at the surgical stage, but it's wise to have her here in case any of them worsen."

The third cow had her full attention when a stethoscope came into view, followed by the person attached to it. She'd been so busy she hadn't even heard the vet pull up in another of the ranch's UTVs. She looked over, and to her surprise, her father emerged as well.

"Didn't expect to find you here," Dad said. "Not with the wedding later today."

She concentrated on the task before her. An animal was in distress, and she couldn't let that go without doing something about it, even if it was supposed to be her wedding day.

Not that she had any intention of going through with the ceremony.

It wasn't that she didn't want to marry Lucky. She did. However, he deserved a wedding and a marriage with love and respect and honesty, and so did she. The cowboy who'd stolen her heart didn't realize everything he did to make others happy, especially her. While she wanted nothing more than to see his smile every day, she couldn't go through with the ceremony like this. Not with a lie between them and the community she loved.

And not without him knowing she loved him.

The cow bleated, and she focused her energy on the animal. Sweat poured down her face, the heat of late summer coming on full force. The brightness of noonday flooded the field, bathing the clumps of wildflowers in a golden glow. Finally, the cow gave a slight bellow, her relief evident, and Lizzie stepped back. Her stomach grumbled, and JR handed her a protein bar. "Thanks."

She ate the energy bar, and another case confronted them. They continued treating the affected cattle. Finally, the vet snapped her bag closed. "I'll consider this a happy ending, since they all survived without surgery."

They listened to the vet as she gave tips about symptoms and treatment. JR pointed to some forage in the distance. "That patch of sweet clover over there. It's most likely the cause of their distress. I'll take care of it now."

Lizzie nodded while JR headed to the UTV for the tools he'd need for that task. While clover didn't usually result in bloat, certain cattle were more susceptible and the wet conditions of the past few days would have exacerbated the likelihood of that being the culprit.

Would her plan for adding Simmentals to the ranch with

their leaner bodies be something that would mean they could avoid this morning's near calamity in the future? Perhaps not, but she'd still need to address this addition with her father. With a half-hour ride back to the ranch, there was no better time for a long-overdue conversation, starting with the cattle and ending with the truth about the fake engagement. Even if he fired her on the spot, the ranch would benefit from her changes.

The vet stayed with JR, leaving her alone with her father. This wouldn't be easy, but she wasn't the same Elizabeth she was when Lucky dropped that fated peppermint in the straw. She could do this.

Her father yielding the driver seat to her came as the latest surprise today. While her brothers had been driving the UTVs as long as she could remember, her father had always assumed he'd drive in her presence. Lizzie took the wheel and eased the UTV onto the dirt path.

"I texted Evie—"

"About today—"

Silence came over them and lasted a moment too long. "You first," she said, keeping her gaze on the road.

"Evie texted the guests and pushed everything to five tonight, not that you've mentioned the wedding once today." Then he sniffed the air. "What's that odor?"

She glanced at the jeans and flannel shirt she had thrown on while it was still dark outside, and they now featured dirt mixed with grass stains. Two showers might start making a dent in the strong stench coming off her. "Me." She took a deep breath and then coughed. "What would you think of introducing Simmentals to the ranch?"

"That you were avoiding the subject of your wedding."

He wasn't wrong, but she had to know one thing before she confided in him the wedding wasn't happening today.

"What if Jeff or Ben had brought up the subject of introducing another breed of cattle to the ranch?"

"I don't know if Jeff could distinguish between an Angus and a Holstein anymore." Dad laughed with a blustery huff. "And Ben? Takes after your mom's side of the family. Military life suits him, just like ranch life suits you."

This didn't make sense to her. "Then why have you treated me different all these years?"

"Huh?" A quick look at her father showed his consternation. "How have I done that?"

"You've always acted one way with Jeff and Ben and another way with me, like you kept forgetting I grew up."

"You're six years younger than Ben and ten years younger than Jeff. Even on a ranch, that's significant." Dad's lack of hesitation cemented his answer. "All three of you are unique, but you're the one I trust running the ranch."

I was taking their individual personalities into account. Audrey is younger than Zack. Lucky's response to her accusation of treating the siblings differently echoed in her mind. All this time she'd thought Dad had been giving preferential treatment to her brothers and while he'd treated her differently, it was out of deference to her younger age, affording her more respect and responsibility as she grew older. She should have seen it for herself, but she'd been too close to look objectively at the whole situation, a lesson she needed if she'd run the ranch someday.

This newfound knowledge gave her added strength. "I stand by the changes I'm proposing as far as the bunkhouses and the Simmentals."

"And that's why I'm glad you found Lucky. Just like Evie keeps me grounded, he's perfect for you. He's the restful calm to your energetic initiative."

Her heart ached at the mention of Lucky's name. This weekend, he'd head to the rodeo, and then there'd be the one after that, his RV/horse trailer combination the only home he'd ever really had. A home on wheels, it took him anywhere he wanted to be, and why would he want to be with her when he could go anyplace at a minute's notice?

The truth came to her in a flash.

She didn't need to pour out her heart to Dad.

She needed to pour out her heart to Lucky.

She stepped on the gas, this newfound realization too important to hold in any longer. Out of the corner of her eye, she saw her father grip the seat, his knuckles turning white. "Speaking of Evie, I'd like to get back to her in one piece."

"I need to talk to Lucky."

"Slow down, and you'll have your whole life to talk to him."

She eased her foot off the pedal as the offensive odor surrounding her almost made her gag. "Maybe I should take a shower first?"

"Only if you want to talk to him in the same room." Dad laughed at his joke as the stable came into view.

She parked the UTV and headed for the guesthouse, where her dress was waiting. There was no time to lose before guests would arrive, and a shower wasn't a luxury but a necessity. After she didn't smell like cattle, she'd share her heart with Lucas Harper.

What they decided to do from there was up to them.

SHORTLY AFTER TWO in the afternoon, Lucky shut the door of Will's truck at the same time Cale Padilla did. Cale let out a long, low whistle. "That's some ranch house."

Lucky agreed with Cale's assessment of the Double I. Not that he had expected Cale to drop everything at the

Cattle Crown Ranch and drive to Violet Ridge with him, but he had.

After Lucky had arrived at Cale's ranch, it was like no time had elapsed, although there were more crow's-feet wrinkles near Cale's brown eyes and a few streaks of silver in his black hair. His mentor was still robust, his heart as big as ever. He and Vivi had listened to Lucky for five minutes before hugging him and sending him to their guest room to sleep for a few hours, but not before admonishing him he shouldn't have waited so long to visit.

When he awakened, a large breakfast awaited him, as did two sets of eyes eager for an explanation. Lucky started with a long overdue apology for staying away so many years.

Lucky had been so certain there was no more room in Vivi's and Cale's hearts for him, so he'd pretty much kept his distance once he'd joined the rodeo. They'd been hurt at his absence, but they understood he needed time to make a life for himself and work things out on his own. They just hadn't expected him to take quite so long.

The four-hour trip to Violet Ridge had given Lucky and Cale more time to finish clearing the air and updating each other on their lives, including details about their respective families, with Lucky telling Cale about the changes in Will's life and Sabrina's.

But now came the biggest risk of his life. He had to lay everything on the line with Lizzie. While he was willing to marry her today, pledge his heart to her for everyone to see, they had to do what was right for them so they could move forward with no false pretenses. She was worth the wait.

And if she didn't love him? Well, last night with Will and today with Cale proved he'd been wrong about how others felt about him in the past. Sometimes the truth hurt, but it was better to be honest and hurt than live with a guilty conscience.

As they approached the front door of the ranch house, Lucky found time for one more apology to Cale. "This might be a wild goose chase. There's no guarantee I'm getting married today," Lucky warned in a tone low enough only for Cale to hear.

"There are no guarantees in life, period." Cale removed his battered brown cowboy hat and placed it against his chest. "But Vivi and I have missed you. Before we left, she told me to tell you she's sorry for missing your big day. Her mare is due any hour now, and she wants to be there to see the new foal. But it took you too long to come back. You're like a son to us, Lucky. We're here for you, no matter what happens today."

Lucky expected the house to be a beehive of activity, considering the wedding was set to start in less than an hour, but no one answered the front door. Cale's gaze almost burned a hole in the back of his head, and Lucky turned with a shrug.

"They must be at the meadow already." He reached into his pocket and checked for any messages from Lizzie, but there were none. "I'll let Lizzie know I'm back."

He shot off a quick text with an urgent plea to talk to her as soon as possible. Only by talking to each other could they determine the path for the rest of their lives.

Then he placed his phone in his jeans, and Cale looked at him. "It is a casual wedding, right?"

"You're my guest, so you're fine," Lucky said, while plucking his own flannel shirt, the worse for wear since he'd driven half the night and quite a while today. "But I've looked better after my dead-last rodeo finishes. I'll take you to the kitchen first and see if I can rummage up a snack for you while I shower and change into something more appropriate for the groom." While his brown cowboy hat and jeans were like a second skin to him, he'd left Ben's tuxedo in one of the guest rooms.

Lucky led Cale past the mudroom into the kitchen.

"Seems as though you know your way around here," Cale said.

Tammy was nowhere to be found, confirming Lucky's guess everyone was already at the meadow. He glanced at his watch. "I'll have to take the fastest shower in the history of showers to make it there by three. You can wait in the living room. If anyone asks, just tell them you're a guest of the groom."

Lucky settled Cale in the formal living room in time to see Gordon's office door open and shut. *Perfect.* He'd just give Gordon a heads-up he had to talk to Lizzie before the wedding and that if they were late to stall everyone.

It was up to Lizzie how long everyone would be waiting, or if they'd explain there'd be no wedding, either today or any other day.

He hurried to the office door and rapped on it a few times before hearing the command to enter. Gordon stood behind the desk, looking through drawers, his gray hair damp. To his surprise, Gordon wore jeans and a plaid shirt, not the attire he expected of the father of the bride.

His breath whooshed out of him. Lizzie must have leveled with him. Lucky didn't know whether to be thankful or devastated. If she loved him, he'd have gone through with the wedding in a heartbeat.

"So you know." Lucky sagged, relieved that Gordon had finally learned what really happened. He only hoped there were no hard feelings since Lizzie had had her father's state of mind at heart when this all started.

"I can't say I really approve at this point. Time will tell whether Lizzie is right. I'm used to calling the shots, but she's all grown up. She's right that I have to give her the same freedom that I afford Jeff and Ben." Gordon gave up his search and stared at Lucky.

That look told Lucky everything. He knew all about the fake engagement. A weight lifted from Lucky's shoulders.

"Then you'll want these back." Lucky pulled out his key ring and extracted the cabin keys, placing them on Gordon's desk. "Who knew a peppermint could cause so much trouble? You're not mad with Lizzie about this engagement farce, are you? I'm as much to blame as she is."

Equal culpability. It was nice to shoulder the blame with her. Even though Lizzie wasn't by his side, he knew she was in this with him. With that in mind, he steeled himself for whatever Gordon had to say.

"Care for a drink?" Gordon reached behind him and placed two rock glasses on the desk, pushing one in Lucky's direction. He produced a decanter and poured a splash of an amber liquid, presumably Scotch, into each. "Why don't you back up and begin at the beginning?"

Lucky accepted the drink and swished it around the cup. "If you've already heard Lizzie's side of the story, why hear the same thing twice?"

"Humor me." Gordon smiled and sat in the plush leather executive chair before he sipped his drink.

Lucky settled across from him and placed his crystal glass next to the keys. "Growing up in foster care, it was nice to be a part of your family for a while. And Lizzie? She went along with all of this so you'd have a happy wedding. That's just who she is. She'd do anything for you, sir." He launched into the story, making sure to paint Lizzie in the best possible light, as she tended to be hard on herself.

Gordon poured another drink and downed it before he stared at Lucky. "Do you love my daughter?"

"Yes, sir."

"And Cale is here?" Gordon tapped his fingers together as if he was forming a steeple. "In my living room?"

"I had to make that right before the ceremony, same as Lizzie, and I knew you had to know the truth." It was the day of reckoning, but he could hold his head high, and did exactly that while he headed for the door. "Thank you for listening to my side of the story."

"You keep talking like the wedding's off." Gordon's words made him pause at the door. "No one's told me any differently."

Lucky faced him, the older rancher's face like stone, not giving away any expression. "It's on as scheduled?"

"As far as I know. Evie's the one in charge." Gordon frowned. "With everything that's happened, I haven't seen her in the past few hours. My gear's at the guest house. I'd better change and then find Evie and Lizzie. See you later."

With a light step, Lucky hurried upstairs and was ready in record time. Even the bow tie, thanks to Will's previous lesson, cooperated. At last, the tide seemed to be turning in his favor.

He and Cale proceeded to the meadow, and what a pair they made with Lucky in Ben's tailored tuxedo and Cale in his boots and jeans. But this was a working ranch, and Lizzie would understand, once he explained Cale's sudden appearance.

Rodeo calves danced in his stomach. This was it. His wedding day. He fidgeted with his tuxedo lapel and thought about changing his clothes into something more comfortable. He decided against it, wanting to look his best for Lizzie, and for himself. There were times as a little boy he asked himself if he was worthy of love and a family. He'd cobbled together the best family, and he wanted Lizzie to be his wife. But before anything else happened, he had to talk to her and find out how she felt about her dad's reaction. That was only part of it. He wanted to scream from the top of the Ferris wheel he loved her and hoped she'd be willing to do the same. Love was within his grasp, and he wanted to claim it, along with their future.

He found Tammy with her arms full, muttering to herself. "First, it was happening in December, then it was happening at three, then it wasn't happening at three."

"Tammy?" Lucky approached the cook carefully, as she was balancing a long sheet cake. "Did I hear you right? The wedding's not at three?"

"Why do you think I'm taking the cake back to the house? The chocolate will melt out here." Tammy swept past him and loaded the cake into the van.

Lucky wobbled, the ground shaking under his feet. He would have preferred hearing the news from Lizzie, not Tammy, but it was true. The wedding was canceled.

Cale rushed over and supported Lucky's elbow. "I heard. I'm sorry, Lucky. Vivi and I would love to have you stay with us for a while."

The rodeo was where he belonged. "I have to be in Williams, Arizona, tomorrow morning." His legs steadied, and he found his phone. "Hold on a minute."

He texted Lizzie regarding the current status of the wedding. Cale stayed silent while Lucky waited. No reply. It was over.

"I'm calling Vivi. See if she can round up the neighbors to help for a few days while I go with you to the rodeo." Cale whipped out his phone and walked over to the front row of seats.

Lucky called Lizzie, and it went to voice mail. He needed more than fifteen seconds to say everything, but this would have to suffice. He poured out his heart. "I've worked my whole life for a chance at the finals, and I'm going to give it my all this weekend, but I'm coming back to Violet Ridge for you, for us." He swallowed and loosened his collar. "I understand why you called off the wedding, considering you told your dad and he listened to my side of it, but I sure would appreciate the honor of taking you out on a date Monday night. Just the two of us. Because I'm in love with you, and I'd like to court you the right way."

The new engagement and wedding ring he'd purchased in Denver earlier today on the drive with Cale weighed heavily in his pocket. He gave a long lingering glance at the arch of flowers with strands of small twinkle lights wound around the arbor and along the framework over the rows of seats. For a second, he saw what could have been the scene later today. Lizzie, looking beautiful in wedding dress with her auburn hair cascading over her shoulders. While her family would have been a bonus, and they were the reason he and Lizzie had even talked in the first place, they were no longer his driving motivation behind wanting to see Lizzie smile or hold her hand through the disappointments.

It was Lizzie herself, a strong and vibrant woman who worked as hard, if not harder, than anyone on this ranch. Being with her boosted his confidence and made him feel like he could conquer the world, or, at the very least, earn a spot at the year-end finals.

She made him feel worthy of her, regardless of his past.

His relationship with Lizzie might be hanging on by the thread of a rope, but it wasn't over, and neither was his shot at the finals. Even if the wedding wasn't happening today, the rodeo would still go on, and he'd give nothing less than his best.

LIZZIE LOOKED AT herself in the guesthouse mirror. Audrey was right. Her bridesmaid dress was the perfect wedding dress. The dusty pink set off her auburn hair, and the delicate embroidered flowers were exactly what she'd have picked out under different circumstances. Who'd have believed that the cowhand covered with dirt and smelling like cattle could transform into someone this beautiful who smelled like a rose garden in the space of two hours?

She turned and faced her sister-in-law and Evie, the women responsible for taking her in hand and delivering someone she hardly recognized in the mirror. "You two are amazing. Thank you."

Evie twisted the mascara wand into its case before embracing Lizzie. "And you, my darling stepdaughter, are also a natural wonder. What's more, you're family. I'd do anything for you or Jeff or Ben." Then Evie reached out and hugged Nicole. "And you and yours."

Nicole plucked out a couple of tissues from the box and approached Lizzie, puckering her lips as a signal for her to blot her lipstick. Lizzie did as directed, and Nicole smiled. "Perfect." She faced Evie, her face blushing a rosy red. "It's still astonishing that my father-in-law married Evalynne."

"He married Evie." Lizzie shook her head. "Evalynne's a bonus."

She smiled at her stepmother, and everything clicked into place. Her family supported and loved her. That was what had drawn Lucky toward accepting her plus-one invitation after the fact. Unlike Jared, who'd been impressed with the Irwin family name and status, Lucky didn't stand on pretense. He'd stood in the creek with her until the calf was free. They'd been drenched and covered with mud, but his relief had been as clear as hers. He didn't brush off Zack and Audrey, but spent time with them, going so far as teaching them how to whittle. He was as happy with a stuffed animal from a carnival stall as he'd been when presented the keys to a luxurious mountain cabin.

Her family had taken in Lucky and, in doing so, given the two of them time and opportunity to find each other and fall in love. That moment on the Ferris wheel had changed everything. Lizzie drew in a deep breath and smoothed the pale pink dress.

"I have to find Lucky. There's something I have to say to him before the wedding."

While that had been her intent all day, the time was finally right. "See you soon."

A light knock at the door caused everyone to look in that direction. Gordon ducked his head into the room. "Is this a good time?"

Lizzie shook her head and gathered her skirt in her hands. "I have to find Lucky first. It can't wait."

Gordon entered the room, his tuxedo perfectly paired with his cowboy hat. He removed his hat and placed it on the dresser. "This can't, either. Can I have a minute with Elizabeth?"

"I'd best check on my family." Nicole brushed past him, and Evie kissed Gordon before leaving the room.

Lizzie tapped her foot, the tip of her cowboy boot coming into contact with the hardwood floor. The order of these conversations was out of whack. She had to talk to Lucky first. Afterward, they'd talk to her father together. From there? Who knew whether the wedding would occur even though she already knew she'd like nothing more than to marry the rodeo cowboy.

"Dad, this really—"

"I had an interesting conversation with Lucky an hour ago," Dad said. "He's a fine man."

One look at her father told her everything. "You know, then?" She gulped. "That I lied."

"I know Lucky's side of it. I'd like to hear yours."

She sank onto the bed, an icy chill running through her,

while Dad sat next to her. "He did it for me." She squared her shoulders and told him everything, fully accepting her part in the charade. "I expect you're disappointed in me. If you want my resignation since I lied to you, I understand."

"That's a bit extreme, don't you think? The ranch will survive, and you're the right Irwin to make sure it does." He reached for her hand and held it in his own. "Lucky told me you didn't want to ruin my wedding. He was rather adamant I understand you went along with this so you wouldn't ruin my day."

"Actually, my pride started all of it. I didn't want everyone to think I couldn't get a date." Getting this off her chest felt like a boulder had lifted off her. "Then it snowballed."

Someone knocked, and Sabrina entered. "Have you seen Lucky?"

That was her entire goal for the day, and the one thing she hadn't accomplished. "No."

Dad stood and headed toward Sabrina. "I talked to him less than an hour ago. He was going to show his guest, Cale, around the ranch while I changed into my tuxedo."

"I thought I saw Lucky's trailer on the highway, heading south." Sabrina frowned and then smiled. "Ty told me I must be mistaken, and I obviously was."

That chill returned, and Lizzie shivered. Lucky's horse trailer/RV was too distinctive. "So he talked to you before you changed?" Dad nodded while Lizzie started putting the pieces together. "Did anyone tell Lucky we pushed the wedding back to five?"

"Evie notified the guests. Let me check with her." Dad rose and left the room. He returned with a grim expression. "Evie thought you told Lucky."

Lizzie entered the bathroom and searched for her phone. It wasn't there. First, the ring. Now her phone. She was losing things left and right, and now she might have lost the most important part of her life. *Lucky.*

Her jacket pocket. She'd left it in the tack room, the odor of the offending outerwear quite pronounced upon their return from the cattle meadow. Wasting no time, she excused herself and hurried to the stable, relieved she'd chosen boots for her wedding rather than heels. She found her phone and gasped at the number of texts and voice mails she missed. Quite a few of them were from Lucky.

Without further ado, she started listening to his voice mail, tuning him out as soon as he said he told her father everything. While she'd taken a shower, he'd discovered the wedding was off. Of course he headed to the next rodeo. He was gone. Without her.

There was only one person for whom she'd have left the Double I.

Lucky.

But he didn't ask her to go with him.

"He told me the same thing," Dad said.

She started at the sound of his voice. She turned around and found him there. "He told you what?" Her voice came out in a whisper. "That he was leaving and returning to the rodeo by himself."

"That he's in love with you." Dad stared at her with thoughtful deliberation. "You only heard the first part, didn't you? Play the message again."

Hadn't she learned anything over these past few weeks but to listen and gather all the facts before jumping to conclusions? She did as her father requested, and joy started spreading through her. "He loves me."

A goofy smile came over her, and she'd never felt this light. Chords of wedding music reached her ears, and her grin faded. It was time to face everyone.

"I'll make the announcement." Dad started for the stable doors.

Lizzie ran and caught up with him. "I got myself into this. I'll say something." She reached up and kissed her father's cheek. "But thanks for offering."

Guests were being seated, and Lizzie steeled herself as she approached the musicians. She whispered to them, and they stopped playing before she proceeded to the front. In the back, she saw her brothers and the rest of the family looking her way. When Jeff and his family arrived for Dad's wedding, she'd hidden in the stable. Now they were all here for her, and she loved them for the support.

Somehow, though, she had to tread carefully as she intended for Lucky to become a part of her family permanently.

"Hello." She stopped talking when a sea of faces looked at her. For a second, she wished she was saying this to Andromeda, but she could, and would, do this. There would be consequences because of the past few weeks, and she'd face them head-on.

"There's been a slight hitch in the proceedings. You see, I thought a date to my father's wedding would get my brother off my case, but instead, that led to a series of misunderstandings that created a false impression that Lucky and I were engaged. We weren't then, but that's not to say we might not become engaged and get married down the road. However, what we decide to do will be between us and it'll be for the right reasons. Today was the right outcome for the wrong reasons, so there won't be a wedding, but rest assured, this is only the beginning, not the end. Thank you."

She hurried into her father's arms, and her family surrounded her in an embrace of love. Her father released her, his eyes full of pride. "You handled that well."

She knew what else she had to do. "Dad, we're short-staffed without Roy, but I need to go talk to Lucky."

"I know." He smiled and nodded. "We'll manage for the weekend."

Audrey tugged on Lizzie's dress, tears in her eyes. "Does this mean I can't call him Uncle Lucky? I want to say goodbye."

"I was going to give this to him for your wedding present," Zack said as he reached into his pocket and pulled out a piece of wood that Lizzie thought sort of resembled an elephant.

Zack handed it to her, and her heart almost burst with how much Zack had grown since he'd arrived. "It's beautiful."

"I've always wanted to see a rodeo," Nicole said, putting her hand on her sister-in-law's arm. "We're supposed to leave tomorrow night, but we can go home on Sunday instead. I hear there's a rodeo this weekend in Arizona we should attend. Show our support for a certain contestant."

Tears formed in Lizzie's eyes at Nicole's unexpected request. While a formidable lawyer, and more than a match for her brother, Nicole had always seemed distant. Once Lizzie got to know her better, she understood her sister-in-law's fear that she didn't belong here. With time, she was learning everyone accepted her, and she was more at ease. The important thing was how much she loved Jeff, her kids and her career. She and Nicole had a lot in common, and Lizzie could see them building a friendship on that foundation.

Lizzie squeezed the elephant and caught sight of her bare ring finger. As much as she'd like nothing better than to leave for the rodeo and Lucky's side immediately, she needed to do something important first, and enlisted her family's help to get it done.

CHAPTER SEVENTEEN

THE NEXT DAY, Lucky opened Butterscotch's grooming kit at the stall assigned to his American quarter horse at the rodeo fairgrounds. With extra care, considering he was running on little, if any, sleep, he cleaned the horse's hooves and then selected the currycomb from the leather kit. Next, he loosened the dirt and dust from the trailer ride to Arizona. The chore was rhythmic and soothing, something he needed since Lizzie hadn't returned his voice mail. He should have found her and confronted her with his feelings right there rather than relying on Gordon's and Tammy's statements.

The hardest part about leaving early was competing tonight. Being distracted in a rodeo arena with an energetic calf was never a good idea.

Should he forfeit his event and head back to the ranch a day early, rather than risk injury in the ring, since his mind wasn't in the best place? He needed the points if he had any chance of making the finals, but there was always next year. A relationship with Lizzie? That was once in a lifetime.

Taking special care of Butterscotch's sensitive shoulders, he dislodged the dirt from the flank and combed in the direction of the hair growth.

The tan horse swished his tail, and Lucky finished his task. He swapped out the comb for a soft body brush. "This will make you shine tonight." His gelding gave a soft snuff, as if setting Lucky to rights about his ability to captivate the crowd no matter how he looked. "Humor me."

"Anytime."

"That settles it, Butterscotch." Lucky reeled and rested his head against his gelding's flank. "I'm going to pull out. I'm hearing her voice."

Something brushed his shoulder, and he almost fell backward. He turned and found Lizzie there, a vision in her red cowboy hat and boots. "Now you're seeing me, too, but I assure you I'm quite real."

His mouth dropped. She was a long way from her beloved Double I. Could it be that, after all these years, someone didn't want to wait another day to see him? Tell him she loved him? While he loved Cale and Vivi, Will and Sabrina, all members of his adopted family, no one had ever dropped everything just for him. Instead, they'd patiently waited for him to realize he wanted them in their lives. Sometimes, though, it was nice to be asked.

Lizzie held out her hand, and the diamond engagement ring sat nestled in her palm. His heart sank. "You found it."

She didn't drive all this way for a big revelation or to join him on the tour. She'd come to return the ring.

Once he accepted it, it would be official. Their fake engagement would come to its fitting end.

"I would have arrived last night, only a few hours behind you, but I wanted—no, needed—to find this and return it to you." She pushed her hand in his direction.

"It's yours." He curled her fingers around the ring. It wasn't his, and in a way, it never had been. "Where was it?"

"We scoured the stable. I was about to give up when I remember I refilled the feed buckets that day. I moved the trough, and it was lodged between the bin and the wall," Lizzie said with a smile. "I left a mess to clean up on Monday."

So much for their date. "You could have left the ring with Will rather than coming all this way to tell me you're busy in person."

"I came all this way to attend a rodeo. You see, the man I love is going to win his event, and I've never even seen him compete in person. He's coming home to Violet Ridge, and on Monday night, we'll talk about every minute of the rodeo on our date." She wiggled the ring onto the fourth finger of her right hand.

Wait! Did she just say she loved him? He almost swooned. "Did it take canceling our wedding to make you realize you love me?"

"I didn't cancel our wedding. I'm hoping it was only postponed." Lizzie stopped talking when other rodeo contestants entered the stable and started grooming their horses. Her gaze darted around as if she was seeing where she was for the first time. "Is there somewhere else we can talk? Don't get me wrong, I love Butterscotch and any stable is like a second home, but we need some privacy. Besides, I have something important to show you."

Curiosity over what that could be compelled him to pick up his grooming kit. He followed her outside the stable, only to find the Irwin family waiting for him.

Audrey launched herself at him. "I couldn't go back to Boston without giving you a hug."

Zack hugged Lucky and presented him with a small wood carving. "It's an elephant. They say elephants don't forget, so I wanted to make you something so you wouldn't forget me."

His throat constricted at the gesture, and he soaked in everyone's presence, making another forever memory. Grandma Eloise's eyes sparkled, Jeff and Nicole nodded his way, and Evie smiled. He didn't know Ben well enough to read his expression, but he looked forward to making his acquaintance. Lizzie hugged his arm close to his side. "Dad is taking over stable duties today."

"And loving every minute." Evie's reassuring tone matched her demeanor, and she reached out her hand to him, keys transferring from her grip to his. "Gordon and I agreed you should have these. The cabin is yours whenever you visit Lizzie. Or even if you're spending time with Sabrina and Ty, or Will and Kelsea."

His heart swelled. "All of you came for me? Even after I lied? Even after the wedding didn't go on as planned?"

Jeff stepped forward and patted him on the back. "Once you save an Irwin, you're part of the family. Lizzie didn't tell you that?"

She hadn't told him many things yet, but Lucky planned on listening to her every day for the rest of his life. That, and ride horses with her, and kiss her. Often.

Somehow, she and her family had made room in their hearts for him, and that sent him clear near over the moon.

"Lizzie and I have a lot to talk about. Why don't you all make yourselves comfortable in my trailer? Especially you, Grandma Eloise."

The older woman smiled and tapped her cane in the dirt. "Evie arranged for a private flight back to Texas tomorrow. I'll be in the stands for your competition tonight, but it was a long drive and I don't mind resting a bit." She fluffed up her hair. "That way, Bob will see me at my best."

Lucky leaned forward and kissed her leathery, wrinkled cheek. "I have a feeling that Bob always sees the best of you."

"You flatterer, you." She hugged Lizzie first before embracing him. "You take good care of my step-granddaughter."

Lucky ushered everyone to his trailer and didn't try to hide the stuffed horse Lizzie won for him from its position of honor at his dinette table. As a matter of fact, there were more signs of his personal life around the trailer now than a few weeks ago: the book JR had lent him, his whittling knife on the nightstand and a framed picture of him and Lizzie from Gordon and Evie's wedding. Sometime in the past few weeks, he'd allowed himself the privilege of attaching sentimental value to objects, ones he'd keep and display, knowing he wouldn't have to shove everything in a garbage bag at a moment's notice. Audrey and Zack were busy bouncing on his bed when he escaped outside with Lizzie. Having her family's support was everything, but there was one person's support he valued above theirs, and he was holding her hand.

THE FAIRGROUNDS BUSTLED with the activity that preceded the start of the rodeo. Lizzie walked alongside Lucky to a trail where silver aspens provided plenty of shade, their leafy branches extending overhead. Black-eyed Susans and marigolds lined the side of the trail, their sweet fragrance a perfect counterpart to the coolness of this last day of August.

She stopped and grasped his hand. "Why did you tell Butterscotch you're going to forfeit? I know how much this means to you."

"There are other rodeos, but only one you."

His words, so simple, carried love in every syllable, and she would make sure he felt that same love and support as long as she had breath in her lungs.

"You'd have driven back to Violet Ridge for me?" She released him and twisted the ring on her right finger. One look at him revealed the answer.

"I love you, Elizabeth Irwin. You'll always be Lizzie to me."

He bent toward her, his hand reaching up and cupping her chin, his callused fingers soft against her skin. He kissed her and the part of her that was anxious, always seeking action on the ranch, settled into a peaceful calm. Somewhere along the line, their relationship had changed from nothing to everything. She let go of the past and embraced the future, the sweetness of this kiss flooding her with him. Lucky loved her, and she'd make sure he knew every day how much love was in his life.

After a few minutes, she touched her forehead to his. "I love you, Lucas Harper, and I'm looking forward to our first date on Monday night."

He laughed, that slow, deep chuckle she wanted to hear often, the one that made her feel all warm and shivery inside. "It seems as though we did this backward. Fell in love and then started dating."

She leaned her head on his shoulder. "You should know I'm not much for half measures."

He tilted his head until it touched hers. "That's what makes you undeniably you."

While she could stay like this for quite a while, she faced him. "I'm staying to watch you compete, of course. We all are."

"Butterscotch and I would be honored." His cheeks reddened as though he wasn't used to people coming out for him.

"The Irwin family is here in force. Audrey and Zack talked Jeff and Nicole into attending before they head back to Boston, and Grandma Eloise will tell her husband all about your performance. Ben hasn't been to a rodeo in years. I think he misses Violet Ridge."

His lips met hers, and she knew without any doubt that someday soon Lucky would be an official part of the Irwin family. But that was the tip of the saddle. Best of all, he loved her for herself. This was the real thing, and she reveled in the joy of his kiss.

EPILOGUE

Eight months later

LUCKY HAD NEVER seen the Silver Horseshoe look so festive as it did on this spring evening. Will and Kelsea were welcoming the new season with a festive celebration. He and Lizzie also suspected there'd be an announcement from the couple about a future addition to their family.

The weather was acting in true Colorado fashion, as he learned to expect from his adopted state. Last week, a blanket of snow greeted him as he and Lizzie walked from the guesthouse to the stable. Today, sunshine had flooded the paddock with warm weather, causing him to shed his jacket before noon.

Fairy lights lit up the barn, which had been transformed into a party space. Half of Violet Ridge mingled inside and outside the barn, as people everywhere enjoyed a bowl of chili or huckleberry cobbler. He accepted two drinks, a beer for himself and a ginger ale for his wife of two months.

Even in a crowd this size, he had no trouble spotting Lizzie, radiant in her red cowboy hat and jeans. This morning, they'd waited together for five minutes until the pregnancy test confirmed they were expecting. He didn't care whether it was a boy or a girl, just as long as the little one was healthy. He'd waited a long time for a family, before he realized he'd had one all along. Now he cherished both of his families, his honorary one of his best friends and the one who possessed his heart.

Sabrina came over and eyed the drinks. "Lizzie's drinking ginger ale?" She glanced Lizzie's way with a grin. "This might be presumptuous, but is Genie gaining another cousin? Are Evie and Gordon going to be grandparents again?"

He and Will and Sabrina were closer than siblings, and together for the long haul. "Stay tuned. Tonight's Will and Kelsea's night, though."

Will headed their way, a goofy smile on his face, and Lucky met Sabrina's gaze. They both laughed, and Will's grin was replaced with a glare that was anything but menacing.

"Are you two planning something?" Will asked, grinning.

"Why, Will." Sabrina crooked her arm through his. "Whatever gave you that idea?"

"That gleam in your eye, my dear Sabrina." Will arched an eyebrow.

"We're just wondering whether you and Kelsea are going to make the announcement about the baby before Snow and Flake break loose of the pen and disrupt the festivities." Sabrina laughed while talking about Will's infamous pair of goats, who loved Kelsea but gave Will a rough time.

"Ha, ha." Will pretended to laugh and then stilled. "Wait. How did you know she's pregnant? We just got off the phone with Kelsea's father and sister a few minutes before the party started."

Lucky leaned against the barn post and smiled. "You know how they say expectant women glow?" He couldn't help but sneak a glance at Lizzie, who was positively radiant, before facing Will. "You're glowing, Will."

"Expectant fathers don't glow." His friend glowered at them and then wiped his face. "That's just sweat."

Will's uncle Barry approached the trio and threw himself at Will in a huge embrace. "I knew it. I knew Kelsea was pregnant. Rocket's been guarding her at all costs. I'm going to be a great-uncle. This is big, really, really big. Snow and Flake are going to be guardian goats." His eyes lit up, and he rubbed his hands together. "That's it. At last I have my million-dollar idea. Guardian goats. I can see it now."

Barry's wife, Regina, came over, shaking her head, her eyes twinkling. "Come with me, my darling husband, and tell me all about it." She shepherded him away, but not before turning her head and whispering that she'd dissuade him before the night ended.

As soon as the pair was out of listening distance, Lucky burst out laughing with his friends, taking care not to spill the drinks.

Will shook his head and then sighed. "Oh, well. If Uncle Barry hadn't had a big idea, the three of us wouldn't be here now."

Lucky nodded, knowing too well that Barry Sullivan was the real reason Kelsea had arrived at the Silver Horseshoe. Then Sabrina had arrived at the ranch, seeking a job so she could support her unborn child. Will had arranged for an interview at the Double I, where Sabrina had worked as the barn manager until Ty reappeared in her life. And now, the Double I was his home base, where he and Lizzie had taken up residence in the guesthouse and where they'd bring home their little pardner in approximately seven and a half months. Making his life complete was the offer Ty and Sabrina extended to become a full partner in their rodeo academy. He'd called Lizzie on the spot and accepted the job without a second thought.

"I don't know about that." Sabrina tugged at one of her long brown braids. "You two are family, so we'd still be together. It's just everyone else wouldn't be here tonight."

She grinned, and Lucky laughed. The three of them were family, through thick and thin, and he loved they'd be alongside him and Lizzie when the time was right for their announcement. If they'd learned anything since their fake engagement, it was communicating with each other and their friends.

The twang of country music came out of the speakers, and guests started tapping their boots along with the rhythm. Ty came over and winked at Sabrina. "While Evie and Gordon have Genie for the evening, may I have this dance with my beautiful wife?"

"Thought you'd never ask. I do love a good dance with my husband." Sabrina kissed Ty and then waved at Will and Lucky.

Will laughed until Kelsea sidled up to him and nudged him. "One dance, and then I'll make sure Snow and Flake are properly penned for the evening and can't get out."

Will tipped his hat, as if he had to give careful consideration to his reputation as a gruff cowboy, but he wasn't fooling Lucky or Kelsea. "Deal."

The two ambled away, Kelsea's sunshine the perfect balance to Will's rougher edges. Lucky tightened his grip on the drinks, but didn't have a long way to walk as Lizzie met him in the middle.

"I thought I'd have to send a search party for you." She accepted her ginger ale with a smile, lifting her glass for good measure.

Lucky sipped his beer and then placed his half-full glass on the closest tray table. "Never. I know a good thing when I see it." Lucky held out his arm. "And you are the best."

She smiled and then situated her empty glass next to

his. Her ruby engagement ring with a cluster of diamonds surrounding the oval gem gleamed in the glow of the fairy lights. "Dance with me?"

"I'd be delighted to have this dance. Lizzie, you always keep me on my toes."

They glided to the makeshift dance area. She fit perfectly in his arms and nestled her head against his shoulder while the slow song played. He'd waited his life for a family, and now he had two. Besides, Lizzie was worth the wait, and so was the newest member they'd greet later this year.

Life didn't get any better than this moment with the woman he loved in his arms. He was a lucky man, indeed.

* * * * *

WESTERN

Rugged men looking for love...

Available Next Month

Starting Over With The Maverick Kathy Douglass
A Family For His Boys M. K. Stelmack

....

Worth A Fortune Nancy Robards Thompson
Her Hometown Secret LeAnne Bristow

....

LOVE INSPIRED

Her Son's Faithful Companion Jill Weatherholt
Sunflower Farms Redemption Stacie Strong

Larger Print

Keep reading for an excerpt of a new title
from the Special Edition series,
A CAPE COD SUMMER by Jo McNally

Chapter One

The Sassy Mermaid Motor Lodge didn't look too terribly bad at night. Thanks to traffic delays, Mom's insistence that they stop at what felt like every other exit to "see what looked interesting" and Lexi getting lost on the dark, winding side roads of Cape Cod, she and her mother didn't arrive at their motel until two in the morning.

Not just the place where they were staying. It was *literally* their motel. Or at least…*Mom's* motel. Phyllis Bellamy had inherited the Sassy Mermaid Motor Lodge from an uncle no one had spoken to in decades. And their first time seeing it was right now. In the dark.

There were a few cars in the parking lot of the long, low, two-story motel, so the place was at least pulling in *some* money. That would make it easier to sell, which would happen just as soon as Lexi could convince her mother to dump this place. But despite the No Vacancy sign being lit, it was definitely not full. The lawyers said the motel had thirty rooms, and there were only ten cars parked there. The reception office was located near the center of the building, but it was dark, too.

"Thank goodness I have the keys, right?" Mom shook the giant ring of keys the attorneys had sent her. Each was carefully labeled—apartment, office, laundry, pool, storage one, storage two, etc. Lexi parked in front of the office and stared into the darkened room beyond the plate glass.

"It feels creepy to just let ourselves in like this."

"Don't be silly." Mom hopped out of the car. "It's *my* motel, so we're not trespassing. Oh, wow—I can smell the ocean!"

Lexi got out and stretched. It had been a long three days since they'd left Des Moines, and she'd driven most of it. Not because Mom hadn't offered to drive, but because her mother was quite possibly the world's worst driver. Lexi's life might be a flaming hot mess right now, but she still wanted to keep *living* it awhile longer.

She took a deep breath as she stretched, and realized what Mom was talking about. The rich, salty aroma of the ocean was heavy in the breeze. She could hear the surf splashing against rocks coming from somewhere out there in the night. For all her doubts about this journey, Lexi was looking forward to spending a little time near the ocean. But right now, exhaustion was catching up with her—she was hitting the proverbial wall, barely able to stay on her feet.

"Let's get inside and hope that mystery uncle of yours left you some comfortable beds."

"Right. Let me find the key here…" Mom flipped through the keys, her bright pink hair falling over her face. It had been a little like watching a butterfly leaving its cocoon to watch her mother transform over the past year. From a meek housewife to a fearlessly liberated woman, and all because her husband—Lexi's father—had left her for a woman younger than two of his children.

Meanwhile, Lexi had followed the opposite path since her own life imploded. She'd gone from being confident and successful to nursing her emotional wounds and avoiding everyone she used to know or work with. Maybe Mom's year of living dangerously would rub off on *her*, now that they'd escaped Des Moines and Chicago. Never mind that neither of them had ever been to Massachusetts before and knew nothing about running a motel. Details, details. With any luck, she'd convince Mom to sell by the end of the summer. That was all the time that Lexi could give to this project. It was mid-April now, so they should be able to get this place on the market and sold by August.

"Okay, sweetie, I got it open." Mom waved her hand to get Lexi's attention. "I feel like this should be a more momentous entrance, but we don't want to wake up our guests by popping champagne in the middle of the night." She pushed the door open and a tiny bell rang above it. They both froze, but they didn't hear any movement inside. Whoever was watching the office had obviously gone home for the night. The lights from the parking lot cast a soft light through the windows into the office. There was nothing surprising—an ice machine, a reception counter, a coffee counter and a few chairs scattered around. All in shades of brown and gold. There was a door in back with a sign that said Private.

Mom giggled, whispering for some reason. "This is so exciting! My very own motel and a brand-new life on the *ocean*. I've seen the ocean exactly once in my life, and your father bitched the entire weekend we spent in Virginia Beach. It was too hot, it was too sandy, there was nothing to do, blah, blah, blah." She pushed the back door open. "This must be the residence. Where's the light switch? Oh, there it is." She hit the switch and the room lit up.

"Jesus," Lexi muttered, "turn them back off."

The sign out front said the Sassy Mermaid had been open since 1948. From the looks of things, this room hadn't been updated once since then. It was wood, layered on wood, layered on wood—parquet wood floors, paneled walls and a plywood-coffered ceiling. There was a well-worn braided rug of brown, gold and orange in front of a brown plaid sofa to the right. Over the sofa was a giant oil painting of a tri-masted schooner speeding across an angry sea. On the left wall was a kitchenette with a small sink, an apartment-size refrigerator and a hot plate. Along the back wall was a twin-size day bed with a rusted white iron frame. Beyond the kitchenette was a staircase that was partially enclosed, showing only the bottom four steps. If this was the so-called living quarters the lawyers emailed her mom about, there was no way the two of them could stay here.

Lexi walked across the room to check out the two doors in the back. The first was a small bathroom with one of those old metal shower stalls that belonged in a camp or cabin somewhere. Spots of rust looked like brown snow-flakes on the sides. The other door led to a weird combina-tion of hallway and storage closet, with painted plywood shelves narrowing the space even more. The shelves were packed to the ceiling with cleaning supplies and boxes of who-knew-what. There was a door marked Exit at the back.

"Do you really think Uncle Tim *lived* in here?" Mom was moving papers around on a small desk in the corner. "The lawyers said—"

"Clearly the lawyers had no clue what they were talking about," Lexi said. "We'll figure it out in the morning, but for now, why don't you take the bed and I'll sleep on the sofa. I'm exhausted—" There was a sound behind her. A footstep on the stairs. *We aren't alone!* She spun toward the narrow, carpeted staircase...

"If you're here looking for drug money, you're going to be very disappointed." A rough male voice spoke coldly, but calmly, with a heavy New England accent. She could see bare feet and legs coming down the stairs—long legs, with one calf sporting a large, ornate tattoo of a ship's anchor. The intruder took another step and Lexi backed up as he spoke again. "If you don't get your dumb *ahsses* out of here, you're going to find yourselves sitting in the back seat of a police *cah*...with fresh bruises." Another step. He was wearing blue boxer briefs, and nothing else.

But Lexi didn't spend much time thinking about the man's physique. Not when he was uttering threats with a dangerous growl. And carrying an iron fireplace poker. She put herself between him and her mother. She was the daughter of one large, angry man and had almost been the wife of another. She didn't intimidate easily. Not anymore.

She didn't see his face until he stepped onto the bottom landing. He was tall, with dark hair and startling blue eyes. Those eyes were cold as steel right now, his square jaw tight. He'd started to raise the fire poker, but he stopped when he got a look at them.

"Who the hell are you?" he asked.

"I think—" Mom was using her full *Mom* voice, low and cold, which had always sent her three children scurrying "—*we* should be asking that question, young man." The guy was at least mid-thirties, maybe even forties. From his tan and the weathered lines on his face, she'd guess he spent a lot of time outdoors. Mom continued. "I *own* this motel, so why don't you tell us who *you* are and what you're doing here. Or maybe we should call the police to sort this out?"

The man's jaw dropped. "*You're* Curly's niece?"

"If by Curly, you mean Timothy Neely, then yes, I am."

He set down the poker in the corner and stepped into the room, apparently forgetting he was in his underwear. "Damn. I didn't think you'd be here until the weekend. Uh...

I'm Sam Knight. The estate lawyers—" he pronounced it *law-yahs* "—have been paying my cousin and I to keep the old place open for, well…you, I guess. Phyllis, right?" He started to step forward as if to shake her hand, then looked down. Color rose in his cheeks. "Oh…son of—excuse me." He stepped into the bathroom just long enough to grab a brightly colored beach towel, which he wrapped around his waist.

Now that he wasn't clutching a weapon in his hand, Lexi tried to shift herself out of fight mode and join the conversation.

"And you *live* here?" That came out as more of an accusation than a question, but she was so damn tired, not to mention being extremely wary of this rough-looking guy making himself at home on her mother's property. Although he didn't look quite as tough now that he was wearing a green beach-towel skirt covered with pink dolphins and yellow starfish.

"No," he answered, having the grace to look a little guilty. "But someone has to take the overnight shift. Tonight was my turn." He glanced up toward the top of the stairs. "I had no idea you'd be here tonight, or I wouldn't have stayed upstairs."

Mom let out a loud sigh of relief. "You mean this isn't the living quarters?"

"For the owners? Hell, no." He glanced around the room with a look that mirrored their first impression. "This is basically just an extension of the office. The bed's there for someone to use if they're covering the office overnight. The upstairs is a full two-bedroom apartment. Do you have luggage to bring in? I can take it up for you."

"But weren't *you* covering the office overnight?" Lexi sounded contrary. She knew it from the warning look on

Mom's face. There was just something about this guy that set her on edge. Or maybe it was the fourteen hours of driving she'd done that day.

His gaze settled fully on her for the first time. He did one of those annoying head-to-toe appraisals, and she bristled. Sam raised one eyebrow, and she could swear she saw a glint of amusement in his eye. "And you are...?"

"Oh, this is my daughter, Lexi," Mom answered for her. She was a thirty-six-year-old woman and didn't need her mother speaking for her. But right now, exhaustion was pressing down on her more every minute.

"The only bags we need tonight are there by the door." Lexi nodded at the two small-wheeled suitcases. "I really need to get some sleep before I start dealing with—" she gestured in his general direction "—this."

Her tone made it sound like he was the bellhop. She really didn't care at this point. She wanted a bed and she wanted it now. She just prayed the upstairs was a hell of a lot nicer than this time capsule from the forties. She brushed past him, being sure to keep her eyes away from the towel around his waist, and headed up the stairs. He scrambled to turn on the light switch on the wall behind her.

"I thought I was sneaking up on a robbery, so I left the lights off."

Mom followed Lexi as he grabbed the bags. "Do you have a lot of robberies here?" Her voice made the question sound naively innocent, as if she was asking how often it rained on Cape Cod.

"At the motel? No. But every small town has its share of bored teenagers looking for mischief. Once tourist season starts, that number goes up substantially." He called up to Lexi. "There's a double light switch at the top of the stairs on the right."

She flipped the switches and looked around with relief. The apartment was, most importantly, clean, and second, *not* brown. The floor plan was open, and it had a nice living area with textured laminate floors the color of driftwood. The decor was a blend of midcentury modern and coastal, with a large blue sofa facing a wall of windows with a sliding glass door. There was a small white brick fireplace in the corner. The beadboard ceiling was vaulted, giving a sense of space. Behind her was a bright kitchen—not huge, but efficient. The counters, including the long peninsula, were blue and white tiles in a checkerboard pattern. A little busy for her taste, but it was cute. A hallway led past the kitchen, presumably to where the bedrooms were. The layout reminded her of the shotgun houses she'd seen in New Orleans—long and narrow. But livable for the short time they'd be here.

Her mom and Sam stepped up into the living room, and he swept his arm around, giving a bullet-point tour as he pointed. "The sliding door leads out to a big deck above the motel office. Obviously, that's the kitchen back there. Bathroom over there with a shower. Two bedrooms share a full bath down the hall. They don't have the view this space does, but they're pretty good sized. The apartment gets wider as it goes back. There's an outside entrance back there with stairs down to a private parking area behind the motel."

Now that he mentioned it, she could see the apartment was pie-shaped, narrowest at the window wall. It certainly wasn't as traditional and ornate as the house she'd grown up in, but it was bright and inviting. This would be her home for a few months, until she could convince Mom that neither of them belonged in Winsome Cove.

That was the deal she'd made with Max and Jennifer.

All three Bellamy siblings agreed someone needed to keep an eye on Mom until she came to her senses. Going a *little* wild after the divorce was one thing. But insisting she was going to move to Cape Cod to run a motel she'd just inherited was a lot more dramatic than dying her hair hot pink, or trading her Talbots wardrobe for one from Forever 21.

Phyllis Bellamy had been the quintessential stay-at-home soccer mom and socialite housewife throughout her forty-year marriage to Bob Bellamy. She'd kept the house spotless. She'd joined Dad at the country club every Friday for dinner. She'd hosted bridge club and run fundraisers for all the most socially acceptable charities. She'd attended the United Methodist Church every Sunday, always sitting in the same center pew. But she'd never once run any kind of business. When she'd insisted she wasn't going to sell the motel until she'd "checked it out," they figured they had to protect her.

Lexi had been first up, since she was unemployed and had already been living with Mom for a few months after losing her job, her Chicago apartment *and* her reputation. Max and Jennifer had promised they'd each take a turn here in New England if she couldn't get Mom to sell right away.

"Point me to the smaller bedroom." Right now, she just wanted to sleep. "And please tell me the bed is made." She took the handle of her suitcase and turned toward the hallway.

"Uh, yeah… I gotta get my stuff out of there first." He moved ahead of her. "That's the room I was using tonight. Like I said, we didn't expect you for a few more days…"

She waved her hand. She didn't care. "Are the sheets clean?"

"Well…they were fresh tonight but I'll change them—"

"Don't bother." What a weird welcome to Cape Cod—a

towel-clad hottie threatening her with a fireplace poker before offering to make her bed.

Sam turned on the light in the bedroom and dashed around, grabbing a T-shirt off the dresser and yanking it over his head. He gripped khaki shorts in one hand while he picked up a small duffel bag. "I'll, uh…give you a better tour of the place tomorrow."

"Yup. Whatever. Good night." She crawled into the bed and fell onto the pillow. "And goodbye."